HANGTOWN
THE DARK NIGHT

HANGTOWN
THE DARK NIGHT

Book Three in the Hangtown Series

JOHN PRATT BINGHAM

BINGHAM BOOKS

Published by John Pratt Bingham at binghambooks.com. Printed in the United States.

www.binghambooks.com

First Edition
ISBN - 978-0-9970061-5-5 (Paper)
ISBN - 978-0-9970061-6-2 (Electronic)

Edited by David Downing of Maxwellian Editorial Services, Inc.
Cover Design by Dave Fymbo of Limelight Book Covers
Back cover photograph by Stringer Productions, Boyce A. Stringer, Photographer
Book Design by Mark D'Antoni of eBook Design Works

Hangtown: The Dark Night
is dedicated to The Reverend Bill Adix

In strange ways hard to know

gods come to men.

Many a thing past hope

they had fulfilled,

and what was looked for

went another way.

A path we never thought to tread

God found for us.

So has this come to pass.

— Euripides

TABLE OF CONTENTS

SATURDAY, AUGUST 14, 1852

IT WAS A hot, dry summer morning in Hangtown when Claire heard the bell of her boarding house ring. Standing on the porch was Rose, watching the butterflies explore the potted roses, zinnias, and violets.

She's right on time, thought Claire, *but she looks exhausted.*

"Come in," said Claire. "You look worn-out. What's going on?"

"I was up most of the night with Kay," said Rose. "She gave birth to a boy she's calling Zachery Bunnell. He's a good-sized lad — he weighs about eight pounds — and looks a lot like Kay. If I didn't need a new nursing uniform and dress so badly, I would have rescheduled our appointment."

So Kay had a boy? Wouldn't you know she'd name him Zachery, after his father? She sure knows how to get under my skin.

"I see blood on your uniform," said Claire, walking with Rose through the front room and into her office. "Did everything go all right?"

"Yes," said Rose. "It was a routine birth, nothing special about it. Being Kay's first, it took a while. How is your pregnancy coming along?"

"My baby is rambunctious," said Claire, smiling. "She kicks a lot, which I can do without, but at least she's full of life. That's good."

"How do you know the child is a girl?" asked Rose, indulging her curiosity over wanting to get on with the meeting.

"My dreams told me," said Claire matter-of-factly. *Now that Kay has a son, I want a boy too; only I want mine to be bigger than Kay's and to look like his dad.*

Rose rubbed her eyes. "You have some sketches to show me?"

"Sorry. I got distracted," said Claire, handing Rose several sketches she'd drawn for her. "Do any of these appeal to you?"

Rose studied the renderings, and then, pointing to the third option, said, "I like this design for a uniform." Shuffling through the remaining sketches, Rose stopped at a blue dress she found attractive.

"Does Stephen like blue?"

"He does," said Claire, "but any of these designs can be made using blue material."

"Do you have a sample I can see?" asked Rose.

"No," said Claire. "I went by Huntington's this morning to see what they had in stock. I found some off-white cotton that'll look sharp as a uniform, but I couldn't find a single piece of blue fabric in the store. That's not like them. Fortunately, they have new material coming in regularly. I'll keep looking."

"Because there's so much blood on this uniform," said Rose, "I can't use it for work anymore. Payday comes soon. Make me two uniforms like the one you've drawn here, and a dress like the blue one. I see myself wearing that blue dress when I'm with Stephen."

"I'm pleased you and my brother enjoy each other," said Claire, setting Rose's choices aside. "You make a lovely couple. Be aware, though, Stephen's a man who loves being a lawyer. You'll have to share him with his work if the two of you are to have a future."

"That's not a problem," said Rose, yawning. "Stephen will have to share me with my nursing responsibilities. We've talked about it, and so far, it hasn't been a problem."

Claire and Rose agreed on a time for a fitting, and when Rose left, Claire resigned herself to the reality her rival didn't die while giving birth to her husband's child. *If Kay had died, it would've solved so many problems*, thought Claire picking at one of her cuticles. *Since she didn't, I hope her labor was excruciating.*

* * *

Zach awoke unaware that overnight he'd become a father, and that his son was named after him. He remembered Claire had an early appointment at the boarding house, which explained why she wasn't still in bed.

Zach strolled to his study and began his day the way he started most days, by reading Morning Prayer. The lesson assigned for the day was Mark 9:17-27, a story about Jesus performing an exorcism.

> "Teacher, I brought you my son; he has a spirit that makes him unable to speak; and whenever it seizes him, it dashes him down; and he foams and grinds his teeth and becomes rigid; and I asked your disciples to cast it out, but they could not do so."

He answered them, "You faithless generation, how much longer must I be among you? How much longer must I put up with you? Bring him to me."

And they brought the boy to him. When the spirit saw him, immediately it convulsed the boy, and he fell on the ground and rolled about, foaming at the mouth. Jesus asked the father, "How long has this been happening to him?" And he said, "From childhood. It has often cast him into the fire and into the water, to destroy him; but if you are able to do anything, have pity on us and help us." Jesus said to him, "If you are able! — All things can be done for the one who believes." Immediately the father of the child cried out, "I believe; help my unbelief!"

When Jesus saw that a crowd came running together, he rebuked the unclean spirit, saying to it, "You spirit that keeps this boy from speaking and hearing, I command you, come out of him, and never enter him again!"

After crying out and convulsing him terribly, it came out, and the boy was like a corpse; so that most of them said, "He is dead."

But Jesus took him by the hand and lifted him up, and he was able to stand."

Zach completed his prayers and went downstairs to the kitchen. He poured himself a cup of coffee to which he added extra honey. Sitting at the kitchen table, he pondered the passage from Mark.

Why does this story quicken my spirit? There is something more to it than Jesus healing a sick boy.

* * *

Yesterday, Zach invited Joe, his younger brother, to come to his house for a visit. While they pitched horseshoes, Zach planned to talk about the infuriating letter Joe had sent to him before coming west. With Claire at work, it was the perfect time to clear the air.

Joe was the son who chose to carry on the family tradition of becoming an Episcopal priest. After completing his education and being ordained, Joe came to Hangtown to start a congregation he called Saint Mary's.

When Joe arrived at Zach's house, they ate lunch, and then went to Zach's side yard.

"The Fergusons lived here before us," said Zach. "They put in a regulation horseshoe court beside the house, which I like, but Claire doesn't. She's been pressuring me to move it to another part of the yard. She wants to grow vegetables here. I've resisted, but it hasn't been easy. The next time you see her, be sure you let her know how much fun you had today, even though you are going to lose."

"Have you gotten better at horseshoes since you left home? You'll recall I beat your brains out when we were boys."

"Though I haven't played since I left Virginia," said Zach, "I'm confident I can beat you."

"I'm glad you believe that. It makes drubbing you all the more satisfying," said Joe. "I'll tell Claire how thrilling it is to humble you."

"As your host," said Zach, "I'll let you go first. I'm glad we're playing. I need to remind you why I'm the superior son."

"You're older, but your immoral behavior has disqualified you from any claim of superiority."

"Whoa," said Zach, watching Joe toss a ringer. "I resent what you just said."

"That's three points for me," said Joe. "Your behavior has become perverse. You're killing people; you get a woman pregnant and then marry someone else. I don't understand what's become of you. You're not living a virtuous life."

"I don't need more of your reprimands," said Zach. "You gave me enough of them in your letter. You may be a priest, but that doesn't give you the right to judge me."

"I love you," said Joe, tossing one of his horseshoes. "It appears I want you to be in God's good graces more than you do. The comments in the letter I sent you were offered in the spirit of returning you to a healthy relationship with our Lord."

"And what makes you think I'm not in one now?" asked Zach, throwing a ringer of his own.

"You aren't following God's commandments or the church's rules. You act as if you can get away with whatever you want. You're wrong. Each of us has to live by the approved teachings of the church, whether we like them or not. I strive to do that and wish you did too."

The play continued with Joe racking up points. When Joe threw another ringer, he had ten points to Zach's five.

"Why don't you acknowledge the truth of what I'm saying?" asked Joe.

"Your criticisms of me, while well-intentioned, are uninformed and misguided. Why can't you trust me to do the right thing?"

"Because you're clearly not!" said Joe, turning to look directly at his brother. "Why can't you follow the church's rules?"

The arguing continued. Zach contended that organized religion's preoccupation with proper behavior impedes individuals from having their own authentic experience of God.

"What I'm seeking," said Zach, "is as many direct experiences of God as I can have. I want to feel touched by God."

Joe walked to the other end of the horseshoe court, pausing to think. He moved the horseshoes back and forth between his hands.

"I need to win before your horseshoes aspirations become as exaggerated as your spiritual ones," he said. "If you want to be close to God, then renew your commitment to the church and return to the Sacraments. That's the proven path to God. Besides, history shows a direct encounter with God happens only to a select few, like Moses and Jesus. Do you really believe God will select you for such a revelation? What happened to your humility?"

Joe went on to decisively win the first game. Zach began the second by overthrowing the stake and bouncing the horseshoe near the gate in the side yard fence.

Joe chuckled and said, "That was ugly!"

"The toss certainly was," said Zach, "but your remark about only a few people being able to experience God directly is not true. Direct, personal experiences of God are common. God speaks to us through our dreams, and everyone dreams. I don't believe what I'm seeking is unrealistic."

"All your efforts have achieved so far," said Joe, "is an invasion of hubris and a lot of sinful behavior. In contrast, if you turn your efforts to engaging God through the Sacraments, you'll be on solid ground. The Sacraments go back to Jesus and the apostles. Who knows where your way originated? Probably in superstition. If you stay on the path you're on, you'll end up worshipping some esoteric god, not the Lord of Christian scripture."

"There's more than one path to the Almighty," said Zach wondering when Joe become so doctrinaire? "If you were open to your dreams, you'd experience God talking directly to you too. Then you'd understand why I yearn for more of these moments."

"I have a question," said Joe. "How do you know your dreams come from God? I suspect dreams arise more from indigestion than they do from God. Who's to say?"

"I can see we aren't going to agree about which of our ways to God is better," said Zach. "The important thing is we support and respect each other, and neither of us criticizes the other."

"I'm concerned about your standing with God," said Joe, preparing to throw. "I reserve the right to speak up when I believe you've gone astray. With the leaner I just threw, I've won both games. Let's have a beer. Loser buys. That's you."

* * *

Claire was walking home when she saw Zach and Joe.

"Join us for a drink," said Joe. "Zach's buying. He lost in horseshoes. I'm glad you kept the court; playing is fun. It provides me the opportunity to remind Zach my ways are better than his ways."

"I need a place to grow vegetables," said Claire. "There isn't room to do both on that side of the house. The horseshoe pit will have to find a new location. Where are you going for a drink?"

"To the El Dorado Hotel," said Joe. "It's the closest place."

"I'll join you," said Claire. *Matilde's hands will be all over Zach if I'm not there.*

As the three of them walked into the hotel, Claire said to them, "I've got news. Kay had her baby this morning."

"Where did you hear that?" asked Zach stiffening.

"Rose was the midwife. She told me when she came to the boarding house to select the outfits she wants me to make for her."

"What'd Kay have?" asked Zach, his face flush.

"A good-sized boy she named Zachery," said Claire. *She won't let go of you. Little Zach will be a constant reminder of your time together.*

"I want to hold my son," said Zach, clearing his throat. "Does he look like me?"

"Rose said he looks like Kay," said Claire. "Now that Kay's back living in Red's Saloon, you won't be able to see, much less hold him. Red has made it clear you're not welcome there."

"You sound angry?" said Joe, taking a seat in the hotel dining room. "Why's that?"

"I hate Kay. She tried to kill me, she's draining Zach and me financially, and she wants my husband to divorce me and marry her," said Claire. "If you were me, wouldn't you'd be angry too?"

"I see your point," said Joe, turning away from Claire and looking at Zach. "I'll find a way to meet my nephew. Red doesn't know me. I'll have a drink and take a peek at the boy. I'll tell you all about him."

"I'd like that," said Zach, ignoring Claire's frown.

Matilde approached their table, her revealing dress attracting both men's eyes. She smiled.

"Joe and I'll have a beer. What would you like?" Zach asked Claire.

"A glass of red wine." *What I'd really like is to have all these lecherous women out of my life.*

"Got it," said Matilde, flipping her hair. "Who's the good-looking fella with you?"

"This is Joe," said Zach. "He's my brother. You met him when he was here last year. He's an Episcopal priest now."

"I remember. You owe me a drink. Come back when you're alone, and I'll take you up on your offer," said Matilde, with a wink. "Do you want to see a menu?"

"Might as well," said Joe, grinning. "Zach's buying."

"I'll be right back with them."

"Watch out for that woman," Claire said after Matilde left. "She'll do anything to satisfy her lust."

"She's a looker, that's for sure, but she's not the type to be a parson's wife," said Joe, shrugging. "Now she knows who I am, I'll be safe."

"Don't count on it," said Zach. "She noticed your interest. She'll take you being a priest as a challenge to seduce you. I agree with Claire, be careful."

Matilde returned with the menus.

"The smoked bear tenderloin with mushrooms and rice is tonight's special," she said. "I recommend it. That's the aroma you smell. Isn't it wonderful? While you're looking over tonight's offerings, I'll get your drinks."

When Matilde went to the bar, Claire asked, "Have you found a place to hold your church services?"

"Not yet," said Joe. "I'm still searching."

"Are folks even interested in having an Episcopal church in Hangtown?" asked Zach.

"I've met many people who say they'll give us a try when Saint Mary's opens," said Joe, sighing.

Matilde returned with their drinks, bewitching the men when she bent-over to serve the drinks.

"Floozy!" mumbled Claire under her breath.

"Are you ready to order?" asked Matilde, putting her hands on Zach's muscular shoulders.

"Not yet," said Zach, shifting in his chair. "We've been too busy to look at the menu. Joe needs a place where he can hold church services."

"Sunday mornings are quiet here," said Matilde. "You're welcome to use the dining area."

"I can't have gambling and drinking going on around us while we are worshipping the Lord," said Joe. "Are you willing to halt them while the service is going on?"

"Having a church here will add respectability to the place. We're talking only an hour or two, right? I'd be willing to do that in exchange for your advertising that you're conducting services here. You'll bring people here who ordinarily wouldn't come, and some of them may stay for lunch. That sounds like a fair trade-off to me. When do you want to begin?"

"What about a week from tomorrow?" asked Joe. "Say at ten o'clock?"

"Starting at ten will give me time to set up for lunch," said Matilde, running her fingers through her hair. "Come back tomorrow morning, and we'll discuss how to arrange the room and whatever else I need to do for you. Partnering with a priest is a new experience for me, one I'm sure I'll like."

"I'll be here at ten o'clock," said Joe, smiling. "That'll give me a sense of what the room is like at that hour."

"Bring a list of things you'll need. I have a table you can use for an altar and a piano for music, but you'll have to find someone who can play church music." The arrival of new diners made Matilde look over her shoulder. "I see other guests need attention. I'll seat them and be right back to take your order."

"Working with Matilde is going to be great," said Joe, beaming.

Walt Selzer burst into the hotel. "An Indian raiding party is coming down the street! Everyone outside. We have to stop them."

All the men left the hotel and drew their weapons, except for Zach and Joe, who don't own guns. After several minutes of waiting, a shout of "all clear" came, and everyone went back inside.

After their meal, Zach said good-bye to Joe, and walked Claire home.

"How was your talk with Joe?" she asked. "Did you clear the air?"

"We clarified our differing approaches to God, but Joe is resistant to accepting my path. He's intent on correcting what he sees as my errors. I told him I don't like that, but he insists on doing it anyway."

"That's the new priest in him. He'll mellow with time, and you'll be close again."

"I hope you're right. I don't like discord."

MONDAY, AUGUST 16, 1852

ZACH BEGAN HIS day reading Morning Prayer. The assigned lesson was Leviticus 19:18, 33-34.

> You shall not take vengeance or bear a grudge against any of your people, but you shall love your neighbor as yourself: I am the Lord.

> When an alien resides with you in your land, you shall not oppress the alien. The alien who resides with you shall be to you as the citizen among you; you shall love the alien as yourself, for you were aliens in the land of Egypt: I am the Lord your God.

Leviticus is telling us we must love our neighbors and immigrants as ourselves if we want to be welcome in God's presence. Here's the Biblical support for my newspaper's editorial position.

"Zach, breakfast is ready. Are you?" asked Claire.

"I got lost in my reflections on today's lesson," replied Zach. "I'll be down in ten minutes."

"I've got a busy day ahead. I'll wait for ten minutes, but then I'm eating."

When Zach joined Claire, she was slicing a grapefruit. "What has you in such a rush?" he asked.

"I have to create a pattern for Rose's uniforms, go to Huntington's to buy the fabric, cut it, and pass the pieces to Alice and Betty so they can sew them. I have to put the finishing touches on Mary's wedding dress. These things will take all day to accomplish. I don't have time to stand around, waiting for you," said Claire. "What kept you?"

"The assigned lesson was from the book of Leviticus. It indicates a part of being right with God involves loving our neighbors and immigrants as ourselves. It supports my conviction that the laws that persecute immigrants, Negroes, and Indians must be repudiated."

"You're consumed with helping the disempowered and with being close to God, aren't you?"

"I am," replied Zach. "I look to the Bible to give me guidance. My challenge is to implement its teachings in my life, which isn't easy. My editorials are where my strivings come to life."

"Clearly, not many in Hangtown agree with you. Have you thought about not being so preachy when you write? That might lead to more subscribers."

"I feel strongly about issues. If that comes across as preachy, so be it. Advocating for what I believe is right is more important to me than making money."

* * *

When Zach went to the newspaper office, Bill, his new pressman, was sweeping the floor.

"What will the paper focus on this week?" asked Bill, looking up.

"With the election less than three months away, I want to start a series of articles that examine the candidates and their stances on the issues."

"Do you have in mind a series of biased stories like the one you did on John Weller when he was elected to replaced John C. Frémont in the Senate?"

"Biased?" a startled Zach responded. "Weller is a haughty, pretentious, doughface. When he was in Congress representing Ohio, he was a Democrat who favored slavery. He's a pompous fool who dresses up even when it's not appropriate. He's already had three wives. Financial scandal follows him wherever he goes. The people of Hangtown deserve to know who's representing them."

"You're the boss, but I believe your piece on Weller wasn't fair." Bill proceeded to refute each of Zach's charges against Weller. He ended his analysis by saying, "Weller wasn't a doughface; he was right to support slavery. The economic future of the South depends on it."

"I don't like Weller," said Zach. "He supports everything I detest."

"That doesn't mean it's okay to demean his character. I'm pleased to be represented by Weller. I hope he can persuade Californians to accept slavery. It's good for business."

"That it is," said Zach. "My profits would soar if I stopped paying you."

"I'm not a Chink, Negro, or savage. None of those lesser beings could do my job. Slaves are intended by God to do what white men want. They don't aspire for more as you and I do. They're grateful for the housing and food white men provide them."

"My first pressman was a Negro. He did an outstanding job."

"Did he operate a rotary press?"

"He did when he worked in San Francisco," said Zach, folding his arms across his chest.

"I find that surprising," said Bill. "He must have some white blood in him."

"To answer your original question, yes, I intend to do a piece on each of the various candidates," said Zach. "I'll continue fighting for the rights of immigrants, and I'll support candidates who agree with me. If you can't join me in this, I'll find a pressman who can."

"You can't ask me to change my mind about what I believe," said Bill. "I do my job, and I do it well. Are you willing to meet me halfway?"

"I'm not sure we can make this work. I agree, you do a good job, but I don't want to fight you along with everyone else," said Zach. "I'll give you another week to see if the tension between us goes away. If it doesn't, I'll have to find a new pressman."

"I can make it work," said Bill, rubbing the back of his neck. "You know where I stand. I don't need to keep telling you."

* * *

To take a break from the strife in the office, Zach went to Wakefield's for lunch. There, he ran into Roberto, who was just starting to eat.

"May I join you?" asked Zach, grasping the back of a chair across from Roberto.

"Of course, my friend. Have a seat. How are you?"

"I'm stressed," said Zach. "Bill, my new pressman got under my skin. He disagrees with most everything I believe. He does his job well, but I don't like the friction our opposing views generate. I told him I'd give it another week, but I'm not sure that was the right decision. If qualified pressmen weren't so hard to find, I would have fired him on the spot."

"Have a piece of Lucy's pie," said Roberto. "That'll make you feel better. What caused the problem today?"

"We disagreed about my report on Senator John Weller. I criticized Weller for being in favor of slavery, and Bill defended him. I don't want to work with someone who is pro-slavery."

"I wouldn't want to either," said Roberto, sipping his steaming coffee. "Is that the extent of it?"

Zach explained the paper was beginning a series of articles on the candidates and where they stand on the issues. Central to the series is the Compromise of 1850. In particular, the revised Fugitive Slave Act requires federal officials in every state, even free states, to return escaped slaves to their masters. Anyone who refuses to enforce this law is subject to a thousand dollar fine.

"That's a steep price to pay for not following the law," said Roberto.

"That's not the worst of it," grumbled Zach. "The law says any white man can make a free Negro his slave simply by claiming the fella is his property and a fugitive. The accused can't defend himself because the law forbids a Negro from testifying on his own behalf. This is horrible! Even though California is a free state, the law requires ordinary citizens like you and me to join a posse in search of a runaway slave. We have to stop what we're doing to assist in that person's capture and custody. We even have to provide the captive with transportation to his hearing. The requirements of this law are abhorrent."

"Why was a provision like that included in the law?" asked Roberto, shaking his head.

"It was inserted so pro-slavery senators would vote for the parts of the bill they regarded insufferable. It's what makes Senator Henry Clay's vision for America a compromise. Senator Clay is convinced the Union can hold together only if both the pro-slavery interests and the abolitionists make concessions."

"What's it have to do with Hangtown?" asked Roberto.

"Hangtown's voters should know if a candidate supports the Compromise, wants it modified, or insists on its repeal. I'll publish their answers. After all, the men elected in November will determine the country's future."

"I wish I knew an unemployed pressman who agreed with you," said Roberto. "I'd like to help you."

"I wish you did too."

* * *

Dave met with Nurse Kellogg in her office at Pastor White's church. Dave wanted to discuss the possibility of acquiring an artificial hand.

"Thank you, and Doc Martin, for saving my life," said Dave. "I'm grateful."

"I'm glad we could," said Rose. "You've been through a lot. I admire your fighting spirit."

"Now that I'm better, I was wondering if Doc Martin knows anyone who makes artificial hands? I'm frustrated by the things I can't do. An artificial hand would make a world of difference."

"The doctor isn't the one to ask. Doctors consider that once their patient is cured, their involvement is no longer needed. I'll try to find someone who can help you, but that won't be easy."

"Why's that?" asked Dave, sighing.

"Several reasons. First, there isn't much of a demand for artificial hands," said Rose. "Most folks who lose their hands or fingers die. You're the exception. Also, hands are complicated mechanisms: they're impossible to replicate. Craftsmen try, but they have to limit artificial hands to doing just one thing."

"That's disappointing," said Dave. "What are my options?"

"They aren't appealing," said Rose reluctantly.

"Whatever they are, I want to know them," said Dave with a pained expression.

"You can wear a device that's a tool, but isn't a hand, or, you can wear a device that looks like a hand, but doesn't move. Artificial hands are expensive, making a collection of them unaffordable. Also, they don't fit well, they wear out quickly, and they're painful to use. The truth is the devices cause more misery than they provide assistance."

"I feel my hope for a better life slipping away," said Dave, looking down.

"I don't want to make you glum, but you wanted to know the reality of having an artificial hand," said Nurse Kellogg. "Think about what you want to do for a couple of days, and let me know what you decide. I've been wondering, how is it to operate both a pub and a buggy business? You must not have much time to sleep!"

"It hasn't gone as well as I'd hoped," said Dave. "Business at the Boomerang is slow. The customers loyal to Slick Sam moved on, and I haven't been able to replace them. I've discovered it's a disadvantage to be located at the far end of town. The people who come my way have used up their money before they arrive, and they want me to run a tab for them. I don't like doing that. I'm barely covering my expenses."

"How are the wagon sales?"

"Johnny Studebaker misled me," muttered Dave. "Johnny promised me a full inventory of products when he recruited me. After I accepted, Johnny told me the first year I'd receive only one work wagon. It's well built, but I can't survive off the sale of one rig. Right now, nothing is going right, and I don't know what to do to make things better."

* * *

Bill was walking home, thinking about his heated exchange with Zach.

We'll never see eye-to-eye on slavery or immigration. While it felt good to speak my mind, it almost cost me my job. I like what I'm doing, I'm well paid, and I certainly don't want to go back to mining.

Bill turned down an alley he used as a shortcut. Suddenly two men on horseback and two men in a wagon surrounded him.

"Are you Bill Miller?" asked the leader.

"I am. What can I do for you?"

"You work at *The New Republican?*"

"I do. What's this about?"

"Grab him," said the man. "He's the one we want."

The other man on horseback threw a lasso around Bill's arms. The men on the wagon jumped down and took hold of him.

"Why are you doing this?" asked Bill frowning.

"You're responsible for printing all that immigration crap. There are people in Hangtown who want it to stop," said the leader, aiming his pistol at Bill's head. "We're here to present you with their ultimatum.'

"Ultimatum? What are you talking about?"

"Quit your job, or we'll kill you."

"I don't like the paper's stance on immigration any more than you do," said Bill, trembling, "but I need the job."

"After we finish with you, you'll view things differently."

"What are you going to do?" asked Bill sweat dripping from his brow.

"Take off his clothes," said the one in charge, "and do what we came for."

When Bill was naked, warm molasses was poured over his head until his body was entirely coated. Next, chicken feathers were applied, and he was tied up. Just before leaving, Bill's captors pushed him to the ground. Bill lay alone in the dark, screaming, but no one came.

* * *

Zach and Claire were cuddling in bed, discussing the day's events.

"I wonder how Joe's meeting with Matilde went?" asked Claire.

"Joe came by the office after the meeting," said Zach. "He told me the space isn't perfect, but it'll work until he finds a better place. Joe asked me to print his Sunday bulletin. I told him Mondays are the only day of the week that'd be possible. He said he'd have his first bulletin ready for printing tomorrow."

"Is Bill okay with this arrangement?" asked Claire.

"He doesn't know yet," replied Zach. "Bill had already left when Joe showed up. If Bill doesn't want to do it, I'll find someone who will."

"I hear irritation in your voice," said Claire. "I thought you liked Bill. Have things changed?"

"Bill berated me for an article I wrote about Senator John Weller," said Zach. "Bill favors slavery and disagrees with my pro-immigration editorials. He believes laws should favor business interests, not human wellbeing."

"What's wrong with that?" asked Claire.

"It makes the pursuit of money more important than having a humane society. That's foolhardy."

"You have such strong opinions," said Claire. "Can you work with someone who doesn't agree with you?"

"I doubt it," said Zach, rolling over onto his back. "I was on edge all day. I don't like working that way."

"I hope the two of you can resolve your differences," said Claire rubbing Zach's chest. "Do you know if Matilde behaved herself when she met with Joe?"

"Joe spoke glowing of her. He said he wished he'd met her under other circumstances."

"That's not good," said Claire, biting her lip. "It sounds like she's getting her hooks into him. I'll have to speak to her. I don't want their relationship turning romantic."

TUESDAY, AUGUST 17, 1852

ZACH BEGAN HIS day reading Morning Prayer. I Kings 3:5-12 was the assigned scripture.

> At Gibeon the Lord appeared to Solomon in a dream by night; and God said, "Ask, what shall I grant you?"

> Solomon said, "You have made Your servant king in place of my father, David, but I am a young lad, with no leadership experience. Your servant finds himself among the people You have chosen, a people too numerous to be numbered or counted. Grant, then, Your servant an understanding mind to judge Your people, to distinguish between good and bad, for who can judge these vast people of Yours?"

> The Lord was pleased that Solomon had asked for this. And God said to him, "Because you asked for this—you did not ask for long life, you did not ask for riches, you did not ask for the life of your enemies, but you asked for discernment in dispensing justice—I now do as you have spoken. I grant you a wise and discerning mind, there has never been anyone like you before, nor will anyone like you arise again."

God asks Solomon what he would like to be granted, and Solomon requests the ability to distinguish between good and evil. I wonder what I would ask for?

What's striking is Solomon's wisdom comes from God; it's not something he was born having, or he acquired through learning. It confirms my conviction God's grace is more important than human attributes and capabilities. I can't wait to tell Joe.

* * *

Joe walked into the newspaper office and tossed a copy of Dr. Kitto's *Journal of Sacred Literature* on Zach's desk.

"What's this?" asked Zach.

"It's a magazine that keeps me informed about what's new in theological writings. I like to read what the best minds are saying."

"Let me look through it when you've finished. I'm curious about what's being said."

"I thought you might be, that's why I brought it. I've read the entire issue. You can keep it."

"Thanks, I'll look at it tonight. I was reading I Kings this morning like you probably were. Did you notice the wisdom of Solomon came to him through a dream? Once again, we see God's grace is superior to human strivings."

"I did read this morning's lesson, but I'm not here to debate it. I've come to find out if you're going to print my bulletin? Here it is."

"I don't see why not. I haven't had a chance to speak with Bill about it, but we'll get it done," said Zach, looking over the order of service. "This hymn is new to me. Where'd you find it?"

"Which one?" asked Joe, twisting his head to see where Zach was pointing.

"*A Closer Walk with Thee.*"

"It's popular among the Negroes when they're working in the fields. I became familiar with it at the anti-slavery rallies I attended with Mother and Dad. Look at the words. They're kind of catchy, don't you think?"

"They certainly are," said Zach, as Bill opened the office door.

Bill's face was haggard, his skin covered with red blotches, and there were rope burns on his wrists. He was rubbing his eyes as he entered.

"What happened to you?" asked Zach, jumping to his feet.

"Last night on my way home from work, I was cornered in an alley by four men who tarred and feathered me. They tied me up, threw me to the ground, and left me in the filth."

"That's awful! How long were you there?"

"I lay in the cold and dark for at least an hour," said Bill wheezing. "I screamed, but no one came. A pack of dogs found me and raised a ruckus. Their barking lasted so long that Walt Selzer came to find out what the problem was. He untied me and took me to Nurse Kellogg."

"Who did this to you?" asked Zach.

"I didn't know. The bastards told me I was chosen because I work for this stupid paper. They gave me an ultimatum: either I quit, or they'll kill me. The tar and feathering was to show me how serious they are."

"That's terrible," said Zach. "I'm sorry you had to go through that. Why didn't you tell them you agree with their point of view? They might've shown mercy."

"I did," said Bill, crossing his arms. "The creeps didn't care. As long as I work here, they'll do whatever it takes to stop your editorials from being printed."

"What's that obnoxious odor?" asked Joe, stepping away from Bill.

"Nurse Kellogg used turpentine to get the molasses and feathers off. That's what you're smelling," said Bill. "It took all night and hurt like hell. I never want to go through that again."

"Sound's awful," said Joe, sighing deeply. "I need my Sunday service bulletins printed. Will you do it?"

"I'm not printing anything. I came to quit," said Bill. "No job is worth dying for. I suggest you sell the paper before you're killed. The swine said they represent people in Hangtown who are intent on shutting you up."

"Even though you're quitting," said Joe, "I need my bulletins printed. Will you do it? Printing them has nothing to do with immigration. I'll pay you well."

After carefully looking around the room, Bill agreed to do it. "I need the money, but don't ask me to do it again."

"While you're helping Joe," said Zach walking to the back of the room where supplies were kept, "I'm going to post the flyers that advertise the pressman position. By chance, do you know someone?"

"I don't, but even if I did, the new fella would be in danger of being killed," said Bill, rubbing his eyes. "A guy would have to be crazy to work here."

* * *

Rose and Stephen met for coffee.

"I've some news," said Stephen. "I'm moving to Sacramento. Alex Hunter and I agreed I should open a branch of his firm in the Capitol."

Damn! Thought Rose. *What's this mean for our future?*

"That's where I need to be if I'm going to change California's child labor laws," continued Stephen. I won't be able to see you as often as I'd like, but I'll be back frequently. You're important to me."

Well, that's good news. Should I tell Stephen he's important to me too?

"I've enjoyed our time together," said Rose. "I'm disappointed you're leaving. I won't ask you to stay because I know how deeply you feel about your work."

Nevertheless, I'd love it if you changed your mind and stayed.

"You're a remarkable woman," said Stephen. "I'd like you to be a part of my life moving forward. Why don't you give up nursing and come with me?"

Is he proposing marriage? I'm not sure.

"I can't quit. Caring for the sick feeds my soul," said Rose. "I have to do it."

"I understand," said Stephen. "Perhaps a church in Sacramento will want your services. I'll look into that."

Things may work out, thought Rose, wiping moisture from her eye.

"Please check and let me know. I have patients waiting," she said, standing.

Rose kissed Stephen on his bald spot and hurried out the door.

* * *

Zach finished posting the flyers and met Claire for a late lunch in the dining room of the El Dorado Hotel. Claire wanted to talk with Matilde about keeping her distance from Joe, and thought it'd be easier to do with Zach present.

"Bill quit this morning. I'll go into why later. It's quite a story. Anyway, because I need a new pressman, I spent the morning posting flyers around town. While I was by the post office, I picked up the mail and in it was this letter to you from the Bishop of Boston. I wonder what he wants?" asked Zach, handing Claire the thick envelope.

Claire opened it and found two letters inside.

Dear Mrs. Johnson:

I regret to inform you that Father Michael died. He had just finished saying mass for a group of union organizers when he fell to the ground. The two of us were to meet that afternoon to discuss a matter of importance to him.

Your brother was a friend, a trusted advisor, and a priest in good standing with the Diocese of Boston. He's buried in the cemetery adjacent to the Cathedral of the Holy Cross. I'm confident our most blessed Savior has delivered Father Michael from the pangs of eternal death.

In Father Michael's possessions was the enclosed letter. Though he didn't complete it, I thought you'd like to see what he was thinking.

Yours in Christ,
The Right Reverend John Bernard Fitzpatrick
Bishop of the Diocese of Boston

Dear Claire:

I received your letter. I'm grateful for your forgiveness for my many failings. I love you. There is nothing more I'd like than to live close to you. I'll speak with Bishop Fitzpatrick about allowing me to move to Hangtown.

Claire gasped and put the letters down. She fell back into her chair, tears trickling down her cheeks.

"What's wrong?" asked Zach, grabbing her arm. "What did Michael say?"

Claire shoved the letters to Zach. The shouts and cursing of the nearby gamblers faded into the distance as Zach read the messages.

"I'm stunned," he said, moving next to Claire, and holding her tightly. "At least Michael wanted to live close to you again. That's a positive thing. It's clear he felt your love and died knowing you'd forgiven him."

Claire squeezed Zach. "You don't have to say anything," she said. "Just hold me." Claire sobbed uncontrollably for several minutes.

Flann approached their table, but when he saw Claire's distress, hesitated.

"Here are your menus," he said, sliding them onto the table. "I'll be back when you're ready to order."

"That might be a while," said Zach, looking up and nodding.

Matilde sauntered up behind Flann. She was carrying a bottle of Zinfandel.

"Bad news?" she asked, putting the bottle in front of Zach.

"Yes," he replied. "Leave us alone for a while. Claire just learned her brother died."

"How'd Stephen die?"

"NOT STEPHEN!" said Zach. "It was her older brother, Michael. Go away, will you?"

"I'm glad it wasn't Joe," said Matilde. "He brings joy to my life. I'd be devastated if he died."

"Keep your hands off of him!" snapped Claire. "He's not right for you, and you're not right for him."

"Joe and I will decide that," smirked Matilde, "not you. I've long thought Matilde Johnson was an appealing name."

"Joe is a priest," screamed Claire. "He shouldn't be married to a harlot."

"You mean like your husband is?"

"Come on, Zach. It's time we leave," said Claire. "I've lost my appetite, and I need to tell Stephen about Michael."

* * *

Dave went to Mary's laundry when he returned from Sly Park. Dave could hear Belle and Ah singing behind the building as they scrubbed miner's trousers. Mary was inside, folding her customer's clothes, and quietly singing along with them. She was eager to hear Dave's report about finding a spot where they could hold their wedding ceremony.

"I found a large, dry pasture that has a spectacular view of the mountains," said Dave. "There're wildflowers, a stream nearby, and plenty of space for people to gather and eat. I think you'll approve."

"It sounds lovely. Is it hard to reach?"

"No. Buggies and wagons shouldn't have any trouble getting there," said Dave walking behind the front counter. "I've got a crew lined up to go with me Friday to set up the tents, tables, and chairs. We'll also bring the Pakua that the Temple is loaning us. Everything will be in place Saturday morning when your cousins bring the food."

Fantastic! Thought Mary. *The wedding is coming together nicely.*

"Claire has altered my mother's wedding dress so that it fits me, and this month has been a record for gold coming off of the miners' clothes. We can pay for everything without having to go into our savings," said Mary hugging Dave. "Isn't that wonderful?"

Dave looked down. "I'm the one who is supposed to be making money and paying for the wedding, not you. It's not right that you're paying the bills."

"Your businesses are just starting. It won't be long before they take off. I've no complaints about the slow start because you're doing the best you can. In the meantime, I'm happy to provide for us."

"I wish I could feel as good about the future as you do," murmured Dave.

"Would you find Zach and remind him he's helping us dig up Anna's bones?" asked Mary. "We'll meet at her grave in an hour. I'd do it, but I have more work to do."

"I'll go," said Dave, looking down at his fingerless right hand and shaking his head. "I'm the strongest guy. I should be doing the digging...."

* * *

It was late afternoon when Zach and Roberto met Claire, Mary, and Dave at Anna's grave. Roberto brought a pickax and two shovels. Mary brought a canvass bag. "It's time we send Anna home," said Mary. "It's a shame we couldn't do it sooner."

"I'll use the pickax," Zach told Roberto. "Your arm hasn't regained full strength yet, has it?"

"It's as good as it's going to be," said Roberto, looking solemnly at the grave. "Let's get started."

Dave stood off to one side, watching. After several minutes of strenuous effort, Zach said, "The ground is hard. This may take me longer than I thought. I hope we finish before dark."

I could have broken up the ground much faster, lamented Dave.

It took forty-five minutes to uncover Anna's remains. Zach said a prayer as they gathered the bones and placed them in the canvass bag.

"Anna liked lavender," said Mary. "I sprinkled some into the bag to accompany her home."

* * *

Zach and Claire sat at their kitchen table, eating supper.

"Did Dave seem all right to you?" asked Claire.

"I'm afraid Dave is slipping into melancholy," said Zach. "I hope he breaks out of it soon. I miss his fighting spirit."

"Mary told me she's doing everything she can to cheer him up, but nothing seems to help. She's afraid he doesn't want to marry her."

"That's not true. Dave loves her and recently told me Mary is the best thing that ever happened to him," said Zach. "The problem is his adjustment to being one-handed. He's finding it tough to live without fingers."

"I hope you're right, and the wedding lifts Dave's spirits," said Claire. "Mary doesn't want to be another thing in his life that isn't right."

FRIDAY, AUGUST 20, 1852

IT WAS DARK when Claire got out of bed. A light breeze moving through the oaks hummed a morning hymn. Claire quietly made her way downstairs to the kitchen, fixed a cup of her favorite tea, found a pencil and paper, and began writing.

> *A spirit takes me on a trip. I don't remember if the spirit has a face or even a head or arms. It is transparent, sometimes glinting in the light, and it is hard to see its form. Anyway, it takes me out from earth deep into space. I hear music, with the feeling that the marvelous music I hear is a small part of the full music. If my human senses didn't limit me, the music would get more and more magnificent. All the stars are dancing, and everything is interconnected. This is all part of a plan.*

> *The spirit shows me back to earth, back to home, and imparts the feeling that I too must dance, that my life is part of the great dance. I awaken.*

"Claire, where are you?" boomed Zach's voice from the bedroom. "Are you and the baby okay?"

"We're fine," replied Claire. "I had another dream. It's special, and I don't want to lose it. I came to the kitchen to record it because I didn't want to disturb you. Now that you're awake, I'd like you to hear it."

"It's too early. I want to hear the dream, but I need more sleep. Come back to bed. We'll talk about it over breakfast."

"I'm going to finish my tea and experience the dream one more time."

Zach was snoring when Claire got into bed. She wasn't ready to let go of the dream; she wanted to keep it alive as long as she could.

* * *

Shortly after seven o'clock, Zach headed to the newspaper office. It was early for him, but he wanted to finish the first draft of his editorial before someone showed up to apply for the pressman's job. This piece was crucial to Zach. After the tar and feathering of Bill, he knew he had to do a better job of persuading his readers to restore the rights of immigrants.

Zach drank several cups of coffee as he struggled to find the words that would spur action. Several revisions later, it was mid-morning, and Zach still wasn't satisfied. He decided to go to the Hangtown Bakery for a blueberry muffin.

Perhaps inspiration will come while I eat.

* * *

Claire woke when Zach shut the front door. It was early, and she hadn't had much sleep, but she dressed, ate a quick breakfast, and went to the boarding house.

"Alice, Betty," she shouted as she entered, "are the outfits for Mary and Rose ready to go?"

Alice, Claire's number one assistant, came out of the upstairs sewing room and scurried to the hallway at the top of the steps. Looking down at Claire, she said, "Miss Mary's wedding dress is finished. I put it in her room. Miss Rose's first uniform will take another half-hour to complete. What time is she coming?"

"Rose will be here at ten-thirty," said Claire. "How far along are you with her second uniform and evening dress?"

"We should have the second uniform completed after lunch. We'll have the dress ready for a fitting tomorrow."

"We'll be at Mary's wedding tomorrow. Rose will have to come back on Monday."

* * *

At ten-thirty, Rose arrived for her fitting. Claire explained to her because of Mary's wedding, the second uniform and evening dress wouldn't be ready until Monday morning.

"I'm excited to have new clothes," said Rose. "Waiting for a couple of days isn't a problem."

Rose took the completed uniform into Claire's office, which doubled as a fitting room. In the corner of the office stood a full-length mirror that Rose used to study how she looked.

"I've lost a few pounds," said Rose. "Can you take in the waist a smidgeon?"

Claire took hold of the material around Rose's waist and tightened it with her fingers.

"How's that?"

"That's too tight. I don't want the uniform to be formfitting," said Rose, smiling. "I'll save that for the evening dress."

They agreed about how much to take in, and Claire asked Betty to make the alterations. When Betty said she could complete the changes in twenty minutes, Rose decided to wait.

"Would you like a cup of tea?" asked Claire. "I have a bit of news."

"Tea and news. Sounds wonderful!" said Rose.

Claire told Rose about her older brother's death. "I loved Michael even though our relationship was rocky. It didn't help that he was a heavy drinker. Despite that, my brothers and I living near each other again would've been fun. Michael was quite the comedian; he made everyone laugh. He would have been a favorite in British music halls. I hope it isn't too long before I can return to Boston to visit his grave."

Rose hugged Claire.

"Miss Claire, the alterations are done," said Betty, carrying the uniform over her right arm.

Rose slipped into the uniform and liked the revised look. As she headed back to work, Rose said, "Look at all the butterflies on your front porch! You've made the boarding house such an appealing place."

* * *

Back inside, Claire told Betty, "You do fine work and so quickly. I admire your skill."

"Thank you, Miss Claire," said Betty. "I love working with clothes."

"There's something else I want to tell you," said Claire. "During Zach's duel, I recalled your advice about the little girl in my life. I didn't allow her to seize control of me. My little girl was terrified that Zach might die, and she pressured me to do something. Following your advice, I told her to calm down, that everything would work out. When I did, she released her iron-grip on me. I wasn't governed by her fears anymore, even as the gunfight proceeded. I want to thank you. You helped me tremendously. The little girl and I are learning to trust each other."

"How exciting!" exclaimed Betty. "Thank you for giving me credit, but you did this yourself."

* * *

Mary, the woman who convinced Claire to create a boarding house to protect Chinese women from sexual exploitation, was about to marry Dave, Zach's good friend, and previous pressman. Mary arrived at her cousin Lily's house mid-morning to have her hair washed and prepared for the wedding. When Lily opened the front door, Mary told her, "You're my good luck woman."

"I'm honored you asked me," said Lily, motioning Mary inside. "Dulun, my husband, took the children to my parent's house so they wouldn't bother us. I know you like to follow tradition, so I put pomegranate leaves around the water bowl I'll use to wash your hair. Their aroma freshens the air, and the presence of the leaves protects you from any evil spirit that might try to take possession of you."

"That was thoughtful," said Mary, moving through the house to the back-yard. "I can smell the leaves. They're heavenly. Where would you like me to sit?"

"I've prepared a place on the lawn where the warmth of the sun, the scent of the pines, and the perfume of pomegranate flowers will combine to wrap you in positive spiritual energy."

"You always know the right way of doing things. That's why you're my good luck woman," said Mary. "Let's get started."

* * *

Joe decided it was time to see his nephew. He entered Red's Saloon, took a seat, and ordered coffee.

"Do I know you?" asked Kay as she poured the coffee.

"I'm Zach's brother, Joe. We met briefly about a year ago. Zach asked me to give you this money."

"The jellyfish couldn't do it himself?" grumbled Kay, putting the money in the pocket of her apron. "Thank you, I can use it."

"May I hold my nephew?"

"No, little Zach is sleeping. Anyway, he's not available to the Johnsons until Zach marries me. Tell that to your brother!" said Kay, turning and strutting to the kitchen.

Maybe little Zach will wake up, and she'll bring him out here. I'll take my time and see what happens.

Kay was taking a break when Joe asked her, "is that fried chicken I smell?"

"It is. Red is cooking up a fresh batch. Do you want an order? It includes a side of German potato salad."

"Perfect!" said Joe. "I love German potato salad. Give me a lot."

Despite eating slowly, little Zach didn't awaken before Joe's bladder insisted on relief. Joe called Kay to his table, hurriedly paid her, and darted up Main Street. Zach was conducting an interview when Joe pushed open the front door.

"Hi," said Zach, looking up. "Can't talk now. Why don't you go somewhere and have a cup of coffee? I'll be free in half an hour."

"I'm full of coffee. I want to use your bathroom to get rid of what I've already drunk," said Joe, hustling out back.

"Sorry for the interruption," Zach said to Chris Clarke, the man he was interviewing. "That's Joe, my brother. He'll be around the office from time to time. I like your work experience. It gives me confidence you can do the job. Now, I need to speak to you about the working conditions. My last two pressmen experienced problems that made it impossible for them to continue. I want you to know about this before you begin."

"Know what?" asked Chris, leaning back in his chair.

"I'm an advocate for immigrants, Negroes, and Indians in a town that doesn't like them. I'm especially outspoken about the repressive laws that Governor Bigler and the legislature have imposed on the Chinese. Since my views aren't popular, my previous pressmen suffered physical harm simply because they worked here. Bill, the man you'll be replacing, was told he'd be killed if he continued working for me. If you accept the job, your life could be at risk too."

"Their lives were threatened because they worked here?"

"Yes. Among those who disagree with me," said Zach, "are a few who want the paper silenced. They're the ones who attacked my pressman."

"I see," said Chris, his muscle's tightening.

"I'm willing to fight for the right of a newspaper to print the truth," said Zach, "even an unpopular truth. The question is: are you? You'll have to have the same convictions I have if you're going to be part of my campaign against prejudice. Do you want to join me?"

"No," said Chris. "What you just said changes everything. I don't want to die fighting for immigrant rights. To be honest with you, I prefer only White Protestants to live in California. Everyone else can go back to where they came from. I'm glad you told me. I don't mind being a crusader for the right cause, but immigrants' rights aren't one of them. I'm no longer interested in the job. Good luck finding someone."

Chris stood up, shook Zach's hand, and left. It wasn't long before Joe came back into the office.

"I gave Kay her money," he said, "but she wouldn't let me see little Zach. I sat in Red's for a long time drinking coffee and eating fried chicken and the best German potato salad I've ever had. Red is a great cook. I was hoping little Zach would wake up, but he didn't."

"Thanks for giving her the money," said Zach, writing a note in his ledger.

"Kay asked me to tell you that no Johnson will ever see or hold little Zach until you agree to marry her," said Joe. You know she's right: you should've married her."

"I love Claire and have no intention of marrying Kay. She knows I'll never marry her. You know that too. Quit telling me that I should have."

* * *

Dave led a crew of men he hired to the Sly Park, where they set up the tents and chairs Roberto loaned him. The sun was bright, and large puffy clouds moved across the sky. Dave had the Pakua placed under a tent. In the middle of the Pakua, facing each other, workers set chairs for the bride and groom. Alongside Dave's chair was put a pot that would hold a lit candle when the service began. Next to Mary's chair, the men put an empty container, which will be filled with water at the beginning of the ceremony. Once the arrangements were to Dave's liking, the men cleared the part of the meadow where the eating and dancing would take place. Five of them volunteered to guard everything until the festivities were over. Dave started to mount his horse to leave when Dan, one of the volunteers, asked, "What's that octagonal-shaped mat called, and why is it being used?"

"It's called a Pakua," said Dave. "It's used in Taoist weddings. Come look."

The men strolled over to the tent that covered the Pakua. The other men gathered around them.

"The design of the outer layers represents the eight forces of nature," said Dave. "Opposite forces of nature are across from each other. See, heaven is at the top, and earth is at the bottom. Moving clockwise, the image of the wind is at one o'clock, and the image of thunder is at seven. That's water at three o'clock and fire at nine. Mountains are at five o'clock, and rivers are at eleven."

"What's the design in the center?" asked Dan squinting.

"That's the yin and yang," said Dave. "The Chinese use those symbols to show how opposites produce wholeness when they come together. A Taoist wedding is a celebration of the opposites uniting."

"I thought that was what the wedding bed was for!" chuckled Dan.

"That's how the festivities conclude," said Dave, winking.

* * *

When Dave got back to Hangtown, he went directly to Jay's to have his haircut and his beard trimmed. From Jay's, Dave went to Kevin Michael's bathhouse.

"Who's your new helper?" asked Dave, grabbing a towel.

"That's Matt Morris. He's Nurse Morris' oldest son. He's a good worker. He'll help me be more efficient and expand my business."

After bathing, Dave went to Claire's boarding house. In the front room, Claire was attaching cypress leaves to the brim of the hat Dave was going to wear during the ceremony.

"Why are you doing that?" asked Dave.

"The Chinese believe cypress leaves protect the groom from evil spirits," said

Claire, "just as pomegranate leaves protect the bride. Both precautions ensure a healthy start to your life together. Mary told me brides and grooms in China wear red for good luck. Are you wearing a red suit?"

"No. I'm not comfortable with every Chinese tradition," said Dave. "The suit I'm wearing is black. I'll wear a red tie, but the tie and this hat are as festive and traditional as I'm going to be."

"I worked on Mary's outfit," said Claire, handing Dave the hat. "I know you'll like it. She's going to look beautiful. Mary told me her mother wore the dress at her wedding."

"That's right," said Dave. "It's something Mary has been looking forward to since she was a little girl. I'm pleased you were able to modify it to fit her."

"It was my pleasure," said Claire, smiling. "Where are you and Mary planning to live?"

"We'll start at the Benham Hotel in Chinatown. Once we find a house we both like, we'll move there. Did Mary tell you she asked Betty to be in charge of the boarding house when you're not around?"

"No, this is the first I've heard of it," said Claire. "Betty is a good choice, but I wish Mary had consulted me first. It wasn't her decision to make."

* * *

When Dave left, Claire started sketching an outfit she thought her client Louise Dombroski would like. Claire was making good progress when the porch bell rang. When she opened the door, there stood a man in his mid-thirties with a distinctive full beard.

"Is this where Claire Johnson operates a dressmaking business and boarding house?" he asked.

"It is. How can I help you?"

"My name is Domingo Ghirardelli. I own a general store in Stockton. Several times a year, I travel throughout gold country selling my products. Today I'm passing through Hangtown and would like to introduce myself. One of my best-selling items is the chocolate I make. Would you like a sample?"

"I would!" exclaimed Claire.

Domingo gave her a chocolate bar. "If you like it, I have more in my wagon.

I also have boxes of chocolates for special occasions. I thought you might want a box or two for your clients to sample."

"This is divine. Where'd you learn to make chocolate like this?"

"An elderly man in my hometown, Rapallo, Italy taught me when I was a boy. He trained me to make the highest quality, best-tasting chocolate there is. Today I appreciate how meticulous and patient he was with me."

"I love the taste. Give me three boxes. One will be a gift for a couple being married tomorrow, one will be for my clients and staff, and the third I'll take home to share with my husband."

"I salute you. You're not only beautiful, but you're also generous. When is your baby due?"

"Late October or early November. The way my baby is responding, I can tell he loves chocolate," said Claire, savoring the taste.

"Liking chocolate is an indication the baby is a girl," said Domingo, smiling.

"No. I'm sure my baby is a boy. Here's your money. Do I have to travel to Stockton to replenish my supply?"

"That'd be the quickest way. I'm opening a second store in San Francisco, but Stockton is closer. I won't be back in Hangtown until next year."

"Twice a year I make a trip to San Francisco to check out fashions. Now I have another reason for making the trip. Where is the store located?"

"It'll be on the corner of Broadway and Battery. I'll look forward to your visit."

* * *

Mid-afternoon, Zach met with James Wilson II, a leader of the Whigs in California. Zach asked Wilson to begin by speaking about himself.

Wilson said he was from the Granite State, where he was Speaker of the New Hampshire House of Representatives. Wilson ran for Governor twice but lost each time. He also served as a Major General in the New Hampshire militia. When Wilson was appointed a California land commissioner, he moved to San Francisco.

Wilson told Zach the Whigs held their nominating convention in June. They met in Baltimore, two weeks after the Democrats held their meeting in the same building.

"They nominated Franklin Pierce," said Wilson. "Pierce is a coward and a drunk."

"Those are strong words," said Zach. "For this story, I want to stay focused on the Whig Party. When President Zachery Taylor, a Whig, died in office, he was replaced by Millard Fillmore, who is also a Whig. Why didn't the Whigs nominate President Fillmore to be the Party's candidate?"

"There are several reasons," said Wilson. "First, Northern Whigs—men like me—didn't believe President Fillmore can beat Franklin Pierce. We supported other candidates. Many Southern Whigs believed Fillmore can win, and they supported him. Also, the Party contains antagonistic factions. The hostility between the abolitionists and the pro-slavery activists was frightful. I just hope the Party can hold together. It took over fifty ballots before we could unite behind a candidate."

Zach asked, "Wasn't Senator Daniel Webster an attractive alternative to President Fillmore?"

"Only a few delegates thought so," said Wilson. "Webster's age and declining health limited the number of people who supported him. The early voting had President Fillmore in the lead, with my candidate, Commanding General Winfield Scott, a few votes behind. By the time we reached the fiftieth ballot, it was clear Senator Webster wasn't going to win. Those voting for him shifted their allegiance to General Scott, which gave my man enough votes to win. I'm pleased because General Scott is a tremendous leader. The Duke of Wellington, who defeated Napoleon at Waterloo, called Winfield Scott the greatest soldier alive."

"That's high praise. What'd Scott do to earn it?"

"When Scott was a young officer, the army was losing the War of 1812. The American troops lacked discipline. To turn the tide of battle, Scott recruited and aggressively trained a group of Northern soldiers. It was these men who drove the British off American soil.

"After the war," said Wilson, "Scott wrote a book that established exacting standards for every aspect of a soldier's life. General Scott is why our country has a professional Army and no longer relies on the poorly trained citizen militias. He'll bring that same vigor and discipline to the Office of President. As you can see, General Scott is a brilliant man that the Whigs can proudly present to voters."

"Tell me about the Whig's platform," said Zach, hurriedly flipping the page of his notebook.

"The Southern delegates presented a strong platform for the convention's consideration. The problem was it kept the voters' attention on the divisive issues of slavery and the Compromise of 1850. Experienced Party leaders felt it was wiser to adopt a weaker platform that was almost identical to the Democrats. If we keep the focus on the candidates and not the platforms," said Wilson, we have a better chance of winning."

"What about the Compromise of 1850?" asked Zach. "Do you still stand behind it?"

"It is our sincere hope the Compromise will keep the Union together," said Wilson. "It took us nine months of ill-tempered wrangling to get the Compromise passed into law. We're not about to abandon it now."

"My readers want to know what your platform has to say about California?" said Zach. "What can you tell them?"

"Whigs want California to remain free and undivided."

"That's good," said Zach, looking up at General Wilson. "What about slavery in the rest of the country?"

"Whigs want to attract voters on both sides of the issue," said Wilson. "Since General Scott is well known for his anti-slavery views, the platform states that the Whig Party supports slavery. We think that's a winning combination."

* * *

During dinner, Zach told Claire about his day. He went into great detail about his interview with Chris Clarke and Joe's experience with Kay. He was telling her about his talk with General Wilson when Claire interrupted him.

"I don't care what the platform of the Whig Party is," she said. "I had a big dream last night that I want to share with you, and you don't seem interested."

"That's right, you did. I remember now. I must've fallen asleep before you came back to bed. I'm interested. Tell me the dream."

Claire recounted it and then asked, "What do you think?"

"My appreciation for Adi's skills grows each time one of us has a dream. I don't know what to make of a dream in which a spirit leads you on a trip into the depths of space, and exposes you to cosmic music and dancing stars. You don't have ordinary dreams, do you?"

"It was remarkable," said Claire softly. "What stood out to me was the message that everything is interconnected, and is part of a plan in which I have a role. I am part of the great dance," said Claire, biting her lip. "It's important I learn my steps and respond to God's reaching out to me."

SATURDAY, AUGUST 21, 1852

ZACH AWOKE EXCITED about Dave's wedding. He went to his study and read Morning Prayer; the psalm assigned for the day was 93.

> The Lord has become king,
> He is robed in majesty;
> The Lord is robed, He is girded
> with strength.
> He has established the world;
> it shall never be shaken.
> Your throne is established from of old;
> You are everlasting.
> The ocean sounds, O Lord,
> the ocean sounds its thunder,
> the ocean sounds its pounding.
> Above the thunder of the mighty waters,
> more majestic than the breakers of the sea
> is the Lord, majestic on high.
> Your decrees are indeed enduring;
> holiness befits Your house,
> O Lord, forevermore.

The psalm speaks of God's enthronement: the Lord is King! As such, he establishes his kingdom, the kingdom of God, of which Jesus spoke at length. This hymn mirrors my experience: I'm increasingly aware of God's presence and feel protected by his rule. I've reached a new level in my spiritual growth, where earthly things matter less than spiritual ones.

"Zach, it's time to get ready for the wedding. Before we leave for Sly Park, I want to help Mary get dressed. Come eat so I can get on with what I need to do. Did you remember to reserve a buggy?"

"I did. I'll dress for the wedding and be right down."

* * *

When Claire entered the boarding house, Mary was already dressed.

"I was too excited to wait for you," she said.

"I understand. Zach held me up. Let me see how you look."

"The qípáo fits comfortably," said Mary. "As tradition dictates, only my hands, toes, and head show. You did a terrific job of altering my mother's dress. I'm thrilled."

Mary showed Claire her embroidered shoes and coronet headdress.

"These were my mother's, too," said Mary. "Her friends helped her decorate them."

"You look elegant," said Claire.

The porch bell rang. It was Dave, dressed in his wedding attire. When he entered and saw Mary, he said, "Wow! You are beautiful! I couldn't feel more blessed than I'm feeling right now." Dave sat in one of the nearby chairs. "Your magnificence is so overwhelming I'm afraid I'm going to forget my vows."

"I feel fortunate to be marrying someone as handsome, kind, and protective as you," said Mary, standing tall.

"If we are going to be in Sly Park on time, we'd better leave," said Dave. "Zach is waiting out front. He arranged for our buggy and horse to be decorated with red roses. It was a lavish thing for him to do. I feel like a king riding in it."

Mary noticed Claire picking up two boxes.

"What are those?" she asked, adjusting her headdress one more time.

"Before you leave, I want to give you a couple of small gifts," said Claire, handing her the items.

Mary looked at Dave, who shrugged about not leaving promptly.

"The top box is filled with chocolates," said Claire. "They're delicious. I have a box of my own. The second box is something Alice told me about. She said in China, it's customary for newlyweds to light a dragon and phoenix candle in their bedroom. Alice helped me find one, and I bought it for you to use tonight."

"You shouldn't have gone to all the trouble. You've done enough already."

"I wanted to do it. God bless your marriage."

"Thank you," said Mary bowing. "You and Zach are making it more than I could've ever hoped it could be. I can't thank you enough."

* * *

When Dave escorted Mary into the Pakua, the guests stood and clapped. Zach and Claire found seats next to Lily.

"I'm glad it's overcast," said Zach. "I was afraid the sun would be unrelenting."

"Let's hope the bugs stay away," said Claire. "I hate the ones that fly."

Dave settled into the chair next to the urn that held the large candle. Dulun acknowledged Dave and lit the candle. Across from Dave, sat Mary. Cheng, Dulun's assistant, nodded to Mary and poured water into the container next to her. The two men stepped outside the Pakua and began lighting eight candles that had been placed around the tent.

"Why are the candles there?" Claire asked Lily.

"A holy circle is being formed to hold the couple and to bring blessings upon them," she whispered.

While the candle lighting ceremony proceeded, Dave studied the crowd and periodically waved.

When all the candles were lit, Dulun invited everyone to meditate.

"We want to fill this space with positive, happy energy," he said.

Dave grew restless during the prolonged silence. He crossed and uncrossed his legs until Mary shot him a stern look.

When the few minutes of quiet ended, Zach stood and read a passage from *The Spiritual Union of Tao*. As Zach read, Dave's attention was drawn to the scratchy cry of a Stellar Jay that circled the unattended food tables. *If only I had my rifle, I'd get rid of that pesky bird*, he thought.

The reading ended, and Dulun addressed the gathering.

"We have reached the point in the ceremony where the bride and groom exchange their vows and rings. I ask you to stand as Mary and Dave create a new life together."

Mary looked up into Dave's blue eyes, smiled, and made her vows. She placed a gold ring on his finger and bowed to him.

"Now is Dave's turn," said Dulun.

Dave hesitated, as the verses he memorized refused to materialize. Slowly, the words came to him. Dave fumbled over a few of them but succeeded in completing the task. He slid a ring on Mary's left hand, bowed, and gave a sigh of relief. Smiles spread throughout the gathering. Mary and Dave moved aside as Dulun offered prayers.

When Dulun finished, everyone sat. Cheng carried a curved pole into the Pakua and placed it between the couple. Dave watched Dulun pick up the container holding the burning candle and put it under the pole. Next, Cheng picked up the pot of water and suspended it from the pole, just above the flame of Dave's candle.

"The union of fire and water creates steam," Dulun said to the gathering. "The joining of these two separate elements symbolizes Mary and David's lives being joined and becoming a new reality."

The ceremony concluded with the extinguishing of the candles outside the Pakua.

"Please join Mary and David," said Dulun," in the open space off to our right. It's time to greet the couple, eat and dance, and celebrate this happy occasion."

Religious ceremonies bored Dave. He could hardly wait to leave the Pakua. He was looking forward to eating and drinking with his friends. He also wanted to chase off that menacing bird, which retreated to the canopy of the nearby pines and waited for its chance to return.

* * *

The sky had turned orange and yellow. Long, flat, dark clouds provided a contrast to the brilliant colors. Mary and Dave said good-bye to everyone and left for Jackson, their honeymoon destination. Zach and Claire helped the crew clean up before they returned to Hangtown.

"Did you see the blue jay flying overhead while we tided up?" asked Claire. "It unnerved me when it landed and began hopping towards me."

"I heard it," said Zach. "Its unrelenting shrieking annoyed me. That bird was up to no good."

Claire talked about what other women were wearing for most of the trip back to town. When their buggy turned onto Main Street, she asked, "Isn't that Joe entering the El Dorado Hotel?"

"It sure looks like him," said Zach. "I bet he's making last-minute preparations for tomorrow's service."

"I hope that's what he's doing," said Claire. "I'd hate to think Joe is on his way to meet Matilde."

"I hadn't considered that," said Zach, reigning in the horses. "Do you want me to stop?"

"There isn't much he can do to prepare for tomorrow while the room is set up for dining and gambling," said Claire. "Let's see what he's up to."

Flann greeted the couple as they entered.

"May I show you to a table, or are you here for a drink?"

"I want to speak with my brother," said Zach. "Did you see where he went?"

"Joe is sitting over there," said Flann pointing to a corner of the dining room. "He's reading a book. He told me he wanted to put the final touches on tomorrow's service."

"There he is," said Claire, advancing toward Joe. Zach followed closely behind.

"Hello," said Joe, putting a marker in his Prayer Book. "How was the wedding?"

"I thought Mary looked like a princess," said Claire. "She wore the dress, headdress, and decorated shoes that her mother wore when she was married. Most things were red, which is a Chinese tradition signifying happiness. It worked! Everyone had fun and laughter filled the air."

"The wedding was unlike any I've ever experienced," said Zach, pulling out a chair for Claire. "Lots of symbolism. There was a blending of the here-and-now with the eternal. I found it fascinating. It's been a while since I've seen Dave that happy. It was like the old Dave reappeared."

"I'm sorry I missed it. I needed to attend to some last-minute details for tomorrow's service," said Joe, noticing Claire's protruding belly. "How are you and the baby?"

"We're great! The baby is getting bigger every day. He's active, which is hard on me, though I'm not complaining. It feels wonderful to have life kicking inside of me."

"That's something I'll never know," said Joe, with a chuckle. "Feeling life inside you is a holy thing. I'm jealous."

"Speaking of experiencing the holy, I had a dream I want to tell you," said Claire. "I welcome your thoughts."

Claire recounted her trip into outer space and the message she's part of a cosmic dance. "What do you think?"

"Dreams don't have meanings," said Joe. "While you may think yours came from God, I don't. Dreams are nothing more than a response to what you last ate. Only diviners look for messages in dreams, and the Bible warns us against diviners."

Claire winced.

Walt Selzer ran into the hotel. "There's a fire up the street. Every man is needed."

"I wonder what's burning?" asked Zach, springing to his feet.

It didn't take long for them to discover it was his newspaper office. Captain Meyer was putting out the fire's last embers when Zach and Joe arrived. The brothers joined the crowd watching the firemen.

"The OSSB is at it again," grumbled Zach.

"It doesn't look like there was much damage," said Joe. "The fire crew must've caught it soon after it started."

Captain Meyer spotted Zach and walked over to him. "Someone blew up the pond behind the laundry. My men and I were making sure nothing flooded when your office caught fire. Because we were close by, we were able to put it out quickly."

"Thank you!" said Zach. "You did a good job. How's the laundry?"

"The building is fine, but its source of water has been destroyed," said Captain Meyer. "I don't know what Mary will do."

"Do you know who did this?" asked Joe.

"One of my men saw several prospectors running from the back of the laundry after the explosion. He had no idea who they were. When I got there, I found a note tacked to a tree. Pulling it from his pocket, Captain Meyer read it to Zach and Joe.

"Mixing races is unnatural and won't be tolerated. Mongrels go away! RICE CRACKERS AREN"T WELCOME IN HANGTOWN!!! OSSB"

"That's appalling," said Zach. "It gives me chills. Let me have a look."

Handing it to Zach, Captain Meyer said, "I agree. I tore it down because I didn't want Mary and Dave to see it."

Zach examined the damage done to his office and was relieved that it wasn't more.

"I can't thank you enough for everything you've done," said Zach, shaking the Captain's hand.

When Zach and Joe returned to the El Dorado Hotel, Claire was talking with Stephen.

"What was burning?" she asked.

"My office. However, Captain Meyer put the fire out before it could do much damage. Clearly, God was looking out for me."

"That's a relief," said Claire. "I'd hate to think of you having to start over again."

"I was lucky," said Zach. "Mary was too."

"What do you mean?" asked Claire.

"Someone blew up the pond behind the laundry," said Zach. "On the way home, I want to stop and see how much damage was done."

"On her wedding day, too," said Claire. "This is terrible. Who'd do such a thing?"

"Captain Meyer said the men who did it left a note that was signed OSSB," said Joe.

"I ran off an Indian who was loitering around your office this afternoon," said Stephen. "Do you think the OSSB hired him?"

"I doubt it," said Zach. "I can't see the OSSB hiring an Indian to do their dirty work. They'd kill him before they'd hire him. Captain Meyer said several prospectors were seen running from the laundry after the explosion. I wouldn't be surprised if they left the laundry and went directly to my office. I'm guessing they're the ones the OSSB hired. Tell me about the Indian."

"When I walked up Main Street about mid-afternoon, the Indian was pacing back and forth," said Stephen. "Periodically, he'd look inside your front window. I figured he must be scouting the place. I shouted at him to move on, and he skedaddled."

"I'll stay alert," said Zach, sighing and shaking his head.

"After I yelled at him, he kept to the shadows," said Stephen. "He clearly didn't want to be seen."

* * *

Zach lit a torch and surveyed the damage done to the laundry's pond. Though the moon was waning, its light helped the explorers navigate the broken ground behind the laundry.

"Whoever did this is familiar with explosives," Zach said to Claire and Joe. "They completely destroyed the pond, but little else."

"Should we send word to Mary and Dave about what happened?" asked Claire.

"Let's not ruin their honeymoon," said Zach. "When Mary's customers discover what's happened and how it affects them, I'll get all the volunteers I need to fix the damage. We'll have the laundry back in operation before they return."

"How are you going to fix this mess?" asked Joe.

"Hangtown Creek is still flowing," said Zach. "The hole the explosives made I can use for a holding pond that'll be deeper than the original. We only need to move some dirt around, and the pond will be functional again. I trust God that it can be done. I see His hand involved in this."

"You do?" asked Joe frowning.

"Absolutely. The explosion is a blessing in disguise," said Zach. "The OSSB wanted to make life more difficult for Mary, but God instead made things better for her. Remember, God works in mysterious ways, His wonder to behold."

"I hope you're right," said Joe, "but I don't see God's involvement. I see intolerant people expressing their anger. Your newly found discernment of God's involvement in everyday life is bizarre. You don't really believe God gets involved in life's minutia, do you?"

"I didn't believe it before the duel," responded Zach. "But after what I experienced during it, I do now."

"That's nonsense!" said Joe. "You're full of shit."

"I'm getting cold," said Claire. "Let's go home."

SUNDAY, AUGUST 22, 1852

IN THE EARLY morning of a warm summer day, Claire rolled over and put her head on Zach's chest.

"What time is Joe's service?" she asked.

"Ten o'clock." *Why's she asking me this? She knows what time the service is.*

"I wonder how many people will be there?"

"I have no idea," sneered Zach. "There're a lot of British miners around; they might come."

"Are they aware of the service?" she asked, delighting in the warmth of his body.

"It's hard to know. Joe did some advertising, but did they see it? How many will show up is anyone's guess. To be honest, right now, I don't give a damn!"

Claire rose up, looked Zach in the eye, and said, "You're kind of grumpy this morning. Is something bothering you?"

"I'm frustrated I don't have a pressman," said Zach with a heavy sigh. "Everything I want to do with the paper is on hold."

Maintaining her gaze, Claire said: "I want you to tell me when something is bothering you. When you don't, you end up grouchy, and I don't like that."

"Yeah, yeah. You're right," responded Zach, rolling over, so his back faced her.

Stop being a jerk! Thought Claire as she recoiled to her side of the bed. *It's not my fault you don't have a pressman.*

* * *

At nine o'clock, Flann closed the bar and asked the gamblers to leave. With Joe's help, he shoved the dining tables out of the way. Together, they arranged the dining chairs into three rows, and Joe placed a service bulletin on each of them. Flann carried a rectangular table from the lobby and put it in front of the chairs. On the table, Joe placed a white tablecloth, and on it he centered a two-foot-high brass cross. Flann pushed the bar's piano over to the right side of the worship space while Joe carried a lectern to the left side. At twenty minutes before ten, Misses Olive Day began playing pieces by Bach.

Promptly at ten o'clock, on Joe's signal, Misses Day launched into the opening hymn, *Praise to the Lord*. Everyone stood as Joe entered from the side of the dining room. He wore a black cassock with a white surplice and a tippet. After the singing concluded, Joe read the opening sentences from Morning Prayer and then asked everyone to sit as Zach stepped to the lectern to read the first lesson: Isaiah 42:6-7.

> I, the Lord, in My grace, have summoned you.
> And I have grasped you by the hand.
> I created you and appointed you
> A covenant people, a light of nations,
> To open the eyes that are blind,
> Rescuing prisoners from confinement,
> From the dungeon, those who sit in darkness.

Following the first lesson, the congregation stood and read Psalm 125, sang a brief canticle, and sat again as Robert Jenner read the second lesson: Romans 7:6.

> But now we are discharged from the law, dead to that which
> held us captive, so that we are slaves not under the old written
> code but in the new life of the Spirit.

Joe walked in front of the gathering and began his sermon. It was based on the readings from Isaiah and Romans.

"A new life is entering Hangtown!" said Joe. "This new life is a congregation of disciples who are obedient to Christ and his teachings. We have been summoned to be a light to the nations, to open eyes that previously were blind. As priest-in-charge, I welcome you to Saint Mary's Episcopal Church."

Joe went on to address the mission of Saint Mary's: to spread the Good News of a spiritual life grounded in love.

"Time is short. Christianity is only one generation away from extinction. If we don't share the Good News, future generations won't know what they're missing. We must act now. With our worship this morning, Saint Mary's vital work has begun. I'm glad you're here and urge you to bring a friend or two to next week's service."

Following Joe's sermon, prayers were offered, an offering taken, and a lively rendition of Isaac Watts' hymn, *Joy to the World!* was sung as the closing hymn.

Joe greeted the congregation as they filed out. Zach and Claire were the last to reach him.

"What are you doing for lunch?" asked Zach.

"I'd like to have it with you," said Joe, smiling. "If you don't mind, on this first Sunday I'd like to eat here at the hotel. I want to repay Matilde for all she's done to help me."

"That's fine with me," said Zach. Turning to Claire, Zach asked, "Is having lunch here okay with you?"

"I don't like being around Matilde, but for Joe, I'll do it."

* * *

Claire used the time before lunch to go to the boarding house. She wanted to speak with Betty about assuming leadership of the women from Mary. While Claire was doing that, Zach went to the post office to pick up Saturday's mail. Two letters were waiting for him.

Lucretia Mott got back to me. I hope she's interested in coming because the people of Hangtown need to hear her message. The other letter is from Norman Asing. I wonder what's on his mind?

Zach opened the letter from Misses Mott as he walked to his office. The sun was already hot.

Dear Mr. Johnson:

Thank you for the invitation to speak in California. I'm delighted word of my efforts to achieve equality for women has reached across the continent. However, I must decline your request; I can't neglect my obligations here. Besides, I'm too old to make the trip.

I have an idea about how I can help you. I've spoken to a young associate of mine, Miss Julia Lynn Powell. She's thirty years younger than I am, and she's eager to bring our message to California. I assure you she'll do an excellent job. Besides being a splendid speaker, she has experience organizing reform movements. She'll teach the women of Hangtown how to become a dynamic force for change.

Julia will arrive in San Francisco in the middle of September on board the Pathfinder. She asked me to tell you she accepts your invitation to stay with you while she's there.

It warms my heart to know you're an advocate for equality. May God bless you in your strivings.

Earnestly,
Lucretia Mott

I can't wait to show Claire her letter. Miss Powell is coming soon! As Joe said, new life is coming to Hangtown, one that'll open the eyes of those who are blind. I can hardly wait.

At the newspaper office, Zach settled into his chair, put his feet on top of his desk, and read Norman Asing's letter.

Dear Zach:

I'm writing to let you know I've heard about the killings and ordeals you've been through since we met. I want to help bring an end to the vexations the OSSB has caused you. I'll say more about this in a moment.

The labor strike being planned when you were here produced the desired results. The significance of the Chinese workforce became apparent to everyone.

My determination to convert the minds of the State leaders continues. I send a steady stream of letters to every legislator, demanding changes to the laws restricting immigrant's rights. Your editorials fill me with hope. I pass them along to the leaders of the State, and I believe your words are making a difference. Keep them coming.

The reason I'm writing is to let you know I've sent a crack reporter your way. His name is Zhang Wei. I'll pay half his salary so that he's free to investigate the leadership of Hangtown's OSSB while he's contributing to the growth of your newspaper. Zhang is fluent in English, Mandarin, and Cantonese, writes well and is a hard worker.

Zhang will come by your office on Monday, August twenty-third. Please forgive my forwardness for sending him before consulting with you. I've been told your hands are full and that you can use all the help you can get. Think of Zhang as the Chinese community's contribution to your success.

To equality for all people, I close, your friend,
Norman Asing

What a generous gift Norman is providing. Halting the oppressive activities of the OSSB would be an answer to prayer, and I certainly can use a good reporter. Zhang's arrival will ease my load, but I still have to find someone who can operate and maintain the press.

Zach left the newspaper office and went directly to the boarding house. Claire was drawing when he rang the porch bell.

"Hi, Claire," said Zach. "Are you finished? I've got some wonderful news to share."

"My meetings have ended, I can go. While I waited for you, I started a picture of my recent dream. I can't wait to show it to you. I need a moment to tidy up. Have a seat and enjoy the butterflies."

It was ten minutes before Claire returned.

"How did your meeting with Betty, go?" asked Zach, walking down the front path to the street.

"Betty and I quickly got on the same page regarding the expected behavior of the borders," said Claire, lifting her dress off the ground as she walked. "I told her my policies about collecting rent, and she's comfortable with them. Betty is a reasonable woman. There won't be any problems she can't handle. After Betty and I met, we gathered the boarders for a house meeting. I felt better once everyone agreed to accept Betty as the new leader. Tell me your news!"

"I got a letter from Lucretia Mott," said Zach.

"Is she coming? When will she be here?"

"As I suspected, she's too old to make the trip."

"That's terrible!" said Claire. "What's wonderful about her not coming? You said you had good news."

"All isn't lost," said Zach. "Hear me out."

"I was looking forward to her staying with us," said Claire. "I wanted to thank her for the difference she's made in my life."

"You can express your gratitude to her when we visit Michael's grave."

"That trip just became a higher priority," said Claire. "Did Misses Mott have anything else to say?"

"I've been trying to tell you she did," responded Zach. "She's sending a colleague in her place. She highly recommends the woman."

"Who is she?"

"Miss Julia Lynn Powell."

"Never heard of her," said Claire. "I hope she's good."

"Misses Mott says she is. I'm grateful Miss Powell is willing to endure the hardships coming here entails," said Zach. "Being thirty years younger than Misses Mott may account for why she's willing to make the trip."

"That means Miss Powell must be our age," said Claire.

"I suppose she is," said Zach. "Miss Powell is scheduled to arrive in the middle of September. She's already on her way. I received a second letter I want to tell you about."

"Who was that from?"

"Norman Asing, the leader of the Chinese community in San Francisco," said Zach. "You remember him. I went to San Francisco to meet him last March. He's sending a fellow named Zhang Wei to assist me. Norman will pay half his salary."

"Why's he doing that?" asked Claire, carefully watching her step.

"Norman has a couple of things in mind. First, he wants Zhang to discover who's leading the OSSB so we can put an end to their harassment. Zhang will also work as a reporter. If he's as good as Norman says he is, the paper will flourish," said Zach. "I'm as excited about this development as I am about Miss Powell coming. God has doubly blessed me."

* * *

When Zach and Claire arrived at the El Dorado Hotel, Joe and Matilde were waiting for them. As they approached, Zach found the couple absorbed in conversation.

"Next week, I'll have Flann set up the chairs in two sections, with an aisle between them," said Matilde.

"Hello," interrupted Claire. "What are you talking about?"

"Hi," said Joe, looking up from his notes. "We're critiquing the service and identifying what we can do to improve it. We're adjusting some minor things. For a first effort, I thought everything went well."

"I agree," said Zach. "You led an inspiring service. I got a lot from it."

"I did too," said Matilde. "I loved your message, and you gave me enough time to set up the dining room before the lunch crowd arrived. That really helped. Working with Joe is a delight. I look forward to a long partnership. How about an appetizer to commemorate the successful start? It'll be on the house."

"That would be terrific!" said Joe, putting aside his notes.

"I'll tell Flann to bring you one," said Matilde. "Enjoy your meal."

"Aren't you joining us?" asked Joe. "I wish you would."

"Not today, sweetie. Sundays are a busy time, but thanks for asking," said Matilde with a squeeze of his shoulder and a wink.

Joe's eyes fixated on Matilde as she strutted across the room and spoke with Flann.

"Be careful, Joe. I don't trust that woman," said Claire, crossing her arms.

"She's a flirt who treats all men the same. I'm nothing special to her, though I wish I were."

"No, you don't," snapped Claire. "Trust me, Matilde is trouble."

"I don't know what you've got against Matilde?" said Joe. "She's always treated me well. What do you think, Zach?"

"I don't want to be in the middle of this," he said. "Claire has her reasons for warning you. She doesn't want to see you hurt, and she doesn't want you doing something you'll regret later."

"Like you did with Kay?"

"That's one possibility, but let's not talk about that," said Zach, looking incredulously at his brother. "I'm proud of how you launched Saint Mary's and preached a compelling sermon. Well done!"

"Thank you. Bishop Kemper inspired me," said Joe. "I'd like to think he'd be proud of me."

"I'm sure he is," said Claire, "whoever Bishop Kemper is."

"He's the first missionary bishop in the Episcopal Church," responded Joe.

Joe said he met Bishop Kemper when the Bishop came to Virginia Seminary to give a series of lectures on evangelism. Bishop Kemper used the occasion to recruit students to join him in his missionary work in Wisconsin among the Oneida Indians.

"Why doesn't he seek out men who are already priests?" asked Claire.

"Fellows who serve parishes on the east coast aren't inclined to give up their comforts for the frontier's hardships. It turns out I'm the only one who responded positively to the Bishop's call."

Flann brought the appetizer and took their lunch order.

"Bishop Kemper's lectures lit a fire in me," said Joe. "He gave my ministry a focus, which is to win souls for Christ. I've felt empowered to do that ever since I heard him speak."

"I know how that feels," said Claire. "I've felt empowered by my dreams. They opened my eyes to see God as I never had before."

"What do you mean?" a wide-eyed Joe asked. "How is that possible?"

"I became aware of a powerful force arising from deep within me," said Claire. "This realization required me to adopt a new attitude about life and myself."

"I still don't understand what you're saying?" said Joe frowning.

"I've found God's majesty resides behind the images depicted in my dreams. Through my dreams, God is urging me to act. I don't feel the need to convert the world, but I do feel responsible for doing something. Your sermon reinforced my conviction to do something. Thank you for that."

"Dreams again? I thought I made it clear that God doesn't speak through dreams," said Joe, looking to Zach for support. "I'm glad you feel motivated to share God's love. That's what matters. I just hope you do it in a church-approved way."

"I once was skeptical about dreams, too," said Zach. "But the more she and I have had, the more I've come to see God's Hand in them. You may want to rethink your attitude and be more open to them."

"Hogwash," said Joe, waving his arms dismissively. How many times do I have to tell you God doesn't speak through dreams? To follow them is an act of defiance and betrayal. The one, true, living Lord won't put up with that. For the sake of your spiritual well-being, repudiate them!"

After several moments of awkward silence, Zach said: "You had more than a dozen people show up this morning. Saint Mary's is off to a good start."

"I counted fifteen to seventeen people," said Joe, settling back in his chair.

"Besides Zach and me, I saw Stephen, Rose, Roberto, Matilde, and Flann," said Claire, finishing her meal. "Who were the others?"

"The couple who brought the two children are the Jenners. Mister Jenner operates a general store in town. Frederick Bee was also present with his wife, Catherine. She told me Fred's brother, Albert, will join us as soon as he returns from his honeymoon on the east coast. Catherine's guess is they'll be back in time for Lent. The others left before I could speak with them," said Joe. "Several looked like miners. I'll have to catch up with them next week. I'm exhausted. I used to be critical of dad for taking naps following Sunday services, but now I understand why he did. Leading worship is invigorating, but it's also draining. Here's money for my lunch. I'm off to take for a nap."

"I'm ready to go too," said Zach to Claire. "Are you?

"I'm ready," said Claire, placing her napkin on the table. "What's your hurry?"

"I want to spruce up the backyard. The hedges need trimming, and the paths need sweeping," said Zach standing. "There's no end to the work in the yard that needs to be done."

As they went home, Claire said, "Despite Joe's lecture, I'll continue to pay attention to my dreams. In fact, while you're doing yard work, I'm going to work on the drawing I started. I've had some stirrings, and I want to see what more might come. Thank you for speaking up on my behalf. That was a loving thing for you to do."

"Joe is a bit rigid about some things, though it wasn't long ago that I shared that same attitude," said Zach.

"Rigidity runs in your family," said Claire. "What made you change your thinking about dreams?"

"Your openness to them and Adi's insights," said Zach. "I spoke up because I want Joe to know he's wrong, as was I."

* * *

The afternoon was hot and humid. By four-thirty, water was pouring off Zach, and he was ready to rap up his yard work. He raked the cuttings into a pile, lit them on fire, and returned the clippers and rake to the shed. When the fire burned out, Zach poured water on the ashes and went inside for a drink. He found Claire in the kitchen, making lemonade.

"That looks delicious. Where'd you get so many lemons? It looks like you've got enough to make a gallon," said Zach, drying his head with a dishtowel.

"Don't use that! I dry our dishes with it."

"Too late!" Zach said with a sheepish grin.

Claire told Zach their neighbor, John Larue, gave her the lemons. His tree was overflowing with them.

"I filled a good-sized bag," she said. "John said there are more if we want them."

"He's a good neighbor," said Zach. "It's time we had John over for horseshoes and a meal. How's your drawing coming along?"

"I'll show you when I finish here," said Claire. "Let's sit on the bench out back. It's too nice a day to be inside, and I want to enjoy the fruits of your labor."

As they relaxed in the shade, a gentle breeze came up. Claire said: "You've made the yard beautiful. Thank you for all your hard work."

"I enjoy a nice-looking yard. Sitting here next to you with a glass of lemonade is sublime. I'm sorry I was irritable this morning," said Zach, taking Claire's hand. "I'll do better next time. Show me your drawing."

"Thank you for saying that," said Claire. "You're forgiven."

Claire handed Zach the drawing she'd been working on, and said, "The picture doesn't do justice to the images I saw in the dream."

Zach studied the picture.

"I like what you've done," he said. "There's a spiritual quality to it. The picture transports me to another realm."

"I wanted those feelings to come through," said Claire, squeezing Zach's hand. "As I drew, God's presence came alive in me. The more I drew, the stronger my awareness of His presence became. Joe is wrong: God does communicate through dreams. What a gift to me this dream has been! I'm eager to find out what my part in the great dance is."

"Does that mean you're leaving me to become a nun?" asked Zach, narrowing his eyes.

"Don't be silly," said Claire, punching Zach on his shoulder. "I want to start a school that's a place where children not only learn to read, write, and do arithmetic but discover the wonders of the world."

"You want to be a teacher?"

"No, I'm not a teacher," said Claire. "I'll fund the school and hire the right woman to guide the students. I'll start my search for her tomorrow."

"Starting a school is an ambitious undertaking," said Zach. "Perhaps you should wait till after the baby is born?"

"I don't want to wait," said Claire. "I have the time and energy to do it now."

"Starting a school won't be easy," said Zach. "I think you should wait."

"I have more time now than I will after I give birth," said Claire, pulling her hand away from Zach's. Turning toward him, she said, "When I tell you my inspirations, your nitpicking robs me of my enthusiasm. I come away feeling unheard. No man...not Joe...not you...is going to squash my response to God's message in my dreams. Do you understand?"

* * *

After dinner, Zach returned to the El Dorado Hotel.

"Excuse me, gentlemen," he shouted while tapping an empty glass with a knife. "I need your attention."

It took several moments of tapping before the talking subsided, and Zach could speak without shouting.

"Yesterday someone blew up the pond behind the laundry. That means there won't be water for the women to clean your clothes. You'll have to send them to Sacramento, San Francisco, or overseas. Not only will that take longer, but it'll also cost you more."

"I don't like that," said Martin Klopp. "The Chink here does a good job at a reasonable price."

"That's right," yelled Dan O'Hare. "Let's string up whoever did this!"

"Who's responsible?" shouted Domenico Freguilia.

"The OSSB left a note saying they did it," said Zach. "I have a plan to fix the problem, but I need your help. I'd like ten of you to join me at the laundry at eight o'clock tomorrow morning. Bring shovels. We'll create a new pond that's superior to the one the miscreants blew up. Who's with me?"

Fifteen hands went up.

"Thank you. I'll see you in the morning behind the laundry. With so many of you volunteering, it shouldn't take us long."

As Zach walked home, thunder rumbled in the distance.

MONDAY, AUGUST 23, 1852

A WINDOW-RATTLING BOOM WOKE Zach to heavy drumbeats on the roof. As his eyes adjusted to the darkness, a flash of light momentarily lit the room. Claire wasn't in bed.

"Claire, where are you?" he yelled.

"Downstairs. I couldn't sleep with all the noise," hollered Claire. "The baby doesn't like it either. I can't sleep with his wiggling and throwing of elbows. I'm having a cup of tea. Will you join me?"

Another loud boom shook the house.

"I'll be right down," he said.

Claire had his tea brewing when Zach arrived in the kitchen.

"The thunder sounds like gigantic rams butting heads," said Claire.

"I imagined a herd of rhinos racing across the night sky. How long have you been up?"

"About an hour. I don't recall it ever raining this hard," said Claire. "I hope the roof doesn't leak."

"I'll check when the sun comes up," said Zach. "Our yard can use the rain, and the wet ground will make it easier for the crew to create the pond at the laundry."

"Be careful," said Claire. "The creek behind the laundry will be full and running fast. I don't want you swept away."

"I hope the storm ends before daybreak. No one will show up if there's lightning around."

"It's only two-thirty. There's plenty of time for the storm to pass," said Claire. "I feel sorry for the fellas who have only a tent to keep themselves dry. They must be miserable."

"I'm going out back to relieve myself."

"Go slowly," continued Claire. "The path is muddy. I almost slipped when I went."

Another flash, followed by a loud boom, greeted Zach as he entered the backyard. The pelting rain drenched him when he fell.

Damn it! He thought as he pulled himself off a rose bush. Zach opened the outhouse door. *At least the wind has reduced the foul smell. I see it's time to remove the waste from the hole. I bet it hasn't been done since Jake Ferguson left for Georgia. I wonder how much trash the Fergusons tossed in here?*

When Zach finished sprinkling lime into the hole, he washed his hands in the kitchen and rejoined Claire in bed.

"I hope you left your shoes on the back porch," she said. "I don't want muddy tracks in the house."

"I took them off outside with the rest of my clothes," said Zach. "I slipped on the way to the privy."

"I warned you."

"The path must be slicker now than when you went," grumbled Zach. "Why didn't you tell me we're running low on newsprint in the privy?"

"Did you have enough?" asked Claire.

"This time, I did," said Zach. "I'll bring more home from work."

Thunder rumbled in the distance as Zach held Claire, and they drifted off to sleep.

* * *

It was seven o'clock when Zach woke. The rain and lightning had stopped, and he was excited he'd be able to fix the pond. Before leaving, Zach checked the house for leaks. Not finding any, he grabbed a shovel and hurried off to the laundry. It wasn't long before the volunteers appeared.

"Here's my plan," said Zach. "We'll dig a channel to the creek so water can flow back into the hole the explosion made. On the other side of the crater, I want to create a place for the women to stand to collect the water they need. Any questions?"

"With due respect for your plan," said Rusty Colter, "it's clear you've never done this before. There's a better way. I'm afraid if we do what you're suggesting, the water will leak until the basin is unusable."

"Tell me what you have in mind," said Zach, leaning on his shovel's handle.

"I grew up in Rock River, Wyoming," said Rusty. "The clay there is a natural sealant. We used it to build all our basins. The clay swells almost twenty times its original size when it gets wet, making it a natural barrier between the ground and the water. If you cover the bottom and sides with this clay before it's filled, I guarantee it won't leak."

"Where do I find clay like that?" asked Zach, rubbing his beard.

"I've got a huge pile of it behind my cabin. You never know when you'll need it. I'll take several men with me, we'll load my wagon, and be back in an hour. While we're gone, I suggest the rest of you refashion the crater into a four-foot deep pond with a channel that connects to the creek. Remove all the rocks and plants you find. They'll interfere with the sealing process. When you're done, compact the ground as best you can."

When Rusty returned, the basin was ready for the clay. Rusty applied it to the bottom and sides while the others made sure the ground was firm and smooth. "Open the channel. Let's see if it holds," said Rusty.

"Look how quickly it's filling," said Zach. "The creek is as full as I've ever seen it."

"I don't see any leaks," said Rusty. "Some of you spread sand around the edge of the pond. That should provide a firm footing for the women."

"The laundry is back in business!" exclaimed Zach. "Thank you, Rusty, for taking the lead on this. I'm afraid if we'd done it my way, it wouldn't have worked."

"You're right, it wouldn't have," said Rusty, chuckling and putting his arm around Zach.

The workers went to the El Dorado Hotel for lunch and a beer. In the middle of the meal, Walt Selzer sprinted into the dining room.

"Zach, there's an Indian loitering outside the newspaper office. He wouldn't tell me anything except he's waiting for you. I told him to move along, or I'd shoot him. He left but returned when he thought I was gone. I fired a round in his direction to show him I meant business. He hid after that. I suspect he's still around, but I couldn't find him. Be careful when you return to your office. He appears to be up to no good."

"Thanks," said Zach. "Gentlemen, I have to leave, but I want to thank you again for your hard work. I'll speak with the laundry owner about giving each of you a discount."

* * *

At ten-thirty, Rose rang the boarding house's bell.

"I'm here for my fitting," she told Claire.

Claire gave Rose her new uniform and evening dress to try on. Rose approved the uniform but wanted the dress top and waist to be tighter.

"Stephen is leaving soon. I want him to take sensual thoughts of me with him."

Claire gave the dress to Alice, who went upstairs to make the changes.

Handing Rose a cup of tea, Claire asked, "Where are you and Stephen going Saturday night?"

"He's taking me to the Empire Theater. We're going to see *Dan Rice's Great Hippodrome and Menagerie*. The show is modified to be indoors, but it'll still have his horse and animal tricks. I'm looking forward to it. Dan Rice is quite the clown. Many say he's the best comedian in America. I'm told his commentaries on current events are unforgettable."

"I've heard the same thing," said Claire. "The show sold out before Zach purchased tickets. I told him to hurry, but he didn't, so we're not going. You'll have to tell me about it."

Alice returned with the evening gown, and Rose put it on. She admired herself in the mirror and thought, *That's tight. I love it.*

* * *

Zach walked up Main Street to Cedar Ravine and on to the boarding house. He didn't see the mysterious Indian as he passed his office.

Walt must've scared him away. I wonder if this is the same Indian Stephen saw?

Belle answered the door.

"Hello. What can I do for you?"

"I wanted you to know the pond behind the laundry is repaired. You can open for business any time you want."

"Thank you! I'll start heating the water right away so we can open in the morning. After last night's storm, there should be a demand for our services."

"Is Claire here?"

"She's with a customer. I'll let her know you asked for her. Do you want to wait?"

"No, I've got to return to my office. I'm expecting a visitor."

As Zach approached the newspaper office, he carefully checked the area around the building.

I don't see an Indian, and there's no indication Zhang Wei has been here.

It wasn't long before Mister Tobey walked in.

"I understand there was another attack on my building," he said, examining the burned area.

"There was, but the damage was minimal," said Zach.

"You'll have to pay for the repairs," Mister Tobey said. "I've arranged for a crew to fix the place. They'll be here in the morning."

"Thank you, Mister Tobey. Tomorrow morning will be fine."

"Listen to me, Zach. You'll have to change your editorial policies if you want to stop these attacks. I don't like my building disfigured. Either you change, or you'll have to move on. Do you hear me?"

"I don't have a pressman. I won't be publishing any time soon."

"This is your last chance. If there's any more damage to my property, you'll have to leave. I'll be back tomorrow afternoon to make sure the repairs were done properly."

* * *

It was two o'clock when Walt Selzer threw open the front door and dragged in an average built man in his late teens. He had dark hair and penetrating brown eyes.

"The Indian came back after I told him not to," said Walt. "What do you want me to do with him?"

"What's your name, and why have you been loitering around my office?" asked Zach.

"My name is Elsu. I've come to apply for the pressman position. You're hiring a pressman, aren't you?"

"I am. I'm looking for a man with experience operating and maintaining an 1848 Hoe rotary press. Can you do these things?"

"I can," said Elsu.

"Where'd you learn to operate and maintain a press like this?" asked Zach, pointing to it.

"Are you questioning my ability because I'm an Indian?"

"Yes," said Zach. "I've never heard of an Indian working in the newspaper business."

"Do you want me to take care of him?" asked Walt. "I can use the money I'll get for his scalp."

"No. I want to find out more about Elsu. He's an unusual fellow. Persistent too. I like that. Thanks for your help," said Zach, holding the door open for Walt. "I can handle things from here."

"I've heard you're a fair man," said Elsu. "Give me a chance to show you what I can do."

"Here's an article. Print it."

"Elsu took Zach's writing, typeset it, and asked, "How many copies do you want?"

"One will do."

"Elsu printed the article, took the press apart, and cleaned it. After reassembling it, asked, "Are you satisfied? Do I get the job?"

"You're good," said Zach. "Where'd you learn to operate a rotary press?"

"Before I tell you, do I get the job?"

"There's another thing we need to discuss first," said Zach. "My editorial policy is to insist on equal rights for immigrants. Some of the townsfolk don't like that. To stop me, they've injured my two previous pressmen. You may be in danger if you take the job."

"I appreciate you telling me," said Elsu, "but I'm a Modoc. My life is in danger every day, whether I work here or not. I'll take the job if you're offering it?"

They discussed salary, Zach's expectations, and a probationary period. When Elsu agreed, Zach said, "You're hired. When can you begin?"

"Today, if you want."

"Tell me how you learned to operate a press like this."

Settling into their chairs, Elsu told Zach his story.

"It was a Sunday, many years ago. My father and his brother went to watch the settlers they liked stack hay. Both families went. Because we already had all the game we needed for winter, we brought the settlers the meat of an elk."

"My cousins and I were bored watching the men stack hay, so we explored a nearby creek. We never saw the two strangers ride up behind our fathers and shoot them. When my father's friends objected, the killers said they knew my dad and uncle were 'damned bad injuns.' That was a lie, but a good enough excuse to justify the killings. After scalping my father and uncle, the killers took my mother, aunt, cousins, and me to Yreka."

"That's horrible! These men make me ashamed I'm white," said Zach, frowning.

"I know there are some decent white men," said Elsu. "I wouldn't have come if I didn't believe you were one of them."

"What happened to you, and your mother, aunt, and cousins?"

"The killers didn't know my father or uncle. They just said they did. They'd seen how pretty my mother and aunt are, and wanted them for themselves. When we arrived in Yreka, no white man said a word about the Indian women being with the bounty hunters, even though they all knew the men were married. I was separated from the others and sold to a man who owned the newspaper. By law, I had to work for him till I was eighteen, and he didn't have to pay me, which he didn't. He was the one who taught me how to operate the press. My cousins were also sold. They tried to run away but were caught and killed.

"It wasn't long before the bounty hunters' wives learned of their husband's private stash. They forced them to sell my mother and aunt. I heard a couple of rich miners purchased them. I haven't seen my mother since she was sold. I don't know if she's alive. I think about her every day."

"How'd you get away?"

"Just before my eighteenth birthday, the owner of the newspaper bought another young Modoc. I was told to teach him how to operate the press. I figured my owner intended to kill me and turn in my scalp for the reward. That's a common practice in Yreka. I fled when the owner wasn't around. Members of other tribes hid me from the posse that came looking for me. One of the chiefs I stayed with told me about you. That's why I'm here. I need a job. I won't disappoint you."

"I'm glad you're here," said Zach, "but why didn't you stay with your tribe?"

"Bows and arrows can't compete with rifles when it comes to hunting game.

Over the years, the whites killed most of the deer and elk. They fenced our traditional land and plowed it. That prevented the women from gathering the roots and acorns we rely upon. As bad as these developments were, even worse was the salmon's failure to swim upstream," said Elsu. "The miners clogged the rivers with their tailings and diked the rivers. This caused the salmon to stay away. Even the trout turned on their sides. Deprived of their food, my people starved. When a few desperate braves entered another tribe's hunting grounds, fighting ensued. The shortage of food affected everyone."

"How have your people been able to survive?" asked Zach.

"Without fish, game, roots, or acorns, not well. I've seen men who've been hunters all their lives go to Yreka to sell their bows and arrows," said Elsu.

"Why'd they do that?"

"Bow and arrows are of no further use. The men used the little money they got to buy bread for their babies. Others begged until the settlers set dogs on them. Thousands of men who once were brave warriors retreated to their lodges and died."

"Why didn't your tribe move to a reservation?"

"The nearest reservation is over by the sea. That's forty or fifty miles away from the Holy Mountain."

"Holy Mountain?"

"You call it Shasta. My people regard it as a sacred place, and the magnificent forest is our home. The Great Spirit made this mountain and gave it to us. We don't dig it up looking for gold, and we don't cut down the pines or muddy the rivers. My people would rather die than defile the mountain."

"Isn't the land by the sea holy too?"

"Not to us. The coast tribes eat fish from the sea. My people eat venison and acorns. The feud between tribes is fierce. Many people on both sides die. Modocs don't want to make a home on the enemy's land. Everything inside of us revolts at the idea."

"I thought life on the reservation was protected by the United States government?"

"They do nothing to protect one tribe from another. Whites believe a dead Indian is a good thing. If we kill each other, it saves them from doing it. My people will stay on the Holy Mountain until the end."

"I want to help you," said Zach. "I'll write an editorial this week about what white men can do to make life better for Indians."

"Thank you," said Elsu. "I doubt it will help, but anything is better than nothing."

The office door opened.

"Hi," said Joe. "I've got next Sunday's bulletin material. Do you have a way to print it?"

"I do. This is Elsu," said Zach. "He's my new printer. He can run off what you need this afternoon. Why don't you show him how you want the finished bulletins to look?"

"You hired an Indian?" asked Joe, creasing his brow. "Are you crazy? If you thought the town was against you before, wait till they learn about this!"

"He's qualified and needs the job. I like him and want to give him a chance," said Zach. "Besides, dad taught us to see Christ in all people. You remember that, don't you?"

"Watch your back," said Joe. "Someone will come gunning for you. Elsu, my name is Joe Johnson. I'm Zach's brother and an Episcopal priest. On Sundays, I hold services at ten o'clock in the El Dorado Hotel. You're welcome to join us. Bring your wife or a friend if you want."

"Show me what you want printed," said Elsu. "I'll get it done for you. Thank you for the invitation, but I'm not a Christian. I find God in the forests and streams of the Holy Mountain you call Shasta. God has been there for my people since the beginning."

"If I weren't in a rush, I'd talk with you about your beliefs," said Joe. "I'm relieved you'll be able to print the bulletin. I'll be back in the morning to pick them up. I'll pay you well for your efforts."

* * *

A little after four o'clock, a Chinese man in his mid-twenties knocked on the office door. He was of average height, slim, wore traditional Chinese clothing, and a queue.

"Hello, I'm Zhang Wei. I'm looking for Mister Johnson. Sang Yuen, I mean Norman Asing, sent me."

"Welcome," said Zach, standing and extending his hand. "I've been expecting you."

"So you got the letter!" said Zhang, smiling. "I hope this is going to work. I'd like to improve the lives of the Chinese any way I can, and I want to learn what it takes to be successful in the newspaper business. When I return to San Francisco, I want to publish the first Chinese-language newspaper."

"This is Elsu," said Zach. "He's my pressman. Today is his first day."

Elsu and Zhang nodded to each other, and Elsu resumed typesetting Joe's bulletin.

"This will be your desk," said Zach, tapping its top. "You'll find office supplies on a shelf in the back."

"I can tell I'm going to like working here," said Zhang, trying out his desk chair.

"Tell me about yourself," said Zach. "How long have you been in California? What brought you across the Pacific? Do you have family here?"

"I'm from Jintian, which is in the province of Guangxi. Guangxi is the most beautiful part of China. It's deep in the south, close to the coast. In the north of the province, you'll find lots of mountains about the Sierra's size. Most of the province is full of rocky hills that are about the same elevation as Hangtown. The soil is red, the rivers plentiful, and the trees in the north are fir, cedar, and rosewood. In the south, orange trees are in profusion. As a boy, I enjoyed exploring the numerous caves that dot the area. I'd marvel at the stalactites and stalagmites, and I'd make boats out of leaves. I'd put them in an underground stream, and watch them journey into the unknown."

"What kind of animals live there?" asked Elsu, who liked that Zhang was a man of the mountains.

"Water buffalos are used by the farmers, but bison, boars, bears, and gibbons run wild. My favorite is the cockatoo. They're intelligent, beautiful, and playful. I've seen them hang upside down from their nest just for the fun of it. I wish Hangtown had cockatoos."

"Why'd you leave such a paradise?" asked Zach.

"There was a rebellion in my hometown, led by one of my neighbors, Hong Xiugua. Our area had suffered a series of natural disasters and was having economic problems. Farmers were heavily taxed, rents were going up, and peasants were moving away. Bandits were numerous. Secret societies—

like the OSSB—were formed. Neighbors fought each other. Everyone in our province hated the Manchus, who were weak and corrupt, but ran the government.

"It was out of these conditions Hong seized power. He pledged to do away with the Manchus' rule and their loyalty to the British oppressors," said Zhang. "When Hong curtailed the bandit's activities, people joined him. Hong attracted more supporters when he pledged to share equally all of the property he seized from the Manchus. By late December 1850, Hong's army was ten thousand men. They attacked and defeated the government forces stationed in Jintian. I wanted no part of the civil war I saw coming. I left for Gold Mountain while I could."

"My paper stands for equality for all people, especially the Chinese, though I see now I need to do more for Indians. As you know, many in Hangtown don't like that. They believe in a white man first policy. They want to keep all others out. They've tried to shut down my paper by intimidation, by turning advertisers against me, destroying my office, and physically harming my employees. Working here will put you in danger. Are you ready to accept that risk?"

"That's why I'm here. I want to help. I learned valuable lessons from Hong about battling oppressive forces. I'll use what I've learned to discover who's behind the OSSB. Secret societies fall apart when light shines on them. I can't wait to get started."

"Excellent! We'll publish this week. Tomorrow I'll introduce you to the church and community leaders who provide us information about their activities. That's the core of our business. I supplement their activities with stories about current affairs and my editorials. Your reporting will give us a broader reach into the community."

Zach and Zhang agreed on a salary, a probationary period, and other details of the job.

"Do you have a place to stay?" asked Zach.

"I'll take a room in Chinatown. Several members of my extended family live in Fiddletown. They don't know I'm here. I want to surprise them."

"I'm blessed to have the two of you working for me. God is good. Enjoy the rest of the day, and I'll see you at eight o'clock tomorrow morning."

* * *

As dusk approached, Elsu finished printing and folding Joe's bulletin.

"I failed to ask if you have a place to stay?" said Zach.

"For now, I'll camp in the trees outside of town. I'm happier there than I am in a building. Don't worry about me. I can take care of myself."

After Elsu left, Zach locked the office door and headed home. He walked a couple of blocks when he remembered the newsprint. He returned to the office, grabbed a substantial supply, and arrived home just in time for dinner.

"I forgot the newsprint and had to go back for it," said Zach. "Otherwise, I would've been here sooner."

"I'm glad you did. I finished what was left," said Claire. "Have you thought about having the waste cleaned out of the privy?"

"I intended to contact Sylvester, the fertilizer guy, but forgot," said Zach, shaking his head. "I'll speak to him tomorrow. Let me tell you the good news about the pond, Zhang, and the pressman."

"You hired a pressman?"

"I did. Elsu is a Modoc Indian. He's familiar with rotary presses. He told me quite a story."

"You hired an Indian after one tried to kidnap me?" asked Claire. "Are you sure he doesn't want revenge?"

"I'm sure," responded Zach. "Elsu has been a slave to the owner of the newspaper in Yreka. He escaped and came to Hangtown seeking employment. I intend to give him a chance."

"Do you think he told a tear-jerker of a story to gain access to you and your family? Indians can't be trusted. I'm worried about this guy," said Claire, her eyes narrowing.

"I believe him," said Zach. "God sent me the person I need. Besides, it's not like there's been a lot of people applying for the position."

Zach and Claire talked about fixing the pond, Zhang, and other matters late into the night. When they climbed into bed, sleep came quickly.

THURSDAY, AUGUST 26, 1852

I'm climbing a large mountain with a group of people, dreamed Zach. *As we follow the path, there are religious stations that block our way. If we're to proceed, we must pass through each station and follow their rules. I feel inconvenienced: I want to get through the stations quickly without being hassled.*

These stations are Buddhist shrines. The workers who take care of the shrines live there. They're poor and uneducated. To pass through a station, climbers are to walk backward with their head and eyes down. Climbers aren't to look at the station keepers, or the walls, or the ceiling. A humble posture is to be maintained.

I've no respect for these customs. I hurry through. I don't raise my head, but I look around to see what the forbidden looks like. I'm arrogant and disrespectful even though I know if I'm caught, I'll be sent back to the previous station, and at least for a while, not be allowed to proceed.

At one of the stations, about two-thirds of the way up the mountain, I'm doing my usual thing. There's another climber present. He's slightly older and more respectful of the process. He observes the regulations. This slows him down, yet he's ahead of me. How can this be? I notice he stays more to the outside of the shrine, whereas I'm cutting through the center. I decide to follow his example. I move to the outer edge.

One of the shrine keepers stops me. He instructs me on the correct way to proceed. He calls my attention to the mahogany strips on the floor. I'm to have my outside arm hang over the outermost edge. This will guide me as I walk backward.

I ask the man what the stations are called. He said each shrine has its own name. This one is Timeless.

I leave the other climbers and explore the station. There are names for God along the walls. Every step there's a new designation: God the Ocean, God the Breath, God the Vastness, etc. Each name is to be used as a meditation. I recite the names a dozen or more times before proceeding up the mountain to the next station.

As I move ahead, I'm ashamed of my previous rushed, disrespectful attitude. I see how much I missed by racing. I realize the climb is a religious trek; one to be undertaken deliberately, and with discipline. The fellow at the previous shrine told me climbers walk backward so we won't be tempted to look ahead. This is because what we're seeking is found on the inside of us, not the outside.

In the morning, Zach recorded the dream and his reflections.

The dream annoys me, and I'm not sure why. I'm surprised it says I have a bad attitude about my spiritual journey. I feel closer to God now than I ever have. I'll keep doing what I've been doing and not worry about what the dream says.

Zach picked up his Prayer Book. When he got to the assigned lesson, it was Luke 17:7-10.

Who among you would say to your slave who has just come in from plowing or tending sheep in the field, "Come here at once and take your place at the table?" Would you not rather say to him, "Prepare supper for me, put on your apron and serve me while I eat and drink; later you may eat and drink?" Do you thank the slave for doing what is commanded? So you also, when you have done all that you were ordered to do, say, "We are worthless slaves; we have done only what we ought to have done!"

Jesus is telling me my service to God isn't worthy of recognition; I'm doing no more than what is expected. The Lord knows I try my best and do more than others.

A repeated rapping on the front door brought Zach out of his musings. When he got downstairs and opened the door, there stood a short, muscular man in work clothes. A wheelbarrow containing a shovel and canvas bags were behind him. It was Sylvester, the fertilizer man. Zach showed him to the side gate and the privy.

"How long will this take?" asked Zach.

"Depending on what I find, an hour or two."

"I'll be at the newspaper office by then. Come by when you're finished, and I'll pay you."

* * *

Back inside, Zach found Claire fixing breakfast. After she commented on how pleased she was the privy was being cleaned, Zach told her his dream.

"Seems to me the dream is telling you to stop taking shortcuts in your quest for God," said Claire. "At least at the end, you have a better attitude than you did at the beginning."

"I work harder on my relationship with God than anyone I know," said Zach. "I deserve a more positive message than 'don't take shortcuts.'"

"Do you believe you're superior to others?" asked Claire, putting Zach's breakfast on the table.

"When it comes to doing God's will, I am. I advocate all people should be treated equally under the law, citizen, and immigrant alike. This is consistent with Jesus' teachings. Those who disagree with me believe economic exploitation is more important than establishing God's Kingdom on earth. It's my responsibility to show them they're wrong."

"I think the dream is warning your pride is obstructing your progress."

"I don't," said Zach. "I've never felt closer to God than I do now. I'm surprised you don't see that."

"Growing up Roman Catholic, I was constantly reminded about the destructive power of pride. I'm pleased that's not a problem for you, and that your journey is going well," said Claire, with a smirk.

Claire changed the subject.

"It's time for me to make a trip to San Francisco, and I want to do it before the baby arrives."

"You shouldn't go alone," said Zach, "but this isn't a good time for me to go. I've got two new employees, and we haven't come together as a team. I don't want to take time off before we do. Give me a few weeks, and I'll go with you."

"The longer I wait, the harder the trip will be," said Claire. "I want to go as soon as possible, with or without you."

"If I don't go with you, who will?" asked Zach.

"Stephen," said Claire.

"Go ahead and ask your brother," said Zach. "I can't leave now."

The meal ended with Claire asking, "Did you remember to include my ad for a teacher in this week's paper?"

"I did," said Zach. "Elsu found a front-page location for it. He's good. If there's someone out there who wants the job, she'll know how to contact you."

* * *

Both Elsu and Zhang were working when Zach arrived at the office.

"I'm glad you're here. Today we print and collate the paper. Elsu, I'll help you as much as I can. Be sure to find space for a banner that says, 'Vote November Second.' I want the banner to run weekly until the election. Zhang, I have a couple of assignments for you."

"What do you want me to do?" asked Zhang.

"First, a human interest piece," said Zach. "The desire to have more women in Hangtown is strong. Women are in such short supply that in saloons, men dance with other men. I want you to write a story about the state's efforts to bring women to California."

"Okay," said Zhang. What's the second assignment?"

"This is a longer investigative piece on the Foreign Miner's Tax," said Zach.

"Write about how it came to be, what its effects are, and what the reactions to it have been."

"I'll start right away. Is there anything else you want me to do?"

"Visit the churches and other organizations I introduced you to the other day. Stay on top of what they're doing and write a report on their activities."

"Will do," said Zhang. "Wasn't your landlord supposed to come by to check out the repairs?"

"He was," said Zach. "It isn't like Mister Tobey not to show up. I wonder what happened?"

* * *

Several hours later, Sylvester entered the newspaper office. He reeked of the work he'd been doing, and his clothes reflected it. He'd come to collect his fee.

"Let's step outside so my colleagues can work undisturbed," said Zach. "What'd you find?"

"As you suspected, there were bottles in the pit. Not as many as some pits have, but more than most. The rest was human waste on its way to becoming fertilizer, which I added to my collection. Your privy is as clean as the day it was dug."

"What'd you do with the bottles?" asked Zach, scratching his beard.

"The ones that aren't broken I clean and sell to Jim Edwards at the hardware store. He resells them."

"You're an industrious fella."

"When I'm cleaned up, I'll be back," said Sylvester, "I have an ad for next week's paper. With your help, my business will blossom."

Mister Tobey appeared just as Zach was paying Sylvester. He made a wide circle around them and entered the office and examined the repairs that'd been made. When Zach reentered the building, he introduced Mister Tobey to Elsu and Zhang and said: "it isn't like you to say you'll be here at a certain time and not show up. What happened?"

"I got sick, really sick," said Tobey. "Doc Martin said it was cholera. I'm feeling better now, but my wife and children have it. It's dreadful stuff."

"Mister Tobey, I'm glad to see you up and around," said Rose, who'd slipped into the office. "Not everyone in Hangtown is as fortunate as you."

"Thank you, Rose. Tell Doc I'm feeling better," said Mister Tobey. "I don't have time to visit; people are waiting for me."

"I'll look in on your family later this afternoon," said Rose as he walked to the door. "It's vital they drink plenty of water."

"It's hard to get the children to drink as much as you recommend," grumbled Tobey. "The children are as headstrong as their mother."

"Hi, Rose," said Zach. "Let me introduce my new staff. Working the press is Elsu, and helping me report stories is Zhang."

Both men acknowledge Rose.

"What brings you?" he asked.

"There's a health problem I want you to publicize," she said. "It's vital that everyone knows about it. Do you have space this week?"

"How much material do you have?" asked Zach. "We're already printing."

"I don't have anything written," said Rose, her cheeks turning red. "I was hoping you'd write it. This is what I want you to say. Cholera has laid siege to Hangtown. It's deadly, especially when it causes diarrhea that drains the body's fluids. You recall that's what killed President Taylor."

"That was about two years ago, wasn't it?" asked Zach writing rapidly.

Rose told Zach to include what a person can do to protect themselves, and what can be done if someone comes down with it.

"In the article, emphasize that the Chinese didn't bring cholera to Hangtown," she said. "They aren't responsible for it. Cholera is the result of local conditions."

"Is there anything else I should say?" asked Zach, putting his pencil in his mouth.

"Despite what some clergy say," said Rose, "cholera isn't divine retribution."

"Divine retribution?" asked Zach. "Why would a pastor say that?"

"Some pastors believe catching cholera is unavoidable and incurable. They're wrong," said Rose. "Nevertheless, many people believe whatever their pastors say."

"How big a problem is this?" asked Zach.

"In Hangtown, about one in twenty people have it," said Rose. "That's why you must get the word out immediately before more people get sick."

"We'll find a place for your information," said Zach, walking with Rose to the door.

After she left, Zach asked Elsu, "Where do you suggest we put the story?

"On a separate page," said Elsu. "That way, the urgency of the message will stand out."

* * *

At four o'clock, Milton Latham walked into the newspaper office. Elsu had the press operating at full capacity. The noise was thunderous.

"Is Zach Johnson available?" he hollered.

"He's over there," mouthed Elsu, pointing to Zach's desk.

Zach was busy finishing the article on cholera and didn't notice his guest until he was standing in front of his desk.

"May I help you?" asked Zach, looking up at the curly-haired man sporting an impressive beard and a bow tie.

"I'm Milton Latham. We had an appointment to discuss Franklin Pierce, the Democratic nominee for President."

"Thank you for coming," said Zach, putting down his pencil and standing to shake Latham's hand. "Why don't we go to Wakefield's? It's too loud in here to talk. I'll buy."

"That's a bloody good idea. I'd like a piece of Lucy's apple pie."

The men walked to Wakefield's, ordered, and found Zach's favorite table. Zach took out a pencil and paper.

"Briefly, tell me about yourself and your career," said Zach.

"I was born in Columbus, Ohio, studied classics in Pennsylvania, and began my career as a teacher in Alabama," said Mister Latham. "I studied law while I taught, and became a lawyer in 1848. When I learned that gold had been discovered in California, I made my way to Sacramento, where I'm now the district attorney. Recently my friends encouraged me to run for the seat in the House of Representatives held by Ed Marshall. I agreed. I hope I can count on your vote."

"It's my job to be a watchdog for the citizens of Hangtown," replied Zach. "The press serves the governed, not the governors. It's my responsibility to report where the various candidates stand on the issues. Please begin by telling me the California Democrats' position on slavery."

"Slavery is an issue that divides the State Party," said Latham. "Democrats in the south want California to be a slave state. Those in the north don't. Southerners are adamant about dividing California into two if slavery isn't allowed. That's a ghastly idea. Consequently, I support the idea of California becoming a slave state. I found when I lived in Alabama that slavery isn't such a bad thing. It's certainly more desirable than splitting the state in two."

"Is one of your supporters James Gadsden?"

"Why, yes, he is," said Latham, with an incredulous stare. "James Gadsden is my largest donor. He has a creative plan for bringing slavery to southern California."

"I've heard that," said Zach. "Gadsden is also a contributor to the Whigs. I guess he doesn't care who wins as long as he obtains approval for his plans."

"I'm surprised you know about his intentions," said Latham. "He told me not to say anything. James is a determined man. He funds those who support him and finds a way to do away with those who don't. I hope you won't print any of this."

"In a democracy, people have a right to know what the government is considering and plans to do. When a free press isn't allowed to print what it knows, it's hard to hold government officials accountable for their missteps."

"I wish I knew this before I spoke," said Latham. "I wouldn't have said anything."

"You didn't tell me anything I didn't know," responded Zach. "What is the national Party's stand on slavery?"

"Nationally, Democrats believe the Constitution doesn't give Congress the power to interfere with a state's legal practices. Therefore, Democrats oppose the federal government's attempts to abolish slavery."

"I don't agree with you," said Zach. "Moving on, how did Franklin Pierce come to be your candidate?"

"Pierce was a compromise, yet he's someone who can beat the Whig's Winfield Scott. Pierce, being from New Hampshire, made our southern delegates uneasy. To appease their concerns, Bill King of Alabama was chosen to be Frank's running mate. Bill reassured the convention Frank is a 'northern man with southern principles.'"

"What's your Party's stance on the Compromise of 1850?"

"We oppose it," replied Latham.

"Why's that?" asked Zach.

"Democrats believe the Constitution gives the federal government only limited powers. The Compromise gives Congress powers it shouldn't have."

"What about immigration?" asked Zach.

"Democrats uphold America as the land of liberty and the asylum for the oppressed of every nation. We'll resist any attempt to abridge a man's privilege to become a citizen and an owner of the soil."

"I like that," said Zach. "Is there anything more you want to tell me?"

"The values that made our country exceptional are under attack. Democrats want to stop these assaults and restore the God-given values to their rightful place of prominence."

"What values are you thinking about?" asked Zach, raising an eyebrow.

"There's a woman's movement back east that diminishes the role of men. It's a vile thing," said Latham. "Equal rights for women aren't good for the country. God decreed that men are the head of the household, the protectors and providers of the family. Women like Lucretia Mott want to do away with what God ordained. If elected, Democrats will do everything in their power to squash Misses Mott's misguided movement."

"Thank you," said Zach. "I'll report what you've told me in next week's paper."

"You're providing a valuable service," said Latham. "I'm pleased to speak with you about these matters, except for Jim Gadsden's plans. Please don't print those."

"I appreciate your candor," said Zach. "When the time is right, I'll expose Gadsden's scheme."

"When you do, don't say I told you," said Latham. "It's dangerous to have Gadsden angry with you. He's vindictive."

"I never divulge my sources," replied Zach, shaking Latham's hand.

* * *

When Zach arrived home for dinner, he found Mary and Dave having a glass of wine with Claire. Dave was wearing a suit and tie.

"Welcome home," said Mary grinning.

"Hello," said Zach. "How was your honeymoon?"

"I can't say enough good things about the National Hotel in Jackson," said Mary. "It's just opened, and they treated us with respect, something Dave and I didn't experience outside their doors. The staff tended to our every wish promptly and graciously."

"I'm glad to hear that," said Zach, thinking about the note that was posted at the laundry. "What'd you do?"

"During the day, we went shopping. Because Dave is now a business owner, he should dress like one. I brought him a trunk full of new clothes. What do you think of his suit?"

"When I walked in, I thought how dapper he looks. To be honest, I wasn't sure it was Dave," said Zach, chuckling. "I thought you had a new companion."

"Come on. I don't look that different," said Dave, crossing his arms.

"You look elegant," said Zach, nudging Dave's shoulder. "It's amazing what a good suit can hide."

"That's enough teasing," said Claire. "I think Dave looks handsome. He caught my eye."

"Thank you," said Dave, smiling and looking down. "Mary and I also went fishing. For her first time with a pole, she did well. The hotel kitchen cooked the trout we caught. It was heavenly."

"Your trip makes me want to get away," said Zach. "I'll see if Joe wants to go sailing on Silver Lake next week. I can use a day away."

"Why don't you come with me to San Francisco?" asked Claire.

"I don't want to be away that long."

"I wish you'd come with me," said Claire, protruding her lips.

When Zach didn't reply, Mary said, "I have some news."

"What's that?" asked Claire.

"Dave and I decided to move the Boomerang from its current location to Chinatown. It'll be more accessible, and it'll cater to the Chinese population instead of miners down on their luck. After the move," said Mary, "there'll be a fast turn-around in profits."

"What a creative idea," said Zach. "I never cared for the Broadway location. If you stayed there, I'm afraid you'd go broke. Speaking of that, did you hear Captain Sutter is penniless? His workers discover gold, and he ends up broke. What a wicked twist of fate."

"I hadn't heard that," said Dave. "I certainly don't want to end up like he did."

"When are you going to move?" asked Claire.

"I'll open my new location in a week or two. Roberto is helping me fix up the place," said Dave. "We'll offer games the Chinese love to play, like mahjong. I plan on having several tables going at all times. That should bring in lots of customers who'll drink while they're playing or waiting to play. That's another of Mary's inspired ideas. It's good she has them because I don't."

"Belle tells me there was a problem at the laundry you had fixed," said Mary. "Thank you for whatever you did. The pond works better than ever."

Zach explained what happened and how it was repaired.

"I promised the men who helped you'd give them a discount on their laundry," said Zach. "I hope I didn't speak out of turn."

"I'll do better than what you offered," said Mary. "I'll give everyone who worked on the pond two free cleanings before their discount starts."

* * *

After dinner, Zach excused himself to return to the office. When he arrived, Elsu was collating the paper.

"While you do that," said Zach, "I'll fold and stack. In an hour, we'll have them ready to pass out."

"Thanks for coming back," said Elsu. "My previous boss never would've. Working for you helps me see things differently. Not all white men are evil; just most of them."

"We'll educate each other," said Zach. "I've no idea what your life has been like, but I'll do what I can to make it better."

SUNDAY, AUGUST 29, 1852

ZACH AND CLAIRE arrived for Joe's church service just as it was starting. The congregation was smaller, but participation was livelier. When it was time for the sermon, Joe chose Matthew 13:44 for his text.

"Jesus says:

> Again, the Kingdom of Heaven is like some treasure, which has been buried in the field. A man finds and buries it again, and goes off overjoyed to sell all his possessions to buy himself that field.

"This teaching of our Lord's," said Joe," is about discovering the Kingdom of Heaven. When it's found, the Kingdom becomes that person's highest priority. Joy fills him. At Saint Mary's, we treasure these moments, celebrate them, and tell the uninitiated about the life-changing experience that awaits them."

After the service, Claire said to Joe: "Zach and I are having a few people over for dinner. We'd like you to join us and to bring a companion."

"I'll do that. What time should we arrive?"

"Zach wants to beat you at horseshoes. Come at four-thirty."

As Claire and Joe spoke, Zach saw Charley Boles standing outside Miner's Drug Store. Zach crossed Main Street to talk to him.

"Hi, Charley," said Zach. "What brings you to town?"

"I'm having a bout of diarrhea," said Charley. "Mister Pettit was kind enough to open his store to get me medicine that he says will stop it."

"Cholera is going around," said Zach. "I wrote about how to deal with it for this week's paper. You may want to pick up a copy."

"I'll ask Mister Pettit if he has any? I'm glad you're here. I have a couple of books for you and Claire."

Charley noticed Mister Pettit motioning to him. He re-entered the pharmacy.

"Here's a potion that should do the trick," Mister Pettit said. "Drink this and chase it down with plenty of water."

"Thanks," said Charley, include the price of a paper in my bill."

When Charley walked out of the store, he saw Claire crossing Main Street on her tiptoes.

"I hope Joe doesn't bring Matilde," Claire told Zach.

"If you don't want Joe to bring Matilde," responded Zach, "why'd you tell him to bring a companion?"

"Hi, Claire," said Charley, swigging the red fluid Mister Pettit sold him. "The horse droppings are bad today, aren't they?"

"They're always bad," she said. "Something needs to be done."

"I've got books I think you'll enjoy," said Charley. "Wait while I get them."

Charley walked over to his backpack and pulled out two books.

"The first is a resource for writers," he said. "A fellow named Peter Mark Roget is a doctor in England. Like you, Zach, his father was a preacher. Roget went to the University of Edinburgh when he was fourteen and had his medical degree by the time he was nineteen. He's a bright fella. As a young man, Roget began keeping words, along with their synonyms. When he turned seventy-three, Roget published his collection in what he calls a thesaurus. You look up a word and find others that have a similar meaning."

"That's quite a resource," said Zach. "Every time I use it, I'll think of you."

"What's your other book?" asked Claire.

"Since you liked *The House of the Seven Gables*, I brought Hawthorne's latest book, *The Scarlet Letter*. It's a story about life in Puritan New England. The heroine wears a scarlet "A" on her chest because she had an adulterous affair, which resulted in a child being born."

"I know that story," said Claire, staring at Zach. "I'd like to see the local woman who was involved wear an 'A' on her chest."

"The last time I was in San Francisco," said Charley, "the merchant who sold me these books, told me about a British magazine that's the first published specifically for women. It's called *Englishwoman's Domestic Magazine*. They advertise that it's for "the improvement of the intellect.""

"That sounds like a magazine I might like," said Claire. "If it's any good, I may want to subscribe to it."

"I'm on my way to San Francisco, I'll ask the merchant how to do that and let you know," said Charley.

"Thank you," said Claire. "I'd like that. We're having a few people over for dinner. Will you join us?"

"I appreciate the offer, but I want to be in Sacramento tonight. I'll take you up on your offer another time."

After Charley left, Zach told Claire about his response to Joe's sermon.

"It upset me," he said. "Joe said the man in the parable gave up everything he possessed to acquire the Kingdom of Heaven. Is he suggesting I should too?"

"Calm down," said Claire. "I think you're making too much out of this."

"I can do without physical comforts, but I'm not willing to let go of you. You're my highest priority. I can't fathom the thought of not having you in my life. Indeed, one of the ways I experience God's love is through you. I won't give you up!"

"I love you too," said Claire, squeezing Zach's hand. "I can't imagine my life without you either, but I don't see this parable demanding a choice. If you do, perhaps talking with Pastor White will help."

"I may do that," said Zach, sighing.

"I need to go to the boarding house and find a time the women can agree upon to have the privy cleaned," said Claire.

"Do you want me to go with you?"

"No. It's too hot for you to sit on the porch waiting for me. Go home, have lunch, and stay cool. While I'm at the boarding house, I'll also prepare for a couple of fittings I have coming up. Don't worry, I'll be home in time to fix dinner."

* * *

Zach was cleaning his front path when Jeb Stuebe strolled up.

"Afternoon, Zach. You're ambitious. It's kind of hot to be out here sweeping, isn't it?"

"It's been a while since I tidied the walkway. The trees provide shade, so it isn't unpleasant. What's new with you?"

"It's that time of year when the Merchant's Association elects a new President. Are you interested?"

"Not this year. I've too much on my plate to head up the Association," said Zach. "Who wants to be President?"

"Right now, Bart Pierce, Alex Hunter, and Robert Jenner," said Jeb. "That's a heavy-weight ballot."

"I should say. Who'll win?"

"I believe it'll be between Hunter and Jenner. Pierce is well qualified, but Alex Hunter has deep ties in the community. He'll be hard to beat," said Jeb. "As for Jenner, he'll have the support of the brothel and bar owners. He'll get enough votes to make it close, but my money is on Hunter."

"You've done a fine job. I'll miss your leadership," said Zach. "May I offer you a glass of fresh lemonade?"

"That sounds delicious, but my wife sent me out to round up the children. I'd better get to it."

* * *

At four-thirty, the dinner guests began arriving. John Larue and his wife, Sophie, were first. They brought a bag of lemons from their tree.

"I'll help Claire make lemonade while you men play horseshoes," said Sophie.

Right behind Zach's neighbors were Rose and Stephen.

"I can't wait to hear about your experience at the circus?" Claire said to Rose.

"It was fun until Stephen went backstage," said Rose.

"Why'd he do that?" asked Claire.

Joe's knocking on the front door interrupted them. With him was Olive Day, who played the piano during the church service.

"The men are out back," said Claire. "They're about to play horseshoes. Olive, the women are in the kitchen. Come this way."

After the women introduced themselves, Claire said: "Rose is going to tell us about her evening at the Empire Theater."

"You saw Dan Rice?" asked Olive. "Is he as handsome as his reputation says he is?"

"Every bit," giggled Rose. "He has a powerful baritone voice, an impressively strong body, and a quick wit. Rice sings, dances, tells jokes, and comments on political affairs. No wonder he's been seen by more Americans than anyone else."

"I saw him perform in San Francisco last year," said Sophie. "He's charismatic, charming, and has a way with animals. I agree. He's an attractive man."

Rose told the women about how Rice mixed animal tricks with acrobatics and clown performances, and how he constantly changed costumes.

"There was always something new going on," she said.

"You said Stephen went backstage," said Claire. "Why'd you do that?"

"Some of the jokes Rice told were about children working. He made light of it. That infuriated Stephen. He went backstage to tell Rice how inappropriate his comments were."

"What was Rice's response?" asked Olive.

"They got into a shouting match. Stephen lectured him about how children belong in school, not working, and Mister Rice told Stephen to quiet down, he was only making a few jokes. Stephen would have none of it," said Rose. "'Children working in mines and factories isn't a laughing matter,' Stephen told him. 'You should be speaking on behalf of children, not be making jokes about them working.'"

"Good for Stephen," said Claire. "I agree with my brother, one-hundred percent."

"The stagehands grabbed Stephen and ushered him outside," said Rose. "They told him not to come back. I was frightened Stephen would be hurt. He wasn't, but the interaction detracted from the enjoyment of the night out."

* * *

Joe was running up the score when Zach asked Stephen: "Is it legal for someone to hold an Indian child in servitude?"

"It is. In 1850, California passed the 'Act for the Government and Protection of the Indians'. The law is supposed to benefit the Indians, but it doesn't," he said. "The law applies to Indians who don't have a way of supporting themselves. White men can seize any Indian they see standing around and use that person as a slave. Indians can't defend themselves because they are forbidden from testifying against white people in court. Some settlers have made a fortune by selling the Indians they captured."

"That's disgusting," said Zach. "The law should be abolished."

"That won't be easy," said Stephen. "There's a good deal of support for it. Not only that but last year, when Peter Burnett was Governor, he promised he'd lead 'a war of extermination' against the Indians. Newspapers cheered him on. There are very few people who support the rights of Indians."

"How's Burnett's 'war' going?" asked Joe.

"I'm told at one time there were between three-hundred thousand and seven-hundred thousand Indians in California. The Spanish and Mexican missionaries brought diseases with them that killed a lot of Indians. By the time gold was discovered, there were only a hundred and fifty thousand Indians left. Today there are less than half that many. Extinction seems probable unless something changes. The war is going well if getting rid of Indians is what you want."

"That's what I want," said John.

"Why's that?" asked Joe, wrinkling his brow.

"Getting rid of Indians keeps Sophie and me safe. We're not alone. Many settlers are afraid," said John. "To keep residents protected, towns offer up to five dollars for every Indian scalp a person brings in. There are reports of men coming into towns like Shasta City leading mule trains with each mule carrying eight to twelve Indian heads."

"What you're telling me must be the exception. This kind of cruelty couldn't be sanctioned by law," said Joe.

"I see no value in living among savages and don't object to their extermination," said John. "What I object to is paying for the scalps. I read in a San Francisco newspaper, in the last year and a half alone, a million dollars has been paid to people who've killed Indians. A million dollars! That's too much money to pay for killing Indians."

"I find the killing of anyone, including Indians, objectionable," said Zach. "The massacre has to stop. Indians have as much right to live as you and I do."

"Most people agree with John," said Stephen. "Zach, your views are in the minority. In fact, the farther north you go, the more pronounced these practices are. Between Marysville and the border, whites search the mountains for Indians. They kill the fathers, take the children, and train them to be servants. It's not uncommon for a miner to pay fifty or sixty dollars for an

Indian girl who'll cook and clean for him. An attractive one will bring one hundred dollars."

"We'd better move on to another topic before Sophie and I have to leave," said John.

The tossing of the horseshoes became more aggressive for the next few minutes. Zach broke the tension when he asked Joe why he didn't bring Matilde.

"I asked her, but she said she couldn't afford the time off. I asked Olive because she's a widow who's helping me with the church music. She seemed to appreciate the invitation. I don't think she gets out much."

"I look forward to speaking with her," said Stephen picking up an errant horseshoe.

"I have some church news," said Joe. "Robert Jenner has agreed to be my Senior Warden. I'm pleased he's willing to take the position. It's a step forward for Saint Mary's."

"I'm glad things are going well," said Stephen. "Not being an Episcopalian, I don't know what a Senior Warden is? Is he the one who keeps you in church?"

"Sounds like it, doesn't it?" chuckled Joe. "There are two prominent lay leaders in an Episcopal church: Senior Warden and Junior Warden. Both are advisors to me and in charge of the congregation when I'm away. Together the Wardens keep me informed about what's going on with the laity that I might be missing. Robert is someone I can bounce ideas off of before I introduce them to the congregation. I'm grateful he's agreed to be Senior Warden."

"Why'd you ask him?" asked Zach.

"He has some exciting ideas about raising money for Saint Mary's. He thinks we should have a church fair. It'll be fun, attract new people, and make money. I like his enthusiasm and creative thinking. That's what drew me to him."

"Doesn't Jenner have a sign in his store window that says 'no injun allowed inside?'" asked Stephen.

"I haven't seen it," said Joe. "I know he has a portion of his store dedicated to the Chinese. That's a plus."

"I hope he's open to changing his mind about Indians," said Zach. "It'll be hard for me to worship alongside someone who doesn't want them around."

"Then you don't want Sophie and me coming to your church," said John.

* * *

"Are you fellas finished?" asked Claire, leaning out the window overlooking the horseshoe pit. "Dinner is about ready. Time to clean up and join the women inside."

Grace was offered, and when everyone was seated, platters of food were passed around the table.

"I saw in the paper that you're looking for someone to be a teacher," said Rose. "Have you had any responses?"

"Not yet," said Claire, "but the paper has been out only a couple of days."

"I'm interested," said Olive. "I like young people. Tell me what you're looking for."

"Someone like Olive Mann Isbell," said Clare. "One of my clients told me about her."

"Who is she?" asked Olive, "and what has she done that warrants imitating?"

"She's the niece of Horace Mann, the famous educator. Misses Isbell and her husband were supposed to come to California with the Donner Party. They missed their connection, and came later with another group."

"That was fortunate," said Rose. "What led her to start a school?"

"During the war with Mexico, the Isbells lived at the Mission Santa Clara de Asis. The mission was about to be attacked by the Mexican soldiers. Colonel John C. Fremont was in charge of the American forces stationed at the mission. The soldier's children ran wild, both inside and outside the compound. That was dangerous, so something had to be done to corral them. Misses Isbell had the children clean a stable, and this became their classroom. Lacking pencils and paper, Misses Isbell wrote the children's lessons in the dirt with a pointed stick. She used charcoal from old fires to write the A-B-Cs on the palms of her student's hands. I'm looking for someone who has the same dedication to teaching, persistence to overcome difficulties, and zeal to succeed."

"That's quite a story. How'd the mission hold up when the Mexicans attacked?" asked John.

"Fortunately, a full assault never happened. When the war ended, Misses Isbell moved to Monterey and started another school above the town's jail."

"I'm your woman," said Olive. "When do you want me to start?"

"Let's talk about the details tomorrow. Come to my boarding house at nine o'clock."

"Is a school really needed?" asked John. "Families need the income children provide. How much will it cost to attend your school?"

"I envision charging those who can afford it eight dollars a month. Right now, there will be six months of schooling."

"Eight dollars a child!" said John. "How's a large family suppose to come up with that kind of money?"

"It'll be a family charge," said Claire. "I don't want the cost of schooling to be a hardship."

"Claire is right," said Zach. "It's time the children of Hangtown receive an education."

"I don't like all the changes women are demanding," said John. "A drinking buddy of mine told me women are insisting the bars and brothels close. Men should decide these things, not women. Another thing: children should help their families prosper, not be a financial burden on them. I'm against these so-called reforms. Hangtown is fine just the way it is."

"I'm sorry you feel that way," said Zach. "Change is coming."

"Not if my friends and I can stop it...and I think we can."

* * *

When Zach saw Joe to the door, he said: "I need some time away. I'm thinking of spending next Monday sailing on Silver Lake. Do you want to join me?"

"I was thinking about watching the steamboat races on the Delta," said Joe. "I'd prefer to do that."

"Sailing is more relaxing," said Zach. "Besides, snow will be coming to the Sierra in a few weeks. I want to go while we still can."

"I'll make you a deal. I'll go sailing with you next Monday if you'll watch the boat races with me the following Monday?" said Joe. "We can catch a small steamer in Coloma that'll take us directly to Sacramento. That beats riding the stage."

"Okay, we have a deal."

* * *

Zach helped Claire clean up after the party. As he did, he shared his thoughts about the evening. Zach was upset his next-door neighbor wants Indians exterminated, and children not to go to school.

"I know attitudes like his exist, but it unsettles me every time I hear someone express them."

Claire agreed and then shared Rose's story about Stephen going backstage to confront Dan Rice.

"I'm proud of my brother," she said, "but instead of apologizing, Rice had Stephen thrown out of the theater. Even bright people like Dan Rice don't see the suffering they perpetuate with their jokes."

WEDNESDAY, SEPTEMBER 1, 1852

CLAIRE AWOKE AMUSED.

"Why are you laughing?" asked Zach.

"I had a dream in which I gave birth to a litter of kittens. They were adorable."

"What's that mean?"

"It means we have to come up with more names, and soon," said Claire, enjoying her humor.

"What do you imagine Adi would say about the dream?" said Zach.

"I don't know," said Claire sitting up, "but the dream brings up my fear of not being a good enough mother. I'm terrified about taking care of a newborn. Do you think I'll be a good mother? You never talk about it."

"Of course, you will," said Zach, kissing her protruding belly. "You'll be great."

"I hope you're right," said Claire. "I'll try my best."

"I've been thinking about moving the horseshoe pit," said Zach. "That way, you can have your garden."

"I'd given up hope you'd do it," responded Claire. "Show me where you intend to put it before you begin. I don't want horseshoes flying near where Cate will be playing."

"I didn't think of that," said Zach. "I may have to come up with a new location. By the way, I'm going to talk with Pastor White Saturday morning."

"Pastor White will show you your concerns are unwarranted. You're good with God. Isn't that's what you've been telling me?"

"Right now, I'm conflicted. Part of me feels close to God, but another part of me doesn't. That's why I want to talk with Pastor White."

"Don't forget, Mary and Dave are coming for dinner. I'd like you home no later than five."

* * *

A little after nine o'clock, Olive Day and Claire met at the boarding house to discuss Claire's teaching position.

"A music friend told me there's a house on Main Street that would be perfect for a school," said Olive. "It has a large yard, so the children have a place to play."

"Let's go see it," said Claire. "What's the address?"

"409 Main," said Olive.

The women got into the buggy Claire brought and set off. "If the people of Hangtown are going to develop an advanced society," said Olive, "we'll need to educate the boys. They're the leaders of tomorrow. It's my job to train them to think for themselves. I'm looking forward to the challenge."

"Educating girls is every bit as important as educating boys," said Claire. "Mothers have a far greater influence on their children than do fathers. I want you to emphasize the girls' education as much you do the boys'."

"I've only a limited amount of time," responded Olive. "Don't you think I should spend the majority of it with the boys? After all, they're the ones who'll be the decision-makers. Men are responsible for the women in their lives. The better educated the boys are, the better job of caring for the girls they'll do."

"Even if you don't agree with me, I want you to give equal time to the girls," said Claire. "I feel strongly about this."

"If you insist," said Olive, shrugging, "but I think your desire to help the girls will hinder the boy's growth."

When they arrived at 409 Main, they found a small, one-story house with a good-sized yard. Oak trees provided shade for the roof and part of the grounds. The women found the house empty, and the front door unlocked. They went in. The front room was large enough to hold twenty desks. A bedroom off the main room could be used to hold supplies, the children's jackets, rain boots, and lunches.

"If I can buy it," said Claire, "would you be comfortable using this building for a school?"

"Oh, yes!" replied Olive. "I'm excited about getting started."

"I'll ask Mister Tobey who the owner is," said Claire. "He knows who owns every building in Hangtown."

As the women rode back to the boarding house, they talked about teaching children of different ages. When they finished, Olive asked: "How was lunch with your brother? Did you find a time for your trip?"

"We did. Originally, we're going to leave for San Francisco on Friday the tenth and return the following Monday. After Stephen told me about Susan Lord, we decided to take an extra day to visit her."

"Who is Susan Lord?" asked Olive.

"She recently opened a school for girls in Benicia," said Claire. "I want to discover what she's learned about running a school."

"I wish I could go with you," said Olive. "Perhaps during vacation, I'll travel to Benicia and speak to Miss Lord."

"That's an excellent idea. I'll alert her you might come."

* * *

When Zach arrived at work, Zhang said, "I put on your desk my report on women coming to California."

Zach started the article. It indicated that in 1849, when California held its constitutional convention, men outnumbered women twenty to one. The first women who came west were as ambitious as the men. Everyone wanted to get rich. While men mined for gold, women sold their companionship. The short supply of women made the bidding for their services frenzied.

To lure more women, the early state leaders created divorce and property laws that gave women rights other states didn't. California's divorce laws made it easy for an unhappy woman to end her marriage. The legislation stipulated that married men and women are partners: they share equally the wealth they accumulate. When a divorce occurs, their money is divided equally. Most men are surprised to learn this, wrote Zhang.

Zach read on. Property laws are similar. They give women the right to control their possessions, whether she had it before she married, received it as a gift, or inherited it while married. If a husband runs up debt, creditors can't claim his wife's separate property to pay off his debt. That's a restriction that has men seething, Zhang noted.

State leaders brought women west with cash incentives, thought Zach, smiling. Zach put down the article, and asked, "Have the laws worked?".

"More women are coming, but I don't know if it's the result of the laws or something else," said Zhang. "My research found these laws have an unexpected consequence."

"What's that?" asked Zach, leaning back in his chair, his hands behind his head.

"The divorce laws have undermined the permanency of marriage. Couples no longer stay together for a lifetime. Ambitious women use the divorce laws to marry a man who's richer than their current husband," said Zhang. "Any time a husband or wife feels mistreated, that person can obtain a divorce and move on to someone new. It's not unheard of for a woman to marry three or four times to increase her wealth."

"Has there been a backlash?" asked Zach.

"Absolutely," replied Zhang. "Newspapers have denounced the laws as evil. Preachers claim Satan contrived them. Judges complain their calendars are full of divorce cases, which prevents them from addressing other matters."

"Your article should stimulate a strong response," said Zach. "That's good."

"If I may," said Zhang, "my friends have alerted me to a story I'd like to investigate."

"What's that?" asked Zach.

"Last Spring whites attacked a gathering of peaceful Chinese miners living along the American River. I don't have all the details, but from what I'm told, it was a massacre."

"Find out what happened," said Zach, putting down his pencil. "I wonder why I didn't hear about it?"

"It occurred some distance from here," said Zhang. "The survivors thought no one would care about what happened, so they kept it to themselves."

"Dig into the incident," said Zach." If it's true, we'll tell the world about it on the front page."

* * *

Roberto walked by the office door, hesitated, turned around, and walked in.

"Morning, Zach," he said. "As I passed your office, I was struck by an idea I want to run by you."

"What's that?" asked Zach.

"Do you have a cradle for your baby? If not, I'd like to make you one."

"That's awfully nice of you," said Zach. "We don't have one."

"You will soon," said Roberto. "This will be my gift to the two—no, make that the three of you."

* * *

Rose met Claire for lunch at Wakefield's.

"I'm glad you could join me," said Rose. "I've had an opportunity to examine Kay's baby, and I thought you'd like to know what I found."

"I would," said Claire. "Kay won't let us near little Zach. We don't even know what he looks like."

"He's healthy," said Rose. "He weighs ten pounds, has brown hair and brown eyes. He's active. It won't be long before he's playing with his toes."

"That's wonderful news," said Claire. "I'm sure Zach will want to know. Someday, Kay will figure out withholding little Zach from his father isn't going to make him want to marry her. I hope that day comes soon."

"For everyone's sake, especially little Zach's, I hope so too," said Rose.

"I've got a gift for you," said Claire.

"You do?" asked Rose, her eyes widening.

"A while back, I promised you the recipe for Mary's tea. Here it is."

Rose looked over the ingredients and asked, "Where does she find the leaves she uses?"

"She goes to Fiddletown, where there's a large Chinese community. Mary told me to buy only from the Chew Kee Store. It's the best," said Claire. "Doctor Yee Fung Cheung owns the store. He's the son of a prominent herb doctor in China, and he's following in his father's footsteps."

"I know nothing about Chinese teas and medicine," said Rose.

"Go to Fiddletown and talk with Doctor Cheung," said Claire. "He'll teach you."

* * *

At three o'clock, Edward Baker walked into the newspaper office with authority. He was dressed in a stylish suit; his vest had a gold watch chain that stretched across his expansive stomach. His receding grey hair added to his commanding presence.

"I'm looking for Zach Johnson," he said with a rich, deep voice that divulged an English upbringing.

"That's me," responded Zach. "You must be Mister Baker."

"Call me, Ed," he said. "I'm here to talk about the Free Soil Party, and our nominee for President, Senator John Parker Hale of New Hampshire."

"Who is the Party's vice-Presidential candidate?" asked Zach.

"Representative George Washington Julian of Indiana. Like Senator Hale, George is an outstanding leader, distinguished family man, and anti-slavery advocate. I urge you to recommend and vote for the Free Soil candidates."

"Before we go further," said Zach, "let's walk to Wakefield's. It's quieter there."

"That's fine with me," said Ed. "I like Wakefield's."

Once the men arrived and settled into Zach's favorite table, Baker told Zach about himself. He was born in London in 1811, the son of poor Quaker educators. Ed's family moved to Philadelphia when he was five and again when Ed was fourteen. This move was to New Harmony, Indiana, where Robert Owen led a utopian community.

"My father believed Owen possessed the secret to a happy life," Ed told Zach. "I could've told them before we moved Owen is a charlatan, but they were starry-eyed and wouldn't listen to me. It took them an entire year to realize he's a fraud."

The family moved again, this time to Belleville in the Illinois Territory, not far from Saint Louis. This move turned out to be fortuitous for Ed. He became friends with the Illinois Governor, Ninian Edwards, who allowed Ed to use his private law library. Ed's love of the law was born in that room. When Ed was nineteen, he was admitted to the Illinois bar. The next year he married Mary Ann Foss, and they have five children.

"It wasn't long after I married that I met the man who changed my life."

"Who was that?" asked Zach.

"Abraham Lincoln. He encouraged me to enter politics. I initially was active on the local level," said Ed. "Eventually, I was elected to the Illinois House of Representatives, and later to the Illinois Senate. 1844 turned out to be a decisive year for me, yet an awkward one."

"Oh," said Zach. "What happened?"

"I ran for Congress, and the man I defeated was Abe Lincoln," said Ed, pie dribbling down his front into his vest pocket. "Nevertheless, we remained good friends, and two years later, he honored me by naming his second son, Edward Baker Lincoln."

I've heard good things about Lincoln. He must not hold grudges.

"When did you come to California?" asked Zach.

"This year. I decided to come when President Taylor refused to give me a position in his Cabinet. I opened a small legal practice in San Francisco. I work with the legislature to keep California a united free state. You know there are men like James Gadsden and his puppet, Senator Gwin, who want to divide California in two with the southern portion being a slave state? I won't allow that to happen."

"I have heard about Gadsden's plans," said Zach. "I'm short on time, so I want to stay focused. What's the Free Soil Party's platform?"

"We're the anti-slavery Party," said Ed. "When we're in control, slavery will be abolished. Our slogan, 'Free soil, free speech, free labor, free men' expresses well what we stand for. There has to be something wrong with someone who can't get behind our vision for America!"

I like the anti-slavery emphasis. I might vote for them.

"I agree with you about the importance of doing away with slavery," said Zach. "It's the morally correct thing to do."

"Allow me to correct your impression," said Ed. "Free Soilers don't oppose slavery on moral grounds. We oppose it because it undermines the dignity of labor and inhibits social mobility. Slavery is an economically inefficient and obsolete institution that's undemocratic. That's why we oppose it. Please emphasize to your readers that the Free Soil Party will fight for the abolition of slavery until we're victorious!"

"Tell me about your nominee, Senator Hale," said Zach, scribbling notes.

"He was born in Rochester, New Hampshire, educated at Phillips Exeter Academy, and attended Bowdoin College, where he was a classmate of Franklin Pierce's," said Ed. "John passed the New Hampshire bar exam in 1830. He married Lucy Lambert, and they have two daughters. John began his political career as a Democratic, and was elected to Congress many times."

"Why'd he leave the Democratic Party?"

"John opposed a pro-slavery resolution supported by both the New Hampshire

Democratic Party, and his Bowdoin classmate, Franklin Pierce. When John wouldn't give in to their pressure, Pierce led an effort to drive John out of the Party. John spent 1845 traveling through New Hampshire seeking to win over the citizens to his anti-slavery cause. John even debated Pierce in Concord's North Church. John's efforts paid off: New Hampshire elected him to their parliament, and he became its Speaker. John has since been elected to the United States Senate."

"What else should I know about Senator Hale?" asked Zach.

"John was one of the strongest opponents of the Mexican-American War. He thought it was wrong and was the only Senator who voted against the resolution thanking Winfield Scott and Zachary Taylor for their wartime service. Another insight into John's character can be seen in his opposition to the Navy's flogging policies. John worked hard to outlaw the practice, which he accomplished in September 1850. You can see that John Hale is a leader who has integrity. He's the man our country needs to be the next President."

That may be true.

"One final question," said Zach. "Being a small party, who are your prominent members?"

"You may have heard of one of our founders, Richard Henry Dana, who wrote *Two Years Before the Mast*," said Ed. "Another leader is David Broderick, who until recently was California's acting Lieutenant Governor. There are at least five United States senators and several congressmen we count among our leaders. Other dignitaries include John Frémont, John Greenleaf Whittier, Walt Whitman, and Horace Mann. We may be small, but we're composed of distinguished men."

"Thank you for your time and valuable information," said Zach, standing. "I have to stop."

Walking to the front counter, Zach told Lucy, "I'll take an apple pie to go."

I like the Free Soil Party's dedication to abolishing slavery and Baker's desire to keep California undivided and free. I wish the Party had different reasons for opposing slavery. Ed expressed no awareness of the crushing impact slavery has on a person's soul, only disdain for its economic dimensions. That gives me pause about voting for them. However, I respect John Hale's integrity and ability to lead, and no other Party is as anti-slavery as they are.

* * *

Mary spoke of her desire to purchase a home as she helped Claire set the dining room table.

"The Benham Hotel is full of drunks who snore loudly. Dave and I hear everything through the hotel's thin walls," she said. "There's a house for sale on Pacific Street that we're going to look at tomorrow, but we're afraid the owner might not sell to us because we're a mixed-race couple."

"I understand your concern," said Claire. "If there's anything Zach or I can do to help, just ask."

"Thank you," said Mary. "You're a special friend."

"I'm glad you feel that way," said Claire. "You know that I love you, but I have to tell you, it upset me to learn you'd asked Betty to be in charge of the boarding house before discussing it with me," said Claire. "I would've selected Betty also, so that isn't the issue. What I'm upset about is you didn't speak to me before you acted."

"I was in a pressured state of mind when I did it," said Mary, lowering her gaze. "You're right, I should've spoken with you first, but with my wedding and honeymoon coming in a day or two, I didn't think I had time. I'd forgotten about your policy that says, when I marry, I have to move out. When I did remember, I realized someone needed to be in charge after I left. I asked Betty and immediately moved on to the wedding details that still needed attention. Please forgive me."

"You're forgiven," said Claire. "I just needed to clear the air. Please call the men to the table while I dish up the food."

* * *

While they ate, Zach said, "Roberto told me the Boomerang is open."

"It is, but to be honest with you, the number of people coming isn't what I hoped it'd be," said Dave. "I expected lots of people who'd be enthusiastic about playing Mahjong, but that hasn't happened."

"It takes a while to build up a new business, especially when the competition is stiff," said Zach. "I believe in you. It'll work."

"Everything I've touched lately has turned out poorly," said Dave. "The statue of Nurse Morris, the Boomerang, even the Studebaker outlet; none of them are going well. I'm not doing much right these days."

"What's wrong with the statue?" asked Zach.

"Before I lost my fingers, I'd lost my way carving it," said Dave. "Fortunately, a man who knew what he was doing finished it for me. The statue turned out well, close to the image Claire drew."

"Where is the statue going to be placed?" asked Claire.

"Pastor Matthews didn't know Nurse Morris, and he isn't supportive of a parish nurse ministry, so Pastor White said he'd take it at his new church. An installation date isn't set, but I imagine it'll be soon. Zach, I have a question for you."

"What's that?"

"Do you still read Morning Prayer every day?"

"I do. It's part of my spiritual discipline. Why do you ask?"

"I don't understand why you spend time in prayer and reading the Bible. What good does it do?"

"It's my way of being close to God," said Zach. "It provides me with a perspective on myself. When I read Morning Prayer, I feel connected to what is Holy, authentic, and loving in the universe."

"Prayer and Bible reading don't do anything for me," said Dave. "They're a waste of time."

"What do you do to be close to God?" asked Zach, putting down his fork.

"That's not something I care about," said Dave. "Despite listening to your God-talk for the past year, I don't believe God exists."

* * *

After Dave and Mary went home, Zach helped Claire with the dishes.

"Thanks for bringing the apple pie from Wakefield's," she said. "It was the perfect conclusion to the meal."

"I'm not sure Dave liked it," said Zach. "He hardly ate any."

"He probably doesn't like apple pie," said Claire. "Mary ate hers, and I thought it was delicious. I'm not going to worry about Dave: he's in a dark mood. Not eating pie isn't going to hurt him. He's got pounds to spare, though recently he looks like he's shed a few."

"I've noticed that too," said Zach.

"Mary is concerned about his melancholy. She fears it's getting worse."

"Maybe there's something I can do to help," said Zach. I'll give it some thought."

MONDAY, SEPTEMBER 6, 1852

ZACH WOKE EARLY; he was eager to sail. He went to his study and began reading Morning Prayer. The lesson was Exodus 20:18-21.

> When all the people witnessed the thunder and lightning, sound of the trumpet, and the mountain smoking, they were afraid and trembled and stood at a distance, and said to Moses, "You speak to us, and we will listen, but do not let God speak to us, or we will die." Moses said to the people, "Do not be afraid; for God has come only to test you and to put the fear of him upon you so that you do not sin. Then the people stood at a distance, while Moses drew near to the thick darkness where God was.

> *This passage impresses me for two reasons. First, Moses indicates God wants us to fear him, so we won't sin. I prefer the alternative approach. I don't sin because I love God and don't want to disappoint him. I value the relationship enough that I don't want to do anything to damage it, which sin does.*

> *The second thing that jumped out to me is the last line of the passage: God is found in thick darkness. Claire's dreams point to God being in bright light, but Moses experienced God in thick darkness. When Moses courageously walked into the darkness to meet God, he was immediately enveloped by lightning, thunder, and the blare of a trumpet. The ground smoked. Given a choice, I prefer Claire's way.*

Zach finished his prayers, dressed, and left for the stables. When he arrived, Joe was waiting. They saddled their horses and spoke of the ride ahead. Kit Carson created the trail to Silver Lake, which is above seven thousand feet. The climb is gradual, and the horses won't be stressed. Zach suggested they go to Jackson, have breakfast, and then head east.

"I'm looking forward to spending time with you," said Joe. "It's been a while since we did something like this."

"It has been. I'm excited too. Whenever I sail, I think of our grandfather. He loved his time on the water."

"Do you still have his watch?"

"I do," said Zach. "I carry it with me every day. It's my good luck charm."

"I'm jealous you got it. I'm the priest who is following grandpa's example," said Joe. "It should've come to me."

"Inheriting the watch is one of the benefits of being the oldest son," said Zach, with a chuckle. "Take the path to the left when you reach the fork that's just ahead. Did you read Morning Prayer this morning?"

"Of course, I did," responded Joe. "Why do you ask?"

"The passage from Exodus brought up the issue of fearing God. The notion of fearing God has bothered me for a long time. I don't believe a God of love wants us to fear Him. He doesn't demand submissiveness, and contrary to your sermon, He doesn't insist we love only Him. Last week you mentioned I have to prove my love for God by letting go of my love for everything else, including Claire. I find that abhorrent."

"You misunderstood me," said Joe, turning left at the fork.

"Perhaps," said Zach. "I discussed the fear of God with Pastor White. His thoughts helped me to understand things differently."

"What'd he say?"

"He said if I were to prioritize my possessions, Claire wouldn't be one of them. I objected, telling him Claire is what I value most. Pastor White grinned and said he's glad she is, but Jesus is talking about giving up things, not people. People aren't possessions. I was relieved to hear that."

"I'm glad Pastor White cleared that up," said Joe. "I made the same point in my sermon. I'm surprised you missed it. Isn't that the Jackson Hotel just ahead? Let's have breakfast there."

When the men entered the hotel, they found the dining room open. After being seated and ordering, Joe said, "Continue with what Pastor White told you."

Zach said Pastor White spoke about how folks are conflicted about having a direct experience of God. While they crave an original, personal encounter, they also fear meeting God face-to-face. The preferred solution is to have someone like Jesus, Mary, or a saint intervene.

"I'm different," said Zach. "I want as many direct experiences of God as I can have."

"There's your inflated sense of importance again. Why would God single you out for a series of revelations?" asked Joe, sighing and shaking his head. "It's time we get going. I'll pay for breakfast."

The men rode single file a good deal of the way up the mountain. When the lake came into view, they led their horses to a meadow near the lake. The boat rental building was at its far end. They tied the horses to a tree and walked to the boat shop.

"The water's calm, and the breeze is light. Does it get any better than this?" asked Zach, wiping his face with a bandanna. "Look at the ducks huddled at the end of the lake."

"Isn't the sky reflected in the water stunning? That peak looming over us appears close enough to touch," said Joe. "I love this place!"

Once they were on the water, they took turns controlling the sail and the rudder. After a couple of hours, Zach saw something swimming in the lake. They were less than ten yards away when Zach said, "It's a bear, and it has something in its mouth. It's headed to shore."

"That's a fish in its mouth!" said Joe. "I've never seen that before."

After swallowing the fish, the bear reentered the water and swam toward the men.

"Let's head back to the dock and have lunch," said Joe, turning the boat away from the approaching bear.

"Good idea," said Zach. "I want to check on the horses. The bear's presence may spook them."

At the shop where they rented the boat, food was for sale. Each bought a sandwich, an apple, and a piece of blueberry pie.

"That'll be five dollars each," said Amy, the shop manager.

"Isn't that a bit steep?" asked Joe.

"Hauling food up the mountain isn't easy or cheap. If you don't want the food, let me know," she said. "I see you left your horses tied to a tree on the edge of the meadow. There are yellow-bellied marmots over there. If you don't want your horse to break a leg by stepping into one of their burrows, use the hitching post on the back of the building. They'll be safe there."

The men moved their horses and ate lunch before returning to the water. In the late afternoon, white caps appeared.

"How fast do you think this thing will go?" asked Joe.

"With two of us squeezed inside, I doubt we'll generate much speed," said Zach, his eyes dancing, "but let's see what you can do."

Joe let out the sail. The boat leaped forward, and the brothers laughed as they bobbed across the lake. When they reached the northern shore, Zach said, "Let me see what I can do. I'll take us home."

Zach tacked back across the lake. It was dusk when they reached the dock and returned to the store.

"I've some money in my saddlebag," said Zach. I'll pay for the boat, but dinner is on you."

* * *

On the way down the mountain, Zach told Joe about Claire's upcoming trip to San Francisco. She likes to see what other dressmakers are doing and discover what their prices are.

"This is her way of staying competitive," said Zach. "Claire also wants to buy chocolates from that Ghirardelli fella. She's become a fan of his."

Zach went on to say Claire planned to stop in Benicia to visit with the director of a girl's school. "She and Stephen will be back Monday night."

"We'll be in Sacramento watching the boat races," said Joe. "Why don't we meet for dinner?"

"That's a great idea. I'll speak to Claire about it," said Zach, examining the path ahead. The trail down the mountain had several switchbacks coming up that required their attention.

"What are you going to do while she's gone?" asked Joe.

"I'll move the horseshoe pit," said Zach. "Claire wants a garden where the pit is now."

"I can help you with that on Saturday," said Joe. "I want to be sure you measure the distance between the posts correctly. When we finish, we can try out the new location. I love beating you."

"I accept your offer," said Zach, smiling. "I can use the help."

"Has Claire found a building for her school yet?" asked Joe, inhaling the pine's fragrance, and watching a squirrel scamper in front of his horse.

"She's found one she likes," said Zach. "Turns out the owner is the same man from whom I rent my office. Claire is negotiating with him. He'd rather rent her the house, but Claire insists on owning it. She wants to be free to make whatever changes she wants. I'm staying out of the haggling."

"Don't you think buying property is a man's responsibility?" asked Joe.

"It usually is. I suspect Mr. Tobey believes he'll get a better deal from Claire than he would from me. He's probably right, but I support Claire's efforts," said Zach. "Unfortunately, Dave and Mary's offer for the house on Pacific Street wasn't accepted."

"They didn't offer enough money?"

"No," said Zach. "Mary and Dave agreed to the asking price. The problem is they're a mixed-race couple. There aren't many people in Hangtown who'll do business with a mixed-race couple."

"I'm not surprised to hear that," said Joe, shielding his eyes from the setting sun. "They're good people, but I wouldn't sell my house to them. Mixing races violates God's laws."

"I don't think so," snapped Zach. "

"What are they going to do?"

"Jim Edwards is the owner," said Zach. "I'll get him to sell me the house. When I own it, Dave and Mary can buy it from me."

"I marvel that we have the same parents. We're different in so many ways. Good thing I love you. Otherwise, I might not have anything to do with you," said Joe, buttoning the upper part of his jacket.

"I have faith you'll grow wiser as you age," said Zach, chuckling. "I see the lights of Jackson. I'm hungry and ready for a break."

"I don't have much money on me," said Joe. "I can't afford to eat at the Jackson Hotel again."

"That's okay. I'm not looking for an elaborate meal," said Zach. "A little food and getting out of the saddle will be enough for me."

In Jackson, they found the streets full of people. When they entered the Astor House for dinner, Joe asked Jane, their waitress: "Why are there so many people in town?"

"The Lee and Marshall circus is here. If you gents aren't here for the show, what brings you?" she asked.

"We sailed all day on Silver Lake. We're on our way back to Hangtown," said Zach. "We saw your place and Tellier's and decided to give you a try."

"Did you notice the large oak tree next to Tellier's?" asked Jane. "The residents of Jackson recently started using it for hangings. Personally, I don't want to eat my meal under a limb where someone was hanged."

The men ordered French onion soup and salad. While they waited, Joe said, "Saint Mary's had a visitor yesterday I want to tell you about."

"Oh, who was that?" asked Zach.

"John Clark. He's just arrived from Cincinnati. He has an interest in getting involved in the life of Saint Mary's."

"That's great news," said Zach. "Why'd he come to Hangtown?"

"He told me he found Hangtown to be 'full of life, full of people, and full of business.' I made sure he felt welcome."

"You have Saint Mary's growing," said Zach. "I did my part by bringing Elsu. He'd never seen a white man's religious service, and he was curious about what went on. The standing, seating, and kneeling confused him, but he's interested in coming back."

"I'm glad you mentioned Elsu," said Joe. "It'd be better if he doesn't return. Several regulars told me if he attends, they won't. You've already scared off John Larue. I can't afford to have you drive more people away."

"If Elsu can't be a part of Saint Mary's," said Zach, sighing, "I don't want to belong either."

"Saint Mary's isn't the only place Indians aren't welcome," said Joe. "You must've gotten a negative response to his hiring."

"I did, but I have to do what's right," said Zach. "I can't let other people's opinions dictate what I do. That includes you."

* * *

After dinner, the brothers rode in silence, the moon illuminating the trail. As they approached Hangtown, Joe said, "I know we have our differences, and I regret that. I yearn to be close to you. It's with trepidation, I tell you a decision I've made."

"What's that?" asked Zach, turning to look at his brother.

"I'm in love with Matilde. I know you and Claire warned me about this, but it happened," said Joe. "I'm going to ask her to marry me. I enjoy being with her, and she supports my church work. I want Matilde at my side for the rest of my life. I have a question for you: will you be my best man?"

"I think she's the wrong woman for you," said Zach, "but if she's the one you want, I'll be your best man."

"Thank you," said Joe, turning his eyes toward heaven.

The men left the horses at the stable and started walking home.

"Have you asked Matilde?"

"Not yet. I thought I'd do that later this week. Please don't tell anyone until I have Matilde's answer. That includes Claire," said Joe. "Today was fun. Let's do it again next month."

"If the weather permits, I'm all for it," said Zach. "I won't tell Claire about your decision. I'll let you tell her."

"I love you," said Joe. "I just wish you weren't so vain and obstinate!"

WEDNESDAY, SEPTEMBER 8, 1852

AFTER READING MORNING Prayer, Zach and Claire shared breakfast. Zach brought up meeting at the Sacramento waterfront Monday night for dinner.

"We won't dock until seven o'clock," said Claire. "The last stage for Coloma leaves at four. If you wait for dinner, you won't return home until Tuesday. I thought you didn't want to be away from work that long, and that's why you're not going with me in the first place?"

"You're right," said Zach. "I didn't think about when the last stage leaves. I do want to be home Monday night. I guess dinner won't work. Rats. I was looking forward to hearing about your trip as we ate alongside the river."

"That's a nice thought," said Claire, "but don't wait for us."

They also spoke of several upcoming special days.

"Monday is also Pete's birthday," said Zach. "I wish he were here to see all that's happened. He'd be astonished."

"I think he would be too. Are you going to do anything to mark the day?"

"I'll get up early and go to the cemetery before I meet Joe," said Zach. "I'll say some prayers, and bring him up-to-date with what's transpired."

Claire noted Dave's birthday is coming soon, as is the first anniversary of his parents' murder.

"That's a day I'm not looking forward to," said Zach. "Thank God I have you to help me through it. I don't know what I'd do without you."

"We'll honor your parents while we prepare for the birth of our first child," said Claire. "That should be in about six weeks!"

"I feel foolish not being able to decide what color to paint the baby's room," said Zach. "Do you have any suggestions?"

"Let's put off painting," said Claire. "I don't want our son sleeping in a pink room. Cate or Zach can sleep with us while you're painting the room."

"Good idea," said Zach. "I can't wait to hold my little girl, look into her eyes, and sing her to sleep. I hope she has your laugh. I love your laugh."

Claire interrupted Zach. "It's time for me to meet Mister Tobey," she said. "I want to finalize the deal today. I'm tired of negotiating."

"Do you want my help?" asked Zach.

"No, I can handle it," said Claire, putting her dishes in the sink.

* * *

When Zach arrived at work, Elsu and Zhang were talking. A young woman dressed in Indian garb stood nearby.

"We'd barely left my campsite when flames lit up the forest," Zach heard Elsu say. "We didn't stop. I followed Tonya to her tribe's camp."

Confused, Zach said, "Morning, men. Who's your friend?"

"This is Tonya Hitchcock," said Elsu. "She's a member of the Nisenan people. Last night, she saved my life."

"Nice to meet you, and thank you for doing that," said Zach, looking at Tonya and smiling. Turning toward Elsu, Zach asked, "What happened?"

"Tonya doesn't speak English," said Elsu. "I'll tell her what you said, then I'll tell you about last night."

When Tonya received Zach's message, she smiled and said something in the Nisenan language.

Zach looked to Elsu for a translation.

"Her elders told her what to do," said Elsu. "She simply carried out their instructions."

"I'm glad she did, but I'm confused," said Zach. "What happened? Start from the beginning."

"After work, I went to my campsite, fixed dinner, and was cleaning up when Tonya appeared," said Elsu. "She told me one of her elders was communing with the spirit world when he was told white men were about to kill me. To be safe, I should leave immediately. 'Come to our camp on the Cosumnes River,' she pleaded. I was stunned, but gathered my valuables and left. It wasn't long before we heard horses and saw flames coming from where I'd camped. Tonya and I pressed on until we made it to her village, where I spent the night."

"Who did this?" asked Zach, "and why?"

"White men. That's all I know," said Elsu. "Does it matter who they are? Indian scalps bring good money. That's why they did it."

"If bounty hunters are looking for you, you're not safe here," said Zach. "Leave before you're killed. I'll find a new pressman."

"I didn't come here to quit. I came to work. Besides, there's no safe place in California for an Indian, not even on reservations," said Elsu. "I like my job. I'm not leaving."

"Stay with me," said Zhang. "You'll be safe in Chinatown. We don't kill Indians."

"Thank you," said Elsu. "I'll do that."

Zhang offered to pick up the belongings Elsu left. "Tell me where you camped," he said. "The men pursuing you may be watching, so it'll be safer for me to go than you. I'll recruit some of my friends. It shouldn't take long."

Tonya moved close to Elsu and spoke to him.

"She wants to know what we're talking about," said Elsu. "I told her it's time she returns to her people. When the danger passes, I'll visit her elders to thank them for saving me."

Tonya slipped out the back door when Zhang left through the front.

* * *

An hour later, the fire chief, Joel Meyer, entered the newspaper office. He came to ask Zach to write another editorial about the importance of acquiring a fire engine. Since Zach's last request, donations had dried up. Joel told Zach while his previous columns raised over five thousand dollars; the steam-powered pumper Hangtown requires costs between fifteen and twenty thousand.

"It's time to ask again," he said.

"I dropped the ball. Immigration concerns and the upcoming election captured my attention," said Zach. "I'll write an editorial reminding the community to contribute. With your help, I'll stay on top of the fundraising until we succeed."

"Tell your readers the longer it takes, the greater the risk a fire will sweep through town. Let's get this done before Hangtown burns out of control."

* * *

Shortly before noon, Zhang returned to the newspaper office. He carried only a few items with him; the campsite had been completely destroyed. The five men Zhang took with him sifted through the ashes, but few things survived.

When Zach asked if anyone watched them, Zhang said, "On the way there, I saw several men using picks and shovels to dig up the riverbed. A few sang while they worked; others bantered back and forth. I felt safe among them. None of my friends saw anyone watching us, though a note was tacked to a tree. Here it is," said Zhang, handing it to Elsu.

Elsu read the note aloud.

"Don't come back to Hangtown. If you do, you'll be killed. Ben Wright."

"Who's Ben Wright?" asked Zach.

"I learned about him when I was in Yreka," said Elsu. "The man lives to kill Indians. He'll act on any excuse to slaughter my people: men, women, children; it doesn't matter to him."

Elsu said Wright began hunting Indians when a few angry braves stole livestock to feed their families. These same men attacked wagon trains and killed packers who came onto our land. The brave's exploits infuriated the people of Yreka.

"Sixty-five men, mostly miners, armed themselves and rode into the foothills looking for the troublemakers. Ben Wright was one of the sixty-five. On the first day, the search party didn't find them, so they camped beside a stream. In the early morning, while it was still dark, warriors from another tribe attacked the vigilantes. Several miners were wounded. Wright vowed revenge. At first light, Wright and the others rode downstream until they came upon fourteen members of my tribe, who were cooking breakfast. Because they had nothing to do with the attack, they greeted the visitors hospitably. Wright and his men shot and scalped every one of them, including the children. Not satisfied, the vigilantes continued their hunt until they came across another band of my people, who asked for food. Instead of the bread, bacon, and coffee they requested, my relatives were massacred. A few days later, I saw their remains on display in Yreka. I puked."

"Did the search party ever find the braves responsible for the attacks?" asked Zhang.

"No. The miners contented themselves by shooting every Indian they saw," said Elsu. "No white man protested or tried to stop them. I hid for days.

"Wright collected most of the money for the scalps and used it to start a business. He hired men who'd failed as miners, trained them, and sold their services to anyone who wanted an armed escort across our lands. The newspaper I worked for viewed Wright as a hero. On their front-page, they told the story of two Indian women, who tried to get away from Wright and his gunmen. Wright chased the women, shooting at them as they ran. One woman was hit and killed, but the other woman almost escaped when she tripped and fell, ripping open her arm. She scrambled behind several large rocks where she tried to stop the bleeding. Wright dismounted, strolled up to her, grabbed her by her hair, and cut her throat. He stood over her watching her bleed until she was dead. That's who Ben Wright is."

"The man is a monster!" said Zach. "The note he left you should be taken seriously. Move on while you can."

"I'm staying," said Elsu. "I feel protected: the ancestors are watching over me. If you're afraid Wright will kill you because I work here, I'll find another job, but I'm not leaving Hangtown."

"Ben Wright wouldn't be the first man who tried to kill me," said Zach, waving his hands dismissively. "If you want to stay, the pressman job is yours. What about you, Zhang? Do you want to stay? There's no disgrace in returning to San Francisco."

"I came to help you," he said. "Nothing has changed. I'm staying."

* * *

After lunch Pastor White opened the newspaper door. He came to put an announcement in the paper that read:

> The ceremony to dedicate the statue of Nurse Morris
> will be held on Sunday, September nineteenth, in front

of Grace Church. Everyone is invited. Refreshments will
be provided following the ceremony.

"Please position this in a prominent place," said Pastor White, handing Zach the announcement. "It's important everyone sees it."

"Is Elsu welcome?" asked Zach, passing the announcement to Elsu.

"Of course he is," replied Pastor White. "Everyone is welcome."

"I won't go to a church where Injuns are present," said a tall man walking in the door. "We're trying to get rid of them, not convert them. The same goes for Chinamen. They're not welcome either."

"Who are you?" asked Zach recoiling.

"I'm Stephen Webb. I represent the Nativist Party. I'm here to speak to Zach Johnson."

"I'm Zach. I'll be with you in a moment. Pastor White, excuse me. I have to interview Mister Webb for an article I'm doing. Elsu will put your notice where everyone can see it."

After Pastor White left, Zach turned to his guest.

"Why don't we go to Wakefield's for our talk? I could use a cup of coffee and a piece of pie."

"That's fine with me," said Webb, stepping outside. "I like coffee and pie, and I don't like being around Injuns and Chinks."

When the men were seated at Wakefield's, Zach said, "Tell me about yourself."

The clean-shaven man with black hair was born in Salem, Massachusetts, graduated from Harvard College, and studied law under the eminent attorney, John Glen King. He married Hannah Hunt Beckford Robinson, and they have one daughter. Following the path of John King, Webb went into politics. He served in the Massachusetts House of Representatives, the Massachusetts Senate, and three terms as mayor of Salem.

"I was a Whig until I found the Nativist agenda more to my liking," he said. "Six months ago, I moved to San Francisco because the Nativists are strong in California. I plan to enter local politics. William Tell Coleman said he'd finance my political ambitions. I'll start with Mayor of San Francisco."

"Why do you want to be a mayor again?" asked Zach, writing quickly.

"It's a job I do well, and it'll propel me to a higher office."

"I'll keep track of your success," said Zach. "Tell me about the Nativist convention and your Party's nominee for President."

"The two-day convention was held in Trenton, New Jersey, immediately after the fourth of July," said Webb. "At this time, our nominee for President is Daniel Webster. George C. Washington, the grandnephew of our first President, is the Party's choice for Vice-President."

"Why'd you say, 'at this time?'" asked Zach.

"The Party hasn't obtained Webster's permission to be our candidate, and his health is failing. He may not have the stamina to undertake a Presidential campaign. If he declines, we'll nominate another candidate," replied Webb. "We won't have trouble finding someone."

No matter who you nominate, you won't get my vote, that's for sure.

"Every day, Nativist policies appeal to more people," said Webb. "Our goal for this election is to grow the Party. Off the record, we don't have a chance of winning the Presidency; however, we do have an excellent chance in several state and local elections, particularly in California."

I hope not. The Nativists give me enough trouble already. I can't imagine what it would be like if they have even more power.

"What makes your platform appealing?" asked Zach, looking up.

"First and foremost, it is to defend America from the influx of Irish Catholic and German immigrants. These people will never be true Americans. They're under the control of priests and the Pope. Our mission is to restore America as a land of temperance, Protestantism, and self-reliance."

"Why, temperance?" asked Zach with a slight frown.

"Irish Catholics like their whiskey and Germans can't do without their beer. These people would rather drink than work. The call for temperance is part of our plan to restore the Protestant work ethic as our country's highest value."

"They're very few Irish Catholics and German immigrants in California," said Zach. "What is the Nativist's position on Chinese immigration?"

"We want to restrict Chinese immigration and limit the number of people who come here from South America. The United States is for native-born citizens, not for whoever shows up on our shores. Our forefathers fought to create a nation where their descendants could prosper. Immigrants make this difficult. They believe they're as entitled to the country's riches as we native sons are. This is wrong. The Whigs and Democrats are doing nothing to protect the rights of the native-born. It falls to us, the Native American Party, to provide the necessary protections."

"What protections do you have in mind?"

"We'll create a twenty-one-year wait before someone can become a naturalized citizen. We'll deport foreign beggars and criminals. We'll bar foreign-born citizens and Catholics from holding public office. We'll require the Bible, the Protestant Bible, to be read in every school, and mandate that only Protestants be employed as teachers."

These guys are scary.

"Throughout the land, there are people like you who are unhappy with the job our country's leaders are doing. The Nativists will replace these do-nothing legislators with inspired Nativist patriots!"

I hope not!

"I've been told there's a secret society within your Party," said Zach. "Is that true?"

"I suppose you're referring to the Order of the Star-Spangled Banner?"

"I am."

"I know nothing about the OSSB," said Webb, putting down his fork.

"I've been told there's an initiation ceremony called 'Seeing Sam'," said Zach, "in which all members are given passwords to memorize and hand signs to use. Members swear never to betray the order, which is only for pureblooded Protestant Anglo-Saxons. Is that correct?"

"I know nothing of these things," said Webb.

"Your answer explains why Nativists are referred to as The Know-Nothing Party."

"I've heard that name applied to us, usually by people who oppose our policies," said Webb. "Please refer to us as the Native American Party, not the Know-Nothings. It's the other parties that know nothing about restoring to prominence the principles of our forefathers. Our Party has a winning agenda for California and for all of America."

"Thank you, Mister Webb. I'll include what you've told me in our next edition."

"May I make a suggestion?"

"What's that?" asked Zach.

"Print extra copies. The Nativists are popular in Hangtown. When people learn you've interviewed me, they'll want to read what I've said."

* * *

Zach returned to his office, sorted his notes, and then went to see Jim Edwards at the hardware store.

"I'm interested in buying the house you own on Pacific Street," said Zach. "How much do you want for it?"

"I won't sell it to you," said Edwards. "You'd let that mixed-race couple use it, and I can't allow that to happen. It's available only to white folks."

"What will it take for you to reconsider?" asked Zach.

"There's nothing you can do that'll change my mind. While you're here, I want to tell you how much I hate that twaddle sheet you publish, and especially the lax immigration laws you champion. They're not only stupid; they're dangerous. What you're preaching will lead to the intermingling of the races, like your friends have done. With your background, you should know mixing races violates God's will. Crossbreeding is not only immoral; it's disgusting. I'll do whatever it takes to prevent your crusade from succeeding."

"I'm sorry you feel that way," said Zach. "If you have a change of heart, let me know."

"Don't hold your breath."

* * *

Over dinner, Zach told Claire about his talk with Jim Edwards.

"He won't sell me the house on Pacific Street. I was confident he would, but I was wrong. He doesn't want a mixed-race couple living there."

"What are you going to do?" asked Claire.

"I'll ask Dave and Mary to find another house they like, but not to make an offer. I'll buy it and sell it to them," said Zach. "That's the only way I know to get around the prejudice they face."

"I hope it works," said Claire, who shared her recent conversation with Mary. "She's concerned about Dave's drinking."

"Dave's a big guy," said Zach. "He can handle more drinks than the rest of us."

"It's not only the amount he drinks," said Claire. "He also refuses to go to work, and Mary has a hard time getting him to even leave the hotel. Coming here to dinner last week was an exception. If you recall, we spoke about how he wasn't his usual self. We were right. Mary confided that he's stopped having sex with her. She's afraid he no longer finds her attractive. Mary doesn't know what to do."

"If Dave doesn't snap out of it soon," said Zach, "I'll take him fishing, and we'll have a man-to-man talk."

"That might help," said Claire. "He told Mary he misses you and being part of the newspaper's team. What do you think about him joining you? You don't have to pay him, just let him be there."

"I'm okay with that, Dave can be a resource for Elsu," said Zach. "I'll invite him the next time I see him."

"You'll have to go to the hotel to speak to him," said Claire. "It's unlikely he'll leave it on his own."

"I'll speak to him on Friday when I'm at the Benham delivering papers," said Zach. "I forgot to ask. Did you buy the school building?"

"Mister Tobey won't sell it to me. After going back and forth several times, he said he doesn't like bargaining with a woman. He said it's too easy for him to take advantage of my inexperience," said Claire. "I thought I'd done a decent job of negotiating. I got him to agree to sell the property instead of renting it."

"That's an accomplishment," said Zach. "Are you pleased?"

"No, I'm frustrated," said Claire. "I won't be pleased until Mister Tobey sells me the property, which he said he'd never do. This isn't easy for me, but will you negotiate on my behalf?"

"I will," said Zach, smiling. "What do you want me to do?"

"His asking price is reasonable," said Claire. "I just need you to close the deal."

"I'll speak to him after I finish distributing papers," said Zach. "I'll have your keys when you return from San Francisco."

"Mary told me another thing that has me upset."

"What was that?" asked Zach, glancing at his grandfather's watch.

"Mary spoke to one of her customers, who is a miner. He brought a baby boy with him to the laundry."

"What's upsetting about that?"

"Miners don't have babies, merchants do," said Claire, folding her arms over her belly, "and the child isn't his."

"How did she know?"

"The boy is Chinese; the miner isn't," said Claire. "When Mary asked him why he had a Chinese baby with him, the man said he's taking care of the boy because he's an orphan."

"The man is a prince," said Zach. "I'll write a story about him so Hangtown can see the extraordinary thing he's doing. He's a model of decency."

"Hold on. There's more to the story," said Claire, pulling on one of her curls. "Mary asked him how he knew the child is an orphan?"

"What'd he say?" asked Zach.

"He said, 'I know because I killed his parents.'"

SATURDAY, SEPTEMBER 11, 1852

WITH CLAIRE IN San Francisco, Zach did not sleep well. After a night of tossing and turning, he rose to read Morning Prayer. The lesson for the day was Proverbs 3:11-12.

> My child, do not despise the Lord's discipline
> or be weary of his reproof,
> for the Lord reproves the one he loves,
> as a father the son in whom he delights.

The author of the proverb tells me I am wrong when I complain about God's rebuke, that the Lord loves the one He admonishes. I hope that's true.

After I grab a bite to eat, I'll see if there's room for the horseshoe pit at the back of the yard.

As Zach measured the space next to the fence, Joe appeared.

"What are you doing back there?" asked Joe.

"Claire convinced me where I wanted to put the horseshoe court won't work," said Zach. "I'm checking to see if there's room here, and it appears there is."

While the men prepared the ground, Zach told Joe about his negotiations with Mister Tobey.

"Claire believed the agreement was in place," said Zach, "but it wasn't. I had to convince Mister Tobey to sell me the property; he still wanted Claire to rent it."

"How'd you change his mind?" asked Joe.

"I told him I'd pay ten percent more than he was asking."

"Was that enough to persuade him?"

"It was," said Zach. "I'll meet with Tobey on Tuesday to finalize the deal. I can't wait to tell Claire she has her school building."

"Congratulations," said Joe. "I'm sure this will please her. How much longer does Claire have before she gives birth?"

"Six weeks is our best guess," said Zach. "Why do you ask?"

"Please don't take offense at what I'm about to say," said Joe, "but it's God's will women experience pain during childbirth. It reminds them of their sinfulness. That's why Claire mustn't use anesthesia when her time comes."

"I want Claire to be in good standing with the church," said Zach, penetrating the ground with his shovel, "but I don't want her to needlessly suffer. Rose says ether and chloroform effectively block the pain, and if Claire wants, she can use one of them."

"I hope you reconsider and insist she not be anesthetized," said Joe, pushing up his shirtsleeves.

"I don't tell Claire what to do," said Zach, chuckling. "She has a mind of her own."

"One thing more," said Joe. "It's important Claire reconciles with the church after she gives birth. She can do this by asking me to officiate at the ceremony designed for the occasion."

"Are you referring to the 'Churching of Women'?" asked Zach, taking a gulp of water.

"I am," said Joe. "The church regards a woman to be unclean after she gives birth. Once Claire stops bleeding, she can request the service of reconciliation."

"It's ridiculous to believe a woman is made unclean by childbirth," said Zach. "Childbirth is a holy event, not an unclean one. Claire doesn't need to be purified after she delivers, she'll be praising God for the miraculous gift she's received."

"Keep in mind an unclean woman isn't able to have direct contact with God until she's purified. Only after Claire's cleanness has been restored can she once again live harmoniously with God. The uncleanness of childbirth is like the uncleanness that comes monthly to a woman," said Joe. "When a woman is bleeding, she isn't welcome to receive the Sacrament. I've never heard you complain about that. This is no different."

"There's only a little more to do," said Zach. "Let's finish before we break for lunch."

"I take it you don't want to talk about the Church's concern for Claire's spiritual wellbeing?" said Joe. "Is that right?"

"That's correct," said Zach.

* * *

Claire's first stop in San Francisco was at Ghirardelli's chocolate shop.

"I want five boxes of your mixed assortment," she said. "I have a depraved appetite for chocolate."

"My mother taught me to indulge a pregnant woman's appetites," said Susan with a wink. "A craving that isn't satisfied will show itself as a birth-mark on the child. You don't want that. Will five boxes be enough?"

"It will," said Claire, giggling. "I don't want to carry them while I'm doing my errands. May I leave them here for a few hours?"

"We're open 'til five," said Susan. "I'll put the boxes in our storage room. Would you like a sample or two before you go?"

"I would," said Claire, with a mischievous grin. "Two should hold me."

* * *

After a stop for coffee, Stephen went to the Jenny Lind Theater. He purchased two tickets for the night's performance.

"Have you heard Eliza Biscaccianti sing?" asked Tom, the ticket agent.

"I haven't," replied Stephen, "but I've heard she's something special."

"She is," said Tom. "Miss Biscaccianti is from Boston, but she's performed for us over thirty times. She's the first American opera star to be invited to sing in Europe. That's how good she is. Locals have taken to calling her, 'The American Thrush.' It's a good thing you purchased your tickets early. I anticipate a sell-out."

"I can't wait," said Stephen, putting the tickets in his coat pocket.

"See you tonight," said Tom, "Next."

On his way back to the Niantic Hotel, Stephen passed a store that had a doll in the window. He looked at it closely, thought a moment, and went inside.

"I'd like to buy the doll in the window," he said. "My sister is pregnant, and I want to give it to her."

"You have a keen eye," said Irwin, the store's owner. "That's an exceptional doll. She's a Jumeau and was awarded a First Place Medal at last year's Great Exhibition in London. I'll sell her to you for fifty dollars."

When Stephen objected to the price, Irwin said, "You won't find a doll anywhere in the city that's as distinguished as this one. Notice the exceptional attention given to the detail of her clothes. She's wearing the latest fashion. Women pay attention to those things. There's only one doll like this in the entire world, and now is your chance to own it."

"I'll take it," said Stephen," but I have to go back to my hotel to get that much money. I'll pick it up after lunch."

"Your sister is a lucky woman. She'll treasure this doll for the rest of her life."

* * *

After moving the horseshoe court, Joe and Zach washed up in the kitchen. "What'd Matilde say when you proposed to her?" asked Zach.

"It was awkward. We were going over the plans for tomorrow's service when I took Matilde's hand and said, 'I love you, and want you to be with me the rest of my life.' Matilde was startled. After what seemed like forever, she said she thinks of me as a good friend, someone special in her life, but not as her husband," said Joe, with a heavy sigh. "I hope she changes her mind. I figure the longer we work together, the greater my chances are she'll come around."

"I don't know about that," said Zach, drying the back of his neck with a dishtowel. "Matilde said she doesn't want to marry you. I know you're disappointed, but I don't think you should fool yourself thinking she'll change her mind. My advice is to accept her answer and look for another woman, one who wants to be with you."

"You never wanted me to marry Matilde, that's why you're pleased she said no," said Joe, scowling. "I won't give up that easily. Matilde is the woman I want, and I'm going to win her over."

"I'm on your side," said Zach, flinching. "I hate to see you living with the hope that something will happen that won't."

"I can't wait to see your face when I tell you she's changed her mind," said Joe.

* * *

Early Saturday morning, Rose left for Fiddletown. When she arrived, Doctor Yee Fong Cheung's herbal medicine store was crowded. She studied the building while she waited. It was a traditional Chinese structure: clay, gravel, and other natural materials rammed together to create a one-story building. A covering protected the front door from the weather.

Inside, Rose saw the building functioned not only as an herb store but also as Doctor Cheung's residence. Doctor Cheung stood behind a counter. Alongside him was a large cabinet with twenty-five small drawers. It held his most precious herbs. Decorated tea boxes from China were stacked nearby. In the back of the building was a wooden table with four chairs, and beside the table was a stove with a built-in wok. Another table with a mat functioned as the doctor's bed. An altar stood in the corner.

Rose held back until Doctor Cheung finished assisting his other customers. When they were alone, Rose said, "My name is Rose Kellogg. I'm a nurse in Hangtown. One of my Chinese patients suggested I meet you and learn about eastern medical practices. Do you have time to speak with me?"

"I can't while I'm serving customers," he said. "There's a tasty eating-house just down the street called the Golden Dragon. When I break for lunch, we can talk there without being interrupted."

* * *

Joe and Zach discussed where they'd like to have lunch. Joe wanted to go to the El Dorado Hotel; he hoped to see Matilde. Zach shook his head and discouraged him. What would he do if Matilde swooned over some other guy? Joe acknowledged it would cut him to the core, and agreed eating at the Virginia House was a better idea.

"Because this coming Monday would have been Pete's birthday," said Zach, "I want to visit his grave before we leave for the boat races. I won't take long."

"I'll rent a wagon and wait for you outside the cemetery," said Joe.

"There's something else I want to tell you," said Zach. "I promised Claire I'd speak to Dave about his drinking and isolation, but I didn't do it."

"That's not like you," said Joe. "What happened?"

"I couldn't find the right words, and I didn't want to face Dave's anger for bringing up how much he drinks," said Zach, dipping the sausage he ordered into a mound of mustard. "I feel awful about avoiding the confrontation. I'm not looking forward to telling Claire I didn't speak to Dave."

"The right words will come," said Joe. "Yesterday wasn't the right moment, but another time will be. Pray about what to say, and you'll do fine. I guarantee it. Let's go back to your place and break out the horseshoes. I want to squash you like a bug."

* * *

Doctor Cheung began his lunch break by walking to the Golden Dragon, where Rose was waiting for him. They began their discussion with Rose asking, "Why did you come to California? Aren't you needed in China?"

"Like many others, I came to California in 1850 to get rich," he said, "but the laws restricting Chinese mining made that impossible. Back home, my father is a highly respected doctor. People travel great distances to receive his advice. I learned a lot from him, so I decided to become a doctor too."

"Why are you in Fiddletown and not San Francisco?" asked Rose.

"I like living here, and after San Francisco, Fiddletown is the largest Chinese community in California," he said.

As they ate, Doctor Cheung explained the basic concepts of Chinese medicine, how teas heal, and the role of herbs in restoring wellbeing. Rose made notes while he spoke. When they returned to his store, Rose thanked him for his willingness to teach her.

"I'll be back for another lesson," she said.

"Any time, my friend. There's much to learn. Be patient. Chinese medicine is worth pursuing."

* * *

In San Francisco, Stephen met Claire for lunch at the Excelsior, a prestigious dining salon.

"Look at this place," he said. "White tablecloths and gold spoons. It makes San Francisco look civilized. The rest of the city may be a quagmire of slushy sand-hills and muddy streets, but this place is elegant. I'm glad we're here."

"I am too," said Claire. "I can't wait to taste the food. The menu says some of the vegetables are from the Sandwich Islands. Coming here was a good idea. How'd you hear about it?"

"On my way to buy tickets for tonight's performance, I stopped for coffee at William Bovee's. It was delicious. You should see all the spices they sell. I felt like I was in the Far East," said Stephen, opening his napkin. "One of Bovee's employees, J.A. Folger, spoke highly of this place."

"I took a break myself," said Claire, shyly looking down. "I went to a French bakery called Boudin. Their coffee may not have been as good as yours, but the scone I ordered melted in my mouth. I love a good bakery. I'll go back this afternoon to stock up on pastries for our trip to Benicia."

"Have you given any thought to whether your child will be a boy or a girl?" asked Stephen.

"Are you kidding?" asked Claire with a grin. "Zach and I talk about it all the time."

"Which is it going to be?"

"I don't know, and won't until the baby is born," said Claire, buttering a slice of sourdough bread.

"You don't have to wait," said Stephen. "Determining the sex is simple. There are two indicators. First, if the father is considerably older than the mother, the child will be a girl."

"That doesn't apply to us," said Claire. "What's your second indicator?"

"If the father is more capable of impressing his personality on to the child, the baby will be a girl. Otherwise, it'll be a boy."

"Have you talked with Rose about your theories?" asked Claire, lifting an eyebrow.

"She has her own," said Stephen. "Rose says it's all about timing. Eggs fertilized early in a woman's cycle are immature. They become girls. Eggs fertilized later in her cycle are strong enough to become boys. Rose claims ranchers figured this out a long time ago."

"These theories don't help," said Claire with a sigh. "Zach and I suspect she'll be a girl."

"You suspect this because...?"

"Woman's intuition," said Claire, grinning.

"How's Zach planning to care for you after the baby is born?" asked Stephen.

"He wants to hire a nanny. I don't like the idea," said Claire. "It seems like a silly extravagance. You and I come from hearty stock. I can take care of my baby."

"Don't be too quick to dismiss Zach's offer," said Stephen. "You'll be in bed for three or four weeks following delivery. The right nanny can advise you about caring for the child, and you'll need someone to help you when you're ready to return to work. Many women have other women breastfeed their babies. You should consider this."

"I'm not a delicate flower," said Claire, looking disapprovingly at her brother. "I'll breastfeed my child, thank you. I note your concern, but trust me, I can handle childbirth, and I can look after my baby."

"One last question," said Stephen, looking earnestly at his sister. "Do you have a will? It's a good idea to have one just in case something goes wrong. After all, childbirth is called a woman's time of trial. It wasn't long ago every woman made out a will when she discovered she was with child."

"I don't have a will and don't want to hex myself by getting one," said Claire. "I'll be fine."

"The lawyer in me had to ask you these things," said Stephen with a half-hearted shrug. "I'm done."

"I'm glad," said Claire. "Your questions annoy me."

* * *

On his way to pick up the doll, Stephen noticed a sign announcing Belle Cora's newest parlor house. It opens in a few weeks on Washington Street and will be the most lavish and opulent parlor in San Francisco.

Business must be good, thought Stephen, chuckling.

After retrieving the doll, Stephen headed for his meeting with Joseph Winans, a San Francisco attorney his partner, Alex Hunter, recommended he meet. Stephen introduced himself by saying his life is dedicated to freeing children from the workforce.

"I want all children to go to school," said Stephen. "Most of my legal work has been in Massachusetts, but I'm opening an office in Sacramento. Any business you can send my way will be appreciated."

"My practice usually doesn't involve children," said Winans, "but if a case comes my way, I'll refer it to you. Senator Henry Clay was my guiding light. Perhaps you heard he died of tuberculosis at the end of June. His passing broke my heart. The Senate honored him by having Senator Clay be the first man to lie in state in the Capitol Rotunda. It was because of Clay's influence that I chose to represent slaves. As you know, California is a free state; slavery isn't allowed. Nevertheless, folks from the South bring their slaves with them when they move here. This creates legal problems I enjoy resolving."

"I imagine working on behalf of slaves isn't easy," said Stephen. "Have you had much success?"

"Recently, I have," said Winans. "A Negro named Charles became involved in a street fight with a white man who claimed to be his owner. Charles hired me to defend him. I pointed out to the judge that California's laws both before and after statehood outlawed slavery; therefore, the white man had no legal right to Charles. The judge agreed and set Charles free."

"It's good to hear success is possible," said Stephen, nodding his approval.

"Not if James Gadsden can stop it," said Winans. "Gadsden has helped the slave owners find someone in the California Assembly who will champion their cause. That man introduced a bill to give white men the power to return Negroes to the states from which they came. The bill, unfortunately, became law."

"Who is the legislator?" asked Stephen, leaning forward.

"Henry A. Crabb. His ancestors were Southern aristocrats. These men want to create in California the conditions they have in the South. James Gadsden funds many of their efforts. I fight Gadsden every step of the way."

"It seems both of us are working to help people who can't defend themselves," said Stephen. "I wish you continued success."

* * *

Claire finished her tour of the dressmakers and returned to Ghirardelli's to collect her package. From there, she went to Boudin's bakery.

Having goodies from the bakery will ensure the trip to Benicia is enjoyable.

From Boudin's, Claire went back to the Niantic Hotel for a rest. Later, she joined Stephen for dinner in the hotel's dining room. Since it wasn't busy, she asked Billie, their server, about the history of the Niantic.

"Was the hotel once a ship?"

"She was," said Billie. "The Niantic was built in Connecticut in 1832 to trade with China. She's had a series of owners and adventures. She's transported silk and tea, was a whaling vessel, and traveled around the Horn of Africa."

"How'd the ship end up in San Francisco?"

"Her final trip was from Panama. She brought hundreds of passengers who were early participants in the gold rush. When the Niantic docked, the crew scattered into the foothills to search for gold," said Billie. "The Niantic was sold to local businessmen who used the high tide to float her into her present location. Initially, the Niantic functioned as a warehouse. Several years later, the owners transformed part of the ship into a hotel. Perhaps you noticed the inscription over the entrance," said Billie. "'Rest for the weary and storage for trunks.' For a long time, that summed up the Niantic's mission."

"This place is too elegant to be the original vessel," said Stephen, looking at the thick carpeting and wood paneling on the walls.

"You're right," said Billie. "There were a series of fires that destroyed not only the Niantic but most of San Francisco. The owners kept rebuilding. Each time the Niantic looked less like a ship and more like a hotel. The latest restoration was completed a year ago, after the fire in May 1851."

"Thank you," said Claire. "If we don't want to be late for tonight's performance, we'd better order."

Following dessert, Stephen gave Claire her gift.

"What's this?" she asked, setting the box on the table next to her.

"I saw it in a store window and had to buy it for you," said Stephen. "Go ahead, open it."

"You didn't need to buy me anything," said Claire. "I only have morning pastries for you."

When Claire saw the doll, tears filled her eyes.

"She's beautiful," said Claire. "Look at how she's dressed! I love her."

Claire jumped up and gave her brother a hug and a kiss on the cheek.

"My mind is swirling with all the clothes I can make for her. Shoes, riding boots, bonnets, handbags, scarfs, jewelry, I can attire her in the latest fashions. Someday I'll pass her on to Cate. She can enjoy the doll and give her to one of her daughters. What a magnificent gift. I'm so excited," said Claire, fluffing the doll's hair. "Thank you."

TUESDAY, SEPTEMBER 14, 1852

CLAIRE WASN'T HOME yet, and Zach was eager to see her. He woke early and read Morning Prayer. The lesson assigned for the day was Isaiah 1:16-17, 10:1-3a, 5:25.

> Wash yourselves, make yourselves clean;
> Remove the evil of your doings before My eyes;
> Cease to do evil, learn to do good;
> Seek justice, rescue the oppressed,
> Defend the orphan, plead for the widow.
> Ha!
> Those who write out evil decrees and compose oppressive statutes,
> To turn aside the needy from justice, to rob the poor of My people of their rights,
> That widows may be your spoil, and orphans your prey!
> What will you do on the day of punishment, in the calamity that will come from afar?
> Therefore the anger of the Lord was kindled against His people and He stretched out His hand against them and struck them;
> The mountains quaked and their corpses were like refuse in the streets,
> For all His anger has not turned away, and His hand is stretched out still.

Isaiah prophesies that on the Day of Judgment, God's wrath will be brought upon the powerful who take advantage of the poor and pervert justice for their own sake. It's teachings like this that motivate me to assist those who are oppressed.

* * *

Zach met Mister Tobey for breakfast at the Hangtown Bakery. With Claire away, Zach didn't want to eat alone.

"Thank you for joining me," said Zach, rubbing the dark circles under his eyes. "I love their blueberry muffins."

"When someone gives me as much money as you are, I'll meet him anywhere," said Tobey, chuckling. "Besides, I own this building, and as you know, I like to support the merchants who rent from me."

"Let's get the financial transaction completed before we eat," said Zach, as he handed Tobey the money due him. Mister Tobey, in turn, gave Zach the keys to the building.

"Claire can't wait to transform the house into a school," said Zach, buttering his muffin.

"She chose well," said Mister Tobey. "The property will make a good school. When is she planning to open?"

"There are changes to the house and grounds that need to be made, and students to recruit," said Zach. "I'm guessing the school will open around the first of November."

* * *

When Zach arrived at his office, Zhang and Elsu were talking.

"That full moon last night made my trip into the forest easy," said Elsu.

"Morning men," interrupted Zach, "What were you doing in the forest?"

"My spirit lives there," said Elsu, looking Zach in the eye. "My name means 'falcon flying.' My spirit soars when I'm among the trees, deer, quail, and bears. I was craving fresh berries, and I know where to find them. That's what led me into the forest, and when I came upon an encampment of my people, I joined them to listen to the elders' stories. I've missed that too. It was a good night."

"I wondered where you were," said Zhang, frowning. "I came to check on you after dinner, and you were gone. I didn't sleep well worrying about you."

"I have to be out in the wild," said Elsu, his voice steady, his chin high. "It's where I connect with life's sacred essence."

"If Ben Wright found you, you might have been killed," said Zach, staring sternly at Elsu.

"There's more than one way of dying," said Elsu, sighing. "There's an invisible reality that coexists with the visible one. My spirit is intertwined with each. Not being connected to these realms will kill me as surely as a bullet will."

"Just be careful," said Zach, tension filling his voice. "I don't want anything to happen to you."

"You need to be careful, too," said Zhang, looking at Zach.

"What do you mean?"

"My friends who work at the Round Tent Café told me they overheard Jim Edwards tell Susie, the waitress, that he wants you silenced," said Zhang. "Edwards is the one who paid to have our office burned."

"Where'd Edwards get the money?" asked Zach, stepping closer. "He's barely able to keep his hardware store open."

"Someone back east sends Edwards money," said Zhang. "I don't know who that person is, but I'll find out."

"Why Edwards?" asked Zach, wrinkling his brow.

"Edwards is the head of Hangtown's OSSB."

"Is he really? You've found out more in a few weeks than I did in a year," said Zach, scratching his hand. "It's Jim Edwards, not Red, who's in charge? I certainly had that wrong. At least now, I know who is out to get me."

"Be careful," said Zhang. "Your enemies are plotting against you."

"Thanks for your efforts," said Zach. "You're doing good work. How near are you to completing your article about the Chinese miners being murdered?"

"I finished it this morning," said Zhang, handing it to Zach.

UNPROVOKED ATTACKS
ON CHINESE MINERS

Over the last five months, there have been a series of unprovoked attacks on Chinese miners by gangs of white men. Here are a few examples.

In May, two hundred Chinese miners in Rich Gulch were attacked and robbed. Four of them were killed. Rich Gulch is in Calaveras County. What makes this attack on the Chinese miners particularly disturbing is the area's diverse population. Until now, Americans, French, Germans, Italians, Jews, English, Irish, Spanish, Mexicans, Chileans, Negroes, and the Chinese have lived together peacefully.

Closer to Hangtown, a gang of sixty white miners, accompanied by a brass band, rode through a chain of Chinese campsites along the American River. They set fire to the miner's tents and equipment.

A brass band? What a brazen group of thugs.

At Weber Creek, they completely destroyed the camp and chased the Chinese away.

At Mormon Bar, in Mariposa County, a group of angry white men attacked two hundred Chinese miners. Encouraged by their success, the attackers rode south and attacked four hundred more Chinese miners who were camped at Horseshoe Bar. All the Chinese fled, abandoning their claims.

In each of these locations, the white men who attacked and killed the Chinese miners must be found and held accountable. The claims must be returned to their rightful owners.

Well said!

In other places, whites haven't directly attacked the Chinese, but have made their lives difficult. Whites set up barricades along the main travel routes to stop and turn back wagons carrying Chinese passengers and freight.

> At Foster and Atchinson's Bar in Yuba County, a resolution
> was passed that denies the Chinese the right to hold
> claims and requires them to leave. Miners in the town of
> Columbia passed a resolution that excludes Asiatic and
> South Sea Islanders from engaging in mining operations.

> *The New Republican* demands Governor Bigler arrest those
> who are responsible for the attacks. The paper insists
> the Governor rescind all state regulations that exclude
> Chinese workers from earning a living or conducting
> business freely.

"You've written a good account of what's going on and how it needs to be corrected," said Zach. "We'll run it on the front page. Your article should give the Governor, Jim Edwards, and the OSSB second thoughts about what they're doing."

* * *

An hour later, Joe entered the newspaper office.

"Hello," said Elsu. "I've completed your bulletins. How were the boat races?"

"Thank you for having the bulletins ready," said Joe. "Even though you're an injun, I'm coming to see I can rely on you. As for the boat races, Zach and I were fortunate to have Captain G. W. Kidd be our companion. He was named after his ancestor, the Scottish pirate who lived two hundred years ago. Zach and I met him while he watched his steamers come and go. He didn't want any of them racing, particularly the *Nevada*, whose captain likes to race the steamer, *New World*."

"Why is that?" asked Elsu, handing Joe the bulletins.

"When steamers race, it's hard on their engines, which can cause the boilers to explode," said Joe. "Also, trying to win, captains take risks that Captain Kidd doesn't like. He told us about the time one of his captains chased *New World* up the Delta. When the ships arrived in Sacramento, *Nevada's* captain turned in front of *New World*, seeking the dock's prime spot. The *New World* responded by ramming *Nevada* and pushing it into a mud bank. It cost Captain Kidd thousands of dollars to retrieve and restore his vessel."

"Then, why do they race?" asked Zhang.

"The faster your ship, the more money you make," said Zach. "When steamboats were new to the run between San Francisco and Sacramento, Captain Kidd charged passengers thirty dollars for a cabin. This enabled him to make sixteen thousand dollars each way. Some months he'd have a sixty thousand dollar profit. With that much money available, bigger and faster steamboats entered the market. The owners of these new steamers lowered their prices to gain quick access to passengers and freight. This forced every other steamer to lower theirs. Profitability plunged until only the largest and fastest ships made money."

"What'd you see?" asked Elsu, looking over the press.

"We watched five or six come up the river and glide into the docks. It's amazing how quickly they offload their passengers and cargo and take on new. We didn't see any boats colliding, boilers exploding, or ships running aground," said Zach. "Still, watching the captains maneuver their steamers was entertaining."

"Thanks again for the bulletins," said Joe, headed for the door. "Be sure to ask Zach, who won at horseshoes."

Joe had barely left when Elsu asked, "Who won at horseshoes?"

"Joe did. He always wins," said Zach, sighing. "I play for fun; he plays to win. We both end up happy."

* * *

A short while later, Pastor White walked into the office. He was pleased with the location of last week's announcement and asked if it could be in the same spot this week? Zach assured him it would be.

"What kind of a turnout do you anticipate for the statue's dedication?" asked Zach.

"Lots of people tell me they're coming," said Pastor White. "The only one I'm not sure about is Dave. I want to thank him publically for his gift, but I can't find him. I slipped a note under his door to remind him."

"Have you spoken to Mary?" asked Zach. "She'll have him there."

"I didn't think of that," said Pastor White. "I'll speak to her. See you Sunday."

* * *

Just before noon Stephen and Claire appeared at the door.

"Surprise, we're home!" shouted Claire, waddling in.

"We had a wonderful trip, and I want to tell you about it," she said, "but I'm starved. Are you ready for lunch?"

Zach popped out of his seat and gave Claire a warm embrace and a kiss.

"Welcome home," he said, beaming. "You look none the worse for the trip."

"It went well," said Stephen. "We were up early this morning to catch the stage. We're dusty and hungry. Claire and I are going to the Ohio House. Can you join us?"

"Yes, give me a moment to write myself a note about where to pick up," said Zach, scribbling furiously.

After arriving at the Ohio House, Claire said, "We've lots of stories to tell, but before we do, how'd it go with Mister Tobey? Did he sell you the house?"

"He did. The keys are in my desk drawer. The property is yours!" said Zach, smiling. "I had to pay him a bit more than anticipated, but the deal is done."

"Thank you. I can't wait to transform the house into a school. I want to accomplish as much as possible before Cate comes."

"Tell me about your trip," said Zach, taking a bite of beef.

"San Francisco is a hard place to get around, especially for women," said Stephen. "While the business district has extensive boardwalks and plank roads, the rest of the city is an unimproved muddy mess. It's hard to go anywhere without putting your foot in the muck. Women can't wear their long, flowing dresses without soiling them, and their dainty shoes aren't suited for the conditions."

"One of the ideas I brought home is the importance of shorter dresses," said Claire. "I also want to design a feminine form of a man's boot that'll help women cross streets. I'll feature both of these in my next collection. After seeing what's available in San Francisco, I'm convinced my creations are the equal of theirs."

Claire spoke about their lunch at the Excelsior, tea at the Niantic, Boudin's Bakery, Ghirardelli's chocolates, and the doll Stephen gave her. Stephen jumped in to tell Zach about the opera and his visit with Joe Winans.

"Sounds like you had a fun and productive time in San Francisco," said Zach. "Tell me about Benicia."

"We slept in Sunday morning and ate French pastries," said Claire. "We caught a two o'clock steamer to Benicia and checked into our hotel. We went for dinner where the concierge suggested. Even though the food was mediocre, the place was crowded, and we waited for a table. I was leaning against a wall when a nice looking Army Major invited us to join him. The Major said I reminded him of his wife, who is as pregnant as I am. He misses her and is disappointed he won't be present when his second child is born."

"What's the Major's name?" asked Zach.

"It's an unusual one," said Stephen. "U. S. Grant."

"Major Grant said he'd arrived in Benicia about a week before we did," continued Claire. "He doesn't expect to be in Benicia long. He's waiting for new orders. Because Grant has organizational skills, the Army made him a quartermaster."

"What's a quartermaster?" asked Zach.

"I had to ask, too," said Claire gently. "The quartermaster procures, manages, and distributes all of the soldiers' supplies, including their food. He's also expected to have their uniforms properly repaired and their graves correctly recorded. Grant said he was responsible for seven hundred men when they left New York in July."

"That's a lot of soldiers," said Zach. "What a nice fella to offer you a seat at his table. Is this the same Grant that Clive Ostroff served under during the Mexican War?"

"I don't know," said Claire. "I didn't talk to Clive about those things. You did."

"Being a West Point graduate," said Stephen, "Grant is qualified to be a quartermaster, but the job bores him. He prefers to be a combat officer."

"Clive said Grant was a brilliant commander," said Zach. "What'd you talk about?"

"The journey here," said Stephen. "In Panama, there was an outbreak of cholera. One of Grant's men died every hour."

"Every hour!" said Zach, wincing. "What'd he do?"

"He sent his regiment ahead, and he stayed behind with the sick and with those who had families," said Stephen. "Out of the original seven hundred men, a hundred fifty died and are buried in Panama."

"When I told Major Grant, I'm glad the rest of his men are well," said Claire, "he laughed. He told me about Lieutenant Slaughter, who joined his unit after they arrived in Benicia. Slaughter suffered from seasickness. He was sick every minute of the journey. When the Lieutenant arrived in California, he received new orders instructing him to immediately return to New York and report for duty at the Northern Lakes. On the return trip, Slaughter was as sick as before. Upon arriving in New York, Slaughter's new orders indicated his original ones had been correct. He was to return to California to assist Major Grant. Once again, Slaughter was sick the entire voyage, but was relieved when there weren't new orders waiting for him in Benicia."

"That poor man," said Zach, chuckling. "How was your meeting with Susan Lord?"

"Benicia is a forward-looking community," said Claire. "The people at our hotel told us it wouldn't be long before Benicia becomes the State Capitol. They've already constructed a building to house the Legislature. With this kind of confidence and ambition, it's not surprising Benicia's leaders insisted on starting a quality girl's school. They want their daughters to receive a lady-like education, one that rivals any school in the East. The school's driving force is a Presbyterian pastor, who made space in his church for the Young Ladies Seminary. Susan Lord was hired to be the school's first principal and one of its three teachers. Soon after Susan started, she fell in love with a judge, and they're engaged. I'm not sure how long she'll continue."

"What'd she tell you about getting started?" asked Zach.

"The first thing I need is a clear purpose. Theirs is to build character. The school's leaders plan is to expose the girls to the ideas of history's great thinkers, poets, and musicians. They want the girls prepared for their roles as wives, mothers, and teachers. The pastor expects the school's graduates to shape the destiny of nations. Like I said, they're an ambitious bunch. I don't intend to compete with their grandiose plans. What's right for Hangtown is a practical education for girls and boys."

"I agree with you," said Zach. "I'm relieved nothing went wrong on your trip."

"There was one setback," said Claire.

"Oh," said Zach. "What was that?"

"On the boat that took us to San Francisco, I was enjoying the cool air blowing in my face when a seagull settled on the railing near me. I absent-mindedly played with my necklace as I watched him. The chain broke, and the amulet

Adi gave me fell into the river. I was heartbroken. After I ate swordfish at the Excelsior, I dreamt I gave birth to a dumb child, just like Adi said I would, if I eat fish while pregnant. I cried when I woke."

"You didn't tell me about this," said Stephen, laying his hand on Claire's.

"I didn't want to burden you with my dream," she said. "We were having such a good time, I didn't want to diminish it. The dream probably means nothing."

"That's right, the dream means nothing," said Zach, smirking. "The amulet falling into the river isn't a loss. Its ability to protect you is fantasy."

"The amulet reminded me of Adi," said Claire, color rising in her cheeks. "I'm going to miss it. Did you visit Pete? How'd your talk with Dave go? Is he going to join you at the office?"

"I had a good visit with Pete," said Zach. "The talk with Dave didn't happen."

"Didn't happen? You promised me it would," said Claire, narrowing her eyes.

"When I got to the hotel's lobby, I couldn't find the right words to use. To be honest, I didn't want Dave angry at me for telling him he drinks too much."

"I'm disappointed in you," said Claire, crossing her arms. "You let Mary down, and you didn't come through for Dave."

"I'll talk to him," said Zach, "but I want to be comfortable with what I'm going to say before I do. Give me some time."

"I hope you talk to him soon. Dave isn't going to get better until you do."

SUNDAY, SEPTEMBER 19, 1852

CLAIRE WAS ASLEEP when Zach woke. He got out of bed and went into his study to read Morning Prayer. Zach discovered the first lesson for the day was Isaiah 6:1-8.

> In the year that King Uzziah died, I beheld my Lord seated on a high and lofty throne; and the skirts of His robe filled the Temple. Seraphs stood in attendance on Him. Each of them had six wings: with two he covered his face, with two he covered his legs, and with two he would fly.
>
> And one would call to the other,
> "Holy, holy, holy!
> The Lord of Hosts!
> His presence fills all the earth!"
>
> The doorposts would shake at the sound of the one who called, and the House kept filling with smoke. I cried,
>
> "Woe is me; I am lost!
> For I am a man of unclean lips
> and I live among people
> of unclean lips;
> yet my eyes have beheld
> the King Lord of Hosts."
>
> Then one of the seraphs flew over to me with a live coal, which he had taken from the altar with a pair of tongs. He touched it to my lips and declared,

Now that this has touched your lips,
your guilt shall depart
and your sin be purged away."

Then I heard the voice of my Lord saying,
"Whom shall I send? Who will go for us?"
And I said, "Here am I; send me."

Over breakfast, Zach told Claire about the reading from Isaiah.

"It's an account of Isaiah's call to be a prophet. After being purified, Isaiah is allowed to speak on behalf of God, which I am trying to do. I wish the OSSB knew the majesty of God like I do. They'd repent of their evil ways, their hearts would be transformed, and an acceptance of immigrants, Indians, Negroes, and women would follow. I long for this to happen."

"You're full of yourself," said Claire. "I can't believe you think you're the next Isaiah. The prophet was humble; you're not. Can't you see your own hubris? Everyone else can, and that's one of the reasons they resist what you're pushing."

"I'm trying to tell you about what motivates me to take on the evil of the OSSB, and you criticize me for it," said Zach, lowering his head.

"I'm sorry I offended you," said Claire. "I love you despite your hubris. I'm giving you honest feedback, which I guess you don't want to hear."

"I have enough people criticizing me already. I don't need you doing it too," grumbled Zach. "Let's talk about something else. How is the school coming along?"

"I showed Olive the list of materials Susan Lord recommended. We decided which of these we need and asked Mister Edwards to order them for us."

"How'd Edwards treat you?" asked Zach. "Zhang told me he's the head of the local OSSB and doesn't like you or me."

"Edwards was professional, but he wasn't in a hurry to order our supplies. It seemed strange at the moment," said Claire, "but his behavior makes sense after what you just said. Why doesn't Edwards like me?"

"He thinks you're too independent and a bad example for other wives. Wait till Edwards hears we're bringing Julia Powell to Hangtown; he'll be in a dither," said Zach, snickering. "We'll have to alert Julia to the danger, though I suspect it's no different than what's happening back east."

"It's time we dress for the dedication service," said Claire. "I don't want to be late: I'm eager to see how folks respond to Dave's statue."

"I hope their response lifts his spirits," said Zach, following Claire up the stairs.

"Don't forget to talk to Dave about his drinking."

"I said I would," said Zach. "Stop nagging me!"

* * *

Zach and Claire rented a buggy and went to the Benham Hotel to pick up Mary and Dave. There was a chill in the air; clouds blocked the sun. Mary was waiting in front of the hotel.

"Where's Dave?" asked Zach as he helped Mary into the back of the buggy.

"He said he'd be right behind me," said Mary, "but I don't see him."

"I'll go to your room and hustle him along," said Zach. "The service is about to begin."

Zach knocked on Dave's door, but there was no response. Zach put his ear to the door but didn't hear anything.

I bet he used the bathroom one last time. He's probably at the buggy right now.

When Zach returned to the women, Dave wasn't there.

"I knocked on your door, but there was no reply. The room was quiet," said Zach. "What should I do?"

"Dave promised me he'd come, but he's hiding somewhere," said Mary. "He hates leaving the hotel, and he's uncomfortable being the guest of honor. I'm embarrassed, but we'll have to go without him."

"It'd be a shame for Dave to miss the unveiling," said Claire, as the buggy lurched forward. "I hope he shows up."

* * *

"Pastor White looks relieved we're here," said Zach under his breath as they walked to the chairs reserved for them at the front of the congregation.

"Where's Dave?" asked Pastor White.

"I'm not sure," said Zach. "I couldn't find him."

"I'll wait another five minutes, but if Dave still isn't here, I'll start without him."

"I understand," said Mary, looking for Dave. "Being here with all these people must've frightened him. I'm surprised because Dave was in such a good mood this morning. He was smiling and didn't seem to have a worry in the world."

After fidgeting for five minutes, Pastor White began.

"Welcome to the dedication of our beloved Gertrude Morris' statue. Gertrude represented the presence of Christ among us, serving and healing not only the members of our congregation but anyone in Hangtown who needed her."

Pastor White scanned the gathering.

"Our guest of honor, Mister David Dodd, has been delayed. I'm going to ask his colleague, Ian Oakland, to do the unveiling. Ian finished the work on the statue after Dave's injury. Ian, please come forward."

"It's my pleasure to be here this morning," said Ian, standing next to Pastor White. "I never met Nurse Morris, but Dave told me she was an exceptional woman, full of warmth, caring, and wisdom. Dave did the bulk of the work creating the statue. My contribution was to give it a few finishing touches."

Ian took hold of the cover.

"I present to you, Nurse Gertrude Morris," he said, pulling off the cloth.

A large gasp followed the unveiling, then excited applause and cheers filled the muggy air.

"That's her likeness," said Matt Morris, wiping tears from his eyes. "That's mom."

"Gertrude will stand outside the entrance to Grace Church as a welcoming presence, and as an example of what Christian service looks like," said Pastor White. "Please bow your heads as I dedicate the statue.

> "O God, who by thy blessed Son has sanctified and transfigured the use of all material things: Bless this statue of Nurse Gertrude Morris, which we humbly set apart to thy service, that it may glorify you and inspire us. This we ask in Jesus' name. Amen."

A girl and boy, age six, carrying bouquets, stood at the back of the gathering.

"Flowers will now be placed at the foot of Gertrude's statue," said Pastor White. "Katherine Grady and Christopher Barnwell will do that for us. Nurse Morris was the midwife at their births."

The children walked solemnly to the statue, placed the bouquets at her feet, bowed, and ran back to their parents as the congregation smiled.

"Thank you, Katy and Chris," said Pastor White, with a broad grin of his own. "This concludes the service. Please join us in the social hall for refreshments."

As they took their turn at the refreshment table, Mary said, "Dave did an incredible job replicating the likeness you put on paper."

"I agree," said Claire. "I'm sorry the day is overcast. I'm eager to see the statue when the sun shines fully upon her."

"The statue is exquisite," said Zach, balancing a cup of punch, a napkin, and a cookie. "I'm sorry Dave missed the enthusiastic response his work received. He's a brave and talented guy. I never would've undertaken a project like this with no previous experience."

Just then, Walt Selzer ran into the room looking for Zach.

"Zach, come with me," said Walt breathlessly. "Dave's been found. He's dead!"

"What are you saying? Dave's dead?" mumbled Zach.

"Step outside with me," said Walt. "I don't want to give you details with everyone listening."

"Mary needs to know. I'll bring her with us," said Zach, his body tightening.

"Come alone," responded Walt whispering. "It isn't pretty."

When the two men were outside, Zach asked, "How'd Dave die? Tell me what happened."

"I was walking up Main Street when I heard a commotion coming from Elstner's hay yard. I went to see what the folks were riled up about and found them cutting down a body from the hanging tree. It was Dave."

"Do you know who did this to him?"

"He did it to himself. He committed suicide," said Walt. "There were two envelopes in his coat pocket. One is for Mary; the other is for you. The people who found Dave didn't know what to do. I told them I'd find you, and that you'd know. They're with him in the hay yard."

Just then, Mary and Claire emerged from the social hall.

"Where's Dave?" screamed Mary. "I want to know!"

"Let me handle this," said Zach. "I'll tell her."

When Mary reached Zach, he said, "Something awful has happened. Dave is dead. It appears he killed himself."

As Claire hugged Mary, Zach continued.

"He left you a note. I'll go fetch it. He also left one for me."

"How'd he do it?" asked Mary, staring off into the distance.

"He hanged himself in Elstner's hay yard. I'm hoping his notes will tell us why. Walt said the people who cut Dave down left his body there. I'll arrange for his burial. People who've been hanged are not a pretty sight. Stay here, and I'll bring you his note."

"I want to see him. I want to know what he was wearing. I want to hold Dave and say good-bye," Mary said in a barely audible voice. "I'm going with you."

By the time Zach brought the buggy to where Mary and Claire were waiting, Pastor White was talking with them.

"Climb in," said Zach, first taking Mary's hand, and then Claire's. "Pastor White, there's room for you. Come with us."

"I will," he said, climbing into the seat next to Zach.

"Walt, thank you," said Zach, as the buggy turned to leave the church.

At the hay yard, two men and a woman stood over Dave's body. Dave's coat had been placed over his head and upper body. When the buggy stopped, Richard, the man who cut Dave down, walked over to them.

"Do you know this man?" he asked. "He's missing a hand. We found him hanging from that tree."

"Let me take a look," said Zach. "I'm afraid he's my friend."

Zach pulled the coat back and saw Dave's anguished face. Zach's knees buckled, and he knelt.

"Why did you do this? You didn't have to die," said Zach, through his tears. "You had so much to live for."

Mary rushed over and threw herself on top of Dave. Claire followed as best she could and touched Zach's shoulder.

"Mary wants to be alone with him," said Claire. "Come with me."

Claire led Zach off to one side while Mary cried and spoke with Dave. After several minutes, Pastor White stepped over to where Dave lay and said:

> "Grant, we beseech thee, Merciful Lord, to thy servant David,
> pardon and peace that he may be cleansed from all his sins, and

serve thee with a quiet mind in thy heavenly kingdom; through Jesus Christ, Our Lord. Amen."

Richard joined Zach and Claire. He handed Zach Dave's notes.

"I hope he said something that explains why he did this," said Richard. "If you ask me, it was a selfish thing to do. Look at all the pain he's caused. He'll pay in hell for what he's done."

"I don't know why Dave did this," replied Zach, clenching his fist, "but I'm sure he thought his reasons were good. Thank you for what you've done. It's time for you to move on."

"All I know is everything happens for a reason," said Richard walking away.

"If I'd been Dave, I would have punched that jerk in the mouth," said Zach to Claire. "I was this close to doing it."

"Richard doesn't know what to say," said Claire. "Finding Dave and cutting him down must've been dreadful. I suspect Richard is angry at Dave for putting him through that."

"What you say may be true, but his words still hurt. He should be careful about what he says."

"What does Dave's note say?" asked Claire.

"I'm afraid to read it. I don't know how much more pain I can take."

"Do you want me to read it? I'll be gentle when I tell you what he wrote."

"No, this is something I need to do," said Zach, wiping the tears from his face. "If you don't mind, I'd like to be alone."

"I'll be with Mary," said Claire. "Give me her note."

Zach walked over to the tree and hit it with his fist. He sat on the ground, leaned against the tree, and opened Dave's note.

Zach:

When you read this, I'll be dead. Thank you for being the best friend I ever had. We had fun together, and I have lots of good memories. I wish I could've continued as your pressman...but that wasn't to be.

You're probably wondering why I did this. Ever since I lost my fingers, I've been in pain, not physical pain, that passed, but the pain of not being a complete man. I think surviving the butchering was worse than if I'd died. The pain I've felt is so awful, I had to find a way to stop it. Today I did.

I know you're a man of faith, and that you know I'm not. I've come to see life is cruel and stupid, that nothing matters. I'm ready to enter the eternal empty.

I have one final request. Watch over Mary for me. Encourage her to marry again, this time to a man who can take care of her.

I hope your life is long and happy. Enjoy your family, and thanks for being an important part of my life.

Dave

Zach sat sobbing till the chill in the air brought him back to the reality of the moment. During the time Zach was lost in grief, Roberto arrived and took charge of the situation.

"I'll arrange for the burial," Roberto told Mary. "You don't have to worry about that. Where do you want Dave buried?"

"City Cemetery is close. I can go there regularly. Bury Dave there."

"I want to buy his headstone if that's all right?" said Zach, drying his face with his hands as he approached the others.

"Dave would like that," said Mary. "Please do."

Just then, Joe arrived.

"I was cleaning up after today's service when word about Dave reached me. I got here as quickly as I could. Where is he? I want to anoint his body."

"Are you okay with that?" Zach asked Mary.

"I don't care," said Mary. "Do what you must."

Kneeling over Dave, Joe took a small jar from his cloak and said:

"I begin by laying hands on his head and anointing his forehead. Dave, I anoint you and lay hands on you in the name of our Lord, Jesus Christ, beseeching him to bring you the peace you so desperately sought.

"I now move to Dave's eyes, anointing the lids and praying, We give You thanks, Almighty God, for these eyes; for all the wonders of Your creation Dave saw, the mountains and the fishing streams, for the first time Dave saw his beloved Mary... we give You thanks, O Lord.

"Moving to the ears, I anoint them, praying, Lord, we give You thanks for all the exhilarating things he heard with these ears, the music Dave enjoyed, the birds singing, water flowing over rocks...we thank You, O Lord.

"For these arms... the heavy loads they lifted for others, for the times they held Mary...we thank You, O Lord.

"I anoint his nose recalling those fragrant flowers Dave enjoyed at his wedding, for the earth after a good rain, and for the aroma of the many meals he enjoyed...we give You thanks, O Lord.

"I anoint his lips with thanks for all his words of wisdom, support, and kindness, and for the sweet kisses Dave gave Mary...we give You thanks, O Lord.

"Finally, I offer thanksgiving for Dave's life among us and pray for his entry into Your Kingdom. May angels and saints surround Dave as he waits for us to join him.

Amen."

"Thank you, Father Joe," said Mary. "That was beautiful. What you said comforted me."

"Mary, why don't you stay with us tonight," said Claire. "We have an extra room."

"I'd like that," responded Mary. "I don't want to be alone...."

* * *

Zach took the women home and helped them settle in.

"I'm going to return the buggy. I'll be right back," he said.

Zach drove the buggy to the stable. As he was paying for its use, Emile told him something strange occurred that afternoon.

"What was that?" asked Zach, struggling to concentrate.

"David Dodd came in, saddled his horse, and rode off without saying a word. That's not like him," said Emile. "Anyway, it wasn't half an hour later his horse came back without him. Dave never returned. We put his horse away, but we're afraid something bad happened to him."

"Dave died," said Zach. "His body was found hanging from the tree in Elstner's hay yard. Dave must have tied a rope around his neck and jumped off his horse. Thank you for taking care of his mount. I'll pay you for your trouble."

"Under the circumstances, they'll be no charge," said Emile. "I'm sorry to hear about Dave. He was a good guy. I enjoyed his company, and he taught me several tricks about blacksmithing. I'm stunned he's dead. I wonder what made Dave do it?"

"Thank you for your kind words," said Zach. "I have to go."

When Zach opened the front door, Mary and Claire were in the kitchen weeping. Zach picked up Dave's note to Mary, which lay open on the dining room table.

Dearest Mary:

You've been a wonderful woman and wife. I adore you and treasure the time we've spent together. You are the best thing that came into my life.

I'll be gone when you read this. It's because I cherish you that I'm removing myself from your life. I'm a failure, and I'm tired of being a burden to you. The disappointment I see when you look at me is unbearable. You'll be better off without me. I find comfort knowing my pain will soon be over.

I have one final request. Marry again. Choose a man who can bring you the fulfillment and happiness I cannot.

I love you with my whole heart.

Dave

As Zach was reading, he could hear Mary whimper, "Dave, I want *you*. I want to spend the rest of my life with *you*. I love *you*...."

TUESDAY, SEPTEMBER 21, 1852

WHEN ZACH AWOKE, he was thinking about how he failed Dave.

I feel awful I didn't speak to you when I had the chance. I might have said something that changed your mind, and you'd be alive. Dave, forgive me for not reaching out to you; you would've reached out to me.

Zach got out of bed, wiped away his tears, and went to his study. He opened his Prayer Book and began reading Morning Prayer. Zach self-consciously said the General Confession, and feeling unworthy of Absolution, skipped it. The lesson for the day was Luke 8:22-25.

> One day Jesus got into a boat with his disciples, and he said to them, 'Let us go across to the other side of the lake.' So they put out, and while they were sailing Jesus fell asleep. A windstorm swept down on the lake, and the boat was filling with water, and they were in danger. The disciples went to Jesus and woke him, shouting, "Master, Master, we are perishing!" And Jesus awoke and rebuked the wind and the raging waves; they ceased, and there was calm. Jesus said to them, "Where is your faith?" They were afraid and amazed, and said to one another, "Who then is this, that he commands even the winds and the water, and they obey him?

Dave didn't believe Jesus could help him. I'm no better. I didn't trust God the right words would come to me. What happened to my faith? Father, forgive my sins and deliver me from the cowardice that afflicts me. Grant me the wisdom and courage to know and do Your will.

Zach finished his prayers and joined Claire for breakfast.

"How are you feeling this morning?" she asked.

"Rotten. If I'd spoken to Dave last Friday, he might be alive today."

"I urged you to speak to him. Why you don't listen to me?"

"Not speaking to Dave is going to torment me the rest of my life," said Zach. "I don't need you to remind me of my inadequacies."

"I'm sorry," said Claire. "I know you're not responsible for Dave's death."

"Thanks for that," said Zach, tossing his napkin on the table.

"Did you know Dave didn't want a memorial service?" asked Claire timidly.

"That's disappointing, but I'm not surprised," said Zach. "I'll visit Dave's grave after work today and ask for his forgiveness. Perhaps we can have a short service when his headstone is installed. What do you think?"

"I like the idea, but I'll ask Mary if she's okay with it," said Claire.

* * *

Zach had just arrived at work when Joe opened the door.

"Where's Elsu?" he asked. "I need my Sunday bulletins."

"I don't know," said Zach. "I just got here."

"I knew I shouldn't trust an injun. Not having the bulletin today is going to mess up my entire week."

"Morning fellas," said Elsu, walking in the back door. "Father Joe, you've come for your bulletins. I'll get them."

Elsu went to the storage shelves and pulled down the bulletins.

"Here you go," he said, handing them to Joe.

"When I didn't see you, I was afraid the bulletins weren't done," said Joe, letting out a big breath.

"I was outside relieving myself," replied Elsu. "Trust me. I won't fail you."

"Zach, when is Dave's memorial service? Mary hasn't asked me to officiate, so I'm assuming Pastor White will."

"Dave didn't want a service," said Zach. "There isn't going to be one."

"That's unfortunate," said Joe. "Funerals aren't for the dead; they're for the living. Closure helps everyone heal."

"Since Dave didn't want a memorial service, I might do something when Dave's headstone is installed. Claire is asking Mary if that's okay."

"Let me know if you want me to have a role," said Joe heading for the door.

Zhang left too. He went to collect the church's information for this week's paper.

After everyone was gone, Elsu said: "I don't understand the need for a headstone. My people burn the dead and their possessions."

"Why's that?" asked Zach, looking at Elsu as he walked to his desk.

"Burials and headstones lead the survivor's mind down into the darkness and decay of the earth. That's no good. When the body is burned, our thoughts rise to heaven's light, where the Spirit resides. That's better. Burning the dead's possessions is a practical matter. We're nomadic people. If we didn't burn the dead's belongings, we'd have to carry them with us."

"I never thought of that," said Zach. "While I like the idea of lifting our heads to heaven, I also like the opportunity to visit the gravesite. Death ends a life, not a relationship. There's merit in both of our approaches."

"I prefer my people's way," said Elsu, thrusting out his chest.

Zach began to read Zhang's article, which was on his desk.

FOREIGN MINER'S ACT

When gold was discovered in California, people rushed to claim their share. At first, foreigners were welcomed, especially Mexicans and Chinese. They'd work for wages far below what whites demanded, and they'd do tasks whites didn't want to do. The only people who objected to their presence were Irish and German miners, who regarded them as competition.

In December 1849, Peter Burnett became the first Governor of California. He was elected amid cries of "California for Americans." Burnett signed the first Foreign Miner's Tax in April 1850. The law required all people who weren't citizens to pay twenty dollars a month for a license to mine. The fee, Burnett promised, would raise two hundred thousand dollars for the state.

The consequences of the law weren't what Burnett anticipated. Miners from Ireland, England, Canada, and Germany complained about the unfairness of the fee. Their objections led to the law being rewritten. In the revision, any miner who is a free white person didn't have to pay.

The new version didn't satisfy everyone. Disgruntled nonwhite miners protested the tax by leaving the mines. Their departure forced merchants to lower their rents and charge less for goods and services. In San Francisco, destitute Chinese miners lived alongside whites. The popularity of Burnett's fee faded.

In January of 1851, John McDougal became the second Governor of California. His attitude toward the Chinese was the opposite of Burnett's. He saw the Chinese as the answer to California's labor shortage and urged them to transform swamps into farmland. When revenues from Burnett's Tax came in significantly below expectations, McDougal pushed the legislature to repeal it. They did.

This period of cooperation between the races didn't last. Severe economic conditions set in. The dirty jobs the Chinese performed were suddenly in demand by the whites. Hostility toward Asian immigrants rekindled.

John Bigler campaigned to be California's third governor on a platform that was similar to Burnett's. He declared the Chinese were avaricious, ignorant of the moral obligations, incapable of being assimilated into American society, and therefore a danger to the public's welfare. Bigler wanted fewer Chinese in California. When he was elected, Bigler had the legislature pass a new Foreign Miner's Tax.

Though the new law reduced the miner's fee to three dollars a month, *The New Republican* believes it is still unfair.

All miners should be treated equally, and prejudice against the Chinese must not be an official state policy. The second Foreign Miner's Tax, like the first, has to be repealed.

When Zhang returned to the office, Zach called him to his desk.

"I like this article," he said. "It's front page-material."

A stranger entered the office.

"May I help you?" asked Zach.

"Yes. My name is F.F. Barss. I want to place an ad announcing the opening of my store. Tell your readers I have a wide selection of exceptional jewelry, fancy clocks and watches, and an outstanding collection of pearls and precious stones."

"We can do that," said Zach. "Is there anything else you want in the ad?"

"Highlight that I'm honest, reliable and that all my work and merchandise is guaranteed."

"Got it," said Zach, scribbling Barss' words. "Welcome to Hangtown, and may you have a long and prosperous stay."

* * *

Zach and Claire met for lunch at Lucy's.

"I spoke with Mary this morning," said Claire. "I told her you plan to visit Dave's grave after work, and we both would like to join you. Can we meet there at four?"

"That's cutting my day short," said Zach. "I'll try. Did you ask Mary about having a service when the headstone goes in?"

"I forgot," said Claire, looking down. "I'll do it tonight. Did you remember Friday is the first anniversary of your grandfather's death?"

"That's right," said Zach sighing. "Life would be different without the money he left us. I'll talk to Joe about a commemoration."

"I want to be a part of whatever you do. I benefitted too," said Claire. "The following Friday is the anniversary of when my dad died. We don't need to do anything to honor his life."

"Does Stephen feel the same way?" asked Zach, rubbing his jaw.

"He does."

* * *

When Zach returned to the office, only Elsu was present.

"What'd you do over the weekend?" asked Zach.

"I went to visit Tonya's tribe. I thanked her elders for saving me and stayed for the stories."

"What kind of stories?"

"At night around campfires, stories are told about the history, traditions, and travels of the tribe. A lot of time is spent describing what different places look like," said Elsu. "Storytellers are held in high esteem."

"Are women storytellers?"

"Women must never attempt to teach anything," said Elsu grimacing.

Stephen opened the office door and asked, "Am I in interrupting?"

"No," responded Zach. "What brings you?"

"I received a letter from Joe Winans that will interest you. He included a copy of Frederick Douglass' speech, *What to the Slave Is the Fourth of July?* I wish I heard him give it: it's terrific. I'll leave my copy with you."

"My parents would've appreciated a good antislavery speech," said Zach, smiling.

"In his letter, Winans mentioned Douglass was the only Negro to attend the Seneca Falls Convention," said Stephen. "When Elizabeth Cady Stanton and Lucretia Mott argued about whether women should have a role in politics, Douglass asked if he could address the gathering. He said the world would be a better place if women were involved in politics because women bring a moral and intellectual power to society that's desperately needed. Denying women the vote degrades half the population and perpetuates a great injustice."

"He's not only for abolishing slavery," said Zach, "but he's also for women's rights!"

"That's right," said Stephen. "Douglass believes in the equality of all people, including Indians and recent immigrants."

"I knew I liked him," said Zach, smiling. "I'd love to chat more, but I've work to do. We'll talk again soon."

"Don't wait too long," said Stephen. "I'm moving to Sacramento next week. I've taken a lease on an office."

"So soon?" asked Zach. "Does Claire know you leaving? She'll want you here when Cate is born. Is that possible?"

"It should be," said Stephen. "The complication is Hunter is pushing me to start in Sacramento."

"Is Rose going with you?"

"Not at this time," said Stephen.

* * *

When Mary, Claire, and Zach arrived at the cemetery, Zach knelt beside Dave's grave. Mary and Claire remained by the buggy.

After a few minutes of quiet, Claire said to Mary, "You look like you've been through hell. You didn't look this way this morning. What happened?"

"People know about Dave," said Mary. "They've been saying hurtful things."

"What'd they said?" asked Claire, taking Mary's hand.

"A Chinese miner came to the laundry to pick up his clothes. When I was alone, he said 'mines are open to all who are willing to work. It's the manliest and most independent way of life on earth. A miner makes five, fifty, or a thousand dollars a day using only his hands and strong determination. Miners' independence and hard work make them the most desirable men to have as one's spouse. You married the wrong man and are better off without him.' Then he proposed to me. I was speechless."

"He didn't mean any disrespect," said Zach, wiping his face as he joined them. "He was merely promoting himself."

"Yes, he did!" said Mary, putting her hands on her hips. "He was telling me I could do better than Dave, that Dave wasn't the highest caliber man. If I weren't numb from my pain, I would've given him a piece of my mind. I just stood there, dazed. How dare he say such things? He wasn't the only one. A woman, a good customer, asked me, 'why didn't I do something to stop Dave?' as if I could have, but didn't?"

"You told her off, didn't you?" asked Zach.

"No, I don't have the energy to argue," said Mary. "Belle ushered her out the door."

"You're strong," said Zach. "You can handle these comments."

"Not as strong as you think. When folks tell me I'll find a new husband, I want to rip their tongues out. Don't they realize I want Dave, not someone new? I actually had a woman ask me, 'what's wrong with you that Dave wanted to die rather than be with you? He seemed so nice and normal when I met him in the hotel restaurant.' Well, in social settings, Dave was amiable. No one could see how much he was struggling. When we'd return to our room, Dave would retreat into a shell I couldn't penetrate. Another woman asked me, 'what did you do to push him over the edge?' I can't take any more of these comments. Betty and Ah are going to run the laundry while I take time off."

"That's an excellent idea," said Claire. "You're welcome to stay with us as long as you want."

"Thank you," said Mary, choking up. "I'd like to be alone with Dave."

"Take all the time you need," said Claire. "We'll wait here."

Zach and Claire couldn't hear what Mary was saying, but it was full of emotion. When Mary finished, she dusted off her outfit and trudged over to where they were standing.

"I have a question for you," said Claire. "Why'd you want to know what Dave was wearing?"

"I wanted to find out if he was wearing his favorite clothes. I was hoping he did."

"Was he?"

"No, he had on what he was wearing when we left for the dedication ceremony. I asked Roberto to put on his favorite outfit before he buried him. He was kind enough to do that."

"The headstone will be ready on Friday," said Zach. "There are some of us who'd like to have a brief ceremony when it's installed. Do you mind?"

"I'm not a Christian, and neither was Dave. What do you have in mind?"

"Saying some prayers, sharing memories, things like that," said Zach.

"I don't have to attend, do I? Right now, being around people is more of a drain than a help."

"You don't need to come," said Zach, "and if the headstone observance makes you uncomfortable, we won't do it."

"Go ahead. It can't hurt anything. I don't understand why you do things for Dave after he's dead, but you wouldn't speak to him when he was alive? I was counting on you."

"I'm sorry I didn't," said Zach. "I feel terrible. Please forgive me."

Mary began to sob.

"You were a good friend to Dave, his best friend. If you'd intervened, he might be alive today. I'd have my Dave…."

Another burst of tears followed. When Mary collected herself, she said, "Forgive me. Today is Dave's birthday. I had a surprise for him that he'll never know."

"What was that?" asked Claire softly.

"I was waiting until today to tell him I'm pregnant."

FRIDAY, SEPTEMBER 24, 1852

ZACH READ MORNING Prayer in his study shortly after waking. The lesson assigned for the day was Psalm 84:5-8.

> Happy is the man who finds refuge in You,
>   whose mind is on the pilgrim highways.
> They pass through the Valley of Baca,
>   regarding it as a place of springs,
>   as if the early rain had covered it with blessings.
> They go from rampart to rampart,
>   appearing before God in Zion.
> O Lord, God of hosts,
>   hear my prayer;
>   give ear, O God of Jacob.

Dad said this psalm is an expression of the joy a pilgrim feels on the way to the temple in Jerusalem. The traveler yearns to be close to God and to find a home near Him. On his journey, the disciple passes through the Valley of Baca, an image for troubles and dangers that are hard to endure. It's a place of sorrow and grief. Nevertheless, the Lord transforms Baca's desolation into an oasis and the seeker's affliction into well-being.

I can't relate to this. My Valley of Baca remains dry and bleak; holy water isn't available to replenish my soul. Lord, why do You spurn me?

* * *

Zhang and Elsu had the papers in wheelbarrows ready to be delivered when Zach entered the office.

"Morning, fellas. Thanks for having the papers ready to pass out," said Zach. "With Dave's service this afternoon, I'm having trouble thinking about anything but the ceremony."

"Missing Dave?" asked Elsu.

"Yes, but the emptiness is more than that," said Zach, rubbing his grandfather's watch. "I'm also feeling the absence of God. All of the time I've spent working on my spiritual development hasn't paid off. My mind is dark, and I'm empty inside. Preoccupation with my quest has distracted me from important matters, like Dave's distress. I'm lost."

"There's an ancient Chinese story that might help," said Zhang.

"Tell me," said Zach, sitting on the edge of his desk.

"A Chinese nobleman was riding through a remote village when he saw a potter at work. He stopped and picked up a pot he found exquisite. As he looked closely, he found the pot to be not only beautiful, but it also contained a crude strength. The nobleman asked the potter, 'How can you form this bowl with grace and strength, yet with a delicacy of design?'

"The potter replied, 'Oh, you're just looking at the outward shape. What I'm forming lies within. I'm interested only in what remains after the pot is broken.'"

"I believe that is what God asks of us," said Zhang. "We are to work on what is forming within and to cultivate what remains after the pot is broken. Your devotion to spiritual matters will be rewarded. Keep at it."

"I hope you're right," said Zach. "God doesn't think much of my efforts. He has abandoned me."

"That's how it feels when you're inside the pot: dark, unseen, and not valued," said Zhang. "Don't despair. You're still in the hands of the potter as he works the wheel."

* * *

Elsu and Zhang had left to distribute the papers when Joe entered the office.

"I'll take Kay her money," he said. "Sorry I wasn't here sooner, but Pastor White and I were discussing the headstone ceremony. Each of us will lead a part of it."

"I like that you're both officiating," said Zach. "Is there a role for me?"

"Of course," said Joe. "You can be the host. I have a question for you. What should we do to commemorate grandpa's passing? I'm stumped."

"Grandpa always liked a good meal. Why don't we go to Tinniman's for dinner? Claire wants to be part of the celebration, and going out to eat will spare her from having to fix another meal."

"We can toast him with a fine glass of wine, tell stories about him, and have a few good laughs. That sounds perfect. If you're bringing Claire, I'll bring Matilde."

* * *

At three o'clock, there were already a large number of people standing around Dave's grave. It wasn't long before Ed von Franz appeared with the headstone. He joined Pastor White, Joe, and Zach.

"Do you want me to put the stone in place now or wait until others arrive?" asked Ed.

"If you have time to wait, that would be best," said Pastor White. "I'm surprised by how many people are still flowing in. Let's give them a few more minutes."

"Who are all these people?" asked Joe. "I recognize many of them, but others I don't."

"That's my wife Mabel talking with Doc Martin," said Pastor White. "Lily and Dulun are the ones kneeling at the grave. You know Zhang and Elsu, Matilde and Flann, Jeb Stuebe, Lucy Wakefield, and Captain Meyer. Walt Selzer is standing next to Gilbert Gardiner and Mel Zombrowski. I hope Mel hasn't been drinking. Walking up now are Alex Hunter, Jim Hume, Walt Tobey, Jim and Sally Tubbs, Kevin Michaels, and Jay, the barber. I don't know the Chinese ladies' names from the boarding house, but there must be half-a-dozen of them huddled over there. Olive Day is standing next to Claire, and Rose and Stephen are standing next to them. In the back are Jim Edwards and Bryan, his assistant, John Larue, Robert Jenner, and Red. Roberto is walking this way. Perhaps he knows some of the others."

"Afternoon, pastors," said Roberto. "Dave would be surprised by how many people are here."

"We were just saying the same thing," said Pastor White, smiling. "Do you know the men standing to the left of the grave?"

"They're the fellas who repaired the pond at the laundry when Dave was on his honeymoon. Rusty Colter, Dan O'Hare, and Martin Klopp are ones I know by name. Standing near them is Mitch, who worked as my security guard for the bear and bullfight. Next to Mitch are Emile and the other guys from the stable."

"Are you ready to get started?" asked Ed.

"Yes," said Pastor White. "Put the headstone in place."

Ed carefully placed the headstone in the hole he'd previously prepared. When the hole was filled and patted flat, the workmen withdrew. Zach stepped forward.

"Thank you, Ed, for making such a handsome headstone. Dave would approve," said Zach. "Pastor White and my brother, Father Joe, will lead the ceremony. After prayers, there'll be an opportunity to share our memories of Dave. We'll begin now with Pastor White."

"I want to say a few words about suicide, which is an awkward and uncomfortable subject," said the pastor. "Those of us left behind struggle to understand why it happened. It seems needless. But the pain Dave felt impaired his thinking and warped his judgment. While you and I could see hope for him, he couldn't see it. Life as Dave was experiencing it was intolerable. Everything he tried to make life better didn't work. To someone in Dave's state of mind, nothing matters but ending the pain. It's time we stop questioning why Dave killed himself. Instead, we can use his death as a reminder to appreciate our friends, value those we love, and reaffirm our commitment to one another.

"Please bow your heads as we pray.

> Almighty God, we ask You to bless this headstone, and to receive
>   David into Your eternal care,
> Make Your face to shine upon him, and grant him peace,
>   forevermore;
> This we ask through Jesus Christ, our Lord. *Amen.*

> O Lord, support us all the day long of our troubled life, until the
>   shadows lengthen and the evening comes, and the busy world
>   is hushed, and the fever of life is over, and our work is done.
> Then in your mercy grant us a safe lodging, and a holy rest, and
>   peace at the last. *Amen.*

Father Joe stepped forward.

"David was a hero. Hero, you ask? He committed suicide. He's a coward, not a hero. Listen to me for a moment. The hero is born of a bitter struggle. One way to be a hero is to die in battle wearing a fancy uniform, surrounded by comrades, with trumpets blaring. But the man who fights a battle with his soul, quietly, patiently, and alone is also a hero. His battle persists year after year, with no one to acknowledge his successes. David was this kind of hero. He battled his inner demons and lost. Nevertheless, he's as much a hero as those who fight and win. That's why I think of Dave as a hero. I hope you will too."

"Let us pray:

"Almighty God, we entrust David, who is dear to us, to your never-failing care and love, knowing You are doing for him better things than we can desire or pray for; through Jesus Christ, our Lord. *Amen.*

"Almighty God, Father of mercies and giver of comfort: Deal graciously, we pray, with all those who mourn; that casting all their cares on You, they may know the consolation of Your love; through Christ, our Lord. *Amen.*

Standing above the grave, Joe raised his right hand and, while making the sign of the cross, said:

"May grace, mercy, and peace from God Almighty, the Father, the Son, and the Holy Ghost, be with you and abide with you, now and always. *Amen.*

Zach stepped forward.

"I want to thank each of you for coming out on a Friday afternoon to say good-bye to Dave. If anyone has a memory of him you'd like to share, please do it now."

Ian Oakland spoke first. "Dave worked hard on the statue of Nurse Morris. He didn't know what he was doing a good deal of the time, but he wasn't afraid to continue. If he hit a hard spot, he'd ask for help and push ahead. His talents were such that the statue turned out well. I was impressed by his willingness to undertake a project he'd never done before and find a way to do it well. Dave was a courageous and adventuresome fella. That's the lasting memory I'll have of him."

Dulun spoke next. Lily stood next to him, holding his hand.

"It was a joy to celebrate Dave's marriage to Mary. His love for her was evident. He was like a silly boy with ceremonies, but he persisted through the awkward moments. Dave was a big, loveable kid. I will miss his enthusiasm for life."

Rose stepped forward. "I worked with Dave after he lost his fingers. We discussed the kind of artificial hands he could purchase. Unfortunately, none of them met his needs. His zest for doing things is what I'll remember. If only we could've found an artificial hand that worked...." Stephen came to Rose's side, put his arm around her as tears ran down her cheeks, and led her back to where they'd been standing.

After a pause, Roberto said, "Dave and I built many things together. He was instrumental in restoring my holding pens and stadium after the Musclemans burned them down. He helped me capture Zanshi, as big and aggressive a bear as I've ever seen. What I'll recall most about Dave is what a good friend he was."

Red indicated he wanted to speak.

"Dave and I didn't get along as many of you know. Despite our differences, I observed he was loyal and stouthearted to his friends. I admire those traits in a man, even one I dislike. I'm here to salute him, and to tell you I wish things had turned out differently. Be at peace, big guy."

Zach stood in front of the gathering.

"Dave was built like a bull, and many times, acted like one. If he could fight someone with his fists, he was happy to do it. Working with him at the paper, I quickly realized he wasn't shy about criticizing my editorials before any of you could." (Snickering spread throughout the gathering.) "When your disapproving responses came in, Dave would defend what I said. He was feisty, that's for sure, but Dave had a tender side also. Inside that hulk of a man was the heart of a lover. There wasn't anything he wouldn't do for someone in need. He'd always be the first to step forward." Zach wiped away a tear and cleared his throat before continuing. "Dave loved to fish. He'd spend his spare time on the rivers and streams in the area, then share what he caught with others. He was truly a special man. I'm going to miss him."

Pastor White was the last to speak.

"It's getting dark. It's time we end our tributes. I want you to leave this ceremony, knowing that life's worst things are never the last things. For in our Father's house, there are many rooms. There's a place reserved for each of us. When a friend of mine was dying, he asked me, 'aren't you afraid of crossing the river of death? I am.' My reply to my friend was 'No, I'm not. I know our Father owns the land on both sides of the river.' On the far side is where we'll find Dave waiting for us. As I look at the sky behind you, I see a large, full moon rising. It reminds me of Dave's presence among us. Use the gift of its light to find your way home safely."

As Zach and Claire walked to their buggy, Zach said, "That was a lovely ceremony. I thought both Joe and Pastor White were outstanding."

"I was surprised by how many folks showed up," said Claire. "Dave touched more lives than I knew."

"I didn't expect that many either. I wonder why Jim Edwards came?"

"He doesn't know that you're aware he's the head of the OSSB. He probably didn't want his absence to raise questions," said Claire. "After all, Dave was one of his better customers."

"I was impressed Red spoke," said Zach. "That man has more character than I gave him credit for."

"I'm feeling better," said Claire. "Joe was right: the service helped. How are you feeling?"

"I was comforted by the large turnout and the kind words shared, but my heart remains cold. As inspiring as Pastor White and Joe were, I didn't feel God's presence," said Zach, starting the buggy toward town. "If anything, their messages accentuated how distant from God I feel."

"What do you need to feel close to God again?" asked Claire, holding on as Zach drove rapidly.

"The words I heard today I've heard all my life," said Zach, "only now they've lost the vitality they once had. I need a new sign of God's mercy, one that indicates He cares about me, and it needs to be something I can grasp."

Zach aggressively turned the buggy onto Main Street.

"You sound like Thomas, wanting proof to dispel your doubt," said Claire. "Slow down, you're making me sick to my stomach."

"I'm sorry. We're almost there," responded Zach. "Perhaps a good meal and sharing memories of grandpa will lift my spirits."

WEDNESDAY, OCTOBER 6, 1852

ZACH SHUDDERED. WITH clammy hands and a palpitating heart, he wrote down the nightmare that woke him. When he joined Claire for breakfast, he told her the dream.

> "I'm in a primeval forest. A large Iron Age man is standing in front of me. He's holding a giant sword. I'm terrified. 'What are you going to do?' I ask. 'Everything must be ruled by the light,' the hairy man says. With a swift stroke, he cuts off my head and sets it aside. He tells me to watch what he's going to do. He cuts off my legs. They're placed away from the rest of my body and from where my head is.
>
> Next, he severed my arms. They're placed so I can see I am in four parts.
>
> The ancient one uses his sword to remove the skin from my head. Some of the removed skin he burns; other skin he feds to wild animals.
>
> My body, though dead, is as white as a star in the heavens. Without skin, my head is a golden color.
>
> 'Why'd you do this?' I ask.
>
> The man replies: 'This is indispensable if you are to fulfill your destiny.'

"That's the end of the dream," said Zach.

"My Gosh," said Claire. "That's grotesque."

"Stunned, I went to my study," said Zach. "I beseeched God to protect me, and I read Morning Prayer. The lesson was a prayer of Saint Paul's. Listen."

Zach opened his Bible and read Ephesians 3:14-21.

> This, then, is what I pray, kneeling before the Father, from whom every family, whether spiritual or natural, takes its name.

Out of His infinite glory, may He give you the power through His Spirit for your hidden self to grow strong, so that Christ may live in your hearts through faith, and then, planted in love and built on love, you will with all the saints have the strength to grasp the breadth and the length, the height and the depth; until knowing the love of Christ, which is beyond all knowledge, you are filled with the utter fullness of God. Glory be to Him whose power, working in us, can do infinitely more than we can ask or imagine. Glory be to him from generation to generation in the Church and in Christ Jesus forever and ever. Amen.

"That's hard to follow," said Claire, pulling on one of her curls.

"Paul is instructing the Ephesians God is at work inside each of us, doing 'infinitely more than we can ask or imagine.' If that's true, I'm supposed to believe God dismembers me in a dream so my destiny can be fulfilled. That's ludicrous."

"I don't know," said Claire, cradling her coffee cup. "I can relate to the hairy man saying, 'everything must be ruled by the light.' That matches my experience, but the other things are bizarre. I don't understand them."

"I don't know why they happened, either," said Zach, rubbing the back of his neck. "In the Old Testament, an animal was slain to renew the tribe. If the dream is suggesting my destiny involves being sacrificed, I prefer a different fate."

"I think you're stressing too much about the dream," said Claire. "It's beyond the reach of reason. Let's talk about something else."

"Alright," said Zach, picking up his coffee cup. "Julia Lynn Powell's ship docked in San Francisco three days ago," said Zach. "That means she should be in Hangtown today. I've left my schedule looser than usual, so I can show her around and bring her to you."

"I can't wait for Olive and all the women of Hangtown to be exposed to her thinking," said Claire, wily. "Change is coming."

* * *

Only Elsu was present when Roberto ambled into the newspaper office.

"I want to place an ad for my gambling pavilion," he said, handing Elsu the wording.

"I can do that," said Elsu. "The fee is up to Zach. He should be here any minute. While we wait, tell me why you switched from staging bull and bear fights to operating a gambling hall?"

Roberto explained there were two primary reasons. One concerned the expense of feeding and maintaining large animals. The other reason, he confessed, stemmed from his love of the beasts. "I hate it when they die."

Roberto went on to say, "The men who settle in Hangtown are already gamblers. They'll participate in any activity that offers them the chance to get rich. I gave them that opportunity with the animal fights, and now I do it with card games. Opening a gambling pavilion isn't really much of a switch."

"I've never gambled," said Elsu. "How's it work?"

"When you come to my place, I'll teach you," said Roberto. "You'll find there are tables where the men wager on card games like Mont, Faro, Rouge Et Noir, and Blackjack. On weekends, the desire is so strong, men stand three deep around each table. At the end of the evening, a typical gambler has a few wins and losses. They leave to play another day. A few, however, bet all they have on a final hand. These men go home rich or penniless, which is the excitement that fuels their lives. If they lose, they go back to work, generate a few bucks, and return convinced this time their fate will be different."

Elsu asked why folks come to Roberto's pavilion instead of one of the other many options?

Roberto smiled before answering. "I employ beautiful women to deal the cards. Some nights I have a band, and the men dance with a senorita. Wealthy men come to my place to get away from the greasy cards and the loud, crude voices that permeate the competition. I direct big betters to a private room, where the drinks are free, and my most attractive women attend to them. Whiskey, women, and cards: that's my winning combination."

Zach entered the office.

"What brings you?" Zach asked his friend.

"I have an ad for my gambling pavilion that I want you to run," said Roberto. "Unlike Dave, Elsu didn't try to sell me a full-page ad."

"I will," said Zach, winking. "That way, you'll be sure everyone sees it!"

"A quarter-page will be large enough," replied Roberto chuckling. "I can't afford to give my profits to you."

After agreeing to a price, Roberto said it was time to move on.

"My supply of whiskey is low," he said, striding to the door. "If I've learned anything, it's to have lots of whiskey on hand!"

A short while after Roberto left, Zach said to Elsu, "With the Presidential election only a month away, I need to make an endorsement."

"Who's it going to be?"

"I'll recommend the Free Soil candidate, John Hale," said Zach. "I don't think he'll win, but he's the most opposed to slavery. That gets my vote."

Just then, Mister Tobey opened the office door.

"I was walking by and thought you'd like to be the first to know a big player is coming to Hangtown."

Turning to see who was speaking, Zach asked, "Who's that?"

"Wells Fargo. They're opening an office down the street. They'll employ a lot of people and be a boon to the business community. Hangtown is growing up."

"How'd you learn this?" asked Zach, stepping closer.

"They just signed a lease for one of my buildings," said Mister Tobey, beaming. In a few years, they intend to add stagecoach service between Hangtown and the East. Wells Fargo will keep us thriving."

* * *

Midmorning, Claire met Olive at the school. They arranged the desks and put away the supplies Claire had ordered.

"How many children have you recruited?" she asked.

"Right now, there are twenty-five," said Olive. "I'm working hard to prepare, and I should be ready to start on November fifteenth."

"Then, that's when we'll open," said Claire. "Are you still planning to visit Susan Lord during the Christmas break?"

"I didn't tell you," said Olive, her cheeks turning red. "I received a letter from Miss Lord a few days ago. She canceled the meeting because she's getting married and leaving Benicia. So far, the school hasn't named her replacement. Miss Lord promised to tell me when they do. Until I hear, I'm not going."

"It shouldn't take them long to find someone," said Claire. "Don't cancel your trip."

* * *

After lunch, Zach spotted Claire crossing Main Street. She was headed to Huntington's to inspect the fabric they had in stock. When Zach caught up to her, Claire filled him in on her meeting with Olive and was curious where he'd been.

"I had lunch with Pastor White," said Zach. "We talked about my dream."

"Was he helpful?"

"He didn't know what to make of it," said Zach, with a heavy sigh. "We talked about the passage from Ephesians, and in particular, Paul's thoughts about spiritual growth. I admitted I'd overlooked them. Pastor White called my attention to Paul's conviction that each of us is 'planted in love.' Isn't that a striking image, 'planted in love?' Because we are, we're able to grasp Christ's love for us and to be filled with the fullness of God. I told him Paul's thought is beautiful, but it doesn't change my plight. I'm still wandering in darkness. That's when Pastor White advised me the way to God is to open up to love."

"I like the idea of you being open to love," said Claire. "You have been distant lately. I thought it was something I did."

"I'm sorry you feel that way," said Zach. "My darkness has nothing to do with you. It's because God abandoned me."

"I hope you follow Pastor White's advice," said Claire. "Living with you hasn't been pleasant. Even Mary asked, what's bothering you? She thought your withdrawal was due to her living with us. I want you to snap out of it before Miss Powell arrives. Since I haven't seen her, I assume she hasn't come?"

"Not yet," said Zach. "I don't know where she is?"

* * *

When Zach returned to work, only Elsu was there.

"Where's Zhang?" he asked, walking to his desk.

"He's gone to the post office," said Elsu. "He's expecting a letter from home."

"As I listened to you and Tonya talk," said Zach, "I noticed your language has few words. Why's that?"

"We have enough," said Elsu. "It doesn't take many words to tell the truth."

"My guess is that English has a hundred words for each of yours," said Zach, playing with his pencil.

"You need all your words," replied Elsu, "we don't. Your people use many words to make long treaties to get what you want from my people. But the treaties are full of lies. Your people make many promises but keep few. My people don't need all your words; we speak truthfully with what we have."

"I heard Ben Wright left," said Zach, leaning forward in his desk chair. "You must be relieved."

"I'm safe for the moment, but my people aren't. A gang of white men attacked one of my people's campsites. It didn't go well for anyone. Wright was brought north to resolve the conflict. He promised to meet with all the chiefs at one time to make a peace agreement. When my leaders came, Wright told them there'd be a feast to celebrate the new peace, and they should return to their camps and bring everyone back with them. My people came in great numbers, laid down their arms, and prepared for the festivities. That's when Wright signaled his men: they murdered everyone. Wright reported to Yreka's leaders he'd achieved a permanent peace with at least a thousand Modocs. Your people lie and can't be trusted. Having lots of words doesn't change that."

As Zach recoiled, Zhang entered the office. He carried several letters. One was tucked under his arm.

"Most of these are requests for ads and information," he said, laying the ones in his hand on Zach's desk. "I got a letter from home. My family is well, and they thanked me for the money I sent." Pointing to the letter on top of the others, Zhang said: "This one is addressed to you."

Zach read it, clenched his teeth, and tossed the paper on his desk.

"Bad news?" asked Zhang.

"It's from Captain T. B. Cropper of the steamship *Cornelia*," said Zach. "He said one of his passengers, Miss Julia Lynn Powell, came down with cholera and died. Her death will set back our efforts to advance women's rights for at least a year. This is terrible news."

MONDAY, OCTOBER 11, 1852

CLAIRE SHOOK ZACH.

"Wake up! I just had a terrifying dream. I need to talk to you. Are you awake?"

"I'm awake," he said. "What time is it?"

"It's three. Listen to me. The dream made my blood curdle," said Claire. "I'm still shaking. Let me tell you what I dreamt."

Zach rolled over, rubbed his eyes, and said, "Okay, tell me the dream."

"I find myself in a dark room, surrounded by a dozen or so small animals," said Claire, grabbing Zach's arm. "They don't like being confined and aren't happy. Their discomfort frightens me. One of the animals, a snake, suddenly grows to an enormous size and devours me. That's when I woke. What do you think? Am I going to die?"

Sitting up and putting an arm around Claire, Zach said, "Are you going to be swallowed by a gigantic snake? I don't think so. Your dream reminds me of Jonah being swallowed by the whale. He came through his experience just fine; you will too."

"I'm scared," said Claire. "I don't like snakes. What does the dream mean?"

"I don't know," said Zach. "It's a dream. Forget it. I'll hold you while we go back to sleep."

"Like you forgot your most recent dream?" responded Claire. "I'm sorry I bothered you. Go back to sleep. I'll deal with it."

"What do you want me to do?" asked Zach, throwing his arms into the air. "I don't know what the dream means? For Jonah, it was part of his renewal. When the whale spits him out, it was like he was born again."

"The snake didn't regurgitate me. I woke up inside it. There's no sense of renewal about the dream," said Claire. "I'm shaking, and you want me to go back to sleep? I can't believe you. What kind of a father are you going to be? Are you going to tell Cate to go back to sleep when she has a nightmare?"

"Getting angry with me isn't going to make things better," said Zach. "Why don't you write it down? When you finish, you'll be ready to go back to sleep."

"I'll put it in my journal, but I won't get back to sleep," said Claire. "First, Julia dies; then a snake swallows me. Bad things are happening, and you don't want to be bothered. I'm scared, and you don't care."

"You're very pregnant. There're a lot of changes going on inside of you," replied Zach. "The dream probably reflects those changes. When I go to the office tomorrow, I'll write Misses Mott about Julia's death. Maybe another of her colleagues will come to work with us."

"I'm afraid Cate is so big I won't be able to push her out. That's what worries me," said Claire, tearfully. "I don't want to die with my baby stuck inside me."

"Everything is going to be fine," said Zach, "really it is. Rose will help you through the birth process. Your mother and sister didn't have problems when they delivered; you won't either. Trust me, I won't let anything happen to you."

Claire kissed Zach.

"Thank you for not ridiculing my fear," she said, getting out of bed. "Go back to sleep. I'll fix some tea and record the dream."

* * *

It was only a couple of hours later that Zach's alarm clock went off. He jolted awake, dressed, grabbed a couple of apples and pears, and headed to the stable.

"Morning, Joe. Have you been here long?" asked Zach, walking to his horse's stall and tossing Joe an apple and a pear. "This should hold you until breakfast."

"Thanks," said Joe. "I've only been here a few minutes. Not long. I want to get up the mountain and our sailing in before the storm arrives."

"It's unusually cold, even for Fall," said Zach, saddling up, "but I didn't notice a storm approaching."

The brothers arrived in Jackson as a red sky appeared over the mountains.

"Let's stop at the Jackson Hotel. It's the only place I know that will be serving breakfast this early," said Zach.

"I hate to spend money on hotel food," said Joe.

"You can afford it. You have more money than I do," said Zach. "Indeed, you should pay for my breakfast."

"I'll pay for your breakfast if you buy my dinner," said Joe, grinning. "Losing all those horseshoe games should cost you something. Do we have a deal?"

"If you insist," said Zach, "but I get to pick where we go."

Pierre showed them to a table and took their orders.

While they waited for their food, Joe said softly, "I've got a confession to make."

"What's that?" asked Zach, leaning forward in his chair.

"I asked the wrong man to be my senior warden."

"What's the problem with Bob Jenner?" asked Zach.

"Bob is constantly saying things that rub me the wrong way. He doesn't like the Chinese, Negroes, Indians, or Catholics. He's only comfortable with white Protestants. While that's not an uncommon attitude, it's not mine, and it certainly wasn't Christ's. At first, I thought I'd help him outgrow his narrow perspective. I regarded it as a challenge. Now, I realize I can't change him. He also uses his power as Senior Warden to stop me from welcoming non-white visitors. He's the one who insisted Elsu not return."

"I'm not surprised to hear that," said Zach. "Who do you prefer?"

"Albert Bee. He'd be far better."

"Perhaps Al can help you ease Bob out when the time comes."

"I like that suggestion," said Joe. "It's people like Bob who make the ministry difficult and unpleasant. If he's typical of what other churches have for parishioners, I understand why so many congregations fail. The clergy give up and move on. I stand in awe of Reverend Mine's achievement. He must have been an extraordinary leader."

When they finished their meal, the men made their way up the Kit Carson Trail. The stiff breeze that accompanied them brought smiles to their faces.

"If the wind holds, we'll have a good day on the water," said Joe.

"I agree. We should rent two boats. I'll show you how to go fast," said a smirking Zach.

"Yes! With my own boat, I won't have to wait while you find your way across the lake," said Joe. "We can race with the loser—that'll be you—paying for the rentals."

"You're on," said Zach, chuckling.

"Be sure you've enough money to pay for the boats and dinner, too," said Joe, his eyes aglow. "Today is going to be an expensive one for you."

When they reached the boathouse, Amy was surprised to see them.

"I'm closed for the winter," she said. "I only came in today to finish boarding up. I wasn't expecting anyone, especially since there's a storm coming."

"Will you rent us two sailboats?" said Zach. "We've come a long way to be here."

"Okay," she said hesitantly. "But keep it brief."

"Do you have any food for sale?" asked Joe.

"I've two sandwiches leftover from yesterday. You can have them at no cost. I was about to toss them."

"We'll take them," said Joe. "Time to get on the water."

The brothers sailed rapidly up and down the lake, taking turns winning races. Around three o'clock, the wind began to blow harder. They were competing through white caps in the middle of the lake when Zach saw a man ride to the boathouse. After speaking to Amy, she rang a bell while the man ran to the dock, waving a towel.

Zach turned his boat toward shore to find out what the problem was. Joe was still in racing mode. He didn't see Zach turn until he reached the far end of the lake. By then, Zach was securing his boat to the dock.

"There's a blizzard coming," the fellow told Zach. "You and your friend need to start down the mountain immediately. You don't want to be here when the storm hits. I'll put your boat away while you pay. Amy wants to leave as soon as she can."

When Joe saw Zach leave his boat and walk toward the rental office, he came about. *I wonder what's going on?* It took Joe fifteen minutes to reach the dock.

"Hi," said Joe to the stranger. "Is there a problem?"

"A blizzard is coming. You better head down the mountain right away. Riding in a snowstorm isn't pleasant and can be dangerous."

"I'm Joe Johnson. What's your name?"

"I'm John Thompson," he said. "My friends call me 'Snowshoe' because of my ability to navigate the mountains in winter. You'd better hustle along. Blizzards don't wait for anyone."

"What's Amy going to do?" asked Joe, stepping out of the boat.

"I'll lead her to Jackson," said Snowshoe. "Please hurry. There isn't much time."

The snow began falling shortly after Zach and Joe started down the mountain. Zach led the way.

"I don't know how long I'll be able to follow the trail," he told Joe.

"Maybe the snow will turn to rain when we're lower. Then it'll be mud we'll have to worry about," said Joe.

"I hope we reach that point soon," said Zach. "I'm not familiar enough with the trail to prevent us from making a wrong turn."

The wet snow changed to powder as the men rode. They were forty-five minutes into their descent when Zach said: "I can't see the way. Can you?"

"No, the snow has blanketed everything. Twilight isn't helping either. What do you think we should do?"

"Keep moving," said Zach. "We have to get lower as quickly as possible."

"I disagree," said Joe. "Let's find a sheltered spot and wait out the storm."

"I see what looks like a cave off to the left. Let's see if it'll protect us," said Zach, turning off the path.

What they found was an indentation in the hillside a miner had created looking for gold.

"This isn't perfect, but it gets us out of the wind. We can stay here till the storm passes," said Zach.

"It's going to be a long night," said Joe. "I hope the women don't panic when we don't return."

The men shielded themselves and the horses the best they could. Joe prayed with conviction.

"Why are you praying now?" asked Zach. "We have work to do."

"Prayer keeps my fear at bay," said Joe. "Have you ever built a snow cave?"

"Can't say I have," said Zach. "Time to learn. It's too bad we don't have shovels."

"I'll gather branches," said Joe. "Look, there's a light over there!"

Zach turned around. "I see it. We're not as far off the trail as I thought."

When the light drew closer, Joe called out to the riders. "Hello. Over here. We're lost."

When the riders reached them, the brothers saw it was Snowshoe and Amy.

"You did pretty well to get this far," Snowshoe said. "I've been looking for you. I thought you might need help."

"You're the answer to prayer," said Joe. "We thought we'd have to spend the night here and find our way out in the morning."

"You were wise to stop," said Snowshoe. "Just ahead, the trail becomes a switchback. If you'd kept going, you probably would've ridden off the mountain. I know the way. Get back on your horses and follow me. We'll go single file. Stay in my tracks."

The men wove their way down the mountain and safely entered Jackson.

"I suggest you stay here," Snowshoe said. "I'm going on to Hangtown."

"We'll go with you," said Zach. "I have a pregnant wife at home who's expecting me. If I don't show up, she'll be upset."

"It's not going to be easy," he said, "but we can do it."

Amy stayed in Jackson as the men pressed on. When the road widened, they rode three abreast.

"Tell me about yourself," said Zach to Snowshoe.

"I'm twenty-five. I was born in Norway and came to California to seek my fortune. I began working as a miner around Hangtown: in Coon Hollow and at Kelsey's Diggings. When I wasn't successful, I became a rancher," he said. "I now make my living in the Sacramento Valley, but I'd prefer to live in the mountains. I explore Sierra's peaks and valleys every chance I get. If I could find a way of earning a living roaming the mountains, I'd do it in a heartbeat. Unfortunately, I haven't found anyone who'll pay me to do that."

"I'm thankful you came along when you did. You saved our lives," said Joe. "How'd you find us?"

"I was coming over the top of the Kit Carson Pass when I saw your sails below me. I was surprised to see boats on the lake. I also saw the storm headed your way. Glad I could help."

* * *

When Zach opened the front door to his house, Claire and Mary ran to greet him.

"I was afraid you were caught in the blizzard," said Claire. "I had visions of you and Joe spending the night on the mountain. I didn't know if I'd ever see you again; if Cate would grow up without a father...."

"How were you able to get home?" asked Mary. "The snow is obscuring everything. How'd you stay on the trail?"

"It's quite a story, but I'm cold and wet. I'll tell you about it after I've changed," said Zach. "How 'bout a steaming cup of your special tea and something to eat when I get back?"

Mary went to the kitchen to fix the tea and food while Claire followed Zach upstairs.

"Don't toss your clothes on the floor, they're too wet to be inside. I'll put them on the porch," said Claire. "Mary can take them with her to the laundry tomorrow."

After Zach changed his clothes, he and Claire joined Mary in the dining room. While he ate, Zach told them about racing the boats, Snowshoe Thompson appearing, the trek down the mountain, and dropping off Amy in Jackson before continuing home."

"Who's Amy?" asked Claire, raising an eyebrow.

"She's the woman who operates the boathouse at Silver Lake. Joe and I had planned to stop in Jackson for dinner, but the blizzard was ferocious, and we didn't want to risk being snowed in. I knew you'd be frightened."

"Thank you for coming home. I'll be able to sleep tonight knowing you're safe. Why'd you go sailing with a blizzard coming?"

"I wanted to sail so badly I ignored the warnings. Meeting Snowshoe was an unexpected blessing. His ability to guide us down the mountain was amazing. There was something more to his rescuing us than pure luck," said Zach. "Perhaps God hasn't abandoned me after all?"

"I'm glad you're safe," said Mary. "Losing you right after Dave would have been too much to handle."

"I can't tell you how good it feels to be home with a blazing fire, a full belly, and the two of you with me. I'm a fortunate fella."

TUESDAY, OCTOBER 12, 1852

ZACH AND CLAIRE cuddled throughout the night. When Zach woke, he went to his study to read Morning Prayer. The lesson for the day was I Thessalonians 5:1-3.

> You will not be expecting us to write anything to you, brothers, about 'times and seasons', since you know very well that the Day of the Lord is going to come like a thief in the night. It is when people are saying, 'How quiet and peaceful it is' that the worst suddenly happens, as suddenly as labor pains come on a pregnant woman; and there will be no way for anybody to evade it.

Paul is talking about the second coming of Christ, which he calls 'the Day of the Lord.' This terrifying day will arrive when it's not expected and that no one can evade its tribulation and desolation. I'm in enough darkness, Lord. Is the approaching ordeal necessary?

"If there're any clothes you'd like Mary to take to the laundry beside the ones you wore to the lake, bring them to me now," shouted Claire from the bottom of the stairs. "Mary is ready to leave."

"I have a few more for her to take," answered Zach. "I'll get them."

When Zach brought Claire the clothes, she asked: "Are you free for lunch? I've something I want to discuss with you."

"Come to my office at noon," said Zach. "We'll go to Lucy's. What's on your mind?"

"I'll tell you then."

* * *

When Zach arrived at work, there was a note on his desk from Zhang.

Sang Yuen (Norman Asing) asked me to return to San Francisco. During the past year, more than twenty thousand Chinese immigrants have arrived. Their needs require his complete attention. He wants me to take over his day-to-day responsibilities.

I'm indebted to you for what you taught me about operating a newspaper. What I've learned will serve me well when I publish my own. I'm sorry I don't have time to speak with you in person. Please keep fighting for equality; many people depend on you.

I've left a detailed report about your antagonists. This information only recently came together. Good luck to you.

Zhang Wei

THOSE WHO OPPOSE YOU

1. James Gadsden

He's a prominent political force in Washington, D.C., and increasingly in California. He was born in South Carolina, where his grandfather was a Revolutionary War hero. His oldest brother was the Episcopal Bishop of South Carolina. He died recently. Both James' grandfather and his brother are buried on the grounds of Saint Philips Church in Charleston. His brother lies under the altar.

Gadsden served General Andrew Jackson as a lieutenant of engineers. His assignment was to build forts. When the Senate refused to certify Gadsden's promotion to Adjutant General, he left military service and moved to Florida. There, Gadsden was a leader of the effort to relocate the Seminole people to Oklahoma.

When California was admitted to the Union as a free state, Gadsden urged South Carolina to secede. He said slavery is a 'social blessing,' and abolitionists are 'the country's greatest curse.'

When Gadsden's efforts to have South Carolina secede failed, he shifted his attention to California. He enlisted Thomas Jefferson Green to introduce legislation to divide the state in two, with the southern portion allowing slavery. Gadsden envisioned a colony of southern farmers growing rice, cotton, and sugar, using two thousand African domestics to do the work. Gadsden also planned to use slave labor to build a railroad between San Antonio and California's goldfields.

Another bill Green introduced would provide Gadsden with a land grant for his colony. It'd be between the thirty-fourth and thirty-sixth parallels. Green's proposals generated considerable debate in the state legislature, but a vote was never taken on either of the bills.

Gadsden regards as abhorrent your efforts to bring equality to all people in California. He contributes generously to Hangtown's OSSB.

2. Senator William McKendree Gwin

Senator Gwin is known as a supporter of southern causes. Gwin was born in a small community outside Nashville, Tennessee. His father, a prominent Methodist minister, named William after his mentor, William McKendree, the first native-born Methodist bishop. Senator Gwin likes to tell people he comes from the first families of the South.

Gwin became a medical doctor in Mississippi until the allure of politics seduced him. His father secured

Gwin the position of personal secretary to President Andrew Jackson. Jackson introduced Gwin to Mississippi politics and taught Gwin how to use political patronage to achieve his objectives. Gwin was elected to the House of Representatives for one term. He refused to run again because he was embarrassed by the small amount of money he possessed.

In 1849, at the urging of his Democratic colleagues, including Gadsden, Gwin moved to California to guide the state's constitutional convention to statehood. As the only experienced politician among the delegates, Gwin's influence was significant. However, local leaders rejected his efforts to become the convention's President. Gwin's arrogance appears to have worked against him. Over Gwin's objections, Mariano Vallejo persuaded the pro-Mexican delegates to vote with their white allies to add a clause to the state constitution prohibiting California from becoming a slave state.

Gwin is recognized as the leader of the pro-slavery wing of the California Democratic Party. He'll say whatever advances his interests, whether it's true or not. Gwin's dishonesty was on full display during his recent tour of the state. He made up stories about Negro revolts, Catholic involvement in politics, and foreigners scheming against native-born concerns. He repeatedly spoke about how Negroes, Indians, and Mexicans are biologically and socially inferior to whites. He continues to tell anyone who'll listen that immigration and assimilation threaten the state's social balance. Even though Gwin doesn't have evidence to support his claims, many people believe him.

Gwin became a millionaire when he purchased a gold mine in Paloma. He used his new financial resources to get elected as California's first senator.

Like Gadsden, Senator Gwin sees you as an obstacle to instituting southern values in California. He, too, gives generously to Hangtown's OSSB.

3. Thomas Jefferson Green

Green was born in North Carolina. His parents were outspoken defenders of slavery. Green, a West Point graduate, brought his family's convictions to Sacramento. He was elected to the California Senate in 1849.

In 1850, Green became a Major General and was placed in charge of the First Division of the California militia. He uses the position to suppress Indian uprisings. Like Gadsden and Gwin, Green wants southern values to prevail in California and opposes everything you strive to achieve.

4. Jim Edwards

Edwards is the leader of Hangtown's OSSB. He struggles financially with his hardware store, which rumor has it he may be forced to sell. Edwards needs the money the OSSB provides him to keep the store running.

Edwards doesn't like any minority group, but he has a particular animus against the Chinese, whom he believes must be kept out of California's mines. Edwards claims Chinese fishermen take money that would otherwise go to whites. He doesn't like Chinese farmers either. He complains they plow land that would be more productive in the hands of Italian immigrants.

Edwards uses the OSSB to promote his belief in the superiority of the native-born. He doesn't like Miss Claire's independence, your editorials, or that you hired Elsu and me. One of Edward's priorities is to silence both Miss Claire and you.

5. Robert Jenner

Robert Jenner is the OSSB's second in command. He came to Hangtown to get rich and to establish a Cornish community in California. Jenner conducted religious services for miners before your brother arrived. He resents that Joe does that now.

Jenner believes only white Protestants should hold positions of authority. He shudders when you insist Catholics, Negroes, Chinese, Mexicans, and Indians should have the same rights that white Protestants have.

That's what I've uncovered. I hope this helps.

All the best,
Zhang

Zach was putting down the report when Joe pushed open the door.

"Morning, Joe," said Zach. "What brings you?"

"I want to talk to you about the conversation I had with Bob Jenner this morning."

"What happened?" asked Zach, motioning to his brother to sit down.

"Bob met me for breakfast and told me I'm not doing a good enough job," said Joe.

"How are you falling short?" asked Zach, scratching his head.

"Bob believes I don't spend enough time recruiting new members. He's upset I took time to go sailing with you and said I shouldn't rest until Saint Mary's has an ample supply of money. He attributes our low attendance to me not associating with the right people. Bob was harsh and indicated a new priest would be recruited if I don't improve my performance. I have no idea where he's going to find a replacement; priests don't want to come to California."

"I just learned Jenner knows James Gadsden, who has ties with the clergy in South Carolina," said Zach. "He'd probably use Gadsden's connections to replace you."

"Do you think Bob is correct that I'm not doing a good job?" asked Joe, pouring himself a cup of coffee.

"I didn't say that," said Zach. "I merely pointed out he has a way of finding a replacement. Besides, I'm told he wants to resume leading worship like he did before you came."

"I'd forgotten he conducted services," said Joe, his face tightening. "Do you think that's what this is all about? He wants to take over?"

"That, and he doesn't like that you're related to me," said Zach, chuckling. "Zhang told me Jenner is second in command of Hangtown's OSSB. He wants to bring an end to my crusade for equality. Getting rid of both of us would ensure there's no one in Hangtown opposing his will."

"What do you think I should do?" asked Joe.

"I know it's early," said Zach, "but can you replace Jenner with Al Bee? That'd end the threat. It's too bad there isn't a bishop you can consult and from whom you can draw support. I'm afraid you're on your own."

"I wish dad or grandpa were alive," said Joe. "They'd help me through this."

"Why don't you write Bishop Kemper? He knows you and may have a recommendation."

"That's a splendid idea!" said Joe. "I'll do it this afternoon."

"I have to pick up the mail," said Zach standing. "If you're going in that direction, why don't you walk with me?"

* * *

When Zach returned from the post office, he said to Elsu, "Save space for two new notices and a quarter-page ad."

"What are they about?" asked Elsu.

"Business activity in Hangtown. The first notice pertains to the Michigan Tavern: it's reducing its prices to call attention to its opening. The second notice is about John Fountain and Ben Tallman. They discovered a freshwater spring in the hillside behind their building. They're adding carbon dioxide to the water and selling it as soda. They want folks to give it a try."

"I'm not interested in the Michigan Tavern," said Elsu, "but I'll visit the soda works."

"Let me know what you think," said Zach, turning to the paid advertisement. "It's from the cartographer George Baker. He wants our readers to know his maps are different because he includes two tables. The first tells the distances between all of California's major towns and Sacramento. The second gives the population of the largest communities in the state. Baker estimates three hundred thousand people live California, with fifty thousand of them calling San Francisco home."

"I don't need a map," said Elsu. "I can find my way without one."

"I can't," said Zach, smiling. "I'll buy one of his."

* * *

Shortly after noon, Zach and Claire entered Lucy's.

"Mary and I talked this morning while you were reading Morning Prayer," said Claire. "I didn't say anything to you about it at breakfast, but I want to now."

"I've wondered all morning what was on your mind," said Zach. "What's going on?"

"I'll tell you when we're seated," said Claire. "Let's find a quiet spot. I don't want folks listening."

Once they ordered, Claire continued.

"Mary is looking for an indication that David is present and that he still loves her."

"I didn't know the Chinese believe in ghosts," said Zach, with a sly grin.

"Let me tell you what happened," said Claire, slapping Zach's hand. "Yesterday, Mary went back to the hotel to pay the rent and to pick up fresh clothes. When she walked into their suite, she sensed a presence in the doorway to their bedroom. Mary looked closely but didn't see anyone. Nothing had been touched, yet despite what her eyes reported, she could feel a presence in the room. She's convinced it was Dave."

"Did she ask the manager to check the room to be sure no one was hiding in it?"

"She wasn't afraid. On the contrary, she was thrilled. Part of her knew there was no one in the room and hadn't been. 'Dave still cares about me,' she exclaimed. 'He's still here!' I haven't seen Mary's spirits so high since Dave died."

"I think Mary's mind is playing tricks on her," said Zach. "I hope this doesn't delay her recovery. I guess there are worse things than imagining Dave was in the room."

"There's more. Mary woke this morning from a dream that had Dave in it. They are holding hands as they walked down Main Street. Dave had all of his fingers, which delighted her. What woke Mary was the last thing Dave said to her."

"What was that?" asked Zach, picking up his sandwich.

"Dave said, 'You're going to be a wonderful mother.' Now, how did Dave know Mary is pregnant?"

"Incredible!" said Zach, putting his sandwich down and leaning back in his chair. "That's quite a dream."

"What do you make of Mary's experiences?" asked Claire, looking into Zach's eyes.

"If you and I hadn't had the dreams we've had, I'd dismiss Mary's dream as nonsense," said Zach. "The realness of Dave's presence gives me chills. I don't know what to say, but something is going on. What are your thoughts?"

"I'm mystified by it," said Claire. "Mary's changed. She told me she intends to move back to the hotel this weekend. She wants to be close to Dave's things since they no longer remind her of his being gone."

* * *

After lunch, Zach returned to the newspaper office. Charley Boles was there.

"How are you?" asked Charley. "I've some news and books for you."

"Charley, it's good to see you," said Zach. "I'm well. How've you been?"

"I'm just back from San Francisco. It wasn't good there. People are dying right and left from cholera. I had to leave before I caught it."

"Cholera is bad in San Francisco? I knew it was in Panama," said Zach, "but I hadn't heard about it being a problem in San Francisco."

"The doctor who advised me to leave said one person out of twenty is dying. Right now, the city is full of misery."

"Claire and her brother were just there," said Zach. "Thank God they missed the outbreak."

"Before I left," said Charley, "I bought Claire a subscription to that British woman's magazine she expressed an interest in."

"How much I owe you?"

"The subscription cost fifty cents," said Charley. "Don't worry about repaying me. It's my gift to your beautiful wife."

"I'm sure she'll appreciate your generosity," said Zach. "What else brings you?"

"My favorite bookstore for American and foreign newspapers, Cooke & Lecount, showed me a new publication, the *New York Daily Times*. I read an issue and thought of you. Here it is," said Charley, handing it to Zach.

"Thank you. I'm always looking for newspapers to emulate," said Zach. "Tell me about the books you have."

"The first is a novel by Victor Hugo, *The Hunchback of Notre-Dame*. It's a love story, which I think Claire will enjoy. Since I prefer poetry to novels, I bought his most famous collection of poems, *Les Rayons et Les Ombres*."

"I don't speak French," said Zach. "What does that mean?"

"Beams and Shadows," said Charley. "It's a collection of forty-four poems. Because of their brilliance, Hugo was elected to the prestigious French *Academy*."

"With the acclaim Hugo has achieved," said Zach, "it's obvious the Muses have been good to him."

"Not entirely. Tragedy stalks the poor man. His first-born and favorite daughter died in a boating accident on the Seine when she was nineteen.

The boat in which she was riding overturned, and the number of skirts she was wearing pulled her down. Her husband tried to save her, but he drowned too. What makes the story especially upsetting is Hugo learned of her death while eating breakfast with his mistress. They were in a café when Hugo read about the accident in a newspaper. Can you imagine learning about your daughter's death from a newspaper article? Her loss torments him. He consoles himself by writing poems. Some of the poems were put into a collection called *À Villequier*, which means, *At Villequier*. That's where his daughter died. One of the poems, *Demain, dès L'aube*, describes a time he visited her grave. People say that poem is his best. I can't wait to read it."

"What does the poem's title mean?" asked Zach.

"*Tomorrow, At Dawn*. Gripping, isn't it? I also have a book for you. It's a story by an Englishman, Wilkie Collins, called *Basil*. It's a man's psychological adventure."

"That's intriguing," said Zach, taking it from Charley. "Tell me something about it."

"The hero, Basil, is enchanted by the beauty of women, as many of us are. Basil's exploits take place in the heart of England's corrupt society," said Charley. "The salesman at the bookstore said *Basil's* readers like the story so much they don't put it down until they finish it. I hope you find it that entertaining."

"You've aroused my interest," said Zach. "What's that other book you have?"

"It's on a subject of interest to me," said Charley, "civil disobedience. It's a commentary on American social issues. It was written by Henry David Thoreau to explain why he refused to pay the government's poll tax."

"Why didn't he?" asked Zach.

"It's Thoreau's way of protesting slavery and our country's imperialism."

"Imperialism?"

"That's how Thoreau describes the war with Mexico," said Charley.

"I like Thoreau already," said Zach, slapping his desk.

"I thought you would," said Charley. "Thoreau grew up twenty miles west of Boston, went to Harvard, and then worked for his father in the family pencil factory. When the opportunity presented itself, Thoreau worked as a handyman for his mentor, Ralph Waldo Emerson. It was Emerson's influence that motivated Thoreau to become a writer."

"I can understand Thoreau's attraction to Emerson," said Zach. "When I was a boy, I admired Emerson too."

"Thoreau is an outspoken abolitionist and a local leader of the Underground Railroad. Among his writings is an attack on the Fugitive Slave Act."

"We have a lot in common," said Zach. "I'd like to meet him someday."

Just then Kay pushed open the office door.

"How dare you act so irresponsibly," she screamed. "You went sailing with a blizzard coming? I should've known you lacked common sense when you refused to marry me. Who's going to support little Zach and me if you die? Your thoughtlessness could've left us destitute. Don't you ever think about anyone besides yourself?"

"This shows why you need to find another source of income," said Zach. "Find a rich miner while you're still attractive. Marry him, and you'll be set for life."

"You want me to marry a rich miner?" asked Kay, placing her hands on her hips. "You don't care who raises your child?"

"You won't let me anywhere near him," said Zach. "How can I be a good father when you keep my son away from me?"

"If you want access to little Zach, dump Claire, and marry me."

"How many times do I have to tell you?" bellowed Zach. "That's not going to happen!"

"Then, we have nothing to talk about," said Kay, turning and rushing out the door.

"I see why you chose Claire," said Charley, shuddering. "I would've too."

TUESDAY, OCTOBER 26, 1852

ZACH BEGAN HIS day reading Morning Prayer. The lesson assigned was Psalm 88:14-15.

> As for me, I cry out to You, O Lord;
> each morning my prayer greets You.
> Why, O Lord, do You reject me,
> do You hide Your face from me?

Lord, what do you want from me? I'm striving to be your faithful servant, but you've turned your back on me. Why are you punishing me? What have I done? I pray you'll become alive in every fiber of my being. Please restore your light to my life and guide me in your ways.

When Zach finished his prayers, he discovered Claire waiting for him in the doorway.

"I had another dream," she said. "It woke me up."

"Tell me the dream," said Zach, returning to his chair.

"I'm in the woods outside of town," said Claire. "It's winter. There's a huge fire. Everything is burning. I'm upset the fire is so destructive. After the flames pass, I find a rock among the ashes, which the fire didn't touch. Next to the rock is a dead blackbird. It's such a beautiful creature; I wonder why it had to die? As I look closely, I see the bird's eye is a diamond. It's shining even in the waning light. I awaken."

"The dead bird nauseates me," said Zach. "What a disturbing image. I don't like it."

"It's unsettling, isn't it?" said Claire.

"I don't know what the dream means," said Zach. "It gives me the feeling something ominous is about to happen. What do you think?"

"My first response was like yours, to focus on the fire's destruction and the dead bird. However, when I told you the dream, my attention went to the bird's eye. It's a diamond, glowing in the fading light. That's a beautiful image. Something extraordinary survived the fire," said Claire.

"The rock survived too," said Zach. "My first thoughts about the dream were too negative. This morning's biblical lesson must've tainted my perspective."

"Oh?" responded Claire, resting her arms on her belly. "How'd it do that?"

"The author of the Psalm I read felt the same way I do. He lamented, 'God, why do you hide your face from me?' At least I'm not the only one who's ever felt this way."

"I imagine not," said Claire. "I'm ready for you to stop your bellyaching. There are important things on the horizon, like the birth of our child. All I hear from you is 'woe is me.'"

"To be honest, I can hardly wait for Cate to be born," said Zach. "She'll be a wonderful addition to our family."

"If you feel that way," said Claire, "act like it. While I'm in labor, it'll help me to know you're excited about Cate's coming. Show some enthusiasm."

Claire started to leave when she suddenly stopped.

"Alice and Betty are bringing my dressmaking tools to the house," she said. "I don't want you to be surprised when you find them here. They think Cate's birth is too close for me to be walking back and forth to the boarding house. They'll work here until a week or so after Cate arrives."

"That's thoughtful of them," said Zach. "I have a question for you: what are your thoughts about using anesthesia?"

"I prefer not to be numbed," said Claire, looking Zach in the eye.

"I hate to see you go through unnecessary pain," said Zach. "I hope you'll use it if Rose says it's okay."

"Women have delivered babies for thousands of years without numbing themselves. If they didn't need anesthesia, I won't either. Let's have breakfast."

As they walked to the kitchen, Claire said, "Do you realize it's been a while since OSSB attacked you or the paper? I wonder why?"

"They're focused on the Presidential election. Jim Edwards paid for a series of ads encouraging people to vote for Daniel Webster, the Nativist Party candidate. It must peeve him to give me money, but he needs the paper to spread his anti-immigration message," said Zach. "I suspect when the election is over, the OSSB will resume its efforts to silence me."

"I'm enjoying the break," said Claire. "I hope it lasts."

* * *

As Zach walked to work, he noticed dark clouds building over Hangtown. A cold wind blew, chilling everything.

"Morning, Elsu," said Zach, entering the newspaper office and standing next to the fire. "What's on tap for today?"

"You asked me to remind you that this week's paper is to have your recommendation for President."

"Put a banner on the front page announcing the paper endorses Senator John Hale," said Zach. "My editorial will explain why."

A little before noon, Zach handed Elsu his editorial.

"I'm going to meet my brother for lunch at the Michigan Tavern. I want to see what kind of place it is."

"Be careful," said Elsu, with a smile. "A storm is coming."

"Very funny," said Zach, grinning. "No snow this afternoon. Maybe a little rain, but I won't need Snowshoe to lead me home."

* * *

Joe greeted Zach when he arrived at the tavern.

"Hi!" he said. "I have a table for us over here. Look at the elk, deer, and bear heads on the walls. Someone's quite the hunter."

"I'm sorry I kept you waiting," said Zach. "I didn't realize the Tavern was so far out of town, and it's starting to rain."

"The tavern's location may explain why there're so few people here," said Joe. "We're the only ones having lunch; everyone else is at the bar. I hope that doesn't mean the food is bad."

"We're about to find out," said Zach, taking his seat.

Joe told Zach Bob Jenner was giving him time to increase Saint Mary's attendance.

"I'm making progress," he said. "A couple of families indicated they'd give Saint Mary's a try. I couldn't tell if they were sincere or just said that so I'd go away? I hope they join us."

"That's good news," said Zach. "Has your relationship with Bob improved?"

"No, it's still icy," groused Joe, looking down.

After ordering, Zach said, "I was thinking about Pete last night. It's amazing how much has happened since he died. Claire and I weren't even involved, now she's having my baby. You hadn't visited yet, now you're a priest with your own church. Mr. Goldman was still alive, and I was a cub reporter. Now I own and publish the paper."

"A lot has happened," said Joe. "God has been gracious to you."

"I don't think so," said Zach. "God abandoned me. I feel alone in a deep, dark valley. There's emptiness all around me."

"I'm sorry you're in such a hard place, but people who say they want to develop their spiritual lives at some time have to go through dark periods like you are," said Joe. "God is trying to show you something that you haven't grasped yet."

"What might that be?" asked Zach, crossing his arms.

"You have to surrender your old way of thinking about God if you want to receive a new, fuller vision of whom God is. This includes letting go of your expectations of how He acts. When we became adults, we had to jettison our childhood understanding of God to make room for a more mature faith. Well, the growth process doesn't stop. Our awareness of God has to continue to evolve. When it doesn't, our beliefs solidify, making it difficult for the Holy Spirit to quicken our souls. That's what's you're experiencing now. Your thinking about God apparently has become too narrow, rigid, and predictable. You need fresh eyes with which to behold the Mystery. What you're going through reminds me of Dad's favorite saying from Aeschylus. Do you remember it? 'He who learns must suffer. And even in our sleep pain that cannot forget falls drop by drop upon the heart, and in our own despair, against our will, comes wisdom to us by the awful grace of God.' Does that sound familiar?"

"It does," said Zach, looking over Joe's shoulder at wet miners coming inside for cover and warmth. "I wonder what happened to dad that drew him to this saying? I don't think of him struggling with doubt."

"That's a good question," said Joe. "I don't either. Maybe he'd already passed through the darkness by the time we were born."

"You might be right," said Zach, finishing his lunch.

"I have an idea for dealing with your despair," said Joe. "On our way back to town, let's stop at Seligman's. Abe and Rudolph have the finest men's store on this side of San Francisco. Buy yourself a new set of clothes to represent the renewed perspective that's coming your way."

"I like that," said Zach. "Claire is constantly urging me to buy clothes. It'll please her if it does nothing else."

"I'll go with you," said Joe. "I want to be sure you buy the right things. When it comes to clothes, your taste is terrible."

* * *

Abe Seligman greeted the brothers as they entered his shop.

"Welcome, gentlemen. If you don't mind, remove your muddy boots and leave them by the door. One of my boys will clean them while you're here. Hang your hats and coats by the fire. How might I help you?"

"We're here to buy my brother a new set of clothes," said Joe. "Suit, shirt, tie, hat, socks, and shoes. Everything," said Joe.

"You've come to the right place," responded Abe, helping Zach take off his dripping coat. "I see by the way you're dressed that you're ready for an upgrade in your attire."

"What do you recommend?" asked Zach.

Abe explained the difference between the standard frock jacket that most merchants wear and the new sack coat, which is the choice of fashion-conscious men.

"Whichever style you prefer, I'll help you to look well-dressed," said Abe.

Next, Abe pointed out that men of conservative taste want trousers that match the frock coat's somber hue, but men who are more daring select striped or checked trousers, often in bright colors, to go with their sack coats. After looking at various combinations, Joe asked about waistcoats.

"The vest of choice is double-breasted and checked," said Abe. It's worn with both outfits; however, if you wear it with a sack coat and slacks, the waistcoat's pattern is different from the trousers because it's boring to have your vest and pants match."

"Zach will need your help determining which vests and trousers look good together," said Joe, snickering. "He has no eye for these things."

"That's why I'm here. I won't let your brother leave until he looks sharp."

Next, Abe turned his attention to shirts and ties.

"Shirts come in linen or cotton. They have high upstanding collars and go well with all my coats and trousers," said Abe. "The silk four-in-hand necktie, either square or rectangular, is what is worn by men of substance."

"What do you recommend for headwear?" asked Zach.

"Tall top hats are reserved for formal occasions," said Abe. "With the outfits we're discussing, a soft-crowned hat with a wide brim would look smart."

"I've heard men talking about bowler hats. What are they?" asked Zach.

"Bowler hats have been around for a couple of years. It's a working-class accessory. I don't recommend it for men of your station."

At the urging of Joe, Zach chose striped trousers with a sack coat, a checked waistcoat, and a soft-crowned hat.

"I have a final recommendation," said Abe. "I hope you won't be offended, but to complete your modern look, consider making your facial hair into large mutton-chops. You can keep the mustache. You'll look as refined as Prince Albert, the man who made the mutton-chop popular. You'll be impeccable."

"I'll have to think about that," said Zach, rubbing his chin. "I like my beard as it is."

"You have the broad face that can wear the mutton-chop with distinction," replied Abe. "I hope you do."

* * *

The clothes Zach ordered lifted his spirits. He was feeling like a new man when he returned to work.

"I had lunch with Joe at the Michigan Tavern. It's a long way to go for an ordinary meal. Then I went to Seligman's and bought new clothes. I like what I bought. I'm going to surprise Claire when I wear the outfit to Cate's baptism. As you can see, I didn't beat the rain," said Zach, hanging his dripping coat next to the fire. "It poured all the way back. The mud is getting deeper by the minute."

"I hope it lets up by quitting time," said Elsu. "I've been wondering, did you ever read that book about civil disobedience? I'm interested in what the author had to say."

"I did. Thoreau believes the government does more harm than good, and that the judgment of an individual's conscience is equal to the decisions made by groups."

"He doesn't believe in democracy?" asked Elsu.

"Apparently not," said Zach. "Thoreau said a law never made a man just, but a person's conscience has. Thoreau thinks laws contribute to injustice just as often as they establish what's right."

"I agree with that!" said Elsu, nodding his head.

"Thoreau maintains each man must do what he thinks is right, regardless of what the law requires. Consequently, Thoreau stopped paying his taxes when he discovered the money was being used to pay for a war he didn't believe in. His civil disobedience was justified, he argued, because the war violated the precepts of his conscience."

"Do you agree with him?" asked Elsu, leaning over the press.

"I like the high value he places on individual conscience. However, I disagree with his assertion that an individual's conscience is equal to the laws created by a majority of people," said Zach. "There are bad laws, as you know. But society would be chaos if every man did only what he wanted. We have a responsibility to our fellow man that's equal to the responsibility we have to our conscience. Living in a community has its obligations that can't be neglected just because we don't like them."

"I have no respect for white men's laws," said Elsu. "I have to live by them, but I don't have to like them. My people believe decisions that govern the tribe are rooted in the community's life, not the individual. Tolerating a member's dissent would destroy the trust we have in our decision-making Councils and divide our community. Thoreau's civil disobedience has no place among my people."

WEDNESDAY, NOVEMBER 3, 1852

ZACH HAD A hard time sleeping. Claire was in obvious discomfort, and her restlessness repeatedly woke him. He finally got up and went to the study to read Morning Prayer. The lesson assigned for the day was Mark 14:32-36.

> They came to a small estate called Gethsemane, and Jesus said to his disciples, 'Stay here while I pray.' He took with him Peter, James, and John, and Jesus became horror-stricken and desperately distressed.
>
> 'My heart is nearly breaking,' he told them. 'Stay here and keep watch for me.'
>
> Going on a little further, he flung himself on the ground, praying that, if it were possible, he might not have to face the ordeal.
>
> 'Dear Father,' he said, 'all things are possible to you. Please— let me not have to drink this cup! Yet it is not what I want but what you want.'

Zach finished his prayers and joined Claire for breakfast.

"Today's lesson shows me how different from Jesus I am," he said.

"What are you talking about?" asked Claire. "No one ever mistook you for Jesus."

Zach read the passage to Claire and said, "The early church undoubtedly concocted the story. The text tells us Jesus was alone; there was no one present to record what he did or prayed, yet Mark tells the story as if someone was there."

"That's strange," said Claire. "Why did Mark do that?

"My guess is Mark's portrayal of Jesus' internal struggles is intended to demonstrate Jesus felt the same things you and I do," said Zach. "Faced with approaching death, Mark depicts Jesus full of tension. Mark has Jesus fling himself onto the ground and pray: 'Let me not have to drink this cup!' Mark is accentuating how much Jesus didn't want to die. Who can blame him for that? I had the same reaction as I prepared to duel Slick Sam. I didn't want to die either."

"I'm confused," said Claire. "I thought you said you weren't like Jesus, but you just told me how you are?"

"That's Mark's point: Jesus had a human side that everyone can relate to," said Zach. "Yet, despite Jesus' desire to avoid the ordeal awaiting him, Jesus overcame his fears by accepting God's will. 'Not what I want but what you want,' he said. That's how we're different. Jesus surrendered his will to do God's. I can't do that."

"I find Jesus' submission inspiring and beautiful," said Claire. "Why can't you do that?"

"I don't trust God enough to relinquish my will," said Zach. "My will is all I have, and I'm clinging to it."

"You are a troubled soul," said Claire, with a deep sigh. "It bothers me to see you this way. I hope you find relief soon."

Zach was having a second cup of coffee when Alice and Betty arrived.

"Morning, Miss Claire," said Alice. "How are you feeling this morning?"

"The birth can't be far off," she said. "Look how big I am. Cate might get stuck inside me."

"You'll be fine," said Betty. "Babies have a way of making themselves small enough to squeeze out the birth canal. I bet your mother was feeling the same way, especially with her first child. Everything will be okay."

"Cate can't come too soon," said Claire, shifting her position. "I'm ready to see my toes again."

"Miss Rose came in the shop the other day," said Alice. "She's ready for a new uniform. We kept the old pattern. Should I buy material and get started?"

"Buy the material. Rose is coming by in a few hours to examine me. I'll ask her if she wants any changes. Check with me before you start cutting."

"I'll leave you woman to your work," said Zach. "It's time I attend to mine."

Zach leaned over Claire's chair, gave her a kiss, and said, "Maybe today will be the day. I hope so."

* * *

When Zach entered the office, he noticed Elsu crying.

"What's wrong?" asked Zach.

"Ben Wright is at it again. After he massacred the Modocs I told you about, a few of the survivors never got over it. Last month a small band of angry braves attacked and killed ten miners outside the town of Amador. Ben Wright went looking for them. What he found was a peaceful Miwok Rancheria on the Cosumnes River. Wright's gang attacked while the Miwoks ate breakfast. Wright killed at least twenty of them. The exact number isn't known since many bodies floated downstream before they could be counted. During the siege, Wright's men set fire to the Miwok homes, and threw everything they could find into the flames."

"How many survived?" asked Zach, sitting down.

"One member of the tribe, Taipa, was bathing upstream when the attack began. She dressed and returned to the Rancheria, where she saw her baby taken from the arms of her dead grandmother and thrown into the fire. The child was still alive. She fled and found her way to Tonya's camp, where she told them what happened. Taipa believes she's the only survivor."

"That's horrible," said Zach. "The image of a mother seeing her baby tossed into the fire will stay with me forever. If something like that happened to my child, I'd go crazy."

"Taipa is being comforted by the women of Tonya's tribe. She lost everyone she loved: her parents, husband, and child. White men are the savages, not my people. I'm so furious I'm having trouble controlling myself. If it weren't for you, I'd return to my father's home on Holy Mountain."

"Why don't you go?" asked Zach.

"Because I made a commitment to you. White men may not keep their pledges, but Modocs do."

"I'm glad you're staying," said Zach. "I need you."

"Work keeps my mind off Wright's butchery," said Elsu. "When I'm alone, I create ways in my head about how I'd like to torture Wright. In each version, I prolong the pain so I can watch him writhe."

"I'll write an account about the incident," said Zach, "and we'll put it on the front page of the paper. That'll turn people against him."

"I doubt it," said Elsu. "It'll just add to Wright's fame and encourage others to imitate him. I'd prefer you not to print the article."

Just then, Alice dashed into the office.

"Miss Claire's water broke," said Alice breathlessly. "I'm looking for Miss Rose. Pastor White told me she's at Huntington's looking for a raincoat. I wanted to tell you before going there. There's no need to hurry home. This will take a while."

"Thanks for letting me know," said Zach. "Keep me informed."

"Will do," shouted Alice, hurrying out the door.

"Congratulations," said Elsu. "I'm happy for you."

"Thank you," said Zach. "I'm too excited to work. I'm off to the barbershop; I want to surprise Claire by getting a haircut and mutton chops. I'll be back in an hour."

When Zach arrived at Jay's, Roberto was in the barber chair.

"Morning, gentlemen. Roberto, I didn't expect to see you here. I have wonderful news. I'm going to be a father today: Claire is in labor."

"Congratulations," responded Roberto and Jay together.

"Your nights of restful sleep are about to vanish," said Jay, changing scissors. The tradeoff is worth it. I remember when my first child was born. I went to Red's and bought drinks for everyone."

"It's going to be a long day," said Zach, waiting his turn in one of the chairs that lined the wall.

"A long day of waiting for you," said Roberto, "but an arduous one for Claire. This is one of those occasions when it's good to be a man. Going through childbirth isn't fun."

"You're right," said Zach, with a sly grin. "Giving birth isn't something I ever want to do. I prefer making the babies...."

"I'm just back from San Francisco," said Roberto. "I don't know if you've heard, but Daniel Webster died a little over a week before the election. The Nativists gambled on him and lost. Everyone who voted for Webster wasted their vote."

"I don't feel bad for the Nativists," said Zach. "The fewer votes they got, the better. Do you know what happens in a situation like this?"

"The party leaders quickly replaced Webster with Jacob Broom. In some states, Webster appeared on the ballot. In other states, it was Broom. If the rest of the country voted like California did, it was a disaster for the Nativists."

"That's wonderful. Do you know how California voted for President?" asked Zach.

"The early results give the Democrat, Franklin Pierce, a decisive lead. It's too early to know the election results elsewhere."

"Did Senator Hale come in second?" asked Zach.

"Winfield Scott, the Whig candidate, came in second," said Roberto. "Pierce and Scott got almost all of California's votes. Senator Hale received only a handful. I guess your endorsement didn't persuade many people. The Democrats, Latham and McDougall, are going to Washington to represent California in the House of Representatives."

"That's too bad," said Zach. "Perhaps the national vote will turn out differently."

"I hope not," said Jay. I voted for Pierce."

"Why did you do that?" asked Zach.

"Because Pierce is for limiting the government's control of our lives."

"The Democrat's idea of limited government means states will continue doing what they want, and that nothing will be done to abolish slavery. Until decisive action is taken nationally to outlaw slavery, there'll be more division and conflict to endure."

"I don't think so," said Jay. "Pierce supports the Compromise of 1850 and the Fugitive Slave Act. He'll unite the country."

"I hope you're right, but I doubt it," said Zach, watching Roberto step out of the chair and Jay brush away the hair that accumulated on it.

"How would you like me to cut your hair?" asked Jay as Zach took his turn in the barber chair.

"Just a trim," said Zach. "However, I want you to transform my beard into mutton chops. Can you do that?"

"Of course I can," said Jay. "When did you become fashion conscious?"

"Abe Seligman suggested I wear mutton chops," said Zach. "I'm going to give them a try and surprise Claire with a new look."

"I'm glad I'm here to see this," said Roberto, smiling. "With your new look, I'm not sure I'd recognize you if I passed you on the street. I'd be asking, 'who is that distinguished-looking gentleman? Does anyone know what happened to Zach? I haven't seen him for days.'"

"The first time I look in the mirror, I probably won't recognize myself either," said Zach, chuckling.

As the men spoke, Zach saw Alice and Rose walk past the barbershop. He jumped out of the barber chair and ran outside.

"Hold up," he yelled.

The women stopped and walked to where Zach stood with a sheet tied around his neck.

"Get back inside," said Rose. "You shouldn't be out in this weather without a coat."

"I want to know your thoughts about Claire using anesthesia," said Zach, as they entered the barbershop.

"I don't have strong feelings either way," said Rose. "I'll do what Claire wants."

"I'd like you to encourage her to use something," said Zach. "I hate to think of her in pain when she doesn't need to be."

"Claire's recovery will be quicker without anesthesia."

"I'll trust your judgment," said Zach, returning to the barber's chair, "but there must be something you can do to reduce her discomfort?"

"We'll do everything we can," said Rose. "I'll keep you informed. This isn't a good time to talk; I need to examine Claire."

"Tell her I'm thinking of her and that I love her," Zach shouted after them.

"Will do," came the muffled reply.

"What took you to San Francisco?" Zach asked Roberto.

"My gambling palace is doing well, but the town leaders want me to shut it down."

"Why?" asked Jay, sharpening his shaving blade.

"The influx of women to Hangtown is changing attitudes about gambling. Wives don't want their husbands losing the family's money," said Roberto. "The women complain to anyone who'll listen."

"Damn women!" grumbled Jay. "They ruin a man's fun every chance they get. I'll never understand why men allow women to do that?"

"Why is your place closing?" asked Zach. "I suppose you want a refund on your ad?"

"No refund is needed," said Roberto. "I can stay open until January, but since my gambling palace was one of the more recent to open, I've been tabbed to be one of the first to close. Older gambling places are pleased because I've taken so many of their customers. I could fight the pressure, but I've made enough money. I don't need more."

"What are you going to do?" asked Zach.

"I'll take down the tent and put up a building that's several stories high," replied Roberto. "I'll rent space to merchants and to people who want an office. I went to San Francisco to see what's been done there."

"Did you find anything you want to replicate?" asked Zach.

"I like the appearance and functionality of brick," said Roberto.

"Won't that be expensive?" asked Jay.

"It will, but it's worth the extra cost to survive a fire. Besides, I can afford it," said Roberto. "I found several buildings in San Francisco that I like. I drew plans and will start construction after the rainy season ends, probably in April."

"Any other news from down there that we should know?" asked Jay.

"Two things. First, the cholera epidemic is still a concern. I cut my visit short to minimize my exposure. And second, ships arriving from Central America brought news that Guatemala invaded Honduras."

"Why they'd do that?" asked Jay.

"I don't know, but armies fighting is never good," said Roberto. "Too many people die. I don't care if Guatemala wins. The cost isn't going to be worth whatever is gained."

"How's your health?" asked Jay. "You aren't going to give me cholera, are you?"

"No, I'm feeling fine," replied Roberto. "I stayed away from large crowds. You're safe."

Jay worked primarily on Zach's face and neck. When he finished, he asked, "How do you like your new look? Not many fellas in Hangtown are wearing mutton chops."

Looking into a mirror, Zach said, "The haircut is perfect, but the mutton chops are going to take some getting used to. They'll go well with my new outfit, but I'm not sure how I feel about them for an everyday look."

"Abe was correct," said Jay. "Mutton chops make you look distinguished."

"I agree," said Roberto, grinning. "I like the look on you. You should keep them. Give Claire my regards and congratulations again on becoming a father. You'll be a good one. It's time for me to get back to work. Good chatting with both of you. Bye."

Zach paid Jay and returned to his office.

Elsu gasped when Zach entered.

"With those mutton chops, I'll call you Mister Johnson from now on," he said. "Zach is too familiar for a man of your eminence."

"Knock it off," said Zach, sheepishly. "I'm the same guy who left. I don't look that different."

"Oh, yes, you do, Mister Johnson. Do you intend to run for office?"

"Okay, that's enough," said Zach, grinning. "I'm glad you're feeling better. Get back to work."

* * *

"I came to see how far along you are," said Rose to Claire. "How are you feeling?"

"The contractions are about ten minutes apart," said Claire. "They're not bad."

"You're just getting started. The contractions will come faster and stronger as the birth nears, but it'll probably be several hours before that occurs. Have a seat on the couch and lay back," said Rose. "My examination won't take long, and it won't hurt. We'll have some tea when I finish."

Claire lay on the couch, and Rose discovered how much progress Claire had made.

"You're underway," said Rose. "The baby will be born today. Relax and breathe deeply. That'll help with the contractions. Would you like something to eat?"

"I'm not hungry," said Claire. "Mary left me a pot of her special tea. That's all I want. My mouth is dry."

"It's important you eat. Later, you'll need the strength the food will provide you. Do you take anything in your tea?"

"No, I like it the way Mary prepares it. What can I do to speed things up?"

"Try walking," said Rose. "Sometimes, that helps."

"What do you hear from Stephen? Since he moved to Sacramento, I hardly hear from him," said Claire. "He's not a good correspondent."

"I got a letter from him yesterday," said Rose. "He became frustrated with Alex Hunter and quit the partnership."

Claire stopped walking and turned toward Rose.

"Why'd he do that?"

"Stephen said Hunter is more interested in the politics of Hangtown than he is in defending the innocent."

"What is my brother going to do?" asked Claire.

"He approached Joe Winans, and they agreed to work together," said Rose. "Stephen is excited about them teaming up; they're kindred spirits. I'm disappointed Stephen decided to stay in Sacramento; I hoped he'd move back to Hangtown. I miss him."

"It's a good thing my labor began, or I might not have heard about this for weeks," said Claire, shaking her head. "I hope the change makes him happy. By the way, the girls tell me you're ready for another uniform."

"That's right, I am."

"Are there any changes you want, or should we make the new one like the others?"

"No changes," said Rose. "I'm pleased with how it fits."

* * *

Zach went to the El Dorado Hotel to see if he could find Joe.

"Let's have lunch," said Zach when he spotted him.

"I have a lot to do," said Joe. "I'd like to eat here if that's alright with you."

"Sure," responded Zach.

"I like your mutton chops," said Joe. "Do you?"

"I'm getting used to them," said Zach. "Claire hasn't seen them yet. I'm going to surprise her."

"She'll like them," said Joe. "How's she feeling?"

"She's in labor. I'm going to be a dad today!"

"Why didn't you tell me sooner?" asked Joe, slugging Zach's shoulder.

"I just got here," said Zach. "You didn't give me a chance."

"Is Claire going to use anesthesia?" Joe asked.

"Rose said the decision is Claire's. I thought we'd already discussed this? You want Claire to suffer; I don't."

"There's more to talk about," said Joe, "and I want to be clear: Claire's suffering isn't what I want; it's God's will that she not use anything to deaden the pain. After our earlier talk, I read more about the use of anesthetics."

"I hope what you read changed your mind," said Zach.

"Not at all," answered Joe. "I'm more convinced than ever about the legitimacy of my beliefs."

"What'd you learn?" asked Zach.

"One writer made the point that when there's no pain during childbirth, the maternal instinct is lost. You and Claire don't want that."

"Originally, you were opposed to the use of anesthesia on religious grounds. Now your worried Claire will lose her maternal instinct?" said Zach, raising an eyebrow. "You don't need to be concerned. Claire will be a terrific mother."

"Despite what you say, there still could be a problem!" replied Joe. "Besides, anesthesia is immoral."

"Immoral?" asked Zach. "How could it be immoral?"

"Anesthesia produces an effect on the user that's similar to being drunk. That can't be good for the baby any more than it is for the mother. Being drunk when you're delivering a baby is immoral."

"Your arguments are ridiculous," said Zach, shaking his head. "Give me a good reason why Claire shouldn't use anesthesia."

"Its use can lead to epilepsy, convulsions, even insanity," said Joe. "Why take the chance of that happening?"

"If that were true, doctors wouldn't use it, especially during childbirth. You've got to have better reasons than those."

"Anesthesia is spiritually negative."

"Spiritually negative?" said Zach. "What does that mean?"

"When a woman suffers during childbirth like the Bible calls for, she'll reach out to God for help. Her pleas for mercy come from a deep, earnest part of her soul. The use of anesthesia deprives God of these prayers. He doesn't like that."

"That's the biggest bunch of crap I've heard from you in a long time," said

Zach. "If you'll recall, God put Adam into a deep sleep when He created Eve. If God didn't want Adam to suffer, why would he want Claire to?"

"Did I hear Claire is in labor?" asked Matilde, walking by the brothers' table.

"You did," said Zach, "She started a couple of hours ago."

"How is she doing?"

"So far, so good," said Zach. "Waiting is difficult."

"I imagine it is. Little Zach is a handsome boy. I'm sure this child will be too. You make good ones," said Matilde, with a wink. "Any woman would love to have your child. I'll put some champagne on ice. We'll have a celebration when you come back with the news she's delivered."

* * *

"Claire, the sun is going down. It's time for me to re-examine you," said Rose. "I want to see where you are now."

After checking, Rose said, "There's a problem."

"Is it serious?" asked Claire. "Am I going to die? I had a dream that said I might."

"Ignore your dream. You're going to be fine, but there's a complication: the baby is coming breech. Cate's feet are where her head should be. Don't worry, I have experience with breech deliveries."

"Is Cate going to die?" asked Claire, tearing up.

"It's possible, but not a certainty. The good news is Cate is coming feet first, not fanny first. The birth is more dangerous when the fanny leads the way. When it does, legs can be broken, hips displaced, the umbilical cord pinched. Children born fanny first often end up in the back of the classroom. Feet first isn't ideal, but it's better than fanny first."

"What did I do wrong?" asked Claire. "Was there something I should have done differently? Maybe Adi was right. I shouldn't have eaten fish while pregnant."

"Calm down. You didn't do anything wrong. These things happen. Be positive. You don't want negative thinking to affect Cate."

"I don't understand?" whimpered Claire.

"Negative thinking disfigures a child or can make her mentally ill. Don't fret. When I was in training, I learned a procedure to use when a baby comes feet first. I should be able to ease Cate out safely. You're going to be okay, and

Cate will probably be too. I'm going to need an extra pair of hands, though. I'm going to ask Doc Martin to assist me."

"I'd prefer Betty," said Claire. "Can't she do what needs to be done?"

"She could," said Rose, "but Doc's experience will make it easier for me. Also, if another complication arises, he'll know what to do. Betty won't."

"Okay, send for Doc," said Claire. "I also want Zach to know what's going on."

"Of course. I'll ask Alice to let him know."

"Can Zach be here?" asked Claire. "I'd like him with me."

"It's better if he's not," said Rose. "You'll feel Zach's anxiety, and that'll cause you to tighten up when you should be relaxing. I recommend Zach stays away until we're finished."

"If Zach can't be here, it'll comfort me to have the doll Stephen gave me. Do you have any objections to that?" asked Claire.

"No objections whatsoever," said Rose, smiling. "Where is it? I'll get it for you."

"She's upstairs in the bedroom. She sits on top of my dresser."

"Keep walking and drinking Mary's tea. I'll be right back."

"Send Alice before you go upstairs. I want Zach to know everything that's happening."

"Will do," said Rose, walking into the dining room to speak with Alice.

* * *

Elsu was closing the newspaper office when Alice appeared.

"Do you know where Mister Zach is?" she asked.

"The last I knew, Zach went to the El Dorado Hotel. Start there," said Elsu. "If he's gone, the staff may know where he went. Has the baby arrived?"

"No, but there's a complication. It's my job to keep Zach informed."

"I hope it's nothing serious," said Elsu. "Zach will be devastated if it is."

"It's too early to know," said Alice. "Have to run. Thanks for your help."

On her way to the hotel, Alice passed Doc Martin's office. The light was on, and she went in.

"Doc, Claire Johnson is in labor. Miss Rose says she's going to need your help because the baby is coming breech."

"Is Claire at home?"

"She is."

"I'll come right after I finish bandaging this man's arm. He's cut himself pretty badly. I've stopped the bleeding, but I still need to wrap the wound."

"Thanks, Doc. I'll let her know."

Zach and Joe were having drinks when Alice entered the hotel.

"Over here," shouted Zach. "Alice, I'm over here."

When Alice arrived at the table, Joe asked: "Has the baby come? Is it a boy?"

"No baby, yet," said Alice, out of breath. "There's a complication. The baby is coming feet first."

"Is that unusual?" asked Zach. "Is Claire going to be okay?"

"That's not the normal way," responded Alice. "Miss Rose told me to tell you, Miss Claire will be fine. The uncertainty is with the baby. Apparently, there are a lot of things that can go wrong. Miss Rose is in control of the situation, but she's asked Doc Martin to help her. I just spoke to him, and he'll go to your house in a few minutes."

"I'm coming with you," said Zach, standing. "I want to be there."

"Miss Rose says 'no'! Your anxiety will make it harder for Claire to relax, which is what's needed for nature to take its course," said Alice. "Stay here; that way, I'll know where to find you."

"I'm coming," said Zach. "I don't care what Rose says. I want to be there."

Joe reached up and grabbed his brother's arm.

"That's not a good idea," said Joe. "Claire's screams will upset you, and that'll add to her distress. I'll stay with you. We'll pray. That's the best thing for you to do while you're waiting. Trust that God will use Rose and Doc to make things turn out right. Now, sit down."

"I'm scared," said Zach. "I want to be there to support Claire."

"Your fear is why you shouldn't go," said Joe. "Your presence will make things worse. They don't need you interfering when things get hectic. Sit down, and we'll say a prayer. Thank you, Alice. We'll be here."

After Alice left, Joe said, "I'm sure you read this morning's lesson. It was about accepting God's will, even when you prefer something else. That's what we'll pray for."

"My faith isn't as strong as Jesus'," said Zach. "I don't trust God like Jesus did."

"Nevertheless, we'll pray God gives you the strength to accept whatever happens," said Joe, rising. "Stay here a moment. There's something in the vesting room I want to get. I'll be right back."

When Joe returned, Zach could see an object in his hand.

"What do you have?" asked Zach.

"It's a cross my favorite seminary professor gave me when I graduated," said Joe. "His mentor gave it to him. It means a lot to me."

"What are you going to do with it?" asked Zach.

"I'm giving it to you to wear tonight," said Joe, "but I want it back after Cate is born. The cross has sharp points on it. When you wear it, it's going to periodically rip your skin. It does that as a reminder that you need to be thinking about God and accepting His will."

"That sounds like a medieval torture device," said Zach. "I won't wear it."

"Keep it in your pocket then," said Joe. "The point won't cut you. Its jabs will remind you to trust God."

Zach wasn't in the mood to argue. He slipped the pointed cross into his coat pocket and joined Joe in prayer. After a few minutes, Zach said, "Stephen needs to know what's happening. I'll ask Walt Selzer to go to Sacramento and bring him back."

"How are you going to find Walt?" asked Joe. "I told Alice we'd stay here."

"Walt likes an afternoon brew. There's a chance he'll come here for it," said Zach. "If he doesn't show up soon, I'll check other bars until I find him."

"No, you won't. Getting word to Stephen will have to wait."

"You're right," said Zach, massaging his temples, "though I want Stephen to know as soon as possible."

"Trust God. The right things will happen."

* * *

"Thanks for coming, Doc," said Betty, opening the front door. "Feels like rain."

"A storm is almost here," said Doc, removing his coat. "Rose, I'd like to examine Claire. I want to know how far along she is. Have her lay on the couch."

Claire was wearing a blouse over a short undershirt, a skirt without a petticoat, warm socks, and bedroom slippers. Doc Martin lifted her dress and slipped two fingers inside her.

"I feel the baby's feet," he said. "It's time to grease the birth canal."

"What are you going to do?" asked Claire, smoothing her skirt.

"Applying lard will make it easier for the baby to come out," said Rose softly. "A lubricated birth canal speeds up the delivery and prevents the child from struggling more than necessary. The quicker the delivery, the better it is for mother and child. Because this is your first birth, your muscles are taut, which makes the delivery more difficult. If this were your fourth child, the baby would slide out without the lard."

"While Rose is doing that, I'm going to tie a towel to the back of one of your dining room chairs," said Doc. "Betty, I'll need you to sit in the chair when it's time for Claire to push."

As Doc tied the towel, traces of blood from his previous patient were left on it.

"Can't you turn the baby?" screamed Claire, as a contraction overtook her. "I'd like her to come out normally."

"Doc, what do you think?" asked Rose.

"I've never had luck turning a baby without going inside the mother. When I've done that, I've broken legs and caused problems that wouldn't have occurred if I hadn't done it. Besides, the baby has already dropped too far for me to try. I think it's best we let nature take her course."

"What about you, Rose? Will you try to turn her? You can give me anesthesia if that'll make a difference," said Claire. "I'm desperate. I don't want to lose Cate."

"Turning the baby is rarely successful," said Rose. "Doc is right: nature's way is best, human intervention makes things worse."

"The contractions really hurt," grimaced Claire. "Give me a dose of ether or chloroform."

"Ether has been found to hurt the lungs," said Doc. "I don't recommend it. You're too far along for chloroform. We're going to need you to be fully awake and engaged. Labor shouldn't last much longer. Drink some water and nibble on something. You'll need your strength."

Rose walked into the kitchen and motioned for Doc to follow as Claire screamed.

"What do you want?" asked Doc, as Claire pleaded with God for relief.

"I'm concerned about the baby's neck breaking when her head gets stuck," said Rose. "I want you to apply pressure to Claire's pubic bone while I rotate her head. If we do this maneuver right, there'll be enough room for the neck and head to come out unharmed."

In the other room, Claire let out another piercing scream. Her face was drawn and pinched, her eyes haggard.

"It won't be much longer," said Rose, as she returned to the living room. "You're a real trouper. I see the contractions are now less than two minutes apart."

"What's that mean?" asked Claire, trying to catch her breath.

"It's almost time to push," said Rose.

* * *

When the time came, Claire put her legs on the back of the chair Betty was sitting in. Claire pulled the towel and pushed on Rose's command. Slowly the child's legs, hips, umbilical cord, and shoulders emerged.

"You have yourself a beautiful girl," said Rose, holding Cate's body on her forearm. "Her head is having trouble coming out, so I'm going to have Doc push on your pubic bone while I put my fingers in Cate's mouth and slowly turn her head. I'll need you to give a big push when I tell you."

"I'll do my best," said Claire nervously. "I'm exhausted."

"We're almost done," said Rose. "Doc, apply the pressure."

When Doc laid his left hand on top of his right and pressed, Rose guided Cate's head and body from a forward-looking position to a rear-facing one. When Cate's head dropped toward her chest, Rose said, 'PUSH!' and Cate slid onto Rose's arm.

Cate's cries indicated their efforts had been successful. Cate was alive and well.

"Well done!" said Rose, handing the cleaned up baby to Claire. "The after-birth needs to come out. After that, your bleeding will stop. Alice, it's time for Zach to join us. Please go get him."

"You did an outstanding job," Doc said to Rose. "You're good."

"Thank you," said Rose. "Hold Cate to your breast," Rose told Claire. "We want her to stimulate your milk. Cate is twenty-one inches long by my calculations, weighs eight pounds ten ounces, and her head is fourteen inches in circumference. You delivered a good-sized child!"

* * *

Alice found Zach in the El Dorado Hotel.

"Congratulations, Mister Zach. You're the father of a healthy girl. It's time for you to come home and be with your family. Miss Claire is fine, and she's eager to see you."

"Coming breech didn't create problems?" asked Zach, standing.

"You're fortunate Miss Rose was the midwife. She handled the situation with incredible skill. Doc helped too, but it was Miss Rose's ability that allowed everything to turn out well."

"This is an answer to our prayers," said Joe, smiling. "I'm coming with you. I want to see my niece. But before we go, I'd like to offer God thanks for how everything turned out."

Zach and Alice stopped near the hotel's front door and turned to face Joe.

"Let us pray," said Joe. Zach and Alice bowed their heads.

> "O Almighty God, we give humble and hearty thanks that You gave safe deliverance to Claire through the perils of childbirth. Watch over mother and child, that they may grow daily in their knowledge and love of thee. This we ask through Jesus Christ, our Lord. Amen."

"Let's go," said Zach, striding rapidly out the door.

Rose intercepted them when they arrived at Zach's house.

"I have a few things to tell you," said Rose, steering them away from Claire and Cate. "Because of the strain of labor, Claire needs quiet and rest. She also needs several hours alone with her baby. For that reason, only Zach will be allowed to visit with them tonight. He'll have five minutes. After that, Zach, you must leave no matter how well Claire says she's feeling. Claire needs to regain her strength, and excitement interferes with that. When Zach's visit is over, I'll arrange a warm milk bath for Claire. This is the best method I've found for reducing the swelling and relaxing the body. If that doesn't work, leeches will be necessary."

"May I at least say hello to Claire and catch a glimpse of my niece?" asked Joe.

"Absolutely not," said Rose. "This isn't the time. Claire has been through a demanding and exhausting experience; she needs quiet and rest. Her body and spirit are fragile."

"When can I see her?" he asked.

"Typically, a woman needs two to three weeks to recover. Talking with a variety of people will deplete Claire's energy. I can't allow that."

"Are you suggesting my saying hello to Claire will delay her recovery?" asked Joe. "That's absurd."

"Come by tomorrow afternoon, and you can have a few minutes with her," said Rose, "but don't plan on staying longer than five minutes."

"I'll be here," said Joe, glaring at Rose."

"How much suffering did she go through?" asked Zach. "Will the experience diminish her desire to have another child?"

"I'd say Claire's experience was taxing. But there's no agony a mother won't forget when she holds her newborn close, gently strokes her soft skin, and kisses her child. Almost instantly, Cate will be more precious to Claire than her own wellbeing. Every woman longs for more of these tender moments. Because each delivery is faster and easier than the one before, her desire for more children won't be a problem."

Zach went to Claire's side while Rose led Joe and Alice into the dining room.

"I got blood on my clothes," Rose told Betty. "How soon can you make me a new uniform?"

"Two days," said Betty. "We purchased the material this morning."

"Begin working on it as soon as you can," said Rose.

Zach found Claire wrapped in a heavy blanket sitting next to the fire. He kissed her and held Cate for the first time.

"You have mutton chops! I love them," said Claire. "They look terrific on you. What inspired the change?"

"I'm glad you like them," said Zach. "They're my birthday surprise for you. I'll tell you all about it when we have more time. How are you feeling?"

"I'm tired but elated. Rose has been wonderful. I don't ever want to go through labor without her," said Claire. "She told me I did well, but I don't know if that's true. I moaned and screamed a lot."

"Why are you sitting here?"

"Rose said being next to the fire would sweat the poisons out of my body. Isn't Cate beautiful?"

"She looks like you," said Zach. "I'm so excited I won't sleep much tonight!"

Zach and Claire were lost in the lushness of the moment when Rose interrupted.

"Five minutes is up," she said. "Zach, tomorrow, you can spend more time with them."

Zach kissed each of his girls and followed Rose into the dining room.

"Do you have a nanny lined up?" asked Rose.

"Claire didn't want one," said Zach. "She insists on doing everything herself."

"I wish she'd talked to me before making her decision," said Rose, frowning. "I'll check to see who I can find. Claire will need help; she's more delicate than she appreciates."

"I tried to tell her, but she wouldn't listen to me," said Zach. "Is there anything I should know about caring for Claire?"

Rose told Zach what to feed Claire for the next five or six days. That included not giving her solid or animal food and not heating what she eats.

"Why's that?" asked Zach, making notes.

"Those things bring on inflammation, which is what we're trying to avoid. Because Claire is nursing, give her a little tea and gruel for breakfast. After a few days, add weak chicken broth to her diet. She can have toasted bread for dinner. No wine or malt liquor. Do you understand? This is important. If you don't follow my instructions, Claire's recovery will be slowed, or worse, she could become ill."

"I'll follow your orders," said Zach. "I don't want anything bad to happen."

"One more thing. You're not to share your bed with Claire until she's fully recovered. Tonight she'll stay in front of the fire, so you can sleep upstairs. Tomorrow you'll have to make plans to sleep somewhere else for the next couple of weeks. I'll stay here tonight to watch over Claire and Cate."

Zach led Doc Martin, Joe, Alice, and Betty to the front door.

"I want to thank each of you for what you did," said Zach. "Each of you made a difference, and I love you for it."

"Zach, come with us to the El Dorado Hotel," said Joe. "Matilde has champagne on ice. It'd be a shame for you to miss out on the fun, and besides, we're counting on you to pay."

"Since Rose won't let me spend any more time with Claire or Cate," said Zach, "I'll go with you. The drinks are on me!"

THURSDAY, NOVEMBER 4, 1852

WHEN ZACH AWOKE, his mouth was dry, his head ached, and he wanted his morning coffee. He dressed and went downstairs where he saw Claire sleeping with Stephen's doll nestled in her arms. Rose was busy in the kitchen, and Cate slept nearby in the cradle Roberto made.

"Morning," he whispered to Rose. "I can use something to drink. Is there any coffee?"

"No. All I have is tea. Do you want me to make coffee?"

"My mouth is parched," said Zach. "I don't want to wait; I'll have tea. I didn't sleep well. How'd you sleep?"

"I didn't sleep much, either," said Rose. "I was teaching Claire how to nurse. Cate is hungry, and Claire's milk isn't providing what she needs. Cate needs a wet-nurse."

"How do I find one?" asked Zach, between gulps of tea. "Who do I ask?"

"When Claire is feeling better, I'll do it," said Rose. "I know a couple mothers who might be willing to help."

"That's a relief. I've no idea where to begin. Asking a woman I don't know to nurse my child is awkward," said Zach, rubbing the back of his neck. "Why is Cate with you?"

"Claire was restless throughout the night. I brought Cate into the kitchen so Claire could get some rest."

"May I hold Cate?" asked Zach, stretching out his arms.

"Yes, but let me show you how to do it properly," said Rose, positioning Cate in Zach's arms.

"I've never held a newborn before," said Zach. "She's delicate."

"It was foolish of Claire to insist on doing everything herself, especially since this is her first child. I'll create a list of things you should be aware of regarding her care," said Rose. "These are things a good nanny knows."

"A nanny is a good idea," said Zach, swirling around the kitchen with Cate. "I need help. How are my girls doing?"

"Be gentle. All that spinning isn't good for her. Cate will be fine once her belly is full. However, I have concerns about Claire."

"Concerns?" asked Zach. "What concerns?"

"Claire doesn't have an appetite. After not eating during labor, it's surprising she doesn't devour everything in sight," said Rose. "By itself, not eating isn't something to worry about, but there's more."

"You're scaring me," said Zach. "What more is there?"

"Even though she's in front of the fire, Claire complains of chills. She must have a fever. She should be watched closely, but I have other patients who need me. You have to find a nanny."

Just then, Claire sat bolt upright.

"Where's Cate?" she screamed. "I want my baby!"

"She's in the kitchen with me," said Zach. "I'll bring her to you."

Rose dipped a washcloth in cold water and put it on Claire's forehead.

"Thank you," said Claire. "That feels good. Could I have another cup of tea?"

"Of course," said Rose. "I'll get it."

While Rose was in the kitchen, Claire told Zach the dream that just jolted her awake.

"I'm in a forest of oak trees. Lightning strikes a particularly beautiful young tree, and it bursts into flames. The tree falls to the ground leaving only a stump.

I see mother, Marion, and Adi walking through the forest in my direction. They're dressed in white. Marion is carrying a white gown in her arms.

'Don't be afraid,' my sister says. 'We've come for you. Look again at the tree stump.'

When I looked, out of the stump, sprouted a new shoot. It was small but sturdy. That's when I woke up."

"I wonder where your mother, Marion, and Adi are taking you?" asked Zach. "The end of the dream was positive. I like the new shoot popping out of the stump. What was your reaction?"

"The dream alarmed me," said Claire coughing. "I don't want to go where mother, Marion, and Adi are. I want to stay here with you and Cate."

"You're not going anywhere," said Zach, brushing Claire's hair. "You'll feel better once you start eating. Then you'll have a new dream that'll reassure you everything is going to be fine. What would you like to eat?"

"Nothing right now. I'm a little nauseated," said Claire. "Cate is fussy. She wants to be fed."

"I'll leave the two of you to that," said Zach. "Thursday is a busy day at work. I'm off to get started. I love you and will be back to see my girls a little later."

Zach gave Claire and Cate kisses on their foreheads and left for work. On his way, Zach stopped at the El Dorado Hotel.

I wonder if they have a room available?

"Flann, I need a room for the next two to three weeks while Claire is recovering from childbirth. Do you have one available?"

"I'll check," he said, going behind the counter and turning the pages of a large book.

As Zach turned to watch, the cross in his coat pocket jabbed him.

Time to trust God that everything is going to work out. Claire's dream must be part of a test to see if I trust God even when He's distant.

"We have a room at the back of the second floor," said Flann. "It's small, but you're not going to be spending much time in it, are you?"

"Not at all. I'll just sleep there and spend my time at work or at home," said Zach. "Being small isn't a problem."

"It'll be two dollars a week," said Flann. "Do you want to pay in advance or as you go?"

"I'll pay for the first two weeks. I should have a better sense of how much I'll need the room at that point. Here are four dollars."

"Thank you. I'll get you a receipt," said Flann, walking back behind the counter.

"I'll get it from you tonight," replied Zach. "I have to get to work. See you later."

Zach was starting a fire to heat the office when Walt Selzer appeared.

"Joe said you're looking for me," said Walt. "Those are some mutton chops you've got. They look great. What can I do for you?"

"Claire gave birth yesterday...."

"Congratulations! Is it a boy or a girl?" asked Walt.

"She's a girl!" said Zach with a gleam in his eye. "Her name is her Bridget Catherine Johnson. We call her Cate. She looks like her mother."

"That's wonderful news," said Walt. "I'm flattered you want to share that with me."

"I have a job for you," said Zach. "Claire's brother, Stephen McCarthy, lives and works in Sacramento. I want you to find him and bring him back to Hangtown immediately. I'll give you ten dollars to do it."

"I can do that," said Walt. "I'll leave midmorning."

"That's not good enough," said Zach. "Claire is in a fragile state, and I want her brother to be able to visit with her as soon as possible. No delays. This is a rush situation. Do you understand?"

"I'll leave now," responded Walt. "Is there extra pay for doing this on short notice in a harsh rainstorm? These aren't ideal conditions for me to be dashing to Sacramento and back."

"If you have Stephen here tonight, there'll be an extra five dollars in it for you," said Zach.

"Consider it done," replied Walt. "I'll have him here before bedtime."

* * *

Midmorning, Rose went to check on Claire. As she approached, Rose detected a foul odor.

"How are you feeling?" she asked, wiping the sweat from Claire's brow.

"I'm still having chills," replied Claire. "I can't get warm."

"I'll add a log to the fire," said Rose. "Is there anything else I should know?"

"I have a nasty headache and a pain below my tummy," said Claire. "Everything exhausts me."

Rose lifted Claire's skirt, and the stench increased. Rose poked around Claire's abdomen until Claire groaned.

"You found the spot that hurts," said Claire, resting her head on the wet pillowcase. Beads of water ran off her brow.

"You need to be drinking more water and tea," said Rose. "I want you to sit up and drink a cup of water while I replace your pillowcase."

"There are several clean ones in the cabinet upstairs," said Claire. "Next time you see Mary, give her this pillowcase. She'll wash it and have it back to us fresh as can be."

"That's a good idea," said Rose. "I'll ask Alice to take it to her."

After changing the pillowcase, Rose went to speak with Alice.

"I need you to do a couple of things for me. First, take this pillowcase to Mary and have her wash it. Then find Zach and tell him Claire's fever hasn't broken. He needs to find a nanny quickly. I don't have time to do it myself. Here's a list of women for him to contact. If he can find someone who can also be a wet-nurse, that'd be even better."

"I'll tell him," said Alice. "Is there anything else you want me to do?"

"Go by Pastor White's office and let him know I'm tied up here. If all goes well, I'll be back in my office seeing patients this afternoon."

* * *

Zach and Elsu were printing and collating the paper when Alice entered the office.

"How's Claire?" asked Zach. "Is she getting better?"

"Not yet. Rose asked me to tell you it's time to find a nanny, and if you can, one that'll be a wet-nurse too. She's busy with Claire, or she'd do it. Here's a list of women she recommends.

"What's a wet-nurse?" asked Elsu.

"That's a nursing mother who agrees to step in if Cate needs more milk than Claire can provide," said Alice. "A wet-nurse isn't needed yet, but will be if Claire doesn't get better soon."

"I know only one woman on the list," said Zach, "and I don't want to ask her. The other women I don't know, and I'm not comfortable asking them."

"I know someone," said Elsu hesitantly.

"You do?" said Zach. "Who do you have in mind?"

"Taipa, the woman who lost her family during Ben Wright's raid," said Elsu. "I don't know if she'd be willing to nurse a white child, but I can ask. I assume you'd be okay with an Indian nursing your daughter? It'd be awful if Taipa agreed, and then you said you prefer the milk of a white woman."

"I'm fine with her acting as Cate's wet-nurse if she can forgive other white people for what Ben Wright did."

"The Miwok have a reputation for being friendly with whites, so she might be willing to help you," said Elsu. "Do you want me to leave now or when we finish printing?"

"Printing can wait. Ask Taipa if she'll be Cate's nanny, even if she doesn't want to be her wet-nurse," said Zach. "Go now; if Taipa doesn't want to do it, I have to find someone who will."

Elsu had been gone several hours when Kay opened the office door.

"I overheard a Chinese woman tell Pastor White Claire needs a nanny and a wet-nurse. I won't be your nanny, but I'll be your daughter's wet-nurse. After all, the girl is little Zach's half-sister."

"Thank you for volunteering," said Zach. "Elsu is asking a woman he knows if she'll do it. If she won't, I'll let you know."

"He's asking an Indian to be your daughter's wet-nurse? You'd prefer to give your child a savage's milk instead of mine? Your values are disgusting, and you're a disgrace to the white race. I'd withdraw my offer if your daughter weren't Zach's little sister. Let me know if you change your mind," said Kay, shaking her head as she left.

* * *

When Elsu arrived at Tonya's village, he went first to speak with Chief Alec Tawec. He found him coming out of the sweat lodge.

"Chief, I have an unusual request," said Elsu.

"What's that?"

"A European man I work for needs a wet-nurse for his newborn daughter," said Elsu. "He's a good man. His wife is ill, and their baby will die if a wet-nurse isn't found soon. I request your permission to speak with Taipa about doing this."

"Taipa has been through a horrible ordeal," said Chief Tawec, pausing to reflect. "She's a visitor. I'll approve the decision she makes. Speak with her, but don't pressure her into doing what you want."

"Thank you," said Elsu. "I will do as you say."

Word of Elsu's presence reached Tonya. She waited for him in a sheltered spot near Chief Tawec's dwelling.

When Elsu emerged from the meeting, Tonya said, "I didn't know you were coming? What brings you?"

"I need to speak with Taipa about being a nanny and wet-nurse for Zach's new child," said Elsu. "Can you take me to her?"

"Follow me," said Tonya. "Taipa is making a basket with some other women in the lodge. She's good with her hands. She makes a pretty basket."

Tonya and Elsu scurried through the rain to the lodge where Taipa was working. Lightning flashed across the sky as they ran.

Taipa heard Elsu's request and was uncertain about what to do.

"I will speak with the shaman. If she approves, I will do it," Taipa said. "Wait here."

"While we're waiting, I'll fix something to eat," said Tonya.

"I'd like that," replied Elsu, appreciating Tonya's thoughtfulness.

It was a long time before Taipa returned.

"I have spoken with the shaman," she said. "She invoked Kü'lem, the woman spirit, through her singing. Kü'lem approved my nurturing the child and assisting the mother. I will do it."

"I'll go with you," Tonya said to Elsu. "I'll translate for Taipa; her English isn't good. I won't have to stay long; she's bright and will learn quickly."

* * *

Tonya, Taipa, and Elsu rode through a downpour to Hangtown.

Zach looked up from his writing as the wet trio entered.

"Let me introduce Taipa," said Elsu, pointing to the woman with her head bowed. "She's agreed to be Cate's nanny and wet-nurse. You already know Tonya. She's volunteered to be Taipa's translator."

"Welcome," said Zach, standing. "Come warm yourselves by the fire. Thank you for agreeing to help. Taipa, I imagine your decision wasn't easy to make."

After Tonya told Taipa what Zach said, Taipa replied softly, "The death of a child is excruciating. If I can prevent someone from experiencing what I did, I want to do it."

Tearing up, Zach nodded and sighed deeply.

"I've got printing to do," said Elsu. "I'll get back to it."

"I'll take the women to meet Claire and Cate," said Zach. "I'll see you in the morning and finish collating the paper."

Zach led the women to his home. The rain didn't let up the entire way. Water rushed down the hill that led to Zach's house, making the climb difficult. Upon entering, Rose rushed to Zach's side.

"Claire isn't doing well. Her chills, sweats, and headache have continued. Her fever has gotten worse, and the pain in her lower abdomen is bothering her more. Her heart is pounding fast. I'm worried," said Rose, tears streaming down her face. "The outlook isn't good, and there's nothing I can do to stop her decline. I'm afraid she isn't going to make it." Rose cried as she embraced Zach.

"Is Claire going to die?" asked Zach.

"She is unless her condition miraculously changes," said Rose, wiping her nose. "I've spoken with Claire, and she understands what's happening. She wants you with her...Who are these Indian women?"

Zach reached into his pant's pocket and pulled out his handkerchief. He wiped his tears and blew his nose. Pointing to the shy woman, he said, "That's Taipa. She's volunteered to be Cate's nanny and wet-nurse. Tonya is here to translate."

"Does Taipa understand what's involved?" asked Rose, taking a deep breath.

"I believe she does," said Zach. "Ask her."

Tonya was speaking softly to Taipa when Rose said, "I wasn't expecting an Indian. What happened to the women on the list I sent you?"

"I wasn't comfortable asking any of them," said Zach. "When Elsu mentioned Taipa, I asked him to find out if she'd do it."

"Are you sure this is what you want?" asked Rose, crossing her arms.

"I'm desperate," said Zach with a trembling voice. "I've done the best I could. I'm grateful to Taipa for agreeing to help; she's just been through a trauma of her own. If she doesn't work out, I'll ask someone else. But Taipa's here and willing. She understands what's going on."

"Let me see what she knows," grumbled Rose. "Introduce me."

"This is Rose," said Zach. "She's my medicine woman. She wants to speak with Taipa."

Taipa stood tall when she heard her name. "I'd like to meet your medicine woman," she said.

While the women talked, Zach went to be with Claire. He put a cold washcloth on her brow and gave her a kiss.

"Rose tells me I'm going to die," said Claire, rocking slightly. "She has no way of curing what's causing my fever. Our life together is almost over...."

"She's wrong," said Zach, shaking his head. "Doc may have an answer. He'll know what to do. I'll get him."

"Stay with me," whispered Claire, placing her hand on his. "There's nothing anyone can do."

"There has to be," cried Zach. "I don't want to lose you. I'm going to pray for God's intervention. He'll save you. I'll send for Joe. He'll pray for your recovery too."

"It's too late," said Claire. "That dream of mother, Marion, and Adi coming for me was right. I won't be alone. I feel their love. They'll help me with the transition."

After a long pause, Claire asked, "Who are the Indian women? Why are they here?"

"Rose said it's urgent I find a nanny and a wet-nurse. Since I wasn't comfortable asking a woman I don't know, Elsu offered to see if Taipa would do it. Taipa discussed the idea with tribal leaders before agreeing to help. She's a warm, friendly woman. I think you'll like her," said Zach. "The woman with Taipa is Tonya. She's here to translate."

"I want to meet Taipa," said Claire, pressing her lips together, sweat and tears mingling on their way down her cheeks.

Zach wiped the moisture from Claire's face, gave her a kiss, and went into the dining room where the women were talking.

"Elsu found you a wonderful woman. I approve," said Rose. "Taipa is very loving and knows what to do. Cate will be in good hands."

"I'm relieved to hear that," said Zach, visibly relaxing. "Claire would like to speak with Taipa. May I send her over?"

"We're finished," said Rose. "Introduce her to Claire."

Zach led Taipa and Tonya to Claire's side and stood nearby until he was confident they could understand each other. Then he sought out Alice.

"Would you find Joe for me? I suspect he's at the El Dorado Hotel. Ask him to come right away; there's no time to waste."

"I'll go immediately," she said, putting on her boots and heavy coat.

I'll pray while I wait for Joe.

After a few minutes, Zach looked up and saw Taipa breastfeeding Cate. The women were smiling, and an aura of well-being surrounded them.

Thank you, God, for Taipa. I don't want to lose Claire or Cate. Watch over my girls, and if it's your will, provide them with good health. Lord, I'll do anything you ask if you'll spare Claire. I love her. Don't take her from me.

Dripping and muddy, Joe burst into the house. Alice trailed behind.

"Where's Claire? I've come to give her last rites," he announced.

Zach intercepted Joe before he got to Claire.

"This isn't the moment," said Zach. "I want you to join me in prayer for Claire's recovery."

"Alice told me it's too late for that," said Joe. "I brought oil to anoint her. I came prepared to baptize Cate too. I figured you'd want Claire to be present for that."

"Slow down," said Zach. "The anointing can wait, but I like the idea of Claire being present for Cate's baptism. Claire will need to rest before we ask more of her. Take off your coat and boots and come to the dining room with me. We'll pray there."

"I'm sorry God is putting you through this," said Joe, fighting off tears. "We'll pray for Claire's comfort and renewal, and strength for you, that you're able to persevere through what is to come."

* * *

It was close to ten o'clock when Walt and Stephen appeared.

"How is she?" asked Stephen, removing his rain gear.

"Not well," said Rose, giving Stephen a hug. "She won't make it through tomorrow."

"Who are these people?" asked Stephen as he inspected the room.

"You know everyone but Taipa and Tonya. Taipa is the woman in blue. She's agreed to be Cate's nanny and wet-nurse. Tonya is the colorfully dressed one. She's here to translate. May I get you something to eat?"

"I'd like that," said Stephen. "I haven't eaten for a while. Zach, why are you using Indians?"

"I'll tell you while you eat," replied Zach. "Excuse me a moment; I have to speak to Walt."

As Stephen and Rose went to the kitchen, Zach went over to where Walt waited.

"Thank you for bringing Stephen so quickly," said Zach, "especially in these conditions. Here's the money I promised you."

"Did Stephen tell you a fire decimated Sacramento a couple of days ago?" asked Walt. "His house and office were destroyed, and that made it difficult to find him. When I did, he was rummaging through the ashes of what had been his office. Stephen didn't want to leave, but he agreed when I told him what was going on. The wind, rain, and mud slowed our progress; otherwise, we could've been here hours ago."

"I'm glad you made it safely. Well done, my friend," said Zach, shaking Walt's hand. "Here's a little extra for your trouble. Tell Flann I'm going to be spending the night here. Have a safe journey back to town."

"I'll give Flann your message," said Walt, lingering at the front door. "Any time I can help, don't hesitate to ask. I hope Claire feels better."

Zach shut the door behind Walt, then joined Stephen and Rose in the kitchen. "I'm sorry to hear about your home and office," said Zach. "Were you able to save anything?"

"Everything was lost, said Stephen, "but I've found someone who will help me rebuild. I wish I could find someone who could rebuild Claire's health…."

Rose flinched.

"I wish there were something that could be done, too," she said.

"Joe will baptize Cate in the morning while Claire can still participate," said Zach. "Claire and I would like you and Rose to be Cate's godparents. What do you say?"

"Of course," said Stephen. "I want to stay involved in Cate's life."

"I'd be honored," responded Rose, hugging Zach.

"May I visit Claire?" asked Stephen, "and see Cate too?"

Rose nodded her approval, and Zach brought Stephen to Claire's side. She was snoozing when they sat on the floor across from her.

"Claire, Stephen is here. He wants to speak with you," said Zach, tearing up again.

When Claire didn't respond, Zach kissed her and repeated his message in her ear. Slowly, Claire opened her eyes and smiled.

"I'm glad you're here," she said. "I'm going to have to trust you to teach Cate our family history, what it means to be a McCarthy."

"I'll do my best," he said, wiping the wetness from his eyes. "Why did this happen to you? Why couldn't it have been me?"

"You're not able to get pregnant," said Claire, chuckling. "Besides, you've got Rose to care for. I won't be present for the wedding, so raise a glass in my memory."

Stephen sobbed while he hugged his sister.

"I'm going to miss you," he said. "I'll watch over Cate, don't you worry about that. Zach asked me to be her godfather. I'll be the best godfather a child ever had."

"Thank you," said Claire, smiling through her pain. "I need a moment to rest. Hold Cate while I doze. I want to know what you think of her."

"I'd love to," said Stephen. "Where is she?"

"Cate is sleeping in the dining room," said Rose. "She needs her rest too. You can hold her later. Let me introduce you to Taipa and Tonya."

The vigil lasted an hour. After feeding and changing Cate, Taipa and Tonya took her upstairs with them. Everyone else slept by the fire.

FRIDAY, NOVEMBER 5, 1852

ZACH WOKE EARLY and went upstairs to his study. He shut the door, cried, and read Morning Prayer. The lesson for the day was I Peter 4:12-13.

> Beloved, do not be surprised at the fiery ordeal that is taking place among you to test you, as though something strange were happening to you. But rejoice insofar as you are sharing Christ's sufferings, so that you may also be glad and shout for joy when his glory is revealed.

What kind of God allows his followers to face a fiery ordeal to qualify for future blessings? Lord, if you love me, prove you care by sparing Claire. Give me more time with her. A knock on Zach's door startled him. When he opened it, there stood Rose. "Claire is sinking fast. Joe is giving her last rites. It's time for good-byes."
"I'll be right down," said Zach sighing.
Zach saw Joe praying with Claire when he reached the bottom of the stairs.

> "The Almighty and merciful Lord grant you pardon and remission of all your sins, and the grace and comfort of the Holy Spirit. Amen."

Joe took oil from a bottle and made the sign of the cross on Claire's forehead. As he did, he said:

> "Almighty God, the Father of our Lord Jesus Christ, who has given you the new birth of water and the Spirit and has forgiven you all your sins, strengthen you with His grace to life everlasting. Amen."

Looking up, Joe saw Zach.

"Come join us for Holy Communion," he said. "This may be the last time the two of you partake of the sacrament together."

"I'd like that," said Zach. "After we finish, I have to let Elsu know I won't be available to help him collate and distribute the paper."

"Betty and I have finished Rose's uniform," said Alice. "There's nothing more for us to do. We'll go in your place."

"Bless you," said Zach, with a voice devoid of emotion, his chin quivering.

Following the abbreviated Eucharist, Joe was preparing to baptize Cate when Claire mumbled she needed to rest.

"Everyone to the kitchen," said Rose. "Claire needs a nap. Let's have breakfast."

While Joe was giving Claire last rites and Holy Communion, Taipa was in the dining room nursing Cate.

"What's going on?" she asked Tonya. "Why is Joe dressed that way?"

"Joe must be a Christian shaman," said Tonya. "He's asking the ancestors to look favorably on Claire."

"Why don't they dance and sing?" asked Taipa.

"I don't know," responded Tonya. "I'll ask him when the time is right. This isn't the moment."

During breakfast, Rose responded to a knock on the door. When she opened it, there stood Mary and Roberto.

"I brought the pillowcase back," Mary said. "It's been cleaned, pressed, and is ready for use."

"Thank you," said Rose. "Claire is sleeping. I'll put it on her pillow when she wakes. Come in."

"I was picking up my clothes at the laundry when Mary told me about Claire," said Roberto, following Mary inside. "I came to offer my best wishes and to lend a hand to what needs doing."

"I'm glad you came," said Zach. "Join us; we're about to baptize Cate."

"I can't stay that long," said Mary. "I have to get back to work."

"Do I hear Mary?" asked Claire.

"I'm here," responded her friend. "May I join you?"

"Please," answered Claire softly.

Before Mary moved, Rose took her arm.

"Claire is near death. She doesn't have much strength. Be brief."

Mary nodded and walked to Claire's side, tears filling her eyes.

"How are you feeling?" she asked.

"Not very well," said Claire, breathing slowly. "Before I die, I want you to agree to buy the boarding house. Zach can't handle the newspaper, the school, Cate, and the boarding house too."

"I don't want to do that," said Mary. "I've made the money I came for; it's time I go home. Sell the boarding house to Betty. She's an ambitious and capable woman, and she'll maintain it as a safe harbor for Chinese women."

"What are you going to do with the laundry?" asked Claire, taking a long pause between breaths.

"My assistants have agreed to pool their money to buy it. They see the gold dust left by the miner's clothes. It won't take them long to pay me."

"We're both going home," said Claire, with a faint smile. "I hope your birth goes better than mine."

"I appreciate everything you've done for the other women and me. Without your help, I'd still be servicing men. Your love transformed my life. I'll always be indebted to you. I'll tell the villagers at home about the beautiful American woman who saved me. We'll pray for you every day."

Claire and Mary were embracing when Rose came to see how Claire was doing.

"Claire needs to rest," said Rose. "I brought Cate for her to hold."

"I'd like some private time with Zach," Claire said. "I don't know how long I have. I want to talk to him now. Will you get him for me?"

"Of course," said Rose, handing Cate to Claire. "I'll send him over."

Zach replaced Mary on the floor next to Claire. He kissed her, held her hand, and stroked Cate's head.

"Take care of our precious one," said Claire. "I'm thankful I've had time with her; I wish I could have more. I'd love to raise her...I'd teach her how to be a woman in a man's society. I know you'll do the best you can."

"I'll make sure Cate has lots of women who'll love her and help her grow into the woman you'd like her to be," said Zach. "Cate will be special. How can she not be carrying you inside her?"

Claire hugged Zach as they wept.

"Keep watch over Olive. She'll favor the boys at the school without me around.

That's not what I want. The girls deserve the same education that the boys receive."

"I'll keep on eye on Olive and the school," said Zach. "I want Cate to have the best education possible."

"Have you thought about how Taipa and Tonya are going to fit into the house?"

"I have," said Zach. "I'll make my study into a bedroom for the women at the same time Cate's room is painted pink. I'll stay at the El Dorado Hotel until all the changes are completed."

"I'm sorry you have to give up your study. I know what an important place that is for you."

"Cate's well-being is worth it. Don't worry, I'll adjust," said Zach.

"Don't antagonize the OSSB," murmured Claire. "Cate needs you to be safe and well."

"Taking care of Cate will be my highest priority," said Zach. "I won't do anything that'll jeopardize that."

"You'll have your hands full. You're going to need help," said Claire, gasping for air. "I want you to marry again. You need a woman to look after you. Pick someone who'll cherish Cate as much as she does the other children the two of you have."

"I love you. The idea of being married to another woman holds no appeal to me," said Zach, tears streaming down his face.

"I have one other request," said Claire. "Give Cate this doll. Tell her I want her to have it. Whenever Cate yearns to feel close to me, all she has to do is hold it."

Joe approached the pair.

"I hate to intrude," he said, "but it's time to baptize Cate."

Another knock on the door interrupted them.

"Pastor White," said Rose. "I'm sorry I haven't returned to work. Claire has needed my full attention."

"I suspected as much," he said, stepping in. "How is Claire doing?"

"Not well," said Rose. "I'm afraid she doesn't have much longer to live."

"We're about to baptize Cate," said Joe, motioning for him to come over. "Would you like to do part of the service?"

"I'd like that," said Pastor White. "A little Methodist influence always makes things better."

"Here's what I'd like you to do," said Joe, showing Pastor White a series of prayers to read.

When the men finished discussing the ceremony, Joe arranged everyone in a semi-circle behind Claire. He stood in front of her and began the service. Stephen took Cate from Claire when the godparents made their vows. He handed her to Joe for the sprinkling of water. When the baptism concluded, Joe reached down to return Cate to Claire, but she was dead.

"Let us pray," he said.

> "Depart, O Christian soul, out of this world, in the name of God the Father Almighty, who created you. In the name of Jesus Christ, who redeemed you. In the name of the Holy Spirit, who sanctified you. May your rest be this day in peace, and your dwelling-place in the Paradise of God. Amen.

> "Into your hands, O merciful Savior, we commend the soul of your servant Claire, now departed from the body. Acknowledge, we humbly beseech you, a sheep of your flock, a sinner of your redeeming. Receive her into the arms of your mercy, into the blessed rest of everlasting peace, and into the glorious company of the saints in light. Amen."

Zach held Claire and sobbed. Everyone else quietly moved into the dining room.

"I'll prepare the burial site for her," said Roberto. "Does anyone know where Zach wants that to be?"

"Next to Pete in the Union Cemetery," said Joe.

"I'll help you," said Pastor White.

"We'll hold the funeral tomorrow," said Joe. "I'll officiate. Would you like to give the homily?"

"I'd be honored," said Pastor White. "May I offer my church for the ceremony? Saturdays at the El Dorado are busy and noisy. There'll be fewer problems if we hold it at my place."

"You're right," said Joe. "Your place will simplify things."

"Did Claire indicate which outfit she wanted to wear?" Rose asked Mary.

"There's a purple dress she liked a lot. I'll show you," said Mary leading Rose upstairs. "After we dress her, I'll fix Claire's hair, if you don't mind. She did so much for me, I'd like to do that for her."

"Of course," said Rose, wiping her eyes.

While the women dressed Claire, Joe, Roberto, and Pastor White left to dig Claire's grave and work out the funeral details.

When the women finished preparing Claire, Mary said, "I have to return to work."

"I have to leave, too," said Rose. "I have patients to see."

When everyone was gone, Zach sat next to Claire.

You look beautiful, he thought. *I'm going to miss you more than you will ever know. Rest comfortably; everything is going to be all right.*

Taipa and Tonya left Zach alone and tended to Cate.

Shortly before dusk, Joe returned.

"It's time we move Claire's body to the church to prepare for tomorrow's service. I brought a wagon."

"It's hard for me to let her go," he said. "I know I must, but I'm not ready."

"It's time," said Joe, hugging his brother. "Help me move her to the church."

The rain was a heavy mist as the men drove to Pastor White's church. Nurse Morris greeted them.

"There are so many memories," said Zach, "tomorrow is going to be difficult."

Pastor White met them at the church entrance and showed them where to place Claire.

"I expect there'll be a large turnout," said Joe. "I've asked several men to pass the word the service will be here."

"I think you're right about the turnout," said Pastor White, putting his arm about Zach. "I've spoken with the head of the churchwomen. They'll provide refreshments in the hall following the service. Do you want everyone to join you for the interment, or do you prefer a private ceremony?"

"I don't think I'll be able to hold myself together during the burial. I prefer a private ceremony with only Claire's closest friends."

"Give me the names of those you want, and I'll make sure they know," said Pastor White.

"Thank you," said Zach. "My head is in a heavy fog. I can't think of anything besides my time with Claire. I'm grateful the two of you are taking care of all the details."

"Time for dinner," said Joe. "The Virginia House is quiet. Let's go there."

Following the meal, Joe dropped Zach off at the El Dorado Hotel.

"Here's the plan for tomorrow morning," said Joe. "I'll pick you up at seven, and we'll go to Lucy's for breakfast. I'll take you home before I join Pastor White. Roberto will come to your house after lunch and bring you to the ceremony."

"Thanks for arranging things," said Zach. "I'm going to lean on you for a while."

"One more thing. I put a Prayer Book and Bible in your room. I thought you'd want them."

"Good thinking," said Zach. "I'll use them in the morning."

Zach made his way through the crowd of drunken gamblers to his room. Opening the door, he found the Prayer Book, Bible, and receipt for the room lying on the bed. He got out of his clothes and slid under the sheets.

"Lord, you didn't answer my prayer to save Claire. You let her die. You don't care about your follower's suffering. I thought you were a loving God, but now I realize you're indifferent.

At this point, grief overwhelmed Zach, and he cried himself to sleep.

SATURDAY, NOVEMBER 6, 1852

ZACH WOKE FROM his disturbed sleep, not sure where he was. Collecting himself, he read Morning Prayer. The lesson for the day was Psalm 22:1-2.

> My God, my God, why have you forsaken me?
> Why are you so far from helping me,
>> from the words of my groaning?
> O my God, I cry by day, but you do not answer;
>> all night long I call, and cannot rest.

Jesus uttered these words when he felt abandoned, neglected, and alone on the cross. I feel this way too. Lord, why don't you care?

At seven o'clock, Joe knocked on Zach's door.

"Are you ready for breakfast," he asked.

"Come in," said Zach. "I'm putting on my boots."

"How'd you sleep?" asked Joe.

"I slept in spurts," replied Zach. "My anger with God kept waking me."

"Why are you angry with God?"

"He let Claire die," said Zach. "He could've saved her but didn't. God is indifferent to human suffering."

"I disagree," said Joe, "but this isn't the time to argue. Let's eat."

"Instead of going to Lucy's, I'd like a blueberry muffin from the Hangtown Bakery. Is that okay with you?"

"Of course," said Joe. "I like their croissants, especially the ones filled with cream cheese and jelly."

As they walked across the street, Joe asked, "Did you remember that it was a year ago today grandpa Johnson died?"

"No, I've been thinking about other things," muttered Zach. "It's been a year? That's hard to believe. Are you sure?"

"I am."

"The darkness of November is unrelenting," said Zach. "Include a prayer for him in today's service."

During breakfast, Zach asked, "Anything new with you and Bob Jenner?"

"Bob has been in a disagreeable mood ever since he learned he lost the election to become the President of the Hangtown Merchant's Association."

"Who won?"

"Alex Hunter," said Joe. "Bob really wanted the position, but he came in a distant second. Bart Pierce apparently received only a few votes and was third. Don't say anything; the results haven't been made public yet."

"How do you know the results?" asked Zach, applying honey butter to his muffin.

"Jeb Stuebe told Bob. Jeb didn't want the official announcement at the Merchant's meeting to catch Bob by surprise."

"I'm glad he lost," said Zach, with a smirk. "It appears Bob's influence is diminishing. That's a good thing."

"I don't know," said Joe. "My sense is Alex Hunter is so popular he'd win any election he entered."

Following breakfast, Joe and Zach walked to Zach's home.

"Roberto will be by after lunch to pick you up," said Joe. "I'll see you later."

"Thanks for everything you're doing," said Zach. "I appreciate it."

Zach opened the front door and shouted, "I'm home."

Tonya came down the stairs to greet him.

"Cate is nursing right now. Taipa will bring her down when she's finished."

"I'd like that," said Zach. "I'm eager to see Cate."

Fifteen minutes later, Taipa appeared. Cate was dressed in one of the outfits Claire made for her.

"There's my little girl," he said, taking her from Taipa. "You look healthy. Is she eating well?"

"Yes," said Tonya chuckling. "She's eating so much; she'll be chubby in no time."

"That's a relief," said Zach, tears filling his eyes. "I'm not prepared to lose her too. She looks beautiful in that outfit. I wish Claire could see her...."

Cate relaxed in Zach's arms and fell asleep.

"I'll put her in her bed. I'm going to my room for a few minutes," said Zach. "I'll dress for the funeral and get out of your way."

Zach put on the outfit he'd purchased from Seligman's.

This isn't the occasion I bought the clothes for, but there isn't a better time to wear them.

Zach went downstairs and was freshening the fire when he heard a knock on the door.

"Mister Tobey is here to see you," said Tonya.

Zach greeted his visitor and invited him to sit by the fire.

"What brings you?" asked Zach.

"I'm sorry to give you more bad news," said Mister Tobey, "but someone broke into the newspaper office last night. They kicked in the back door and destroyed everything inside, including your press. The interior will have to be repaired and repainted. That isn't going to be cheap. You'll pay, of course."

"I'm sorry this happened," said Zach. "How long will the repairs take?"

"That's no longer your concern," said Jeb. "You'll recall I told you you'd have to leave the next time my property was damaged. Well, that moment has come. I'll give you two weeks to get out."

"Do you know who did it?" asked Zach.

"There was a note nailed to the wall. It said, 'Stop protecting Indians. OSSB'"

"I see," said Zach. "I'll look for a new location next week."

"A couple of fellows who intend to publish a daily paper approached me about renting the space. They want it expanded. I've been holding them off, but now I won't. After the first of the year, you'll have competition for readers."

"Claire's funeral is in a few hours," said Zach. "I don't care about them."

As Mister Tobey left, Betty and Alice arrived.

"The newspapers were distributed yesterday on time," said Betty. "Is there something else we can do for you?"

"Yes," said Zach. "Cate will need larger clothes soon. Make some for her. Here's the money I owe you for Rose's new uniform and a little extra for helping Elsu."

"What's going to happen to Claire's dressmaking business?" asked Betty. "If you don't have other plans, I'd like to buy it from you, along with the sewing machine and the other supplies she had."

"I'm going to offer the business to Mary," said Zach. "If, for some reason, she doesn't want it, I'll sell it to you."

"I don't think Mary is interested. She's telling people she is going back to China," said Betty. "She's selling the laundry."

"I haven't heard that," said Zach. "To be honest with you, selling the business is too much for me to think about at the moment. Let's talk about it next week."

* * *

Roberto knocked on the front door shortly after lunch.

"You look spiffy," he said. "Claire would be impressed."

"I wanted to surprise her but never got the chance," said Zach. "It's time to go, isn't it? I'm not looking forward to this."

"It won't be bad," said Roberto. "You'll be surrounded by friends who loved Claire and care about you. They'll help you get through this afternoon. If you need anything, I'll be at your side."

Zach hugged Roberto, and they left for Grace church. When they arrived, it was clear there was a large turnout.

"Look at all those people," said Zach. "I wonder how many of them are wearing clothes Claire made for them?"

After Zach sat in the front pew, Joe and Pastor White began the service by walking down the aisle together. Joe said in a loud voice, "I am the resurrection and the life, says the Lord: he that believes in me, though he were dead, yet shall he live: and whosoever lives and believes in me, shall never die."

Zach's mind couldn't concentrate on the words: he could only think about Claire.

When Pastor White read Matthew 11:28-30, Zach's mind momentarily paid attention.

> Come to me, all you that are weary
>> and carrying heavy burdens,
>> and I will give you rest.
> Take my yoke upon you and learn from me;
>> for I am gentle and humble in heart,
>> and you will find rest for your souls.
> For my yoke is easy,
>> and my burden is light.

Oh, how I wish that were true. I once believed those words, but now I see I was wrong. The loss of Claire is a heavy burden, and I am weary, yet God provides no relief for my suffering. My ambition to grow spiritually is pointless. God doesn't care. Life is hell.

Pastor White's homily and the prayers that followed ran together in Zach's mind. When he looked up, Joe and Pastor White were standing beside him, urging him to stand and walk out with them.

The service is over already?

Zach stepped out of the pew and walked down the aisle with the clergy. Pastor White positioned himself at the church door, with Joe and Zach standing alongside him.

"Thank you for coming," Pastor White told the congregation. "The interment will be private, but you're invited to join us for refreshments in the church hall next door."

The number of people who streamed by Zach, shaking his hand, giving him hugs or advice, was a blur. He found himself in the church hall with a cookie in his hand, talking with people whose names he couldn't recall and whose words didn't penetrate the fog that enveloped his mind.

"I'll be opening the school on the fifteenth like I promised Claire," said Olive Day.

"Good," replied Zach, without thinking, "Claire would like that."

"You were a lucky man to have someone as beautiful as Claire to be your wife," said Charley Boles. "She's the kind of woman I'd like to find."

"Thank you for your kind words," Zach heard himself saying.

"Did you hear about the damage the storm caused in San Francisco?" continued Charley.

"No, I haven't paid attention to the storm," said Zach.

"The wind was so wild in San Francisco, I had to leave early again. It's a good thing I did, or I would've missed Claire's funeral."

"I'm glad you're here," said Zach. "Claire would be too."

"Sixty feet of Law's Wharf at Clark's Point disappeared," persisted Charley. "The waves were ferocious, and the wind delayed the installation of the poles that are going to be used for telegraph service between San Francisco and the surrounding cities. When they're finally in place, California will be part of the nineteenth century."

"An important part of my life was lost during the storm," mumbled Zach. Next in line was Mary.

"You look stylish in that outfit. I bet Claire loved seeing you in it," she said. "Is there anything I can do for you or Cate?"

"The only thing I want is Claire," said Zach. "Can you bring her back to life? She never saw me dressed this way; she died before I could surprise her."

"I wish I could bring Claire back," replied Mary. "I miss her too. Did anyone tell you I'm leaving for home in a few weeks? I urged Claire to sell the boarding house to Betty. Did she tell you?"

"So it's true, you are returning to China," said Zach. "I was hoping to sell you the boarding house and dressmaking business. If you're not going to be here, I'll sell them to Betty."

"That's a good idea," said Mary, hugging Zach.

Zach's next awareness was Roberto leading him to the buggy and driving him to the cemetery.

"You did a good job getting through the service," said Roberto. "Time will help you feel better."

I'm ready for the pain to go away now. How long do I have to suffer before I feel better? When I do feel better, does that mean I've lost my connection with Claire? That's an awful price to pay for feeling better. I'd rather hurt and feel close to Claire than feel better and be disconnected from her.

As Zach approached Claire's grave, he saw Joe arranging candles around the burial site. When everyone arrived, Joe began the service.

"The words from the twenty-fourth verse of the twelfth chapter of the Gospel of John provide me with comfort at moments like this," said Joe. "Saint John put these words into the mouth of Jesus:

> Truly, I tell you, unless a grain of wheat falls into the earth and dies, it remains just a single grain; but if it dies, it bears much fruit. Those who love their life lose it, and those who hate their life in this world will keep it for eternal life.

Now there's a thought. Claire had to die because she loved life and wanted more of it, especially with Cate. In contrast, I hate my life without Claire, so I'm stuck with more? I don't want eternal life; I want Claire. I wonder why Joe selected such a stupid passage?

The last thing Zach recalled about the graveside ceremony was throwing clumps of wet dirt on the casket that Roberto purchased for Claire. It wasn't long before Zach found himself sitting in the buggy beside his buddy on their way back to town.

"I'll buy you dinner at the El Dorado Hotel," said Roberto. "You shouldn't be alone."

During the meal, Zach recalls Roberto talking and talking.

"I liked the candles around the grave and Joe's comment that new life is found in the coming of the light. The idea that death leads to new life is a powerful one, don't you think? I'm confident Claire is with the Lord, rejuvenated."

"I don't see anything but darkness," said Zach. "Saint John's words didn't nourish my soul; God doesn't care if we suffer. All I see is the emptiness of my life without Claire."

The men ate the rest of their meal in silence. When Zach finished, he said, "Thank you for transporting me around today, buying Claire's casket, and having dinner with me. You're a special friend. I want to retire now. I'll see you soon."

Zach made his way up the stairs and down the hall to his room. He got out of his clothes and was in bed talking with God when he fell asleep. A knock on the door woke him. In a stupor, he opened the door to discover Matilde standing in front of him.

"I came to tell you how sorry I am that you lost Claire. I know how much you loved her. It was a beautiful thing. Someday I hope to find someone like you to marry."

"Thank you," Zach was saying when Matilde hugged him and gave him a kiss.

Just as she did, Joe walked up to say goodnight to his brother. When Joe saw the two of them kissing, he turned and fled.

"Joe!" called Matilde, running after him. "Come back! I can explain."

Zach shut the door, returned to bed, and grumbled, "Nothing is going right." He rolled over and cried.

Nothing matters. Life is stupid and cruel. It's a steady descent into suffering and death. If there's any meaning to be found in existence, death will destroy it.

SATURDAY, MAY 5, 1906

"**W**ELCOME TO DAD'S memorial. I'm Cate Johnson Winans, Zach and Claire's child. Standing next to me is Father Zach Bunnell, dad and Kay's son. We want to thank each of you for making the trip to Placerville. We especially want to thank the Reverend Thomas P. Boyd for making Our Savior available to us. Deacon Tom is known for his ability to inspire spiritual awakenings wherever he goes. He's dad's kind of clergyman. Deacon Tom asked to say a few words, so I'll turn things over to him."

"Thank you, Cate. Our bishop, William Hall Moreland, sends his greetings. He can't be here because he's busy with the parishes damaged by the San Francisco earthquake.

Zach Johnson was one of Placerville's first prominent citizens. His efforts to bring equality to immigrants, Negroes, Indians, and women are a testament to his faith. Zach's unrelenting efforts to have Bishop Moreland reach out to the Chinese and Indian communities paid off. Bishop Moreland recently instructed the churches in Benicia and Vallejo to provide housing to the Chinese who lost their homes in the devastation. And two years ago, Bishop Moreland started a mission to the Hoopa Indians. A generation ago, we were at war with them. Today we worship together.

"To help with the heat, I've opened all the windows and doors to let in the breeze. The twittering sound you hear is the Western Martins flying about. I hope they don't annoy you."

"Not at all," said Cate. "I love the sound of nature."

"Good. I do too," said Deacon Tom. "When you're finished, please join me across the room for refreshments."

"Thank you, said Cate, moving back in front of the gathering. "Your hospitality brightens our spirits."

"I'll begin by telling you about dad's death," said Cate. "The night before the earthquake, dad attended the Metropolitan Opera Company's production of *Carmen*. Enrico Caruso was the tenor; Olive Fremstad sang the lead role. Tickets were expensive and hard to come by. Dad asked me to join him, but I said 'no.' Now, I wish I'd gone.

"After the performance, dad returned to the Saint Francis Hotel. The initial quake hit a little after five in the morning and lasted about twenty-five seconds. Dad rushed outside, wearing his bathrobe and slippers. That's when the more violent shaking began. It lasted for almost a minute, causing the building next to dad to collapse. It upsets me to think of him dying alone in the rubble.

Cate paused to gather herself and then continued.

"When I was a newborn, dad hired a woman from the Miwok tribe to look after me. Taipa treated me like I was her own, and I think of her as my mom. I call my biological mother, whom I never knew, Claire. Growing up, whenever I wanted to feel close to Claire, Taipa had me hold the doll Claire left me. I also feel close to her when I eat chocolate. Dad said Claire loved chocolate as much as I do." Smiles radiate throughout the room.

"Dad told me stories about Claire's struggles with patriarchal attitudes and her pursuit of equality with men. On my twenty-first birthday, dad gave me a diamond necklace, which I'm wearing today. He said there was a diamond in one of Claire's final dreams, and the stone in my necklace is a reminder to be the self-reliant woman Claire wanted me to be.

"I like to read, so Dad encouraged me to study English Literature at Willamette University. Today, I'm the librarian at the University of the Pacific.

"I married Lee Winans, the son of Uncle Stephen's law partner. Lee became a lawyer too and works alongside John Muir at the Sierra Club. We have three children and two grandchildren, all of whom are here," she said, motioning for them to stand.

After they were acknowledged, Cate said, "The school Claire started lasted one year. Miss Day gave the majority of her time to the boys, and because dad promised Claire he wouldn't let her do that, he fired her. Dad sold the school a few months later to a woman who promised to provide the girls with the same attention she gave the boys. Dad was pleased that he honored Claire's wishes.

"Some of you may be wondering why dad never married Taipa? I certainly did. The answer is he never got over his love for Claire. He was devoted to Taipa and pampered her, but he couldn't bring himself to marry her. I didn't like that, and we'd argue, but dad was resolute. When Taipa died in '98, he buried her in the family plot. She is on dad's left side; Claire is on his right. You may have noticed Taipa's headstone when we laid dad to rest.

After a pause, Cate asked Robert Gonzalez, Zach's closest friend, to come forward. Using a cane, Roberto hobbled to the front of the room, wearing his signature hat with a Red Hawk feather in it. Roberto settled into an overstuffed chair that Father Zach slid in front of the gathering for him.

"Tell us about dad," said Cate.

"Following Claire's death, Zach was in a low spot, mentally and spiritually," said Roberto. "Things immediately got worse. When Elsu, Zach's pressman, learned the newspaper office had been wrecked and Zach wasn't going to start over, he returned to Mount Shasta, his ancestral home. Tonya, Elsu's girlfriend, went with him. They'd been on the mountain only a short time when settlers killed them for their scalps. I'd never seen Zach so despondent.

"Cate, I don't know if you're aware that your dad stopped publishing the newspaper to protect you. He'd promised Claire he wouldn't do anything that would put you at risk. The OSSB hated Zach and was determined to stop his crusade for equality, even if that meant killing him. Zach gave up the newspaper so the OSSB wouldn't make you an orphan.

"What's the OSSB?" asked Cate.

"The OSSB was a secret group of ruffians active in the 1850s. They belonged to the Nativist Party. Let me tell you, they were a nasty, intolerant bunch. Nativists wanted Chinese immigration to stop, Negroes to remain slaves, Indians eradicated, and women kept in their place. Though the OSSB and the Nativists are gone, their attitudes remain. Those of us who share Zach's values still have work to do.

"Zach sold the paper to the men who started the *Mountain Democrat*, with the understanding he'd periodically contribute a guest column. The OSSB rejoiced when the new owners' editorials sought to silence the 'wailing abolitionists.' They didn't gloat for long. Zach's first piece in the *Mountain Democrat* identified Jim Edwards as the leader of Hangtown's OSSB. Public humiliation forced Jim to sell his hardware store and move to Marysville.

"Another of Zach's columns exposed James Gadsden's efforts to establish slavery in California and divide the state in two. For this disclosure, the prominent San Francisco newspaper, *Daily Alta California*, gave Zach a glowing tribute.

"Why did dad leave Hangtown?" asked Cate.

"Zach had an unfulfilled ambition to write a book about the Indian War in Mariposa," said Roberto. "Zach told people he moved to Mariposa to research the book, but he told me he wanted to get away from the darkness that tormented him here. The first time I visited Zach in his new home, he confessed his anguish was still with him.

"Zach wasn't the only one who departed Hangtown at that time," said Roberto. "Nurse Rose Kellogg left too. She moved to Sacramento, married Claire's brother, Stephen, and worked as a parish nurse until Barbara was born."

"Barbara McCarthy Gibson, please stand," interjected Father Zach in a loud voice from the back of the room. A smart-looking woman in her forties stood.

"Barbara, tell us about yourself," said Father Zach.

"There isn't much to say," said Barbara. "I became a nurse like my mother and worked in the children's ward of a San Francisco hospital until the quake struck. Now I don't know where I'll work. I'm married to a doctor, Ben Gibson. We have two sons and a daughter." Doctor Gibson and the children stood as the gathering welcomed them.

"Do you have any recollections of my dad you'd like to share?" asked Cate.

"You know, I do," said Barbara. "When I was a child, my folks would take me with them when they visited Uncle Zach. While the adults talked, Cate and I played in the creek behind the house. There were books to read and a stack of women's magazines I found fascinating. Uncle Zach taught me to play horseshoes. He said it was a family tradition. I beat him every time we played, and I enjoyed teasing him about his lack of skill. When my folks weren't around, Uncle Zach gave me five dollars, which I used for anything I wanted. It was our secret."

"I looked forward to your visits," said Cate. "If I'd known dad slipped you money, I would have had my hand out too!"

Laughter erupts around the room.

"What's new with your parents?" asked Roberto. "I haven't heard about them for a long time."

"My parents survived Sacramento's great flood of 1862," said Barbara, "but now mom is concerned about dad's mental decline. Dad has difficulty remembering things, so he can't practice law. Also, dad is increasingly frightened when he's not home, which is why they aren't here. Mom sends her love."

"I had no idea," said Roberto, as Barbara sat down. "I am so sorry...."

"Uncle Roberto, please continue," said Cate sighing.

"Zach bought a house in Mariposa near John Frémont's estate. The two spent so many nights talking that Zach considered writing Frémont's biography. However, in 1863, before Zach proposed the idea to him, Frémont sold his land to a New York banker. The new owner hired Frederick Law Olmsted to manage the grounds. When Zach discovered Olmsted once had been a journalist who opposed slavery, they became constant companions. Olmsted, who came west after designing Central Park in New York City, fell in love with Yosemite. As the Civil War ended, Olmsted brought Zach into the conservation movement and introduced him to John Muir. The three of them, along with others, lobbied Congress to preserve Yosemite, not just for the wealthy, but for the free enjoyment of all people for all time. The men were jubilant when President Lincoln signed their legislation into law. What a glorious day that was.

"I've gotten a bit ahead of myself," said Roberto. "Zach almost didn't move to Mariposa. Taipa was afraid of Joaquin Murrieta, an outlaw terrorizing central California. Taipa insisted it was too risky to live in Mariposa. Zach contended they'd be safe; Murrieta had no reason to harm them. Taipa went with Zach despite the danger his naiveté exposed them to. Fortunately, Murrieta was killed shortly after they arrived in Mariposa.

"Did Taipa resent Zach for moving when she didn't want him to?" asked Cate.

"No, she forgave him," said Roberto. "She stayed with Zach even though her services were no longer needed. Zach liked that.

"Taipa helped Zach with his book by introducing him to Chief Teneiya of the Ahwahneechee tribe. The Chief told Zach the hostilities started when the Ahwahneechee defended their land from the ranchers and miners who illegally settled on it. Chief Teneiya tried to get the trespassers to leave peacefully. When they didn't, the Ahwahneechee used weapons to drive them out. Many people died, and the Mariposa Battalion was formed to stop the killings. The troops chased Chief Teneiya and his followers into a valley, where they captured them. The soldiers who did this were the first white people to gaze upon the beauty of Yosemite.

"Taipa appreciated Zach for telling the Ahwahneechee's side of the story. The residents of Mariposa felt differently. They burned his book in front of the courthouse.

"I'll turn the conversation back to Cate," said Roberto.

"I have one more question for you," she said, walking up to Roberto and putting her hand on his shoulder. "Tell us about Mary's child, the one born in China."

"Mary named her son, David, after her dead husband," said Roberto. "When I learned David moved to Sacramento, I went to see him. He's built like an ox, just like his dad. David works for the railroad. Because David speaks both English and Cantonese, he was made the foreman of a maintenance crew. A few years later, David was promoted to Chief of Maintenance for all of the tracks between Sacramento and Nevada. He's doing well."

"Why'd he leave China?" asked Father Zach, fanning himself.

"David told me he wasn't treated well. Being of mixed races, David was tolerated only because his mother had more money than everyone else. When she died, the villagers started calling him 'barbarian devil.' That's what caused David to leave. Each time I visit him," said Roberto, "I tell David about his father. David liked hearing about his dad's role in capturing Zanshi, the ferocious grizzly bear, and how his dad made the statue of Nurse Morris. He was shocked to learn his dad almost killed a man with his bare hands.

"David isn't young anymore. He's fifty-three, married, and has three children and one grandson. He's supervising an emergency repair near Donner Pass, or he'd be here."

"Whatever happened to Pastor White?" asked Cate. "Wasn't Nurse Morris' statue on the grounds of his church?"

"You're right; that's where it was," said Roberto. "Pastor White built Grace Community Church into the largest congregation in Placerville. Toward the end of his time at Grace, Pastor White's old friend, the Reverend Charles Maclay, invited him to join the faculty of a fledgling Methodist seminary in San Fernando. He decided to do it. The last I knew, Pastor White was living in the Los Angeles area."

"Thank you," said Cate. "A lot of what you told us I didn't know."

"Yosemite made a tremendous impression on dad," said Cate. "Through his love of the place, he counted as friends not only John Muir, but also Galen Clark, Josiah Whitney, and John Burroughs. When Muir invited Ralph Waldo Emerson to camp in Yosemite, dad joined them. This was a couple of years before I went to college, and I remember how excited dad was when he got back. Emerson and dad had spent the night by the campfire, talking about the meaning of life. It was extraordinary, he said.

"Three years ago, Muir introduced dad to Teddy Roosevelt," she said. "The three of them camped in Yosemite at seven thousand feet. Dad was impressed by the President's rugged spirit, love of the outdoors, and how full of himself he was. Dad never forgot that trip. It was May, and they didn't bring tents. It snowed all night. When they woke, Roosevelt and Muir were ecstatic; dad wasn't. The snow didn't bother dad. He was upset Roosevelt and Muir belittled Negroes and saw nothing wrong about doing it.

"While dad lived in Mariposa, he also got to know Samuel Clemens and Bret Harte. They discussed the newspaper business, novels, and stories about the gold rush. Dad looked forward to their visits."

"I'd like to hear more about the early history of this area," said Deacon Tom. "When did Hangtown become Placerville?"

When no one spoke up, Roberto said, "In June of 1854. Alex Hunter, Placerville's first mayor, pushed for the change because Placerville is a better name for doing business.

"A couple of years later, in April 1856, a fire broke out that swept through town. Without a fire engine, the flames ran free in the business district. What saved Placerville from complete destruction was a shift in the wind that halted the fire's progress.

"A second fire broke out in July of that same year," said Roberto. "This time, the wind didn't shift, and all of Placerville burned. It appeared to be the work of an arsonist, though the culprit was never caught. That fire changed the life of little Zach, who was about to turn four. I'll let him tell you about it.

"A third blaze occurred in October. A drunk staying at the Pittsburg House started it. He died before the flames could be put out.

"After three fires in one year, the town leaders decided they had to improve the way fires were fought. They purchased Placerville's first fire engine along with two hundred fifty feet of hose. They also ordered a large bell from England. It's in the center of town and rung whenever a fire starts.

"Just down the street from the bell was the office of the Pony Express. For the eighteen months the Pony Express operated, Placerville was the western terminus for its riders. To replace the prestige the Pony Express brought to

Placerville, the Merchants Association lobbied the Central Pacific Railroad to run its tracks through town. When the railroad chose a different route, Placerville's leaders were irate. They assumed since Huntington, one of the railroad's owners, got his start in Hangtown, he'd persuade the other owners to run the tracks through town. They were wrong.

"I'm tired," said Roberto, removing his hat and wiping his forehead. "It's time for someone else to take over."

"I'll share my memories," said Father Zach, striding to the front of the room. "I want to thank Deacon Tom for inviting me to preside at the requiem. That meant a lot to me.

"You're welcome," said Deacon Tom, nodding to him.

"Mom was Zach's first love, but he was adamant he wouldn't marry her. This infuriated her. It wasn't until Zach moved to Mariposa that mom opened her heart to Red, the man for whom she'd been working. Red had always looked after mom and was thrilled to marry her. Though Red had a gruff appearance, he was a gentle soul. They'd been married three years when the fire of July 1856 started. Red was fighting it, and mom was protecting the saloon when the flames reached the building. The firemen said the firestorm was too fast for mom to escape. I wasn't hurt because mom had taken me to a friend's house outside of town. Once I was safe, she returned to the saloon. Mom knew how much the place meant to Red. He cried for days after Captain Meyer recovered her body.

Father Zach paused before he continued.

"Red raised me alone. Though I think of him as my father, he encouraged me to visit Zach every summer. I resisted because I thought Zach didn't care about me. Red insisted I go anyway.

"During my visits, I discovered Zach wasn't the cold-hearted man mom said he was. He repeatedly asked me to live with him, but I declined. I couldn't leave Red alone.

"While I was in Mariposa, I rode horses with Cate and read books. Zach introduced me to Yosemite, where I loved to camp with family and friends. Zach's stories around a crackling fire were spellbinding. Like Cousin Barbara, Zach taught me to play horseshoes. Unlike Barbara, Zach and I were evenly matched." Chuckles spread across the room.

"Red wanted me to take over his saloon, but that lifestyle never appealed to me," said Father Zach. "As most of you know, there's been an ordained Johnson in the Anglican tradition for at least two centuries. It was a visit to Uncle Joe's that persuaded me to carry on the tradition. I'm currently the Associate Rector of Saint Paul's Episcopal Church in Oakland, where Zach worshipped the last years of his life. One of the reasons Zach joined us is Saint Paul's long history of service to the Chinese. Saint Paul's became a congregation in 1861 when Chinese children were prohibited from attending public schools. Members of the church responded by teaching the children themselves. Today, Saint Paul's continues its outreach by assisting anyone affected by the earthquake and fire. We don't ask what nationality the people in need are. We see their distress and, in the name of Christ, provide them with food, clothing, and shelter.

"I'm married to Victoria, the most wonderful woman I know. She's here with me. Vicki, please stand."

Victoria stood and waved to everyone as they clapped.

"We have two sons, Edwin and Joshua." The boys stood, awkwardly greeting those around them. "Ed is in seminary," said Father Zach. "It appears the tradition will continue."

"Tell us about Uncle Joe," said Cate. "You visited him?"

"I did. I was fifteen when I spent two weeks in Wisconsin. I made the trip by myself, and it was terrific. Uncle Joe told me how he started a church in Hangtown but was forced out by the Senior Warden. Roberto, do you remember that fella's name?"

"Robert Jenner," said Roberto disgustedly.

"That's right! Robert Jenner fired Uncle Joe because he refused to limit the congregation's membership to white men and their families. When Jenner was unable to find a replacement for Uncle Joe, Saint Mary's closed its doors."

"I've heard rumors about an Episcopal church in Placerville during the early years," said Deacon Tom, "but there aren't any records that show its existence. Your story explains why."

"Besides being without a church, there was another reason Uncle Joe left Hangtown," said Father Zach. "He loved a woman who didn't love him. Her name was Matilde. She owned a hotel that had a bar, card room, and brothel. Uncle Joe fell in love with her flirtatious ways but was broken-hearted when he caught Matilde kissing Zach. Uncle Joe didn't believe Zach's story that Matilde was consoling him about the loss of Claire. Zach tried to clear the air, but Uncle Joe was too hurt and stubborn to reconcile. When Bishop Kemper summoned Uncle Joe to Wisconsin, he went. There he married Anne Leveroos, a member of his new congregation. They have three children: Sarah, Emma, and Megan. Yesterday, I received a telegram from Uncle Joe expressing his sorrow about Zach's passing and how he wished he could be with us. I'm disappointed Uncle Joe isn't here too.

Father Zach rubbed the back of his neck and said, "Matilde sold her hotel to William Cary. He expanded it and changed its name to the Cary House. A picture of Matilde hangs in the lobby. If you're staying there like I am, take a look.

"With her fortune, Matilde moved to San Francisco. She never married but was notorious for the men she entertained. I wanted to meet her, but Matilde was an old woman by the time I found her. I started to ask her about Zach and Uncle Joe when she winked at me, and my courage evaporated. That's one of those experiences I wish I could do-over...."

"Keep going," shouted Cate from the back of the room. "Say more about dad's life."

"During the 1880s, Zach's focus shifted from Indian affairs back to helping the Chinese," said Father Zach. "When I arrived in Placerville, there was a letter waiting for me from Zhang Wei, the fellow who briefly worked for Zach. Zhang started the first Chinese language newspaper in San Francisco, *THE GOLDEN HILLS*. Here is what he wrote:

GREETINGS TO ALL THE FRIENDS
OF MISTER ZACH JOHNSON:

I worked for Mister Zach as a special project reporter in the 1850s. He was one of the few white men who spoke up for the Chinese. After I left, we kept in touch. Mister Zach helped me learn how to run a newspaper and supported my efforts to be successful. He was a faithful and honorable friend. You should hold your head high whenever his name is mentioned.

In 1882 Congress passed the Chinese Exclusion Act. Since the Chinese represented less than one percent of the nation's population; the law wasn't intended to fix an ill but to demonstrate Washington's preference for white people. Mister Zach was outraged by the ten-year moratorium placed on Chinese immigration. He wrote letters to members of Congress objecting to the law. In 1892, the ban was extended another ten years. Your dad was beside himself. Mister Zach wrote to everyone he believed could change things, but his pleas were ignored.

In 1902, Congress made Chinese immigration permanently illegal. The law requires every Chinese person in the United States to register or face deportation. Again, Mister Zach did everything he could to repeal the law, but his efforts failed. To honor Mister Zach, I request you join me in the fight to do away with these restrictions.

With best wishes, I close,
Zhang Wei

"I'm going to do what I can to repeal the law," said Father Zach. "I hope you will too. That's what Zach would want. ...It's time to turn things back to Cate."

"I'll work with you to rid the nation of this spiteful legislation," said Cate, returning to the front of the room. "I have a few more things to cover before we conclude.

"The first concerns the trial of Charley Boles, the infamous Black Bart. Dad testified as a character witness, and during a recess, he asked Boles why he robbed stagecoaches? Boles replied he wanted revenge for an ugly interaction he had with some of Wells Fargo's agents. Twenty-eight times over the next six years, Boles stole thousands of dollars and would've taken more, but his Hangtown merchant friend, James Hume, arrested him before he could. Boles' rancor surprised dad. He'd never seen this side of his friend and was sad when the court sentenced Boles to six years in San Quintin.

"As I said earlier, dad was in a dark mood when I was born. He'd given up reading Morning Prayer and abandoned his quest to connect with God. A few years before dad moved to Berkeley, he had a vision. This is what I recall he told me."

Cate took a deep breath and a sip of water before proceeding.

"Dad had gone to his favorite place along the creek behind our house. He liked to sit by a small waterfall. On this day, the sun was shining, and there was a gentle breeze. While dad was reading, his surroundings suddenly disappeared. He was immersed in a mist that blinded him. Dad tried to regain his bearings by blinking, but the blackness wouldn't go away. Eventually—he wasn't sure how long it was—a light appeared as if someone was looking for him. Dad wanted that person's help, but the light-bearer never came near. Later, dad realized no one was carrying the light; it had a different source.

"The light grew more intense. The air around dad became bright before shattering into a thousand colors. He felt like he was inside a kaleidoscope. Each color made a sound, and dad's body vibrated to the music of the invisible world. It was as if everything was part of a whole.

"As suddenly as the vision began, it disappeared. Dad found himself alone by the waterfall, the sun shining brightly, the breeze refreshing him, his book on the ground beside him. Dad was in awe. He didn't move as he tried to hold onto the experience.

"After the vision, dad changed. The negativity he'd been living with went away. 'All my life,' he said, 'I've been pounding on a door that I thought was bolted shut, begging God to unlock it. Following my vision, I understood I no longer needed to keep knocking: the door was open all along. There never was anything separating us.'

"I don't know what to make of dad's experience," said Cate, playing with a curl near her ear, "but he was different after it."

"It's getting late," said Father Zach. "Time to wrap up."

"There's one more thing," said Cate, biting her lip. "Zach, please join me."

Father Zach came forward and stood next to Cate, unsure of what she had in mind.

"George Johnson was Father Zach's and my great grandfather," she said. "He was the Dean of Saint Paul's Cathedral in London. For his distinguished service, the Archbishop of Canterbury gave Dean Johnson an inscribed pocket watch. It was his most prized possession.

"Dean Johnson's son, our grandfather, joined the British navy as a chaplain. Grandpa wanted to be a part of the war effort that defeated Napoleon. However, his orders brought him to the United States, and that's how the Johnsons arrived here.

"As grandpa prepared to sail from London, his father gave him the pocket watch. Grandpa cherished it and always had it with him.

"On the day dad left home to come to California, grandpa gave him the watch. Like his father and grandfather before him, dad treasured it. On one occasion, the watch deflected a bullet that would've killed him."

Cate reached into her purse, took out the watch, and held it up.

"If you look closely, you'll see the crease in the casing where the shot struck. When Claire had the watch repaired, dad was elated. The men who found dad's body said he was grasping it.

"The watch has passed from father to oldest son, and today, on behalf of dad, I give the watch to my brother. Addressing Zach directly, Cate said, "Dad told me he wanted you to have it. Now it's yours."

"What a surprise!" exclaimed Father Zach, taking the watch. Tears ran down his cheeks as he stared at it. "I promise you I'll take good care of it."

Turning back to the gathering, Cate said, "My brother and I are grateful all of you came; your presence means everything to us. We hope you'll stay in touch. We're done. It's time for refreshments."

The End

ACKNOWLEDGEMENTS

FOLLOWING MY FIRST YEAR of seminary, I spent the summer at Emmanuel Hospital, Portland, Oregon. I trained as a hospital chaplain under the supervision of the Reverend Bill Adix. Bill is a special man who exudes God's grace. I was fortunate to have Bill as my supervisor and dedicate this book to him.

My editor, David Downing of Maxwellian Editorial Services, told me what I needed to hear to improve the manuscript. He was delightful to work with and I want to thank him for his many contributions.

The cover for the book was the inspiration of Dave Fymbo of Limelight Book Covers. I am indebted to him for his vision and skill.

Boyce A. Stringer of Boyce Stringer Productions photographed me. His creativity, talent, and patience are truly appreciated.

I live in a community where friends have nurtured my writing. Among them are Michael Drouilhet and Kris Rickards, Dan and Michelle Oakland, Larry and Billie Kroepel, Jon and Susan Christ, Neal and Mary Olsen. Individuals who live far away yet found time to show interest in my writing are Bart White, Joe Flemming, Sr., Sam and Karen Pierce, Donald Coe, and David Baskins. A heartfelt "thank you" to each of you.

My wife deserves special thanks for putting up with me during the ups and downs of the writing process. I love you, Barbara.

ABOUT JOHN PRATT BINGHAM

John was born and raised in California. He attended Willamette University and the Virginia Theological Seminary. While in seminary, he interned for a year in the office of Senator Philip Hart, Michigan.

As an Episcopal priest, John served as an associate at Saint Paul's, San Diego, and as rector of Saint Luke's, Monrovia.

A series of dreams led John to leave the parish ministry. While he trained at the C.G. Jung Institute of Los Angeles, John earned a master's degree in psychology from Antioch University.

Beginning in 1980, John was either in private practice as a marriage and family therapist or serving as the Executive Director of the Samaritan Counseling Center of Greater Sacramento. He was named a Sacramento Hero in Healthcare in 1999.

John retired in 2013 and moved to San Diego to be with his five children and nine grandchildren. He writes, plays euchre, and works on his pickleball game.

CONNECT WITH JOHN

www. binghambooks.com
Facebook: binghambooks

Please Review Hangtown, *The Dark Night*
Writing an honest review is an important way to help other readers. Please share your opinion at your favorite book site, so others may benefit from your appraisal. Most reviews are a sentence or two, though longer contributions are particularly valued. Thank you.

OTHER PUBLICATIONS

Inner Treasure, Reflections on Teachings of Jesus
(Dove Publications, Pecos, New Mexico, 1989).
www.pecosmonastery.org/Dove Publications.htm.
505-757-6597.

God and Dreams, Is There A Connection?
(Resource Publications, Eugene, Oregon, 2010)
www.wipfandstock.com
541-344-1528.

Hangtown
(binghambooks, San Diego, California, 2015),
www.binghambooks.com.

Hangtown, Secrets & Schemes
(binghambooks, San Diego, California, 2018).
www.binghambooks.com.

Hangtown III